I0581252

The Ungovernable series:

Zero Day Threat
Jailbreak
Time Bomb
Insider Threat
Firewall
Trojan Horse
Security Incident
Threat Agent
Attack Path

INSIDER THREAT

R.M. OLSON

ISBN-13: 978-1-7771778-6-7

To Camilla, Liz, Cam, Tiff, Em (Um), Christin, and Micah—for keeping me sane through university and beyond, and being the best friends I could ask for.

INSIDER THREAT

*A person or group of persons who pose a security risk
due to their ability to violate or compromise security
policies and procedures*

1

Jez crouched in the entrance to the narrow alley. The bare cement of the streets was filthy from years of too many boots and indifferent street cleaners, and the faint scent of garbage wafted from the dark alley behind her, drafted in on the clammy Prasvishoni air.

She was grinning like an idiot.

Beside her, Tae was definitely not grinning, and Masha looked positively grim.

"He'll be here any minute now," Masha said, her lips thin. "Are you ready, Jez?"

"Born ready, you bastard," she said.

"You remember the name of the student we baited him with, right?" asked Tae wearily. His wavy hair was falling over his eyes, like usual, and between that and his ragged street-kid clothes, which he'd started wearing again now that they were back in the city, he looked even younger than his twenty years.

She rolled her eyes at him. "I told you, I'm crap at remembering names, OK?"

"Yula," Tae said through gritted teeth. "Her name is Yula. I swear I've told you that a hundred times."

"Well, maybe I wasn't listening," she countered.

"Remind me why we're letting Jez do this?" grumbled Lev through her earpiece. She grinned and hit her com.

"Easy, genius. Because this idiot likes women, and I'm basically the hottest person on this crew." She paused. "No offence, Ysbel. You're pretty hot too. But not everyone gets off on people threatening to blow them up."

"I think you are the only person who gets off on people threatening to blow them up," grunted Ysbel, from behind her.

"Also," said Tanya over the com, "Ysbel happens to be married to me, and I promise you, Jez, I would do a lot worse to you than just blow you up."

"OK, changed my mind," Jez drawled. "Tanya's also pretty hot."

"Piss off, Jez," said Ysbel in a flat voice. Her heavy outer-rim accent made the words sound like "Pees oaf," but her tone made the meaning very clear anyways.

"He's here," Tae hissed. "Jez, go."

She grinned at him, straightened, and sauntered out of the alley and down the street, then slipped into the side street they'd chosen for a meeting place.

A tall, thin man who looked to be in his early fifties came around the corner at a brisk pace. He had a sharp, predatory look to his face, and it sharpened further when he saw her.

"Hey, Professor Gurin," she drawled. He glanced over at her, looking her up and down.

"Who are you?" he snapped impatiently.

"Me? I'm Jez. Friend of Yula. She said she was going to meet you here, discuss grades and whatever." She shrugged. "Wasn't feeling too good, so I told her I'd come in her place."

The man cocked his head to one side, looking her up and down again in an appraising fashion. "Well," he said at last, "I suppose I could arrange for a substitution. I suppose she, ah, informed you of our arrangement?"

Jez's grin widened. "Yep. She told me that you were a dirty plaguer who sold grades for favours. And here's the thing, I'm really damn good at favours."

He was still looking at her, but his eyes had gone cold. "Really. And what kind of favours are you willing to trade?"

She sauntered over a little closer, letting her eyes drift over him dismissively.

Not much to look at, if she were being perfectly honest. But then again, corrupt mud-sucking bastards generally weren't, in her experience.

"Well," she whispered, "figure I could get you a couple favours with my boss."

He raised an eyebrow. "And who's your boss?"

She lowered her voice theatrically. "Marina Kaschak."

His eyes widened, his expression going suddenly wary. "Marina Kaschak? The mafia avtoritet?"

"Pretty sure that's what I said."

The man glanced around him nervously. "I—Yula never told me —"

"Never told you she was friends with someone who was connected to Marina Kaschak?" She tried to look menacing, but hell, it was hard to look menacing when you were trying not to laugh your plaguing head off. "And also that you were threatening to lower her grade until she could pony you up some favours?"

His face was slightly panic-stricken now, and she felt a warm glow in her chest. This was always her favourite part.

"Well, you scum-sucker, guess you should have asked," she said, stepping closer to him.

"What do you want?" he asked, his voice higher than it had been. She took another step, and he backed away from her.

"Me?" She was grinning so wide it hardly fit on her face. "Well, mostly I'd just like to do this." She grabbed him by the front of the suit and slapped her open palm on the back of his neck. The small patch Masha had given her stuck to his bare skin, and there was barely time for the shock to register on his face before his eyes rolled back in his head and his body went limp.

"Got him," she said in satisfaction, slapping her com. "Lev, hope this wasn't anyone you know, because I'll tell you, I'm going to have a lot less respect for your choice of friends if you say yes."

"Jez." He sounded faintly irritated. "Having taken a class from someone is not necessarily the equivalent of having that person as a friend. For the record, yes, I did know him, and also, I agree with your assessment of his personality."

"And?" she prompted, leaning down over the professor's prone form.

"And," he continued, slightly grudgingly, "I may have once messed with his class files such that he ended up teaching an entire classroom full of students an equation that was an easily-broken code for a seditious message that got him called up in front of the university president."

"See genius? That's why I like you." She rummaged inside the man's jacket and carefully extracted a small, wrinkled card. "You just need the card, Masha?"

"No Jez. As I told you at least half a dozen times in the last fifteen minutes, I also need the chip from his com, and there should be an ID token somewhere on him." She couldn't see Masha, but she could picture the ice in her expression. She rolled her eyes.

"On it, you bastard."

The com chip was easy. She grabbed the credit chip as well, make it look a little more like a robbery. She went through his coat pockets a couple of times, then his trouser pockets, then patted down the front of his shirt.

"Masha, you sure—"

"Jez!" It was Tae, and his voice was strained. "What happened?"

She frowned. "Nothing. I mean, other than the fact that I just knocked out a professor and am robbing him blind."

"Because there are a whole lot of police heading to your coordinates as we speak. You have about thirty-five seconds."

She glanced around.

Damn.

She patted him down again, rolled his limp body over, and yanked off his jacket.

"Where the hell would a professor keep his damn ID, Masha?" she growled into the com.

"Jez! Get out of there!" Tae hissed.

From around the corner, she could hear the faint hum of skybikes.

Damn, damn, damn.

She jerked the professor's shirt open.

There, on a thin chain around his neck.

"Got it!" she whispered, breaking the chain with a quick jerk of her wrist and shoving the ID in her pocket.

Five police bikes shot around the corner. She straightened, and gave them a grin.

The officers slid off their bikes, weapons drawn. A black, cylindrical drone hovered over their heads, red light blinking.

Weapons drone.

Hell, this job had been pretty boring up to this point anyways.

"Raise your hands and step away from the body," called an officer, com amplifying her voice.

Jez stepped back, slinging the jacket over her shoulder, and tried to put a haughty look on her face.

"Hey," she drawled. "Took your time getting here. This plaguer attacked me. I barely managed to fight him off."

The police officer frowned at her. "What?" she said, at the same moment Tae hissed into her earpiece, "What the hell are you doing?"

"I said, you dirty plaguers, it took you long enough to get here. This man jumped me, tried to steal my credits."

"We got here as soon as we got the emergency alert," the woman said, straightening slightly.

"Yeah? Well, last time I trust your damn emergency alerts, then," said Jez, trying to make her voice as arrogant as possible. "Could have been killed."

The woman was still frowning at her. "He jumped you, you say?"

"Yep. But we're all good now. You can go. Maybe call a medic for this idiot on your way out."

"Because the emergency call came from someone named Stanislav Gurin. A professor at the University of Prasvishoni. Fifty-five years old."

Damn.

She put on her best smile. "Always did look young for my age."

The officer straightened and muttered something into her com. Behind Jez, the other officers tensed. The red light on the drone began to flash slowly.

This was going sideways quickly.

"Jez—" Tae sounded distinctly worried.

She dived to one side as a laser-blast from the drone scarred a smoking hole in the concrete where she'd been only a moment before, rolled to her feet, and grabbed the prone form of the professor, hauling him up as a sort of shield.

"Hands up!" the police officer shouted.

"In your damn dreams," Jez shot back. She chucked the professor's limp form at the officer, and as the woman instinctively stepped back, Jez yanked out her own modded heat gun, pointed it at the drone, and fired.

There was a crackle of sparks as the drone's shields overheated in the face of whatever the hell Ysbel had modded Jez's pistol with, and then it dropped to the ground in a heap of misshapen, melted metal. Jez took advantage of the police officers' momentary distraction and ran for her life.

Over her shoulder she caught the mad scramble of officers for skybikes, and then she was around the corner, pounding down the street.

"They're calling in reinforcements," Tae said in a strangled voice. "What were you thinking?"

She shrugged. "Almost worked."

"It did not almost work!"

The bikes rounded the corner, and she barely dodged a heat blast. She swung around another corner and ducked behind an open door. As a police skybike rounded the corner after her, she lunged forward. The man was riding low, and she managed to grab him around the waist as he shot past, swinging her legs up behind him.

"What the hell—" he began, half-turning in his seat. She reached around him and jerked up on the handles, and the bike shot towards the sky. She fumbled for the restraint release. He figured out what she was doing a split second later and grabbed her arms, trying to pry her off him. His free hand groped for his gun. She brought up one knee, jamming his hand hard against the frame of the bike. He howled and tried to shake her off. She clung on grimly.

"What the hell are you doing, Jez?" Lev was speaking through his teeth.

"Busy now," she grunted.

The officer's fingers were prying her hands loose from his waist, his short fingernails cutting into the meaty part of her palms. She retaliated by smacking her forehead hard into the base of his skull. He grunted, and she blinked back stars.

Bastard had a hard head.

They were out of the buildings, and screaming towards the city force-field now. An impact at this speed would turn both of them into an impressive fireworks display.

The officer seemed to have figured this out as well, and he let go his grip on her hands to yank the handles down. Now they were heading for the buildings, and neither of them were in a position to steer.

There. Her fumbling fingers found the release, and she hit it. The restraints strapping the officer to the bike flipped back.

He hit the restraints again, but she was close enough that the thin bands caught both of them, strapping them to the bike and shoving her up against his back.

Jez grinned. "Just couldn't get close enough, could you?" She jerked the handles from his nerveless fingers just before they hit the surface of the nearest apartment complex, leaned hard to the right, and skinned the bike along the surface of the roof, the rough prefab blocks almost scraping her boots. Then she dove back between the buildings.

"What's happening?" she muttered into the com as she threaded a narrow street, whipped around a corner, and shot down an alley.

The officer finally seemed to come out of his shock, and he grabbed instinctively at the restraints. She couldn't see his face, but from the way his hands were shaking, she assumed he liked this just about as much as Lev did. She grinned, flipped the bike upside down, and shot over a crowd of pedestrians, her short hair almost brushing their drab coats and colourful scarves. Someone looked up and swore, and she grinned back cheerily and made a rude gesture.

The officer had completely given up on knocking her off the bike, and now seemed fully focused on staying on himself.

"You've got about fourteen officers on you now." Tae's voice was a sort of resigned horror. "Pull up your com screen, I'll shoot you the specs. Looks like they've shut off the bike's com."

She pulled the bike upright and slapped her com against her knee, and a holoscreen popped up over her wrist.

Red dots were converging on her from all sides.

She yanked the handles and leaned hard, and the bike flipped a hairpin turn in an alley almost too narrow to permit it and shot off in the other direction.

The officer glanced down at the screen hovering over her wrist and seemed to regain some of his equilibrium. He grabbed for the handles, and for a second the bike jerked as they fought for control. She leaned forward, forcing his body down, and the bike picked up speed, almost scraping the dirty walls of the alley. At the last second, she jerked the handles back again, pointing the bike at the sky and missing the dead-end by millimetres. The officer gave a sort of strangled scream and went limp.

She grinned. "Hey Lev, this guy actually fainted! Guess I can't complain about you throwing up anymore."

Lev muttered something that sounded like, 'I don't blame him.'

She leaned forward over the officer's limp body, dropped down until they were skimming along the ground, and hit the restraints. He slumped to one side, and reluctantly she straightened slightly, slowing the bike just a touch as he rolled off.

"Got him," she whispered in satisfaction.

"Yes, well that will be a relief when the rest of the police blow you out of the sky," said Ysbel dryly.

"That assumes they can catch me," said Jez with a grin.

"Jez." Masha's voice was cold, and for just a moment Jez's muscles tightened instinctively at the tone. "Bring the bike back around, and come by the entrance to the alley. And please be ready to roll off."

Jez rolled her eyes and sighed. "Yes, cap'n."

A heat blast seared over her head, and she glanced quickly over her shoulder.

Drone. Figured. They weren't going to send an officer in after her between the buildings, considering they'd probably figured out by now that there wasn't a damn officer on the force who could keep up. She yanked out her heat pistol and cracked off a couple shots over her shoulder.

The drone exploded.

The wind through her hair, the tingle in her hands, the air whipping her face, the cursing through her com—you couldn't get a whole lot better than this, honestly.

She glanced down at the map on her com.

Not good.

Four police bikes surrounded the entrance to the alley she was heading down, and on the other side, four more bikes. Three others hovered over top.

She straightened abruptly, and the bike jerked and slowed to an idle.

"Jez." Tae sounded frantic. "Can you get back here?"

She took a deep breath, loosened her hands on the handles, and half-closed her eyes. "On it," she murmured.

"What are you—"

She leaned forward, and the bike shot towards the entrance to the street again.

They must have had a bead on her, because the heat-blasts were flying before her bike exited the alley. At the last second she jerked back on the handles and the bike shot upwards, missing the shimmering fizz of the heat-blasts by centimetres, and before they had time to re-calibrate their aim, she spun the bike and shot back down the alley in the opposite direction.

The four bikes shot in after her.

She leaned until she was almost flat against the bike. The speed sucked the air from her lungs and pulled tears from her eyes, and she would have been laughing with sheer delight if she had any breath. Heat blasts sizzled past her, and one caught the back end of her bike, sending the controls momentarily haywire. She glanced over her shoulder to make sure they were following close enough, and just as the front of her bike would have come through the entrance to the alley, just as the heat-blasts from the four officers stationed at that exit lit the air, she flipped her bike upside down in an abrupt maneuver that sent her over the heads of the startled officers and back in the other direction.

Behind her she could hear the shouts and curses as the four police bikes shot into the firefight, the heat-shields in their uniforms sparking and glowing, and then she was out the opposite now-clear exit and speeding back towards the alley where it had all started.

"What the actual *hell* was that?" Lev's voice sounded strangled.

"Called flying, genius-boy. Hey Tae, be there in about twenty seconds, if they don't shoot me down first," she said into the com.

"I—" Tae sounded almost speechless.

"When you come by, I'm going to spray some explosive gel onto your bike," interrupted Ysbel. "Roll off when you pass the alley. Tae has already programmed your signature into the bike com, so when it blows it will look like you were still on it. And my explosives will blow it into small enough pieces they won't be able to tell you weren't."

"And that, Ysbel, is why you're so hot," she said, grinning.

She slowed slightly as she approached the alley. Technically, it had been long enough since her most recent stint in jail that her ribs were technically not broken. Still, she was pretty sure they wouldn't appreciate her hitting the ground at this speed. She dropped the bike lower, until again she was almost scraping the concrete with her boots, and then at the last second she jerked the bike to one side and hit the restraints, letting the momentum throw her off just as the bike shot past the alley. A spatter of a sharp-smelling, viscous liquid sprayed above her head as her shoulder hit the concrete, and then the world was a blur of sky and pavement and a scream of protest from her tender ribs as she rolled and came up hard against the wall of the alley.

Not as hard as she'd expected, though. She'd assumed she'd have at least another broken arm to show for the day's escapade.

In the distance, a low 'boom' that sounded like thunder, if thunder was loud enough to blow your eardrums, echoed through the street, and she glanced up. The world was still spinning madly, but she could feel something soft under her, which was—not what she'd expected. She blinked, trying to get the world back into focus, and found she was looking into Tae's spinning, scowling face, and Masha's spinning, cold one.

"I'm going to have so many bruises from this," Tae grumbled. She grinned at him reflexively, still blinking.

He'd braced himself, and broken her momentum with his body. He and Masha, which was honestly a little shocking.

And the most shocking part of all of it was—well, she wasn't even that shocked.

"Thanks," she said, after a moment. He glowered at her and shoved her off him.

"What in the system were you thinking, Jez?" he grumbled. "I told you the police were on their way."

She pushed herself into a sitting position, although the world was still spinning dizzily. "Just figured we didn't want to make this thing too boring," she said with a smirk. She tried to reach into her pocket, and almost fell over. A muscular pair of arms hoisted her to her feet.

"We'd best get moving," said Ysbel's voice from behind her. "They're going to come check it out soon enough." She let go of Jez's shoulders, and Jez staggered, caught herself, and shook her head, blinking hard. Then the four of them ran, Ysbel catching Jez when she weaved too far to one side or the other, police sirens wailing behind them.

When they finally turned down the small, grungy street to Jez's old apartment, the dizziness from her rolling fall had finally dissipated.

"No tracking?" Ysbel grunted, pausing at the steps that led down to the apartment. Tae pulled up his com and checked carefully.

"No. Doesn't look like it."

"Good," she said. "I suppose we go in and find out if Lev has had a heart attack yet."

"And," Jez said, grinning, "I suppose we figure out if Masha can do what she said she could do. Because I—" she reached into her pocket, "did exactly what I said I would do." She pulled out the ID and held it up with satisfaction. "Guess it's your turn now, you bastard."

15

2

Lev glanced up as the others came through the door. His heart jumped into his mouth at the sight of Jez's bloodied face and torn clothes. He closed his eyes for half a second and took a deep breath.

"So," he said after a moment. "I assume you were successful?"

"'Course we were, genius," said Jez, with a smirk. "I was the one doing the important stuff, remember?" She reached into her pockets and emptied an assortment of wrenches, ration-pack wrappers, assorted screws and bolts and bits of wire, and, last of all, a credit chip, a university chip, and an ID token wrapped in a bit of broken jewelry-chain. He sighed, and she winked at him, and his heart gave that strange stutter that every sideways look from her prompted these days.

He cleared his throat and leaned forward, inspecting the pile of junk.

The sight of the university ID sent a strange shiver up his back—it had been such a long time. His whole childhood, his life-long dream, everything that token represented.

It had been a very, very long time.

And in a few weeks, he was going back into the university he'd once called home. They all were.

They were breaking in, of course, under false names, to find some secretive government plot over which the government had already tried once to kill all of them, but still …

It was a strange feeling, and the sight of the ID brought back for half a moment the mildewy smell of his old run-down student apartment, the staticky, electric scent of information chips, the dreary cold of the large, echo-y classrooms that somehow still managed to feel like home, the hard seats and the splintery writing tools and everything that had made up his childhood and youth.

Jez dropped into a seat across from him, long limbs splayed out, cocky grin on her tawny face, black hair disheveled. He glanced up at her surreptitiously.

He was never one hundred percent sure what she was thinking. And after that day in the cockpit, when they'd barely escaped from Lena, their ship broken, both of them bruised and exhausted, and they'd kissed—he could still picture the look on her face when he drew back, her eyes wide, her lips parted, her body leaning into him almost unconsciously.

The memory made something catch in his throat and his heart beat far more quickly than it should, and somehow he couldn't picture that without also remembering the feel of her lips on his, the giddy dizziness of his face pressed against hers and her breath on his skin, the faint taste of her that had lingered on his lips for a long, long time afterwards, and somehow that memory made it much more difficult to concentrate on what he was actually supposed to be concentrating on.

And it wasn't just that. It was the fact that during the last few months—well, the thought of life without Jez in it had become increasingly unimaginable. Her loud laughter at some probably-inappropriate joke, that funny, soft half-smile she got when she looked at any one of their little crew and she thought they weren't looking back. The way she'd throw herself recklessly into something to help one of them out, the faint look of shock on her face every time one of them did something for her in return, the look he wanted to make go away and never come back because she'd finally understand that he—that all of them—cared about her as much as she cared about them, even if she'd never admit it. Her sharp intelligence, the frightened vulnerability that she'd only barely begun to let him see. The way he could stand next to her and stare out at deep space and feel an echo of freedom and bright, sharp joy that was almost too much to bear. The way being with her made him feel whole, and grounded, and alive, and being apart from her was a sort of ache that wouldn't go away.

He sighed.

It wasn't exactly like they'd had any time to discuss it. They'd limped the *Ungovernable* planet-side near a small, out-of-the-way zestava and had spent the next three weeks trying to put the ship back together, and Jez had had them pulling fourteen-hour shifts, and she hadn't even taken shifts, working until she passed out, and then waking up and going straight back to work. More than once he'd found her slumped over her tools, ship parts spread out on the floor around her, fast asleep, and had tucked something under her head as a pillow and covered her in a blanket, pulled the wrench or mallet or socket out of her limp hand and set it gently beside her. And she never said anything about it, but he could sense her eyes on him when she thought he wasn't looking. But they'd both been so busy that that was the best either of them could do, and he hadn't been alone with her since the day in the cockpit. And the week and a half since they'd arrived on Prasvishoni had been just as busy, if not busier, and they'd been crammed into this tiny one-room apartment, and …

Well, and if he didn't get to talk to her by herself soon, he thought he might go completely out of his mind.

"Hey genius, what you thinking?"

He blinked and looked up at her, and her dark eyes twinkled with that familiar spark of mischief, and there was something about the way she was smiling, and damn it to hell, why couldn't he just focus on what he was actually supposed to be doing?

He sighed. "Nothing. Just—brought back memories."

"Yeah? Well, guess that professor we jumped will have some memories to think about." She was still grinning.

He shook his head and pushed back his chair. "I suppose there's no point in saying anything about the fact that you were almost shot down by an entire squad of police?"

She leaned back luxuriously. "Nope."

From across the room, Tae muttered something in a sour tone. Lev shook his head.

They were crowded into Jez's old basement apartment. Despite Tae and Tanya's best efforts with a broom and a mop and probably ten litres of soap, it still looked and smelled like a place on the edge of a biohazard warning. When they'd landed on Prasvishoni a week and a half ago and stored the *Ungovernable* in an abandoned hangar bay owned, apparently, by Masha, and Jez had led them to her old basement apartment and let them in, he'd thought Tae might have an actual heart attack.

'What?' Jez had said with a shrug when Tae had sputtered out a comment on the mess. 'Not like I spent much time here.' And despite himself, Lev had almost laughed at the blank look on Jez's face when Tae, with a long-suffering sigh, asked if she had a broom, and the even blanker look when he'd asked about a mop.

Masha pulled up a chair at the table next to him and sat down, digging through to extract the chip and card from the jumbled mess on the table with mild distaste.

"Masha," he said, turning away from Jez with an effort, and towards the pleasant-looking woman, with her average face and average brown skin and shoulder-length hair pulled back into a practical rat-tail. Average, of course, unless you caught a glimpse of the sharp intensity behind her bland eyes. "Do you have what you need?"

"I told you—" Jez broke in.

"Yes," said Masha, her voice still cold. She and Jez seemed to have come to some sort of truce since their encounter with Lena, but to call it a friendship would have been a stretch. "I believe I did get what I need, at least to forge documents for whichever of us is going in as a professor. Assuming there's not a wanted notice up for Jez by the end of the day, which would, at this point, be unsurprising." She paused. "And were you able to find anything new?"

He pulled up the screen on his com and spread his fingers to enlarge it, then pulled it around in front of both of them. "Next term starts in three days' time. That should solve the problem of getting Tae in, if he's going in as a student. There are four openings they've been advertising for in administration, and there's always support-staff positions—cooks, security guards, janitors. And," he scrolled down the screen until he found the piece of data he was looking for, "you can see here. They're scheduled to be audited by the education department sometime in the next six months or so. That's another in, if we need one."

"And that professor Jez knocked out will be in the hospital for how long?" asked Ysbel. She'd come around to join them, and Jez scooted her chair to one side to make room.

"Two months, give or take," said Masha calmly. "The neurological damage should subside by then, and he should be back as good as new. But until then, they'll need a substitute."

Tae pulled up a chair, and again Jez scooted over to make room. Tanya poked her head out from behind one of the blankets she'd hung to give the children a quiet place to sleep, and, Lev suspected, her and Ysbel some privacy. Despite the fact it felt like at least a decade, it had only been a little over a month since they'd broken Tanya and the children out of prison, and Ysbel and Tanya had five and a half years to catch up on.

"Do you need me out there, my heart?" Tanya asked. Her words had the same heavy outer-rim accent as Ysbel's, but her voice was slightly lighter, and wry with an undercurrent of humour.

"I always need you," said Ysbel, her stoic expression replaced instantly by a soft smile that only Tanya was able to pull out of her. Tanya smiled back, and for a moment the two of them could have been the only people in the room. Then she crossed over and took a seat beside her wife. Jez shifted again, and Lev realized suddenly how close she was sitting to him. He closed his eyes, trying to pull his focus back to what was happening around the table.

Jez was watching him from the corner of her eyes, and there was an expression on her face as if she'd just noticed how close they were as well.

"Lev?"

He looked up with a start. Masha was looking at him, one eyebrow raised, and Ysbel was trying, not very hard, to hide an amused grin.

"I'm sorry, Masha," he said. "What did you ask?"

"I asked, Lev, if you'd managed to find anything else out on your old professor."

He frowned. "Nothing. I've looked through everything you sent me, every database in the university that Tae was able to hack me into—nothing. You'd think she never existed."

"And the cargo that Jez stole, back when she was still smuggling for Lena?"

He shook his head. "Nothing on that, either. There's the newscoms about the theft, but besides that—" He spread his hands.

"This help?" asked Jez. She fished in one pocket of her disreputable jacket, then the other, and finally pulled her closed hand out in a triumphant gesture. She spread her palm open on the table.

In the centre of her palm sat a small pellet of a shiny black material that he didn't recognize, about the width of the tip of his thumb. He frowned and glanced up at Jez, then back at the thing in her hand.

"What is it?" asked Ysbel finally.

"Piece of the cargo I stole," said Jez, dropping it onto the table. It fell with a 'thud' that sounded much too loud for its size.

They all turned to stare at her.

"Jez," he said at last, carefully. "You mean to say that this entire time we've been talking about how to get into the university, and how to figure out why the government was hunting us and what they wanted, and why it was that the government blew up an entire apartment building three years ago just so they could kill you, presumably because of the cargo you stole, this entire time you had that in your pocket?"

She grinned at him. "Yep."

He opened his mouth, then closed it.

Masha's eyes were narrowed. "And might I ask why you didn't mention this before?" she said, her voice calm and dangerous.

Jez shrugged. "Forgot."

Masha sucked in a breath, and not for the first time in the last four and a half weeks, Lev wondered if this was the moment that the Masha-Jez cease-fire finally broke. But at last Masha blew out a long breath through her nose, shot Jez a disgusted look that had absolutely no effect on the pilot whatsoever, and turned back to the small black ball in the centre of the table.

After a moment, Lev reached out. "May I?" he asked. Masha nodded coldly, and he picked up the sphere, cradling it in the palm of his hand.

It was cool, and too heavy for its size, smooth and hard like metal. But it wasn't any metal he'd seen before.

Ysbel reached out her hand, and he dropped the ball into it. She tipped it back and forth, and held it out for Tanya to look at. "Do you recognize this?" she asked her wife. Tanya touched the sphere delicately with the tip of one finger, then shook her head.

"I'll do an analysis on it," said Ysbel, closing her hand around the small object. "Maybe once we get the chemical composition, we'll have a better idea of why this was so important."

Masha nodded. "That's a good idea. Do you have everything you need to do an analysis?"

His hand, dropped down beside his chair, brushed Jez's, and he glanced at her quickly. She was staring straight ahead, conscientiously avoiding his eyes.

Carefully, his breath coming slightly too fast, he hooked his little finger around hers. She stiffened, and he dropped her hand and shot her a wry glance. When she finally caught his eye, he mouthed, 'sorry.'

There was a look in her face, half panic, half something else. She closed her eyes, then he felt her hand slip into his, her fingers twining through his own. He turned to stare at her, but she was avoiding his eyes again.

Ysbel was still talking, but she shot him an amused look that told him she suspected exactly what was going on under the table. He glared at her, but he was having a strangely difficult time breathing. He glanced at Jez again from the corner of his eye, and after a moment, began tracing slow circles with his thumb on the soft hollow of her wrist.

She stiffened again, swallowing visibly, but didn't pull her hand from his.

Masha and Ysbel were talking, but he honestly couldn't make out a single word either of them were saying through the pounding of his heart, and he probably should be paying attention, but there was something like jolts of electricity shooting up his arm where her fingers were tangled with his, and damn it, this was actually getting ridiculous, and maybe the most ridiculous part of it was that he didn't actually care. Her hand was warm, her skin rough, with a thick callous across her palm where a ship wrench would fit, but the skin of her wrist was soft, the sinews standing out beneath the skin. And her hand was trembling slightly, and he could feel her pulse pounding under his thumb, although in reality it could just as well be his pulse, because it was galloping much faster than was strictly necessary.

"—what we'll do then," Masha was saying, and after a moment, the others pushed their chairs back. Ysbel pulled Tanya close for a lingering kiss, and followed her back towards the blanketed-off makeshift room. Masha gave him a piercing glance but didn't say anything, just stood and turned towards the door. Tae got to his feet and followed her out the narrow doorway to the dirty, tumbledown steps beyond.

Once they were gone, he sighed ruefully and glanced over at Jez. She glanced at him from the corner of her eye. For a moment, as their eyes caught, he felt that same dizzy disorientation he'd felt that day in the cockpit. Then she looked away and stood, and he stood as well.

Just as well, really. They all had plenty to do, if he was being logical.

He took a deep breath, and, with more reluctance than actually made sense, made to pull his hand from Jez's. She didn't let go, though, and when he glanced at her over his shoulder, she yanked him back towards her. He turned, half off-balance, and caught himself with a hand against the wall.

His hand had landed right beside her head, and he was leaning against the wall, which meant he was leaning into her, and she was still holding his hand and grinning at him with an expression that made his head spin strangely.

Their faces were only centimetres apart.

She stared at him, and again, there was that mix of mischief and snark and panic in her eyes, and without even thinking about it, he found himself leaning in towards her. She swallowed hard, grabbed the back of his neck, and pulled him forward. His brain, which had already clearly been on the blink, shorted out completely, and the only thing he was aware of was her lips on his, and the taste of her on his tongue, and the fact that, no matter how close her body was to his, it wasn't close enough. His arm had come around her back, and he pulled her in against him, tugging his other hand free from hers and sliding it up the back of her neck into her hair.

She leaned into him, and her wiry body against his was everything he'd imagined it would be, like she was a part of him that he'd never realized he'd been missing until this moment. She caught his bottom lip between her teeth, and he groaned helplessly, pushing her up against the wall, and he slid his hands down her hips and snugged her body tighter against his, and her mouth was moving on his in a way he hadn't actually realized was possible, and every nerve ending in his body hummed—

There was a strangled yelp from the doorway, and they managed to detach themselves from each other and spin towards the sound.

Tae stood there, eyes averted, looking a little bit like he wanted to melt through the floor.

"Um—" he managed. "Lev—Masha wanted—you know what, I'll come back later."

Jez was still very, very close to him, her body pressed up against his, her arms tangled around him, her hands grasping the back of his shirt, and he could feel the angular shape of her hips, and damn it to hell, his brain wasn't even trying at this point.

There were footsteps on the stairs, and Jez tightened her fingers in his shirt reflexively as Masha came through the door.

She glanced from one of them to the other, one eyebrow raised, expression unreadable. Jez managed a slight smirk.

"Hey Masha," she drawled. "Didn't realize we were going to be putting on a show here."

"Neither did I, Jez," said Masha, her voice cold.

There was a snort of badly-concealed laughter from behind the hung blankets, and Lev took a deep breath and shook his head ruefully.

Apparently, being alone with Jez was an aspiration he was unlikely to achieve for as long as the eight of them were crammed into this dirty one-room basement apartment.

Still—

He swore he could still taste her kiss. He'd be tasting her for days.

If he'd thought concentrating was difficult before—

"Lev," said Masha, turning to him. "If you happen to get a moment, I would appreciate your help procuring what Ysbel needs. I've told Tae to take the rest of the evening off."

He cleared his throat. "Of course. Let me get my jacket."

Somehow, he managed to convince his hands to let go of Jez's hips, and she reluctantly loosened her grip on the back of his shirt.

He pulled on his jacket, his hands shakier than they should have been, and followed Masha out the door. But he couldn't resist a look over his shoulder, where Jez was still leaned up against the wall, a dreamy expression on her face that made his stomach turn flip-flops.

Conning and forging their way into the most prestigious university in the Svodrani system was always going to be difficult. As was staying alive while the government was actively hunting them down, and figuring out why the government was trying to kill them in the first place.

But there were two things that were always going to be more difficult than any of that.

Going back to his old university, where he'd grown up, where everything would remind him of what he'd always dreamed of, and what he'd lost.

And … well, trying to keep his mind on the job instead of on the fact that apparently Jez wanted to kiss him just as much as he wanted to kiss her.

3

Tanya was smiling slightly when Ysbel turned back to her.

"I thought they'd never get around to actually kissing," Tanya whispered. Ysbel buried her face in her wife's hair and kissed it.

"You owe me five credits. I told you they wouldn't make it past the end of the day."

"Of course, my heart." Tanya's voice was muffled, her breath warm against Ysbel's neck, sending a pleasant shiver up Ysbel's back. "I'll pay you those five credits as soon as you pay me the five credits that you owe me, for guessing Tae would be the one to walk in on it."

Ysbel chuckled. "I suppose you're right. We're even." She glanced around the small space, enclosed by blankets. "Are the children asleep?"

"Lying down, anyways. I had them tidying all day, and Misko fell asleep in the middle of telling me he wasn't tired."

"Good," said Ysbel. She looked down at Tanya's face, the lines of care that cut into those familiar features. "I think it's time that you and I took a walk or something. You've been out of prison for four and a half weeks, and for once we are going to have a relaxing evening, just the two of us, with no one trying to kill us. We can't analyze that metal that idiot pilot apparently had this whole time until Lev and Masha come back. Jez is still here, if I can get her head back into the atmosphere. She can keep an eye on the children."

Tanya gave her a skeptical look, then shook her head, smiling slightly. "I suppose she can't teach them any more swear words while they're sleeping."

"I wouldn't put it beyond her to try," Ysbel muttered, with an answering grin. She pulled back the curtain and stepped out into the main room.

Jez was still exactly where they'd left her, with the same dreamy expression on her face and faraway look in her eyes. Ysbel bit back a smile.

"Jez," she said, taking a step towards the lanky pilot.

"Mmm?" said Jez in a dazed sort of tone.

"Jez!"

Jez started slightly and looked up, as if she'd just barely noticed that Ysbel was in the room. "Mmm."

"Jez," said Ysbel patiently, "I'm going to go on a walk with Tanya. Do you think you can keep an eye on the children? They're sleeping, so just make sure nothing happens.

"Mmm?"

"Jez!"

"What?"

She sighed. "Were you even listening?"

"To what?"

"Jez." Tanya stepped out to stand beside Ysbel. "I am going to take a walk with my wife. You are in charge of Misko and Olya. Nothing is going to happen while we're gone, because you are going to make very certain that nothing does. Do you understand me?"

Jez gave a long, dreamy sigh. "Fine. OK. Use me as a babysitter, I don't care."

"You can daydream about kissing Lev all you want, but just please make sure that nothing happens to my babies."

"Mmm."

Ysbel exchanged glances with Tanya. This was clearly the best they were going to get out of the pilot in her current state. Still, she'd managed a full sentence, so that was a good sign. Ysbel shook her head, and the two of them ducked through the narrow door and up the filthy stairway into the drab Prasvishoni streets.

The sky was the cool, dusky colour of early evening, and the air nipped at her skin in a way that reminded Ysbel of her very early childhood. She took Tanya's hand, and they wandered wordlessly down the half-deserted streets towards the river. When she'd lived in Prasvishoni as a child, their home had been on the other side of the city, but her father and mother had taken them out to the river often on their off days, to watch the dirty water swirl and foam under the pedestrian bridges, between the concrete banks.

"I used to walk down by the river when I was at school here," said Tanya, nostalgia in her voice. "I would stand by it, and close my eyes, and pretend it was that creek at home, and that when I opened my eyes you'd be standing beside me, and we'd sit together and watch the water and talk, like we did before I left." She paused a moment, tightening her grip on Ysbel's hand. "I was standing by the river the day I decided to leave, and to come back to you. Because I couldn't bear to open my eyes one more time, and not see you there."

There was something slightly choked under her light tone, and Ysbel squeezed her hand wordlessly.

They walked alongside the river for a while in the gathering dark.

"How are you doing, my love?" asked Ysbel at last. Tanya turned and smiled up at her, and a last gleam of sunlight illuminated her features, and for a moment, Ysbel could almost imagine it was the light from her wife's face casting the glow across the city.

"I don't know," Tanya said at last, turning away and looking over the water. "I—you know, Ysi, I didn't think we would ever get out of prison. I thought our children would grow up there, and that I would die there. And so I stopped thinking of anything else, because it was too painful. But now? Now, it's like I was living on a ship's cabin, and trying to pretend it was the whole system, and now I'm out of the cabin and planet-side and—I don't know what to do with myself any more. I don't know who I am anymore."

Ysbel put an arm around her wife's waist and pulled her close, resting her head against Tanya's.

"And you?" asked Tanya softly. "How are you?"

Ysbel smiled slightly. "I'm getting better. Every day I spend with you, with Olya and Misko—I'm getting better, I think."

And strangely enough, it was true. She would still wake up at nights, sometimes, tears streaming down her cheeks, to nightmares, but Tanya was there to kiss the tears away, and—well, and watching Olya and Lev together—

She could have killed him for what he'd done. But knowing that she could have, and that she hadn't, because she'd chosen not to— somehow that made it easier to let it go.

They stood like that for a while, looking out at the river, not speaking, because they didn't need to speak. The cool breeze brushed their skin, and Tanya leaned her head against Ysbel's shoulder. "You were right," she murmured. "I think I needed this. Just one evening with no one trying to kill us."

From the other side of the water, a work crew was coming towards them in the dimming light, talking and grumbling loudly.

Tanya laughed fondly. "Prasvishoni never changes. Like we used to say in university, it may be a cold, miserable dump of a city, but it's our cold miserable dump of a city."

The workers crossed the bridge in front of them. They were wearing familiar non-reactive aprons over their government-issue tunics and trousers, and Ysbel smiled despite herself. "Working explosives at this time of night?" she called.

"Working explosive, or being worked over by them, depending on the day," the woman leading the crew called back.

"Or depending on how fast you move your feet, right?"

The woman leading the crew grinned at her. "You don't sound like you're from Prasvishoni."

"No. I was born here, but I grew up Outer Rim."

"I can tell. You could crack concrete with that accent."

The workers had drifted closer, the prospect of a healthy exchange of insults more exciting than whatever it was they'd been contracted to do.

"It's late for demolition work," said Ysbel, raising an eyebrow.

The woman nodded. "You know how this government works. Urgent, they told us, but then we had to sit on our hands for a month while the paperwork went through. I think it's done this time, though—if it's not, they'll have another crew glueing the pieces back together again. I'm going to get it done before they have time to change their minds again. We planted the charges a month ago, when word first came, but of course—" she shrugged eloquently. "Now it's rained enough times that we have to go back and replace the controller. But what can you do? Lady have mercy on all of us." She shook her head again, glancing up at the sky in mock prayer.

Ysbel chuckled. "Of course. What would the world come to if the government gave up on its paperwork? Where's the site you're taking down?"

"Apartment building," said the woman casually. "179 Rybachka street."

Ysbel's bones turned suddenly to ice. She met Tanya's eyes and saw the same sudden terror.

Jez's building.

She'd been stupid to imagine that they could spend five minutes not running for their lives.

Without stopping even to make an excuse, she and Tanya turned and sprinted back up the street.

"Jez!"

Jez blinked, and glanced at her com.

"Jez, you idiot! Answer your com!"

It was Ysbel, and she sounded frantic. Jez hit the button. "What?"

"The apartment is going to be blown up. Get the children, and get out, now. Tanya and I are on our way back."

Jez stared at her com for a moment, waiting for her mind to compute the words instead of trying very hard to remember exactly what it had felt like to kiss Lev. When it finally did, she jumped to her feet, swearing.

The door swung open, and Masha stepped into the apartment. She was frowning—damn woman was basically always frowning, at least whenever she looked at Jez.

"What's—" she began. Jez gave her a quick grin.

"Apparently we're about to be blown up. Might want to go back out."

"What?" Lev's voice came from behind Masha, and for a second

Jez almost completely lost her focus.

She shook her head. Nope, not the time.

Masha was sputtering something behind her, but she didn't have time to listen. She ducked under the curtain and glanced quickly around the darkened space. Misko and Olya were curled up on a pile of blankets in one corner. She bent over Olya and touched her shoulder.

"Hey. Kid. Time to get up. We have to go."

"Aunty?" asked Olya sleepily.

"Let me." It was Lev. She nodded, and snatched up Misko.

"Come on, gotta go."

Behind her, Lev scooped the sleepy Olya into his arms, and she blinked up at him.

"Put me down, Uncle Lev. I can walk."

"Alright, but you have to walk quickly."

Jez slapped her com against her thigh with her free hand. "Ysbel. How long do we have?"

There was a pause.

"Maybe fifteen minutes. Get the children out, we'll worry about the rest later."

"Yeah. On our way." She ducked out through the blankets, and came face to face with Masha, who was shoving documents, information chips, and bits of tech into an old leather satchel. Her face was grim.

"Masha—"

"Get the kids out," said Masha shortly. "I'll be there in a moment."

She shrugged, and crossed to the door in three long strides. She worked one hand free of Misko and jerked it open, and came face to face with Ysbel.

The woman took in the scene in a glance, then stepped back wordlessly and beckoned her out.

"Mama?" asked Olya sleepily as she and Lev passed them.

"Come on, Olya," she heard Lev whisper behind her, "They'll come in a minute."

Jez took the stairs two at a time, and when she reached the street, glanced around quickly. The neighbourhood was disreputable, the buildings tumbledown and the alleys lined with trash, but the space around the old building that contained her basement apartment was surprisingly clear. For a moment, her mind flashed back to that day three years ago, her first safe house apartment erupting into a fountain of flame, the sight of the neighbour woman lying in a pool of her own blood—she settled Misko more firmly on her hip, swallowing down the taste of vomit, and ran.

She didn't slow until they were a block and a half away. Lev was panting behind her, and Olya was whimpering softly. She leaned back against a wall, and a moment later, Lev came up beside her.

"Should be safe enough here, I think, until the others get out," she whispered. He nodded, breathless.

"If they're going to take down the building, rather than the whole block, I assume they'll use a block explosive, which should have quite a narrow blast radius," he said. "Stay with Olya. I'm going back to help Masha."

"Like hell I will," she said, her grin turning dangerous. "Listen to me, genius, I'm a hell of a lot faster than you. If anyone's going back —"

"Perhaps, but it also so happens that you also have absolutely no sense of self-preservation," he shot back, speaking through his teeth.

She set Misko down carefully against the wall of the alley, tucking the blanket he'd been wrapped in under and around him. He'd blinked awake, and was looking around with a disoriented expression. "You stay here with Uncle Lev," she whispered. "I'll be right back."

"Jez—"

She grinned at him, turned, and sprinted back down the street. She hit her com to Tae's line as she ran.

"Hey tech-head," she whispered into it. "Probably don't want to come back to the apartment anytime soon."

There was a moment's pause, then Tae's familiar, concerned voice in her earpiece. "What? Jez, is everyone alright? What's—"

"It's all good. I'll explain later." She hit the com off and took the stairs to the basement in three steps. She ducked through the door, into a scene of controlled chaos. Ysbel turned and opened her mouth.

"Kids are fine, a block and a half away, Lev's with them, before you ask," said Jez. "What do we need?"

"The rest of Tae's tech," Masha snapped. Jez nodded and dodged around the three women. She yanked a blanket down from where Tanya had attached it to the ceiling, and when she reached the corner that Tae had made into his tech space, she shoved chips, wires, tools, and bits of tech haphazardly into it. She grabbed the edges of it and pulled it up into a bulky bundle.

"We done here?" she asked, jumping to her feet. "Because you said fifteen minutes, and I'd say we've already spent about—"

"We're done," said Tanya shortly. "Out."

Masha slung the leather satchel over her shoulder, Ysbel and Tanya grabbed their own blanket bundles, and the four of them pelted up the dirty staircase and into the street.

When she reached the children and a very irritated Lev, they slowed.

"Mamochka?" Misko whimpered, and Tanya took him from Lev and held him, pushing his head down into her shoulder.

"Shhh, my heart, shhh," she whispered. "It's still night time. You'll go back to sleep in a moment."

"Mama?" asked Olya, detaching her hand from Lev's and grabbing Ysbel's. "Why did we have to—"

"I'll tell you in a moment, my sweet," said Ysbel. "Right now, we need to run."

Lev glared at Jez as they started off. She grinned back at him.

"Jez—" he began.

And then, from behind them, came a low *boom* that reverberated over and over through the streets, a blinding, incandescent flash that jagged across the back of her vision like lightning. She spun.

Behind her, where her old apartment building had once sat, there was ... nothing. A cloud of white prefab dust, rising slowly into the air like a fog.

She swallowed hard.

This was the second safe house she'd lived in that had blown up, and she wasn't sure she wanted to make this a habit.

They'd all paused, looking behind them. For a few moments, no one spoke. At last Masha said, grimly, "Back to the hangar bay, then."

Jez nodded.

Already in the distance, she could hear police bikes heading towards the scene, probably to try to keep order in the rapidly-filling streets. She glanced at the others, and they started off at a run down the narrow, darkening streets, almost deserted now in the dusky half-light of late evening.

At last, Masha shoved open a small door into the wide, echo-y space of the dusty hangar bay, and they followed her in. She hit the light bar, and a dim, flickering blueish-white light sputtered to life overhead, illuminating the graceful bulk of a ship.

Despite everything, Jez's heart stuttered slightly at the sight of it, a mixture of panic and desperate relief and pure, unadulterated happiness.

Yes, someone had just tried to blow them up, and her old apartment was nothing but a cloud of white prefab dust, and yes, this was the second safe-house that had been blown to rubble in the last three years, but—

But this ship.

There were tears in the corners of her eyes, and she brushed them away with the sleeve of her jacket.

Four and a half weeks ago, she'd never have dreamed she'd see it like this. Back together. All in one piece, glowing softly in the faint light, every thruster working, every control as responsive under her fingers as it had been when she'd first flown this beautiful, beautiful angel. But here it was, real and solid and perfect, waiting for her, like she'd known it would be. If she was being honest, that was what had kept her sane all these weeks of being grounded—the thought that here, right here, her perfect, perfect, beautiful ship was waiting for her, every part of it repaired, every piece longing to take her back into the sky the moment she set foot inside its perfect, beautifully old-fashioned corridors.

"Jez!"

She glanced up. Ysbel, eyes narrowed, gestured with her head towards Masha.

Now that Ysbel mentioned it, she remembered hearing Masha's voice start a while back.

She looked back at her ship once more, then finally managed to drag her eyes off its perfect, elegant, beautiful curves and over to

Masha.

Yep. From the look on her face, Masha'd definitely been considering killing her.

"—utmost importance if we want to actually stay alive, do you understand that, Jez?"

She gave Masha an easy smile. "'Course, you bastard." She paused. "Understand what?"

A muscle in Masha's jaw tightened. Then a voice crackled over Jez's com, making her jump.

"Jez. You alright?"

It was Tae. She hit her com, grinning. "Yep, told you. All good."

His voice was tight with strain. "Jez, listen. I—I need help. I found Caz and Peti and the others, but they're in trouble."

She frowned. "Where are you?"

"I'll send you the coordinates. I—I'm sorry. I need help getting them out of here."

She glanced at Masha. To her credit, the woman didn't hesitate. She tapped her com. "Tae, let's get them back to the hangar. It should be safe for the time being. There's plenty of room."

"Yeah," said Tae shortly.

"Hang tight, tech-head," Jez said. "We'll be there in a jiff."

She glanced quickly around the hangar bay. "Masha? You have any bikes?"

Masha jerked her head curtly towards the back of the bay, and Jez sprinted towards them, Lev and Ysbel on her heels. She swung her leg over one of the bikes, and Ysbel jumped onto another. Jez rolled her eyes at Lev. "Hop on behind me, genius, come on. We have to go."

He drew in a deep breath, his face already slightly pale, and, shaking his head, mounted up behind her. He put his arms around her waist and she hit the restraints, locking them down.

Despite the urgent tone in Tae's voice, the feeling of Lev's body pressed against hers by the restraints was not unpleasant.

She glanced at Ysbel and grinned. Ysbel shot her a flat look and hit her com. "If you get us killed with your flying, pilot-girl—"

"Come on, Ysbel. You've seen me fly."

"Yes. I have. That's the problem."

She gave Ysbel a wink, leaned forward, and the bike shot out the door Tanya had pulled open, barely high enough to admit them.

4

Tae slipped through the streets in the cool of the early evening. As he walked through the dirty alleys, the memories came back to him in physical sensations—the eternal, ever-present cold, huddling under blankets that always seemed to be a little too small and a little too thin, sitting awake, blinking his eyes against the exhaustion as he listened for the sound of the others' breathing. The smell of the streets, the taste of half-spoiled ration-packs, the thin sound of children crying. The ever-present alertness, and the ever-present fear.

He shivered, and walked faster.

It had only been a couple of months, but somehow he already felt like a stranger in this place that had once been his home—or as much of a home as he'd ever had.

He stepped out of a narrow side-street into a larger road. The familiar drab Prasvishoni apartment complexes lined the street on both sides, their dirty white walls marred with mildew and riddled with cracks where the moisture had oozed into the pre-fab and frozen, setting the edges and the corners crumbling. Dim, sputtering orange lights shone through some of the apartment windows above him, but most had already closed their curtains, and the only light was what seeped around the edges. How often as a kid had he watched those lights, sick with a sort of envy mixed with desperation, and wondered what it would be like to have somewhere warm to go home to in the cold evenings, even if was just a mouldy apartment with a flickering artificial light?

He swallowed hard.

And here, these last few months, he'd been sleeping on a comfortable cot in the *Ungovernable*, warm and well-fed, while Caz and Peti and the others slept in the streets, huddled together for warmth, looking at those dirty apartments with the same desperate longing he'd once felt.

How had he left them for this long?

He'd already passed the place they used to camp out when he was with them. He'd glanced at it as he went by, and it was as bare and uninhabited as it had been when he'd first come upon it a week ago. And the same panic snaked through his body now as it had then.

He tapped a number into his com and tried again, hopelessly. "Caz?" he whispered. "You there? Can you hear me?"

Nothing. There had been nothing all week.

He shook his head, lips pressed together, and kept walking. It was all he could do at this point. If you'd grown up as a street kid, you knew how to find the places that might keep you warm, so he'd walk the city streets until he found something. Masha wouldn't need him again until the morning, probably, and he knew how to stay alive at night in Prasvishoni.

The light was fading, the dirty glow of the sunset reflecting through the city force-field. His com crackled, and he jumped.

"Hey tech-head," came Jez's whispered voice through his earpiece. "Probably don't want to come back to the apartment anytime soon."

He slapped his own com. "What? Jez, is everyone alright? What's
—"

"It's all good. I'll explain later."

He gritted his teeth and glanced around. He knew Jez well enough
to know that whatever it was, it likely wasn't "all good."

This was the only time he was going to get today to look for the
street-kids, but—

He swore softly. Damn Jez to hell. For once in his life, he was
actually going to do what he'd planned on doing, instead of jumping
in to rescue everyone else. If Jez needed him, she'd have to actually
ask.

But his stomach was tight as he walked, and he kept glancing over
his shoulder.

He paused a moment in the entrance to a dark alley with a dead-
end wall on one side and shook his head in disgust.

This was ridiculous. Jez and the others could take care of
themselves. Why was he even—

And then the muffled 'boom' of an explosion shook through the
streets, and his heart almost stopped.

It had come from the direction of their apartment.

Damn it, he should have gone back, something had happened and
he hadn't been there, and—he'd already turned, without conscious
thought, poised to sprint back towards the apartment, or whatever
was left of it.

Something grabbed his arm. He whirled around, bringing his
hands up defensively—and he was looking straight into a thin,
terrified face that made his heart skip a beat and every thought of
the explosion disappear.

"Peti?" he whispered after a moment. She was staring at him, like
she wasn't entirely sure he was real. "Peti. It's me. Tae. What

happened?"

Her eyes were wide, and the hollows under her cheekbones stood out sharply in the dying light. She looked half-starved.

"Tae?" she whispered at last. He nodded, and her eyes filled with tears.

"Tae," she whispered again, and fell against him in an exhausted gesture that could have been an embrace or a collapse. He caught her, his heart racing, a sick fear spreading through his stomach.

"Peti. I'm right here. It's alright. What happened? Where's Caz and the others? Are you OK?"

She drew back finally, blinking hard. "Tae, I—we thought you were dead. We were sure you were dead. Why didn't you come back?"

The sickness twisted harder in his stomach. "I—I'm sorry. I was —"

"We watched on the newscoms. They said you'd died. They said you were a terrorist, and you'd escaped prison, and you and a bunch of other convicts were trying to steal weapons from Vitali Dobrev to kill people, and they shot you down. They had footage of the explosion."

"I—"

"We thought you were dead. Why didn't you come back?"

He blinked hard against tears in his own eyes, stress and worry and sick guilt. "I'm sorry, Peti. I—things happened. Lots of things. This was the first time—I haven't been back to Prasvishoni until now, and since we landed a week and a half ago, I've been looking for you. I'm sorry. I—" He swallowed hard. "Where are the others? Are they—" He suddenly realized he couldn't finish the sentence, and he wasn't certain he wanted Peti to answer.

He'd never seen her like this. She was usually joking and laughing and making the best of whatever situation they got into. This Peti, terrified and starving and accusing—he hardly knew her.

His heart was pounding so hard he felt dizzy.

"Are—you aren't still working for the government, are you?" she asked at last, her voice low. He stared at her.

But, then again, he supposed he deserved it at this point.

"No," he said in a low voice. "No. I'm not."

She watched him for a long moment, and the mistrust in her eyes cut him. Finally, though, she shook her head wearily. "I'll show you," she said, turning away from him. He followed, dread knotting in his stomach and tightening around his chest.

She slipped down the alley, and just before the dead-end wall, slid through a small gap between two buildings that he would have missed if he hadn't seen her go through it. He followed, squeezing his way sideways down the claustrophobically-narrow space until it broke out into a wider, hollowed-out opening in between two tall buildings, the white pre-fab blocks of the walls grimy from years of disuse and the dying light barely filtering in through the slit of sky far above them. He blinked, letting his eyes adjust to the dimness, and then something slammed into him, and he took a step back, catching himself against a wall.

"Tae!" said a childish voice, and with a painful lurch, he recognized it.

"Mila?" he asked, kneeling down so he was at her eye level. "Mila, is that you?"

She buried her face in his shoulder and nodded without looking up. "They told me you were dead," she whispered. "Caz and Peti told me you were dead."

"It's alright, Mila," he said, trying to choke back the tears in his voice. "I'm fine. I'm sorry. I didn't—I'm sorry. I'm so sorry." He thought he might actually throw up, the guilt squeezing so tightly that he could hardly breathe. He held Mila for a few moments, and he could feel the pathetic shape of her bones under the layers of dirty clothes she was wearing, and see the hollows under her eyes and beneath her cheekbones, standing out as starkly as Peti's.

Finally he stood and looked around him. Now that his eyes had adjusted he could make out the shapes of the other children, huddled against the walls.

They all looked thin, and in the dim light he could see the whites of their eyes, wide and frightened. But. But—

He counted quickly, once, then a second time, and slowly, something in his chest loosened. They were all here. All of them except Peti, who was standing beside him, and—

His chest tightened again.

"Caz?" he asked quietly, turning to Peti.

And then a figure slipped through the alley behind him, and he turned, and for a moment he thought he might pass out from relief.

The tall boy was skin and bones, and there was a wary fear in his expression that made him look much older than his seventeen years, his young face creased with lines of care and worry that hadn't been there when Tae had last seen him. But he was alive.

He stared at Tae as if he'd seen a ghost. "Tae?" he said at last, his voice cracking with emotion. "Is that you?"

Tae grabbed him in a hug, and Caz stiffened for a moment, then threw his arms around Tae. When Tae drew back, Caz pulled away, wiping tears from his face.

"Tae," he whispered frantic relief in his tone.

"What's been happening?" Tae asked, gesturing around.

"It's been bad," said Caz. His voice was choked, and he couldn't seem to stop the tears dripping down his cheeks. "It's been really bad since you left. They're alive, but I don't—I don't know for how much longer. Thank the Lady you're back. Thank—" he broke down, shoulders shaking in heavy, choking sobs. Tae watched him, helplessly, until Peti slipped around him and grabbed her brother in an embrace. Caz cried on her shoulder for a few minutes, his thin body shaking, and Peti was crying too. The other children watched silently, mute fear on their faces.

"I'm sorry," Tae whispered. "I'm so sorry. I'm sorry I wasn't here."

Finally, Caz straightened, wiping his eyes. He tried to smile. "Sorry, Tae. I—I just—"

He didn't have to finish the sentence. Tae had been fifteen when Kira had died, and he'd abruptly become the oldest kid in their street gang, the one responsible for everyone else. He couldn't count how many times he'd cried when the others were asleep, huddled into a ball, the terror and pressure and fear almost choking him.

And then he'd let the same thing happen to Caz.

"What happened?" he asked again, when it looked like Caz was able to speak. Caz took a deep breath and shook his head.

"They've been coming after the street kids. Like I told you that last time, before you—" he broke off abruptly. "Anyways, it's gotten worse since then. It's almost impossible to get food these days. Before, we could do odd jobs or whatever, go through the garbage dumps, but now, you get seen by the police and they'll take you. Doesn't matter what you were doing. Being a street kid is the only crime they need. I—we were trying—" he broke off again, shaking his head. When he spoke again, his voice was thick. "If it hadn't been for those credits you left, we'd all be dead. I don't even know what happened to the other street kid gangs. I didn't have time to look. We don't see anyone anymore, and we always have to be on the move. They catch us, we're dead."

"They've just been killing street kids? Like that?" asked Tae, horror tightening in his throat. Peti shrugged.

"I don't know what they do to them. They take them, and we never see them or hear from them again. Dead, in jail—don't know that it makes that much of a difference."

For a moment, he didn't speak. He couldn't, through the tightness in his throat.

"Caz," said Peti urgently. "What happened out there?"

Caz's face tightened instantly, his posture stiffening. "We have to go. That explosion? There's going to be cops all through this sector tonight. We've got to get out."

Tae caught their quick glance in his direction, but maybe for once they were right, he could actually help, because—

Damn it.

Sharp fear caught at his throat.

If everyone else wasn't already dead.

He tapped his com. "Jez. You alright?"

For an unbearable second, no one answered. Then her lazy drawl came through his earpiece. "Yep, told you. All good."

He slumped back against the wall in relief. "Jez, listen. I—I need help. I found Caz and Peti, but they're in trouble."

Her voice changed abruptly to sharp concern. "Where are you?"

He glanced at the others. "I'll send you the coordinates. I—I'm sorry. I need help getting them out of here."

Masha's voice crackled through the earpiece. "Tae, let's get them back to the hangar. It should be safe for the time being. There's plenty of room."

"Yeah." His voice was tight. He glanced up at Caz. "How much time do we have, do you think?"

Caz gave a helpless shrug. "I don't know. Who—"

"Just trust me, OK?"

He tapped coordinates into his com, and sent them over to Jez.

"Hang tight, tech-head," Jez said over the earpiece. "I'll be there in a jiff."

He felt his shoulders relax, for the first time since he'd seen Peti. He turned to the kids.

"Alright, listen. I have a place we can go. We should be safe. But it's a ways to walk. My friends are coming with backup."

"Your friends?" Peti's face was tight with worry and cut with mistrust. He put a hand on her shoulder.

"Peti, listen to me. This is our best chance at this point. OK?"

She stared into his eyes for a long, long time. At last she nodded.

"Alright, Tae. We'll trust you."

"It's not like we have a lot of options, anyways," said Caz in a low voice behind him. Tae turned and tried to smile.

"Caz, listen. It's going to be alright. I—I promised I'd come back, and that I'd take care of you, OK? I'm sorry it took me so long. But I will take care of you. I'll get you out of this somehow."

"I know," Caz said, his voice barely a whisper. "I trust you, Tae. I —" he swallowed hard, and stopped speaking.

Tae glanced around quickly. The space they were in had only one exit, the way they'd come.

Not good.

"Out," he said. "That's the first thing. If there are police coming, we'll be trapped in here."

Caz and Peti nodded wordlessly, and between the three of them, they roused the younger children and herded them gently through the narrow passageway back into the dead-end alley. When they were out, Tae counted quickly, his heart pounding too fast.

Yes. They were all there, Caz and Peti too. Now, all they had to do was—

"You! In there. Come out."

The voice was amplified by a com, and Tae's stomach dropped. Caz was frozen in place, Peti's expression terrified. He gestured them to stay behind.

"Don't move," he whispered. "I'll distract them. When they're gone, run."

He'd promised them, after all. He hadn't been there when this all started happening, hadn't been here to keep them fed, somehow, and warm, and alive.

This was the least he could do.

He took a deep breath, and stepped out of the alley.

Three police officers surrounded the entrance to the alley, weapons drawn. The captain, a tall, thin man, grey hair poking out from his helmet, gave a cold smile and turned to the others.

"Pretty well-fed for a street kid," he said, body relaxing slightly. "Go on, take him."

Tae barely had time to tense before one of the officers grabbed for him—and then the woman was thrown forward, bouncing face-first off the rough cement, and came to a skidding halt at his feet. He stared at her for a moment, then looked up.

Jez was grinning, the back end of her skybike swung around where it must have hit the officer. Lev, behind her, was pale-faced, his teeth gritted hard.

"He may be a street kid, but he's also my damn friend," Jez said. "And you will leave him the hell alone if you know what's good for you. Or—" she shrugged. "Haven't been in a decent fight for a while, so if you wanted to—"

The captain, recovering from his shock, grabbed for his weapon.

The skybike beside him exploded in a ball of flames, and he yelped and jumped back.

"You might rethink your strategy," came Ysbel's heavily-accented voice. She sounded smug.

The two officers looked at her, and then at Jez.

Then they ran.

Jez turned to him and grinned. "So, tech-head. Think those friends of yours want to sleep somewhere warm tonight?"

He didn't answer. He couldn't answer, through the sudden tears in his eyes and the lump in his throat.

"Go on," she said with a broad grin. "Those scum-suckers probably put a call out. But hell, I figure if we take out the whole damn squad, they might have other things on their mind than a bunch of street kids. Right Ysbel?"

"I think you're right, you idiot," said Ysbel with an answering smile, and Tae just caught a glimpse of the resigned look on Lev's face before Jez leaned forwards and shot off.

"Caz, Peti," he called back into the alley, his voice choking just a little. "Come on. We've got to go, quickly. But—I think we have a chance."

5

When they reached the hangar, Lev slid carefully off the bike. Jez was already on the ground, grinning around her in a self-satisfied way. He shook his head and leaned against the wall for a moment, fighting back the nausea. Then he glanced around the room.

The street kids Tae had brought back were huddled in one corner of the hangar bay, and his stomach twisted at the sight of them. They looked like they were about half-way starved, eyes wide and frightened and much too big for their faces.

And beside them, Tae, breathing heavily, but with a desperate relief in his expression.

"Hey tech-head," said Jez with a grin. "Made it, did you?"

Tae looked up at her, a faint, wondering smile on his face, but before he could answer, Tanya straightened from where she'd been bending over one of the younger children.

"Jez, get into the *Ungovernable* and bring out every blanket and sleeping mat you can find, please. These children are exhausted. Lev, get me the ration packs. Go on, quickly. Olya, please help him, my sweet. Tae, no. Stay where you are. Jez and Lev are perfectly capable."

Jez grinned and sauntered into the ship, and Lev looked after her for a moment. He glanced down when Olya's hand slipped into his.

"Hello Olya," he said, smiling despite himself.

"You're thinking about kissing Aunty Jez, aren't you?" she asked, a knowing look on her face. He felt his smile turn rueful.

"Well, Olya, to be honest, I do think about that sometimes. But at the moment, I think we should worry about getting some food for these kids."

"I heard you kissing her, you know. Back in the apartment, before we almost got blown up. You're pretty loud kissers."

Behind him, Ysbel snickered loudly. He could feel his face warming.

"Yes. Thank you, Olya. But I think the other children are hungry, so let's just get the ration packs."

By the time he and Olya had gathered a basket full of the ship's ration packs, Jez was already on the loading ramp, almost staggering under a pile of blankets and sleeping mats. She dumped them in a heap on the hangar floor and went back for a second load. Tanya, Ysbel, and Tae set about arranging them into a comfortable nest in one corner as Lev and Olya passed out the ration packs. The children stared at them warily for a few moments, but they were too hungry to be cautious, and soon they were all eating ravenously.

"Just one or two each for now, please," said Tanya over her shoulder. "I don't want them to get sick. They haven't eaten enough for a while, I don't know what they'll be able to handle."

The smallest girl, Mila, he was pretty sure Tae had called her, was the first to succumb to exhaustion. She slumped back against the wall, empty wrapper from her ration pack still clutched in her grimy hand. Tae, who had come to stand beside him, watched her with a mixture of concern and fond tenderness. He bent and scooped her up, and carried her over to where Tanya and Ysbel had arranged the beds, tucking her in gently. Another boy, maybe thirteen or fourteen, whose features were similar enough to hers that he must be related, watched with an expression of concern and relief that was almost tangible.

One by one, the children dropped off to sleep, lulled by the food and the warmth and the lateness of the hour. Finally, the only ones still awake were the oldest boy and girl, who must be Caz and Peti. They both had the exhausted look he'd learned to recognize in Tae, of someone who's learned to fight back their exhaustion because the alternative would likely be dying in all sorts of unpleasant ways.

They'd stood and tried to help pass out the rations, until Tanya had seen them and insisted that they sit and eat their own food.

"So," said Tae finally. "Could someone tell me why we aren't in the apartment?"

Jez came over and dropped down beside Lev, leaning back against the wall with a luxurious sigh, and Lev felt himself relaxing at the nearness of her, smiling despite himself.

"I mean, we could go back there," she said. "But probably wouldn't be all that helpful, since it was pretty much blown into dust last time I checked."

Tae turned to her with a look of blank shock on his face. "What—who—"

Lev shook his head wryly, pulling his mind away from the fact that Jez was sitting close enough to him that their shoulders brushed, and that even that touch set his body tingling. "We haven't ascertained that quite yet. It's been a busy night."

"And perhaps now would be a good time to do so," said Masha sharply, coming over and taking a seat beside them. "Jez, considering it was your apartment, do you have any ideas?"

Lev glanced over at Jez.

She shrugged, considering. "Well—" she began, "I mean, any of the smugglers I worked with would have probably wanted to blow me up. And I'd say there's a fair number of ex-lovers who probably wouldn't mind blowing me up if they knew I was here. I mean, I know I'm hot and all, but honestly, no need to be that sort of jealous. And—"

"Yes, Jez," said Masha patiently. "We're all aware of the fact that the list of people who would like to blow you up is probably longer than we have time to listen to at the moment. However, if what Ysbel heard is correct, this was planned, or at least approved, by the government. Whoever this was would have enough influence—"

"It could have simply been the government," Lev put in quietly. "As you recall, we're here because someone in the government has a very vested interest in none of us surviving this."

Masha turned to him. "Of course. But if they knew we were here, why would they have set the explosives a month ago? And why not booby-trap the door, like they did the first time they came after Jez? It doesn't fit."

He frowned, something that had been nagging at the back of his mind finally clicking into place. "And why," he said slowly, "did they warn everyone else in the apartment to get out? Because clearly they did. Do you recall seeing anyone else in that building in the last three days, Ysbel?"

Ysbel shook her head. "Now that you mention it, I don't."

Masha turned to Jez. "How did they usually put out announcements in the building?"

She shrugged. "Never spent much time there, to be honest, but I think they usually sent out info chips. Or stuck notices in the mail slot."

Masha nodded. "And you didn't receive a notice, I assume?"

Jez shrugged again. "I basically never check my mail."

Lev drew in a long, disbelieving breath as everyone turned to stare at Jez.

"So," he said carefully, after a moment. "What you're saying is, it's very possible that we were, in fact, warned to evacuate the building. And that the only reason that we were all almost blown sky high is not, in fact, that there was some nefarious government plot to kill us all, it was, instead, the fact that you didn't. Check. Your damn. Mail."

Jez shrugged again, still grinning. "What? You expect me to read through all the crap they put in there?"

He pinched the bridge of his nose to stave off a headache "That … is what most people do, Jez."

Jez quirked an eyebrow skeptically.

How was it even possible to want so badly to both kiss someone and to actually strangle them?

He took a deep breath. "So. Apparently, Tae, to answer your question, Jez neglected to check her mail. At all. For the last ten days. Which meant we missed the fact that the building was going to be brought down. Thankfully, Ysbel and Tanya found out in time and we got everything out. Including your tech," he added, as Tae opened his mouth.

Tae relaxed back against the wall, frowning. "So—the whole building was condemned?" He asked after a moment. He shook his head. "That seems a bit convenient, don't you think?"

"I don't know," said Ysbel. "Apparently, the explosives were placed a month ago. And, as Lev pointed out earlier, if they'd wanted to kill us, they could have set a booby trap, so that it would go off if Jez came back. Like the last time they tried to blow up Jez, when it was wired through the door frame."

"Still," said Tae slowly, "a month ago. Which would be right around the time we shot Lena down. Again, that seems very convenient."

"Wait," said Caz, blinking hard. He was clearly almost nodding off. "What happened? Tae?"

"It's nothing," said Tae, turning to him. "It's fine. My friends and I—it's kind of a long story."

"Tae," said Peti, struggling into a sitting position. "What's going on?" There was a sharp concern in her voice. Tae sighed.

"Peti. Caz. It's fine. It's nothing to do with you. We—ran into some trouble. With the government. It's fine."

'Fine' wasn't exactly how Lev would have put it, considering that there were apparently C level credit rewards for each of their deaths. Still—

"Where was this apartment?" asked Caz in a low voice.

"179 Rybachka street," drawled Jez.

Caz and Peti exchanged glances.

"What is it?" asked Tae. Caz glanced at the others uncertainly.

"Caz," said Tae quietly. "You can trust these people. I trust them with my life. I—trusted them with your lives."

Caz looked at him for a long time. Finally he nodded, slowly. "Remember how we used to hang around that section sometimes?" he said, his voice quiet.

Tae nodded.

"Well—we haven't. None of the street kids have, for the last month or so. There was word out that the building was condemned, but … you've seen condemned buildings. That one was in better shape than at least half of the apartment building still standing. Peti tried to find out more, and—" He turned to the skinny girl who looked like she must be his sister. She was frowning as well, mistrust sharp on her face. She glanced at Tae, and then at the rest of them.

"It wasn't structural," she said slowly. "It was—I don't know what it was. They said one of the basement apartments might have been contaminated. They were warning everyone that if they found any sort of material there, any sort of metal, it was contaminated and they should leave it alone until the building was brought down. I don't know what it was, but—" she broke off, shaking her head.

"Any sort of metal," said Ysbel slowly. She reached into her pocket and pulled out a small black sphere, about the size of the tip of her thumb. It gleamed in the dull, flickering artificial light. "How much do you want to bet that they found out where our pilot had gone to ground, and wanted to make sure there wasn't any of this left lying around?"

Lev stared at the small black ball that sat in Ysbel's palm, looking heavier than it had any right to be, and felt a small tendril of worry twist through his mind.

The thing was, it was certainly possible.

What was the government doing, that they were so desperate to hide?

"That's not all," said Caz at last, looking back and forth between them. "I—Tae." He turned to Tae. "I don't know what's going on, Tae. I don't know anything about these people, except that you trust them. And if you trust them, I—I'll trust them too." He had the weary, desperate expression on his young face of someone who didn't have much of a choice. "But listen. If you're really on the run from the government, you have to know. The mayor put a new system in place over the past month. It measures your biometrics when you come in through the force field. It can't track down your precise location, but they can find your general vicinity as long as you're in the city. They'll have known you're here from the moment you came in through the force field. For us, I don't think they ever went to the bother of tracking street kids individually. They'd just look for places where there were lots of people clustered together outside after dark. They won't come after us in here, because we're in a building, so we're not street kids. At least," he amended, glancing guiltily at Masha, "they won't come after us until we leave in the morning."

Tae glanced reflexively towards Masha, but before he could open his mouth, she held up a hand.

"Caz, Peti. I'm sorry," she began.

For a moment, Lev saw the sick disappointment on Tae's face, a sort of hurt that was almost a physical pain.

Masha continued, "you are not leaving tomorrow morning, unless you'd like to. Tae is part of my crew, and you are friends of his. For as long as you would like, this hangar is your home."

Tae turned to stare at her, and Lev had to bite back a slight smile at the expression on his face.

"Tae?" asked Caz after a moment. There was a sort of awed disbelief in his voice. "Is—"

Tae swallowed hard, still staring at the woman in the battered pilot's coat. She gave him a faint nod.

"I—yes," Tae said at last. His voice sounded a little choked. "I— you can stay. If you want to."

Caz was blinking back tears as well now. Finally, he nodded.

"Thank you," he said in a choked voice to Masha. She shook her head briskly.

"Thank Tae." She paused. "You're lucky to have a friend like him. From the moment I met him, he's spoken of nothing but finding a way to come back here and get you somewhere safe."

Caz and Peti were both staring at Tae. He tried to smile, but didn't seem to be able to quite manage it through the emotion in his face.

Lev felt Jez shift beside him. He glanced over to see her grinning broadly, but there was the hint of tears in her eyes. She paused a moment, then slipped her hand into his and squeezed slightly, and, of course, as always, despite his frustration with her, he momentarily forgot how to breathe. He squeezed her hand back and twined their fingers together, and she gave him a wink which made him forget how to breathe all over again.

"Well, this is all very lovely," said Ysbel in a voice that was half amused. "But I believe that Caz was saying the government knows we're here. So, I'm currently wondering why we're not all dead."

Jez grinned. "Easy. I took a whole damn bucket of non-reactive ship coating and painted the entire apartment with it when I moved in."

Lev turned to stare at her. "What? That stuff costs—"

She shrugged. "Not much, when you steal it off your smuggling cargo. Told you, Lena's been trying to kill me since basically forever, and besides, there was usually a bunch of people who wanted to kill me. Happened pretty often. Figured better safe than sorry."

Tae was staring at her as well. "You know," he said at last. "That is actually really smart."

She smirked at him. "Don't have to act so surprised, tech-head. I am pretty smart."

Lev had to bite back a chuckle at the look on Tae's face.

"So you're saying that dump we lived in, that hadn't seen a broom or a mop for probably the entire time that Jez lived there, was likely the only place on Prasvishoni that the government couldn't have tracked us," said Ysbel at last, shaking her head. "I don't even know what to say about that."

"You could admit that I'm a damn genius," said Jez, still grinning.

"A damn genius who didn't check her mail and almost got our entire crew blown into bits of rubble," muttered Ysbel.

"Alright," said Masha, holding up a hand. "Caz. How long do we have before the government can find us, with their new system?"

Caz frowned and glanced at Peti. "I don't know. It may take them a couple days to narrow it down. But they'd know you're in this sector by—" he shrugged. "Tomorrow, maybe? The day after?"

Masha nodded.

"Very well then." She paused a moment. "Lev. Send me everything you've found. I'll go through it tonight, and I'll get the documents forged. The day after tomorrow is the start of term, so this may not be bad timing after all. In the meantime—" she glanced around. "In the meantime, I suggest we all get some sleep."

Lev followed her glance to where Caz and Peti were leaned up against the wall, the hollows under their eyes black against their brown skin. He caught Tae's eye and gave him a quick smile.

"I agree, Masha." He squeezed Jez's hand before he let go, then stood and put out a hand to Peti. She hesitated, then took it warily and he helped her to her feet, and led her, half-staggering, over to the pile of bed-pads and blankets. Tae was helping Caz over, and the tall boy was leaning against Tae as if he hardly had the strength to stand. When the two street kids had both collapsed onto the makeshift beds, he turned to Tae.

"Masha was right, you know," he said quietly. "They're lucky to have you."

Even through the exhaustion in Tae's eyes, he could see the tight ball of relief and hope. Tae blinked a couple of times, and there was something glinting in the corners of his eyes. Lev smiled.

"Go to bed, Tae."

Tae nodded, and, after a moment, lay down beside the other street kids.

He was probably asleep before Lev finished turning away.

When Lev woke the next morning, Masha was still sitting in a corner of the hangar bay, a chair pulled up against a makeshift table, illuminated with a flickering orange halo of artificial light. She looked as if she'd just finished a delightful night's sleep and had a good breakfast, instead of sitting up all night forging documents, which is what he was certain she'd actually done.

"Hello Lev," she whispered when she saw him awake.

"Masha." He blinked the sleep out of his eyes, pushed himself up off the mattress that he'd thrown out on the floor, and crossed the dimly-lit hangar bay, stepping softly to avoid waking anyone. He reached her and bent over the table, peering at the documents spread across the table. "What do you have?"

She turned in her chair and smiled, but now that he was closer, he saw the tightness behind her eyes, the way her face was drawn from lack of sleep. "Well, Lev, I believe I have enough documents to get us all through the door, at least. Whether they will hold up under scrutiny will depend, ultimately, on our actions once inside."

He frowned slightly and pulled up a chair. "Masha," he said quietly, "you're worried about something."

She studied him for a moment, and for a moment he wasn't certain she'd answer. But at last, to his surprise, she sighed and gave him a slight, rueful smile.

"I was … unpleasantly surprised by how fast the government is moving," she said. "The fact that they tried to destroy Jez's apartment without even waiting for her to come back so they could set a trap—that isn't a good sign. It means they believe that whatever it is they're doing is either so dangerous, or coming so quickly, that getting rid of the evidence is more important than a chance to kill us."

"And do you have any idea what the government is moving so quickly on?" he asked. Again, she studied him.

"No," she said at last. "I'm afraid I don't."

He watched her, but she was Masha, and he had no idea whether or not she was telling him the truth.

At last he sighed and stood. "Well, I suppose I may as well help get breakfast. It looks like there will be enough people eating." He paused a moment. "I'm—glad. That you let the street kids stay here."

She smiled slightly. "This may shock you, Lev, but I'm not a complete monster. As I said last night, after everything Tae has done, I believe this is the least we could do in return." She glanced over at Tae, and Lev followed her gaze across the hanger bay, lit by the dim morning light seeping in through the high, dirty windows. Tae was awake, talking in a low voice with Caz and Peti, there was a soft look on his face, a sort of glowing joy and desperate relief that made him look almost not tired.

Lev smiled to himself. He hadn't actually realized how good it would feel to see Tae like this.

It wasn't until they'd all eaten, and Tae had finished going through the group of children, embracing them, talking, laughing in a low voice, and then he'd turned away and finished wiping the tears from his face, and he looked like once again he'd regained his composure, that Masha stood.

Lev suspected the delay was on purpose. He'd glanced over the table when he'd spoken with her that morning, and he was fairly certain she'd been done whatever it was she was doing before they'd even finished preparing breakfast.

He smiled to himself again.

He hadn't been wrong. These last couple months had changed even Masha.

"Alright," said Masha in her typical pleasant tone, crossing around the bow of the *Ungovernable* to stand in front of them. "The sooner we get into the university, the better. We're being hunted, and if the government can only track our general location, the sooner we get into a place with lots of people, the harder we'll be to find. So." She bent down and picked up a handful of chips. "Tae. As we discussed earlier, you'll go in as a student. Here's your student ID, your paperwork, and an assignment to your room in one of the dorms. Classes start tomorrow. As a new student, you won't be expected to know much. However, it might not be a bad idea to familiarize yourself with the layout of the university and as much of the internal politics as possible. You're listening for rumours, any sort of school gossip, about strange research, a professor that disappeared— anything."

She glanced back at the chips in her hand. "Lev." She paused. "You've been hired, starting tomorrow, as a member of the Academic Standards Board. That should get you access into the curriculum being taught, as well as access to records of past professors, and some contact with both the government liaison and the financing department. I have your job history and skills base here, if you'd like to take a look."

He nodded, and caught the chip Masha tossed to him, with a strange feeling in his stomach.

He had, for one brief moment, when they'd discussed this, thought that for just a few weeks, he'd have his dream of being a professor.

Although in reality, pretending to be a professor would likely have been even more painful than returning to the university already was going to be.

And it would be. No matter how many times he told himself it would be fine, that he'd gotten over it, that the life he had now was a good one and that everything he'd left behind had been inevitable— he knew, somehow, that stepping through those familiar gates would feel like a knife jabbed between his ribs, a sort of hopeless pain of what might have been and what could have been, and what he'd really have done if life had somehow been a little less ugly and a little less hardscrabble and a little less—well, life.

"Tanya, you're a security guard. Your credentials are here. I suggest you come up with a coherent backstory for continuity's sake, but really, you could use your own history almost verbatim, I suspect. There won't be much digging into the background of a security guard, I imagine. Although we will have to figure out what to do with the children."

Tanya nodded shortly, and caught the chip Masha tossed. "Ysbel and I talked about this last night. I think it will be safest if the children stay here—the government will be tracking us, not them. Ysi and I will come back and check on them when we can, but—I've spoken with Caz and Peti. They said they will care for them while we're gone."

"And me?" asked Ysbel.

"You will be a professor. Chemistry. You'll be taking the place of the man Jez knocked out in the alley, and listening for anything the other professors might let slip."

Ysbel frowned. "Why am I the professor? Wouldn't Lev be more suited?"

"There are too many other professors who might recognize me," he said. "I'd have to be constantly on guard. No one will recognize you there, since you have no previous ties."

Ysbel nodded slowly, but she didn't look happy. "Alright. But I will warn you, I am not a person who enjoys teaching. Or students. Or people in general."

Lev gave a slight smile. "You'll fit right in, then," he said. "I don't believe caring about students was ever a prerequisite."

"What about me?" asked Jez. "I could be a professor. Bet I'd be good at it."

Lev, for one horrifying moment, let himself contemplate the possibility. It was not a comfortable one.

"You, Jez," said Masha, her expression grim, "will be coming in as a government auditor. That will get you access to most of the internal records of the university."

Jez grinned. "Well, guess that isn't all bad. Although if you expect me to actually read through that kind of crap—"

"Which is why, Jez, I will be going with you, as the other auditor." There was a grim resignation in Masha's voice.

"Hold on just a minute," said Jez, narrowing her eyes. "You mean I have to work with you? The whole damn time we're in the university?"

"Yes, Jez." The tone in Masha's voice told him she wasn't any more thrilled about the arrangement than Jez was. "As you stated, you don't enjoy reading through documents. I, however, can—"

"You're damn well babysitting me, that's what this is about, isn't it, you bastard? You're plaguing well coming along to babysit me!"

"Jez—"

Jez took a step towards Masha, glowering. "Listen, you dirty plaguer, if you think—"

"Jez." Masha's eyes were narrowed as well. "Believe me. This is not something I am doing for my own enjoyment. But this is not about either of our personal enjoyment at this point. This is about finding out what exactly the government is trying to do that is so important that there were C level credit rewards for each of our deaths. You do understand that, I presume?"

"You know what I damn well understand, you mud-sucker? I understand that you—"

Lev sighed and took a step forward. "Jez."

She turned, glaring at him.

He held up his hands. "Jez, listen. We need to get in there, and Masha's right, having two auditors makes more sense than just having one."

"No, you listen to me genius." Her eyes were narrowed, her expression dangerous. "I'm letting this damn bastard babysit me over my cold dead body."

"Jez—" he was speaking through his teeth now.

"Listen, pilot-girl," Ysbel broke in. "I'm going in as a professor, which I do not want to do, under any circumstance at all. Lev is going as some administration hack, and I think you know as well as I do how much he would have preferred to be a professor. Tanya and I are both leaving our children, and I believe if you were to ask Tae if he'd like to enrol in the University of Prasvishoni as a first-year student, it would not have been high on his list of things to do. We're going in to get information, and then we get back out, and you will go in under whatever damn papers Masha has forged for you, because you can't forge your own way in. You do not have to like it. Do you understand?"

Jez glared at Ysbel, and muttered something about a damn plaguing sellout. Ysbel's expression didn't change, and finally Jez turned away in disgust.

"Very well," said Masha, her pleasant tone returning. "Now that that's settled, I advise we each get to work memorizing our backstory and whatever other information each of us need in our positions." She sighed and looked around. "We'll go in tomorrow. I hope this will be a short excursion—we go in, get what we need, and get out a few days later. But I suspect, based on the degree to which the government seems determined to go, that it will not be that simple. Therefore, I suggest we prepare as if we'll be in here for some time." She glanced around. "Does anyone have questions?"

No one spoke.

"Good. We'll go in tomorrow morning." She turned back to her table, and Lev watched her, biting the inside of his lip.

Tomorrow. Tomorrow he'd be back at the university where he'd grown up, not as a student, or as a professor, which had been his lifelong dream. As a thief and saboteur.

It had been a long, long time, and there had been plenty of life that had happened in the interim. But he could still taste the sick despair of that day, standing in front of the university commission, when he'd resigned his professorial application and told them, quietly, that he'd decided instead to take a job with the government. And he could still feel the sick weight in his stomach as he'd cleared out his university dorm room, his meagre belongings packed neatly into his battered suitcase, the permanent, heavy weight of the knowledge that no matter where life took him, no matter what else happened, he would never be coming back.

And now he was.

He turned away and took a deep breath.

He only hoped he'd be able to stand it.

Tomorrow.

6

Jez, day 1

Jez swallowed hard, trying to shove down her nerves as she idled her bike down towards the entrance arch.

It was a damn university. She'd flown jobs with seven escort ships trying to shoot her down, and there was absolutely no reason she should be worried about a damn university.

From above, the campus stretched out across several blocks, a cluster of tall buildings and identical, white-walled prefab dorms, and here and there a small, sad patch of grass, trapped in between the building walls rising on all sides.

It looked like an actual prison.

Genius-boy had come here on purpose, by choice, because he'd wanted to. She wasn't sure she'd be able to keep calling him genius-boy after this.

She glanced over her shoulder at Masha, who had managed to keep up better than Jez had expected on the ride over, and dropped down to street level. Masha pulled in front of her as they idled their bikes through the large arched entranceway, down a claustrophobically-narrow passageway between buildings, and onto the parking space on the roof of a high, sprawling building.

Jez dismounted, every muscle in her body tight with adrenalin. She scowled at Masha, who had just dismounted herself and pulled off her helmet, revealing an expression exactly as calm and pleasant as if parking damn bikes in damn universities that felt a whole damn lot like prisons was a normal thing.

And Jez had plaguing well kissed Lev again that morning before they left, and she was still feeling shaky, which didn't help matters at all.

Masha glanced at her and raised an eyebrow. "Jez. We're going in to introduce ourselves. So you are aware, the goal at this stage is to get the university president on our side. If she's on our side, we'll be able to get what we need practically unhindered. If she's not, I can't describe to you the barriers she'll be able to throw up. With that in mind, I need you on your best behaviour. Leave the talking to me. Are you ready?"

Jez managed a grin. "Come on, Masha, you know me."

"I do," said Masha grimly. "That is precisely why I'm worried." She turned. "Come on."

Jez watched her for a moment before she strode forward to catch up.

Maybe that crap with getting the university president on her side was Masha's goal. Jez just basically wanted to figure out a way to survive this somehow. And working with Masha, walking into a university that could have been a damn prison—well, it wasn't looking good.

They took an ancient lift down from the rooftop and into the depths of the massive administration building. Jez shifted uncomfortably in the drab government-issued uniform Masha had somehow procured as the lift made its shuddering way down. The clothing was was stiff and itchy, and not nearly as comfortable as the loose smuggler gear she usually wore. Hell, maybe that was why the government bureaucrats were all basically bastards.

When it shuddered to a halt and the ancient doors creaked and groaned their way open, they stepped out into a huge rotunda, with a domed roof that rose twenty metres over her head. The floor beneath them was polished black stone, smooth under her feet, and the internal walls were a sort of red brick that looked almost decadent in comparison with the dirty-white prefab walls she was used to.

Masha must have noticed her gaping, because she said in a low voice, "This is one of the older city buildings. Most of the rest of the university won't look like this, but they like to keep up appearances."

Jez nodded dazedly, still staring around her.

Who knew there were buildings like this in Prasvishoni?

Well, Lev did, obviously, and Masha, but then again, they were the kind of people who'd probably find this kind of crap important.

She took a deep breath.

She was in the University of Prasvishoni. She was going to be a government auditor, and she was going to be babysat by plaguing Masha. She didn't want to be here, in fact, there was basically nothing about this situation that she liked. But—well, hell. She was here now.

She felt a grin spread slowly across her face.

Masha glanced over at her, and her eyes narrowed in suspicion. "Jez, what—" she began.

"Nothing," said Jez, still grinning. "Anyways, guess you're right. Better introduce ourselves." Before Masha could respond, she strode across the massive open area towards a desk in the back corner.

The man behind the desk looked up at their approach and

frowned. "Did you need something?" he asked in clipped tones.

"Yep," drawled Jez. "You can let your boss know that we're here to audit the hell out of this place."

"You're—" he frowned, looking at her more closely, then his eyes widened and he reached surreptitiously for a red call-button under his desk.

She caught his arm. "Figure you don't want to do that."

"I—" His eyes darted around frantically, and Jez realized suddenly that he could probably see the outline of the heat pistol she'd shoved into her jacket pocket.

She winked at him.

He attempted a look of indignation, but only managed to look slightly sick. "If you're here to rob—"

She let go of his arm, still grinning, and reached into her pocket.

There was the crash of a falling chair as he dived for the ground.

"Hey now, figure if you do that every time someone tries to show you their ID, you'll probably end up with a lot of bruises," she called, leaning over the desk and letting the ID dangle from her hand.

After a long, long moment, the man emerged from under the desk. He straightened his jacket, glaring at her, but his hands were trembling.

"So," she prompted. "You going to call your damn boss?"

Behind her, she heard Masha let out a long, exasperated breath.

"I—" The man cleared his throat. "I didn't realize—I apologize." He smoothed down his jacket. "We weren't expecting you quite so— I can take you directly to the president, if you'd like." He paused a moment. "Uh. The." He gestured to her jacket pocket.

She settled the heat gun a little more firmly in place, and grinned at him. "Never know when one of those will come in handy.

Government buildings are pretty damn dangerous places."

He looked like he was about to protest, then appeared to think better of it, tapping the com on his desk and speaking into it in a low voice.

Jez didn't turn to look at Masha, but she could hear the sound of someone breathing out through clenched teeth, so she figured she basically didn't have to.

The man came out from behind his desk and, with a last nervous look at Jez's jacket pocket, led them hastily down the hallway, up a staircase, through several sets of doors and up more stairs, and finally, knocked on a door at the end of an expansive hallway, decorated with portraits of what looked like a bunch of stuffy old idiots who, from the expressions on their faces, had died of boredom at some point in the process of having their damn likenesses taken.

"Come in," said an impatient voice over the com, and their guide pushed open the doors with a grand gesture, and, beckoning them to follow, stepped inside the room.

"Jez—" began Masha in a low voice. Jez winked at her, then followed their guide into the office.

It was a large, circular room, with a long table in the shape of a half-moon. There were chairs around it, and each chair was occupied by a person who looked, basically, like they were bored enough and half-way dead enough to match the portraits hanging on the walls.

"These are Jez Petrova and Masha Ivanov," the man was saying as she entered. "They're the government auditors we were informed of yesterday."

Jez gave them a sharp grin.

They stared back at her with expressions that reminded her of Lena on a bad day.

"President." Masha stepped forward, addressing the woman at the head of the table. "I'm glad to meet you."

"And you," said the woman, her expression not changing. She didn't actually look like she knew what the word 'glad' meant. "You will be Senior Auditor Masha, and that must be Junior Auditor Jez."

Jez shot Masha a poisonous glance. Masha hadn't said anything about junior damn auditor.

"Yes." Masha was wearing her pleasant, bland smile.

"I assume that since the government sent you at this particular time, you're aware of the … projects we've been carrying out?" asked the president, her voice delicately probing.

"Of course," said Masha, and as Jez watched, she could practically see the people at the table relaxing under the undiluted power of Masha's charisma. "We're well aware of the … arrangement. In fact, one of our main objectives with this audit is to ensure that everything is proceeding as planned, on all levels. As I'm certain you understand, this will require our access to all levels of your classified information, in order for us to verify all the parameters, but …" she shrugged offhandedly. "I'm certain that will pose no problem."

"I am sure we can figure out a mutually beneficial way to provide you with the information you need." The president's voice was still slightly cautious, but it was also clear that she was more than half way to trusting Masha.

"I am very certain my employers will make your cooperation well worth your time," said Masha blandly.

"That's very good," said the woman, a small, rusty smile on her face that looked like an experiment gone wrong. "I've put up with enough while I've been here in efforts to do what your employers requested." She shook her head in disgust. "The students who can't afford to pay for their own education, and get stipends and scholarships, as if they actually provide some value that's worth the expenditure. I understand one professor your employers took a … special interest in some of those students. But as far as I'm concerned, if you or your family aren't industrious enough to pay for your schooling, you have no right to be here."

"Certainly," murmured Masha. Jez narrowed her eyes.

She didn't know all of Lev's story, but she knew enough. And he could probably think circles around this damn self-important bureaucrat.

Masha, as if reading her thoughts, shot her a warning glance, then turned back to the president.

"And the street kids. Street kids on my campus," the president continued, distaste evident in her voice. "Dirty, disgusting things. Like swamp rats." She gave a small shudder.

"I am entirely of your opinion," said Masha blandly.

Jez glowered.

She'd seen those kids last night, with their wide eyes and their starved, terrified faces. As between any one of them and this bastard, if the system could stand to be rid of someone, she knew who she'd pick.

The damn plaguer was still talking.

"I, for one, am glad our current mayor has taken a stricter view on them. It's long past time."

"Of course," said Masha. Jez couldn't see her face, but she could damn well picture it.

"As far as I'm concerned, the sooner he exterminates them, the better for all concerned. In fact, as part of your audit, I'd like you to take a look at a proposal I've put together regarding the elimination of the street child infestation through means of cutting off their access to food sources and removing any extraneous materials they could use for warmth."

"An intriguing proposal," murmured Masha. "I shall certainly review it."

Jez took a deep breath, gritting her teeth so hard they hurt. Her hands were clenched into fists, because that was basically the only thing stopping her from going for her pistol right now. Or else punching this idiot right in the middle of her damn face.

"And you, Junior Auditor," said the woman, turning to her with a condescending smile. "I assume you are in agreement as to the matter of street children?"

Masha looked like she was trying to catch Jez's eye, but frankly, right now Jez was too damn angry to care.

She gave the woman a dangerous grin. "Well," she said, drawing out the words. "Figure you're right that there's an infestation."

She waited a moment, just long enough to see the faint satisfaction beginning to spread across the woman's face. She took a step closer to the table, resting her hands on it comfortably and leaning forward. "See," she said in a chatty tone, "I had no idea how bad things had got. Because before I came here to audit this place, I didn't realize that we had a damn swamp-rat running the university."

For a moment, every person around the table seemed to stop breathing.

"Junior Auditor Jez," said the university president at last, in a dangerous tone. "I must say, I'm not accustomed—"

She could practically feel Masha's eyes boring into the back of her shirt, but hell, that was basically the story of her entire life since she'd met the plaguer.

Anyways, she was in too deep to back out now, even if she'd wanted to.

She gave the woman in front of her a smile that showed every one of her teeth. "Well, President Whatever-the-hell-your-name-is—you may as well start getting accustomed to it."

The woman looked, for a moment, unable to speak, her face a delightful mixture of shock, horror, and apoplectic rage. "Junior Auditor—" she began again, her voice shaking.

Jez shrugged casually. "Hey now, I may be a junior auditor, but at least I'm not a shrivelled-up skin-sack who couldn't find her bum with both hands and a map."

For a moment she thought the woman might actually stand up and try to hit her.

There was a long moment of deathly silence. At last the woman seemed to recover herself.

"Junior auditor," she said again, as if the words tasted rotten in her mouth. "You and your, ah, companion, will have all the access I am legally required to give you. As I stated. Now, I am busy, and I expect you have somewhere you need to be."

Jez grinned. "Well, here's the thing. Figure we do have places to go, seeing as we can't possibly—"

"Yes, I believe the junior auditor and I do have pressing business," said Masha through her teeth, grabbing Jez by the arm and pulling her around. "We will discuss this matter later."

Jez winked at the woman over her shoulder as Masha dragged her from the room, down the hall, and into a side corridor.

Masha turned on her, lips pressed into a thin line. "Jez Solokov," she hissed. "What in the system were you thinking?"

Jez narrowed her eyes, adrenalin still pulsing through her. "What? I thought that went pretty well, all things considered. I mean, I didn't punch her in the damn face, for one thing."

"Jez." Masha's jaw was set, and, Jez considered nostalgically, it had been a long time since she'd seen Masha so angry. "We have one chance at this. Now the president of the university will make it her personal mission to keep us from getting any useful information whatsoever."

Something twisted in Jez's stomach. Because hell, Masha was probably right, but the thing was, she'd actually been trying. Until the dirty scum-sucker had asked her opinion, she'd actually been trying to keep her damn mouth shut.

Not that plaguing Masha would care.

Not that it bloody well mattered.

"Yeah? Well, from the look of her, I'm not sure that she could keep—"

"Jez! This is not a joke. You will stop this immediately, or—"

Jez leaned back against the wall, still grinning dangerously, heart still beating too fast. "Or what, you bastard? You're the one who wanted me to work with you."

"Believe me," hissed Masha, "it was not because I enjoy your company. You need to sit down and figure out what you're doing here—insulting people because you think it's funny, or actually trying to keep every last one of us from being killed."

Jez raised an eyebrow. "She was the one who asked my opinion. I didn't say one damn thing before she did, and—"

"I hope," Masha snapped, glaring at her, "that when the government manages to find us and kill us because we couldn't get the information we've come to find, that you still think it was worth it."

7

Lev, day 1

Lev stood at the front gate to the university. He'd watched from the street as Tae walked in, the kid's posture tense, his entire body on edge as if waiting for the chance to run.

And—well, to be honest, Lev wasn't certain his own posture was any different.

He knew every cobblestone here, every dip in the street that could trip the unwary, every loose stone on every building, the way the rising Prasvishoni sun would glint off the long, high windows, which courtyards were sunlit at which time of day. He could have walked from here to his old dorm blindfolded, where he'd stayed up through the night and into the early morning studying, lost in the sheets and sheets of letters on his com screen, where sometimes he'd brought back a girl, both of them laughing and drunk on sump and hormones and as careless and stupid as any of the students he could see now, crossing the campus.

It was so familiar he could taste it, but, as he looked across the campus now, it felt a million years ago, like a story that had happened to someone else.

He took a deep breath and stepped through the archway.

He knew exactly where he was going, but he wandered between some of the old buildings, looking around as if admiring the sights.

That building, there, on the far side. That was the sciences. That was where Ysbel would be teaching, if he had to guess, although they occasionally put the newer professors in another building that wasn't theirs, crammed into the schedule somehow. And there, the government aptitudes building. He'd always done well in those classes, although he'd never dreamed that it was those skills, not his theory skills, that he'd ultimately use in his job. And there, the narrow courtyard with the fountain. He used to nap in it's shadow when he'd get out of his 0700 morning class.

And across the way, the massive bulk of the administration building, the largest on campus, and probably the grandest.

He sighed, and started towards it.

Just as well to get this over with. No point in nostalgia right now.

He stepped inside and glanced around, waiting for his eyes to adjust from the bright sunlight of the large, open courtyard in front of the building. When he was able to make out his surroundings, he noticed a harried-looking man at the desk. He walked over to him and held out his ID.

"Hello Jakob," he said, noting the tag on the man's shirt. "Academic standards board. Newest member. Would you be so kind as to page them?"

"Of—of course, sir."

Lev frowned at the man. He looked flustered.

"Is there something wrong?" he asked, keeping his tone one of polite interest, although something in his stomach dropped.

"No, no. I'm sorry. It's—been a rather eventful morning, is all. The new, uh, government auditors arrived." There was a tone in his voice that Lev now recognized as that of someone, innocent and unwarned, who had encountered Jez. He relaxed slightly, biting back a smile.

"I see. And were they—difficult?"

The man glanced around reflexively, and leaned forward. "I don't think there's a word to describe what they were," he muttered. "I would watch out for them, if I were you. At least the tall one. If they weren't government, I suspect they wouldn't have lived through the meeting with the president today."

Lev raised one eyebrow, somehow managing to keep his face perfectly straight. "That bad?"

The man shook his head. "No. Worse. Whatever you're imagining—worse."

"Ah." Lev still, somehow, was wearing a neutral expression, his voice the perfectly-modulated tones of polite interest.

"I'll call the Academic Standards and let them know you're on your way," the man said. "I assume you know your way there?"

Lev shook his head and gave a polite smile. "No. I was interviewed via com. I did study here, but that was years ago. But I'm certain I'll find my way, if you can page them."

The man tapped the com on his desk and spoke into it. He glanced up at Lev. "Your name, sir?"

"Lev Preobrazhensky."

"Lev Preobrazhensky," the man repeated into his com. He listened for a moment, then turned to Lev.

"Go ahead. They're waiting for you. Straight ahead, up to the fourth floor, right out of the lift, and the fourth door on your left."

When Lev reached the correct door, he paused for a moment.

He was back. Officially part of the university.

He took a deep breath, straightened his jacket, and stepped

through the door.

The entire board, it appeared, was waiting for him, and he saw the expressions that flashed over their faces at his entrance.

He didn't blame them. From his resume, they'd likely expected he'd be at least in his early forties.

He gave them a pleasant smile, and studied their reactions.

The man in one corner was almost certainly Maxim, the president of the committee, and beside him would be Klava.

She had an interesting history. The kind of woman who would sit back and watch, likely, see which way the wind was blowing.

It would be instructive to see how she responded to this.

"You are Lev?" Maxim asked. Lev nodded, keeping his smile pleasant, and ignoring the insult in the man's tone. There was that instant re-evaluation in the man's eyes, and the expression that flickered over his face was transparently easy to read.

Someone who backed down from a conflict, the man was thinking. Someone who was easily intimidated.

The man narrowed his eyes. "Good. I'm glad to have you here. I'll admit, we were expecting someone a little older, but then, fresh blood is never a bad thing."

Lev nodded again, pleasant and self-effacing.

Klava was watching him from the corner, but even she seemed to be on the point of making up her mind about him.

"Well," Maxim continued, a jovial note creeping into his tone, "As I was saying, I'm glad to have you. I've been looking for someone to act as head of the student advisory department."

Head of the student advisory department. The president assumed he'd be impressed by the title.

If he'd done his research a little more, though, he'd know that it was a dead-end job of bumping your head against a wall, over and over and over again. But impressive to a dewy-eyed innocent who was easily impressed, and easily fooled. Or else, acceptable to someone educated, but too unambitious and afraid of conflict to object.

The man was watching him closely, gauging his reaction.

He wanted to know which one Lev was.

Lev didn't let his smile drop.

The thing was about politics—you needed to know exactly what you wanted. You needed to understand everyone who planned to stop you. And you had to be able to be pleasant, quiet, and completely ruthless.

He'd spent seven years in the government. And he was very, very good at it.

"Thank you," he said smoothly. "I'd be happy to take on that job."

He paused for a moment to allow them to react.

He was the first, then, they'd be thinking. A dewy-eyed innocent.

He could see the faint disappointment in Klava's eyes. She'd apparently read through his resume, and she'd expected more.

"Of course," he added carefully after a moment. "I'm certain you are aware of everything that goes along with that position."

Maxim frowned at him, his pinched face creasing. "Everything—"

"It's in the old university rules," Lev continued, his voice still mild. "The position of head of student advisement carries with it a responsibility for not only knowing the curriculum, in order to advise students, but understanding how the curriculum was developed and its purposes."

The man's face cleared. "Ah. Yes, I'm aware of—"

"Which means," Lev continued, "that I will have to have access to every record for every other branch of this department. Because, as you know, we are the academic standards committee, and everything we do touches on the students' experience." He gave them a bland smile. "I accept the position, of course, and I'm duly honoured by your trust. I will begin inspecting each of your reports and your internal records for each of your departments starting tomorrow. I'll collect my access from the university administration aid on my way out, if you'll be so kind as to confirm my position with them."

Klava was looking at him with a new respect, and he had to bite back a smile at the look on the president's face.

He was neither of the two possible options they'd considered, of course, innocent or unambitious. He was the third—someone who knew the rules of the university inside out, had access to files most of the people in this room could only dream about—had, in fact, been thrown in jail for reading things even he shouldn't have had access to —and had a photographic memory.

"I—you know, now that I think about it, there is another position I could offer you," began the president. "One with significantly more prestige, as well as—"

Klava lifted her hand. "Come now, Maxim," she said. "You offered him the position—let him do it. We do need someone to head that department, after all." She was smiling, but her smile was cold and challenging. Lev raised an eyebrow.

He'd suspected, from reading the reports, and, it appeared, he'd been correct. She was the real power here.

He smiled back, pleasantly, and caught the faint respect in her eyes, and the note of challenge.

She was telling him that she would be harder to dupe than the president, and less likely to walk into her own trap. And his own bland smile was telling her absolutely nothing. But then, if he was right about her, she wouldn't need him to tell her anything.

Still, he'd always enjoyed a challenge.

"I'm sorry," he said, "I realize I haven't been introduced to each of you."

The president narrowed his eyes. "I do apologize, Lev." He paused, and gestured to the woman beside him. "This is Klava."

He introduced her first. So she wasn't just a power behind the scenes, then—the president was fully aware that she ran the department.

Lev, still smiling, gave a small, respectful nod as the president finished the introductions. "A pleasure to meet each of you," he said. He waited until Maxim had relaxed slightly, once more in control of the situation, then added, "I generally begin my work day early, while I'm still fresh. I'll expect access to all your reports tomorrow by 0600 hours. I'd hate to disturb anyone by waking them, but as there's nothing really for you to prepare—I assume it will not be a bother."

They stared at him, and there was something approaching panic in each of their eyes.

Because of course. He'd worked in the university before. There was always something to hide. And unless he was much mistaken, they'd spend the hours between now and 0600 tomorrow morning hiding everything they could manage.

And he, beginning at 0600 Standard tomorrow, would have a clear trail into whatever it was that these people in the university thought it prudent to keep secret.

He gave them all one last, bland smile. "Now, I believe I will get settled in my apartment. I'll see you tomorrow. I look forward to working with each of you."

He turned on his heel and walked out of the room, closing the door firmly behind him. Turning his back was always a risk, here in the university, but he suspected no one would try to murder him in the main boardroom in broad daylight in the administration building.

Give him at least another week to find out secrets about them before they'd be desperate enough for something like that.

He smiled to himself as he walked down the hallway.

He took a circuitous route to the faculty and administration housing, across the square from the student apartments.

He'd looked at these apartments as a student, across from his own tiny dorm. He'd assumed he'd live in them one day.

And now—well, here he was.

Klava was waiting by the door to the building, as he'd expected she'd be.

"Lev," she said.

He turned to her, still smiling slightly. "Hello, Klava."

She studied him for a long moment. Her records said she was seventy-three, and she looked every one of her years, but that did nothing to detract from the sharp intelligence in her gaze.

"You're remarkably well informed for someone on their first day on the job," she said at last.

He spread his hands depreciatingly. "I prefer to go into a job having done my homework."

She nodded, still watching him thoughtfully. "It does make one wonder how much homework you've done on your colleagues."

He gave a non-committal shrug. "I wouldn't dream of prying into any information that would be untoward."

The look she gave him told him she knew exactly what he was saying.

"Well," she said at last. "I worked with a professor once. She was a close friend, inasmuch as there are close friendships in these departments. And she believed the same thing you do about privacy, for most of her tenure. Except towards the very end." She paused.

"That was almost nine years ago, of course, but things haven't changed that much."

Lev's heart gave a strange jolt.

Nine years.

Evka had disappeared nine years ago.

"Do you recall her name?" he asked, offhandedly. Klava studied him for a moment, then gave another of those sharp, warning smiles.

"I do not. I do hope, Lev, you find our department a place where you can comfortably grow old."

The threat—or warning—was hardly veiled.

He nodded, still smiling, although his heart was pounding. "As do I," he murmured.

She stepped aside. "I don't want to keep you. Please, make yourself comfortable. I hope you find your quarters to your taste."

"I'm certain I will," he murmured. He unlocked the door with his key card and stepped past her into the hallway, letting the door swing shut behind him.

He felt faintly dizzy.

Evka. Why had she brought up Evka? Because he was almost certain that was who Klava had been referring to.

His apartment, when he pulled open the door, was larger and more spacious than he'd imagined. There was a main room, with a couch, a small coffee table, and a couple high-backed chairs, the walls lined by bookshelves. Through one doorway he could see a study, laid out with a large, if ancient, desk, more bookshelves and chip storages, and a large, comfortable-looking faux-leather easy chair. There was a bathroom at the end of the hall, larger than the ones in the student dorms, although that wasn't saying much, and across from it, a bedroom. Through the bedroom door, slightly ajar, he caught a glimpse of a window looking out on the square.

He dropped his luggage on the floor in the main room and pushed the door to the bedroom open carefully. It took him a moment to see it, but then, he'd been half-way expecting it.

Stuck deep into the headboard of the bed was long, thin, deadly-looking knife.

He scanned the room quickly with his com.

No heat signal. So whoever it was had likely left.

He stepped inside, and, wrapping his hand in the sleeve of his jacket, gingerly pulled the knife free. He turned it over in his hands, examining it. Nothing particularly noteworthy, except the fact that it had been imbedded in his headboard.

The question now of course was, who was worried enough about what he'd dig up in their reports to threaten to kill him? And Klava —had she caught him at the door to protect whoever left the knife? Or to protect him?

And what did all of this have to do with Evka?

He walked over to the window and dug under the frame with the tip of the knife, until he removed the tiny recording device whoever it was had left. He crushed it delicately under his heel. Then he locked the window and made his way back into the main room. He placed the knife on the small coffee table in the centre of the room and dropped into the easy chair.

All things considered, he'd uncovered a surprising amount of information for having been here less than an hour.

The problem now appeared to be living long enough to figure out what it all meant.

8

Tae, day 1

Tae kept his head down as he stepped under the archway into the body of the university.

He'd memorized the layout of the university campus Lev had given him, but he stopped for a moment at the large map, trying to control his breathing.

There was no way going in as a new university student could possibly be worse than breaking into Vitali's compound, or into prison, or trying desperately to find a way to keep everyone alive when their ship was dead in deep space and they were being hunted by a murderous smuggler boss.

But somehow, he couldn't convince his nerves of that.

Get inside, find the information Masha was looking for somehow, then get back out. That was all.

He closed his eyes for a moment, trying to slow his racing pulse.

"New here?"

He whirled around.

A young man was studying him. He looked maybe a couple years older than Tae, with a handsome, friendly face, pale skin, long-ish, sandy-brown hair, and striking green eyes. He had a self-confident, almost cocky air, but his smile was friendly.

"Um," muttered Tae, "yes. I'm—I just—"

"That's OK," the boy said. "It's a bit confusing when you first get here. Let me see your card."

Wordlessly, Tae fumbled for his student card and held it out. The older boy scanned it quickly with his com, and his smile broadened. For a moment Tae almost flinched, expecting some insult, but the boy said, "Must be fate—you're rooming in the same hall I am. You got all your paperwork? Come on, I'll take you back there and you can drop off your suitcase." He started off, then turned back, holding out his hand. "Sorry. I'm Dmitri."

"Tae," Tae mumbled, taking the proffered hand. Dmitri's hand was the soft of someone who hadn't had to do much physical labour, but his grip was pleasantly firm. There was, Tae noticed, a slight dimple in the side of his mouth when he smiled.

"Nice to meet you, Tae. You want a hand with that bag?"

"I—no. I'm fine. Thank you."

Dmitri shrugged, still smiling. "Well, let me know if you get tired. It's a long walk."

It wasn't actually that long of a walk—twenty standard minutes, maybe. But considering all of it was within the campus, and considering the massive buildings rising around them, the small, closed-in courtyards full of grass and the ever-present evergreen trees like the ones that surrounded the city—Tae shook his head.

For a street-kid who's biggest dream in life had been a one-room dirty apartment in the bad part of town, this much luxury, these many buildings, hallways open and classrooms lying empty every night while Caz and Peti and a thousand other kids like them slept huddled in dirty corners of alleyways—it was like a slap in the face.

At what must be the far end of campus, Dmitri stopped in front of a row of dingy white buildings, their walls constructed with the familiar pre-fab blocks Tae recognized from the typical Prasvishoni apartment complexes. Dmitri gestured to them with a depreciating smile.

"Sorry, the student dorms aren't fancy. But, not too far from classes. You can roll out of bed hungover and still get to class before it ends, as long as you've chosen your schedule wisely." He gave a small smirk, and pulled out his own student card. "Card here. That'll let you in the building. Don't lose it. I did once, and I couldn't get back in. Had to stand out here at three in the morning shouting until someone woke up and let me in." He chuckled. "I was actually surprised no one called the police on me."

Tae froze. Dmitri laughed. "Family would lose their minds if you got a police report?"

Tae nodded dumbly, and Dmitri chuckled. "Don't worry about it. They're used to drunken university students causing a ruckus. If they'd come, they would probably have given me a warning and unlocked the door with their master-key, honestly. At the very worst, they throw you in a cell to sleep it off and let you out once you're sober."

Tae's breath was still coming a little too quickly.

He would never fit in here. He would never fit in to a place where having the police called on you was a joke, where the worst thing you had to look forward to was a hangover, or maybe an evening in the cells before you were let go. Caz, back at the hangar, Peti, the rest of them, would have been killed if the police had caught up to them, and he'd spent five months in jail, certain he'd never walk the streets freely again, and—panic clutched at his chest so tightly that he wasn't certain he could still pull air into his lungs.

"Tae? You alright?" Dmitri was frowning at him. Tae closed his eyes for a moment, forcing himself to draw in a long breath, then another. He opened his eyes and tried to smile.

"Yeah. Sorry. I'm fine. I just—I—"

Dmitri was still watching him curiously, but he gave him a sympathetic smile. "First time away from home?"

"I—yes. I suppose."

Dmitri shrugged. "Don't feel bad. I think everyone gets a bit of a panic attack the first time they get here. It's a big university." He pulled open the door and gestured Tae inside. "Get into your room, get unpacked. You'll feel better."

"Yeah. Thanks," Tae muttered. He followed Dmitri into the dingy hallway, up three flights of stairs dirty from hundreds of boots, and down another dingy hallway. The dim overhead light flickered a dull whitish-blue, making the hallway look even starker and colder than it felt.

"What's your room?" asked Dmitri. Tae glanced down at his com.

"Um. Thirty-seven."

"That's you at the end, then," said Dmitri, gesturing. "I'm a few doors down on this side."

Tae nodded again. He felt like an idiot, but at the same time, he had no idea how a college student would react, because he'd never been a damn college student, just a scared street-kid, with every waking thought consumed with staying alive just one more day, and keeping the rest of the kids he was responsible for alive as well.

"Nice to meet you, Tae. You should come down for dinner. We're going to Stolovaya 734. It's a hole-in-the-wall, but the food is decent. A bunch of us are getting together. Celebrating our last evening of freedom."

"I—I'm sorry. I'll—probably be busy. Getting ready for

tomorrow."

Dmitri shrugged. "Let me know if you change your mind. I'll see you around, Tae."

"Yeah. Um. Thanks for showing me around." Tae felt his cheeks warming. Dmitri gave him that easy smile.

"No trouble. I was going this way anyways." He turned and held his card up to one of the doors. It clicked open, and he stepped through, leaving Tae alone in the hallway. Tae closed his eyes again for a moment, clenching his teeth against the sick feeling in his stomach. Then he pulled the battered suitcase Lev had lent him down the corridor to the last door, with a faded "37" painted in black paint that was already worn so thin that it was difficult to make out exactly what they numbers referred to, unless you already knew what you were looking for. He held up his student chip-card, and the door lock clicked. He pushed it open with his foot and stepped through.

The room itself was tiny, almost as small as the cell on the prison planet where they'd found Tanya. On one side, there was a narrow cot that looked about as comfortable as the prison cots, and on the other, a long desk with a hard-backed, battered chair. There was a sink and a small mirror in one corner, and a door that led to a bathroom small enough that the toilet was almost inside the shower. A battered bureau completed the furnishings.

Tae sighed and dropped his suitcase on the cot. He pulled it open, but there was depressingly little to unpack. Masha had insisted on buying a few clothes that would look like something a university student might wear, and some school uniforms, and he shoved those into one of the drawers. Under them, he shoved the tech he'd brought, just in case. If this was just a matter of hacking into something, he wouldn't have the tight knot in his stomach he had now. He knew how to hack into things.

What he didn't know—what he'd realized he didn't know, the moment he met Dmitri—was this.

He was here to get information, that was all, although how the hell he was supposed to do that he had no idea, because he had no idea how to make friends with people like this, kids who'd grown up in a world so different than his own that it could have been a whole different system.

His life on the streets had prepared him for a lot of things, but this wasn't one of them.

He glanced out the narrow window. Three stories below, students were clustering around the doorway, talking animatedly, laughing and gesturing, and suddenly he felt a sharp pang of loneliness.

Those kids—they looked like they'd never wondered where their next meal was coming from. They'd had time to learn how to do things like make friends, joke and laugh and take classes for fun, complain light-heartedly about the dorms, because they'd never slept in the street. The way they laughed and talked, they'd never learned the wary, haunted silence he'd learned from before his first memory, that all the street kids had. That even Olya and Misko had.

He turned away from the window and dropped onto his cot, and dropped his head wearily in his hands.

He was here, in a university, in his own private room, with credits on his com chip and no shortage of food, surrounded by people. And he couldn't remember a time in his life he'd ever felt quite so alone.

By mid-day he'd finished unpacking, made a couple half-hearted attempts to hack into the university system—it had been so easy that it hardly seemed worth the effort—and gone over Lev's and Masha's instructions at least three more times.

Talk to the students, make friends, track down rumours about strange things happening.

He tried to shove down the sick panic that started in his stomach at the thought of what he was supposed to be doing, what he had no idea how to do.

Finally, shaking his head, he stood reluctantly.

He should wander around the university grounds, probably, get to know the area.

He changed from his street clothes into one of the drab school uniforms and made his way down the dingy corridors and out of the apartment, and wandered through the maze of buildings, towering over the narrow green courtyards. These buildings weren't made from pre-fab. They were red brick, accented with white brick that managed to look actually white, instead of the colour of grime and mildew that passed as white on the pre-fab buildings he was accustomed to. High windows rose in every wall, arched with brick, with one block of shiny stone set as the capstone to each arch. They looked old, and venerable, and forbidding, and he couldn't help but shiver. He found his way to the buildings noted in his class schedule for the next day, which took longer than he'd anticipated. Clusters of students wandered past him, but he seemed to exist in a sort of bubble, and they separated around him almost subconsciously. He kept his eyes firmly on the ground, and swallowed down the lump in his throat.

He wasn't actually a student here, and he was never meant to be.

He was almost back to his dorm when someone shouted, "Tae!"

He looked up quickly, frowning.

"Tae! Over here!" Across one of the courtyards, a familiar figure with sandy-brown hair was striding towards him, that easy, friendly smile on his face, and again Tae had to swallow down the knot in his throat.

"Tae!" said Dmitri, when he was close enough to be heard without shouting. "I thought you were going to be busy all afternoon." He slapped Tae on the shoulder, his expression teasing.

"I—I was—"

"Come on. You don't even have classes until tomorrow. We're going out, and you're here—may as well come with. You haven't eaten yet, have you?"

"I—no. But—"

"No buts. Come on, there's a whole group of us going." He turned to a tall girl with dark hair and dark skin beside him. "Vera, this is Tae. It's his first day here, and I'm trying to talk him into not being a stick-in-the-mud."

Vera laughed, and held out a hand. "Hi Tae. Vera. Nice to meet you. Sorry you had to run into this idiot first. I promise the rest of us are pretty normal." Her voice was husky, and warm with affection.

He took her hand, and found he was half-smiling despite himself. "Hi Vera."

"So," said Dmitri, grinning. "You coming?"

Tae sighed internally. "I—sure," he said. "Thanks."

Dmitri's grin widened. "Good! I was hoping you would. Come on, I'll introduce you to everyone once we get there."

'There' turned out to be a small, cramped diner a block away from the university, and five standard minutes in, Tae had already forgotten at least half of the names that had been shouted at him from around the three tables Dmitri and his friends had commandeered in the back. They were an eclectic mix, friendly and talkative. Vera asked him about his family, and he stammered through the cover story Masha had created for him—parents from the poor part of town, both working, he'd gotten a scholarship somehow—but she didn't even question it, just nodded with polite interest. A boy named Leonid asked what his class schedule was, and they all gave a collective groan of sympathy when they discovered he had a class starting at 0900 standard every morning. And somehow, in the noise and the chatter and the laughter, he found the tight knot in his stomach had begun to loosen.

It didn't make sense, of course. He had plenty of things to worry about, and he couldn't afford to relax, not yet.

But—

But somehow, when it was far too late and they made their laughing, shouting way back to the university dorms, he found himself smiling at the jokes and the banter. When he reached his dorm, the others waved and shouted their farewells as he passed the key-card over the outside door lock.

"See you around, Tae!" called Vera. Dmitri turned from an animated conversation he'd been having with Leonid and two other kids whose names Tae had already forgotten.

He caught Tae's eyes and grinned. "Glad you could make time in your schedule, Tae," he called, and for some reason, Tae found himself smiling back.

It was just because now, now that these students could be, maybe, friends, perhaps he could do what Masha and the others needed him to do. That was the only reason he felt so much lighter.

But—he pictured for a moment Dmitri's smile, the way the corner of his mouth dimpled.

He was still smiling when he reached his dorm. It was still tiny, but it felt, somehow, less grim than it had that morning.

9

Ysbel, day 3

Ysbel dropped a case onto the long desk at the front of the classroom.

Lev had warned her that they might try to assign her to a different building as a power play, since she was a new professor. However … she smiled to herself slightly.

It appeared that the ability of intimidation she'd honed in prison worked just as well in a university setting as it did in a jail. The administration officer had looked so relieved when she'd left the office with her classroom assignment—to what appeared to be the most convenient classroom in the science building—that she'd thought he might faint.

She pulled out the chip they'd given her, with the term's curriculum and schedule on it. She'd sat in on a faculty meeting two days ago. Apparently, she was supposed to show this to the students, with a schedule of what they'd be learning which day. And then, apparently, she was supposed to follow the schedule herself.

Which she had no intention whatsoever of doing. She'd looked at the schedule, and it was ridiculous. How they expected these students to understand chemistry by learning this was beyond her.

She shrugged internally, and dropped the chip into the trashcan.

They'd hired her to teach chemistry, and she was going to teach chemistry. Until they found out what in this corrupt hole of a place needed to be stolen, or destroyed, or blown up, after which she would happily leave these idiots to their own devices.

Anyway, it had been a strange schedule. Some of it was, she supposed, natural enough. But there'd been an emphasis on solubility of various metals in liquids and solids. An odd subject, but nothing too strange.

Except—except she and Tanya had finally managed to do a chemical analysis on the metal that had come from Jez's jacket pocket.

It was highly, highly soluble.

Nothing dangerous, certainly, no reason she could see why the government was so protective of it. And yet, with what she knew, combined with this odd schedule ...

A bell rang in the hallway, and she glanced up, narrowing her eyes slightly.

This was the part she'd wanted nothing to do with—the actual students. Chemistry was fine. You couldn't blow things up effectively if you didn't have a broad working knowledge of chemistry. Even the faculty meetings she'd discovered she could navigate with surprising facility. But university students were not something she had any desire to have close contact with.

The first of them began filtering in a few moments later. She ignored them, unpacking the padded case she'd brought with her.

From the corner of her eye she saw a couple of the students glance at her, then at their coms.

"I am taking over from Professor Gurin," she said, without

looking up.

The back of the classroom filled up quickly, as if the students were doing their best to stay as far away from her as possible. There was, in fact, a short scuffle for a chair in the farthest corner, but when she glanced up with her flattest expression on her face, the scuffle ceased instantly. As more and more students arrived, the closer rows filled reluctantly until most of the seats in the room were taken.

The bell rang a second time, and Ysbel sighed and straightened, looking grimly out over her class.

They were young. That was the first thing she noticed. Tae was young, and Jez, and even Lev. But they had lived their lives, and it showed. Not one of them had the babyish youth of these children, who reminded her more of Olya than of Tae.

They also looked mildly terrified, which, she supposed, was fair.

And then, in the corner, she caught a glimpse of a familiar face.

Speaking of Tae—

He sat with his head down, long hair falling into his eyes, shoulders hunched slightly, and she felt a sudden pang of pity.

He wouldn't feel any more at home in this place than she did.

He glanced up and caught her eye, then looked away quickly, and she sighed internally and shook her head.

Tae was smart, and he'd be able to take care of himself.

And furthermore, if anyone in this classroom tried to bother him, she would vaporize them, which might help.

At any rate, best to get started.

"Hello," she said. "I am Ysbel Kuznetsov, your new professor. Professor Gurin was in an—unfortunate accident, and was unable to teach this term, so I am taking his place."

From the looks the students were giving her, they were fairly certain she'd murdered Professor Gurin and hidden the body.

Which, to be fair, was not entirely divorced from the truth.

"They gave me a syllabus," she continued, her tone completely flat. "It was a stupid syllabus, and I am not using it."

The students, who had all bent over their coms, looked up in faint confusion. At last, one of the students in the front timidly raised her hand.

"Professor. Professor Gurin told us that if we wanted to pass the class this term, we'd need to know specifically the topics he set out in the schedule. He—he was very insistent, especially for the first couple weeks. And besides, if we don't have the syllabus, how are we supposed to—" she noticed Ysbel's expression, and swallowed hard. "I mean, what would you suggest for us to study between classes?"

"I will give you something to study between classes," said Ysbel in a tone which she'd used to successfully intimidate prison gang leaders. "In the mean time, you will pay attention to what I teach you. Because the thing about chemistry is, if you get it wrong—" she made a quick motion across her throat. "You die. So it's important to know what you're doing."

They were all staring at her now, wide-eyed with terror. She gave a long sigh.

"I'm not planning on killing you, you idiots. I won't need to. Because if you can't grasp the basics of chemistry, you will probably end up inadvertently killing yourselves before the end of the term. So I suggest you pay attention. Do I make myself clear?"

There were scattered, terrified nods.

In the back of the room, Tae raised his head and this time gave her a slightly amused look. She managed not to crack a smile at him.

"Alright then. I think we understand each other. So." She reached into her bag and brought out a fine powder. "Can anyone tell me what this is?"

They stared at her blankly.

She sighed and shook her head. "Look at this," she said slowly, as if talking to an infant. "I would like you, please, to tell me how you would determine the chemical composition of this."

For a few moments there was terrified silence. At last one student raised a timid hand.

"Yes?" grunted Ysbel.

"I—would do a chromospectrum scan," she said, voice shaking slightly.

Ysbel raised an eyebrow. "Very well. I will do that." She pulled out a scanner and waved it in front of the tube, then shook it. "There. Carbon, hydrogen, and oxygen, in a ratio of 3-6-2."

Considering what she'd seen of them so far, she was hardly surprised at their lack of reaction.

"And is that all you'd like to know?" she prompted.

"Maybe an acid test?" volunteered another student from the back.

"That's not a terrible idea, generally speaking." She pulled up a holoscreen and expanded it, and with the tip of her finger, wrote down a line of figures. "If you were to do an acid test, this is what you'd see. Anyone else?" She turned back to the class.

No one moved.

"Very well," she said. She took one of the test tubes gently. "With what we know of it, how should I treat this compound?"

There was another silence.

"I will show you, then," she said. She placed the test tube into a holder on the non-reactive counter, stepped back, then, with the long teacher's pointer, tapped the base of the tube smartly.

The test tube exploded, a jet of white-hot flame bursting up to the ceiling, the *crack* of it enough to temporarily deafen her.

When the thick smoke cleared slightly, she glanced around the classroom.

The students sat completely petrified, all except Tae, who appeared to be trying, unsuccessfully, to cover his laugh with a cough.

"So, you see?" she said, waving smoke away from her face with one hand. "Those were not bad ideas to analyze the compound. But none of you knew what to do with the information once you had it. If I'd passed that around and one of you bumped it, there would have been none of you left sitting here, because you'd have been blown into pieces so small that it wouldn't have been worth gathering them up to take home to your parents. So, can you see why I told you that it was important to understand chemistry?"

No one moved, apparently convinced that any movement at this juncture might be their last. Ysbel shook her head.

"That will do for a lesson for today. I'm going to let you go early. But before I do, I will tell you what I expect in my classroom. You will pay attention. You will ask questions if you don't know. You will do the homework, and you will do it carefully. And in return, I will try to keep you alive, although after what I've seen today, I don't think I can promise anything. I also expect you to bring goggles and explosive-level ear protection, because what I did today was something very, very minor compared to what might happen in this class if you get answers wrong. Do you understand me?"

This time they did nod.

"Good. You may go."

For a long moment, no one moved. Then, at last, the braver of the students stood, stricken looks on their faces, and began filing out the door in a sort of stunned trance.

Tae, in the back, stood to go, but as he reached down to gather his materials someone bumped him, and his info chips went flying across the floor. Even from here she could see his shoulders tense, and she felt her own shoulders tense in sympathy. A tall girl, who was sitting across from him, stood quickly, and Ysbel narrowed her eyes.

Perhaps it wasn't what that idiot Masha would have wanted, but she wasn't going to stand by and let Tae be beat up by the other students.

But instead, the girl knelt and began scooping the chips up and handing them back up to Tae. He looked up, frowning. She smiled at him, and offered the chips again. He took them carefully, as if he wasn't entirely sure what she was doing. Another boy knelt beside her, and grabbed a couple more chips that had slid under the chair, and dropped them into Tae's outstretched hand. Tae was still frowning in confusion, but Ysbel felt a small smile spreading on her face.

The boy reached out his hand and helped Tae to his feet, and the three of them walked out of the classroom.

Ysbel watched them go.

These idiots were certainly young, and they were almost certainly stupid.

But—perhaps not as bad as all that after all.

She found she was actually, reluctantly, smiling.

Then she frowned suddenly. What had that student said about that other stupid professor? He'd specifically asked them to study the first part of the schedule, which was that strange unit on metal solubility.

She reached into the trash can and pulled out the chip from where she'd thrown it. She studied it for a moment, then slipped it into her pocket.

Perhaps it was worth looking a little deeper into whatever it was Professor Gurin had set the students to study.

* * *

When she stepped out into the hallway, Tanya was waiting for her. Somehow, even her security-guard uniform—dark navy slacks and button-down shirt, heavy black boots—she could still take Ysbel's breath away.

"Hello, my heart," Tanya whispered teasingly.

Ysbel smiled, and pulled her in for a kiss. "My Tanya."

Tanya had called her on the com the evening before, told her that she had arrived, that there had been no trouble when she'd come in, and that the children were fine. But still—the small bed in Ysbel's faculty apartment had felt empty and cold without Tanya's familiar warmth beside her.

"Have you terrified the students already?" There was a smile in Tanya's voice, and once again Ysbel was reminded how much she loved this woman. "I saw them walking out. They looked like you'd threatened them with violent death."

"I did not threaten them with violent death," Ysbel grumbled, smiling despite herself. "I only warned them of the dangers of making a mistake in your chemistry compositions."

Tanya chuckled, and Ysbel drew in a long breath and pulled her close. She'd almost forgotten, in the five and a half years they'd been apart, how having Tanya here was somehow as good as food and water and shelter and warmth together.

"So, you are a security guard now?" whispered Ysbel into Tanya's hair.

"Yes." Tanya pulled back slightly to look into her face. Her expression had sobered. "Yes, my heart, I'm a security guard, and they were telling me what I was expected to do as part of my duties."

Ysbel frowned. "What?"

Tanya paused for a moment. "They told me that in a few weeks, it was possible that there'd be a disturbance. They wouldn't give me more details than that. But whatever it is—" she shook her head. "There is something that's going to happen, soon, and they're worried about it. Or, more accurately, they're worried how the students and faculty will react to it. I don't like it, Ysbel."

Ysbel frowned as well.

The children were safe. She'd spoken to them the previous night as well—the street children, now that they were warm and fed and no longer in danger of being disappeared by the police, seemed to have taken to the two youngest members of the 'gang' with absolute delight.

Still—

There was something coming.

For a moment she remembered, once again, the look on her father's face as they'd fled Prasvishoni in the early hours of the morning, when she was a child almost too young to remember it, the explosion that could have killed the three of them as easily as smashing an insect.

And here she was, back in Prasvishoni, fighting to find out how to keep her own family safe.

She leaned in and kissed Tanya once more. "It's alright, my Tanya. We'll figure this out."

Tanya smiled slightly, then sobered. "Be careful, Ysi. There is something wrong here. I have only been here three days, but I can tell. There are too many secrets."

Ysbel nodded without speaking. She'd felt it too.

Whatever was coming, it had permeated this whole rotten place like gas through air.

10

"Jez." There was a sharp tap at the door. Jez blinked and rolled groggily to her feet, trying to remember where she was. Prison? No, she was pretty sure she'd gotten out of that. She rubbed her eyes hard, blinked again, and looked around her more carefully.

She was in a room, small-ish, with the same white pre-fab blocks as a prison cell, but more of a nod to comfort. There was a window, and a door that didn't look sturdy enough to be an outside door, and

—

Oh. University. She was in Lev's university. And she was starting to wonder more and more why in the system he'd ever wanted to come back here. And the voice outside her door was Masha.

"Jez!" The knocking came again.

"Coming," she shouted back. She pulled on some clothes, splashed water from the sink on her face, and made her unsteady way out of the room, through the small cramped study, and to the front door, which she yanked open.

She'd never actually had this much space to herself, and she wasn't completely sure she liked it.

Masha stood there, her expression one of cold resignation.

"Jez. I'm glad to see you decided to get up. Considering that in exactly—" she glanced at her com, "three hours, we have an appointment with the finance department. And in the meantime, I would like to go through as much of the information we have on them as possible. As much as I would have enjoyed doing that on my own, it will look suspicious if my junior auditor—" she was so obviously holding herself back from putting an emphasis on the words that it almost made it worse, "is not with me. So I'd appreciate your punctuality."

"Yeah? Well I'd appreciate not having to look at your damn face first thing in the morning, you plaguer," Jez muttered under her breath.

"And this time, Jez," Masha continued, "I would appreciate you letting me deal with the financial department, considering the … difficulties we had last time."

Jez smiled at the recollection, and Masha's face hardened.

"Jez?"

Jez rolled her eyes. Masha turned away, lips pinched, and walked briskly up the corridor.

Jez followed her as she made her way across the campus to a tall, narrow building next to the administration building where they'd made their appearance yesterday.

"The records building," said Masha shortly, after they'd showed their IDs and entered. "I highly doubt they'll have stored anything important here, but I refuse to go into a meeting anything less than fully prepared."

She led them to the lift, which was, if anything, even more ancient than the ones in the rest of the university, and to a small room on the fifth floor, with narrow slots for windows that looked down into the walkway below, and an orangey artificial light that almost seemed to make things darker, rather than lighter.

Masha, who seemed completely familiar with the layout of every damn room in this damn maze of a place, scanned the shelves until she came to a centre shelf far back in the room. She pulled out three com-chips and handed one to Jez.

"Start looking through this, please. I'd like you to be familiar with the way the financial records are prepared."

Jez stared at her, open-mouthed. "Listen, Masha," she said, once she'd regained her power of speech. "I agreed to break into a university and steal crap. And maybe blow crap up, I'm ok with that too. But I never said I'd spend my damn life going through—"

"Jez." Masha's voice was one of sorely-tried patience. "If you don't look through this, it will be difficult to ascertain what exact 'crap' we are supposed to steal. So I would appreciate it if you would please at least attempt to do what we are here to do."

Jez narrowed her eyes, but managed to bite back her retort. She took the chip from Masha's hand, shoved it into her com, and pulled up her holoscreen with bad grace.

Damn Masha, and damn Lev, and damn every single damn person who'd agreed to put her with this damn, plaguing idiot.

She dropped into a chair and began scrolling aimlessly through the long columns of numbers. Looked like someone was trying to mark down how many credits each department had used for what, but honestly, it was almost impossible to keep her mind on the task. She bounced one leg against the leg of her chair, then tipped her chair back and leaned up, pushing the holoscreen so it reflected against the ceiling, to see if that would help.

It didn't.

She rocked her chair back and forth absently for a few minutes, then dropped it to the ground abruptly, pulled the holoscreen back over her wrist, and paced across the room a few times. Plaguing Masha seemed completely absorbed in what she was doing.

Figured.

She wandered over to the window and hopped up on the narrow sill so she could peer out.

It was still early in the morning, and the dim rays of sun that managed to penetrate the grimy air of the city made the faint dusting of frost on the grass sparkle dully. A couple of students made their way down the walkway, with the dazed, half-awake half-stagger of someone who had been awake much too late, and woken again much too early, but other than that, the broad walkway and the brick courtyard outside the administration building was almost deserted.

Then she frowned.

Almost deserted. But there was one track of footsteps across the rapidly-melting frost that seemed—off. They didn't seem to be heading towards any building on campus. Instead, they were crossing to—she squinted. It looked like a narrow space between two buildings. Like an alley, except it didn't look like it went all the way through.

And there were no footsteps leading out.

There was no reason the sight of those footsteps should send a strange sense of unease up the back of her neck. Probably just a student, who wanted to—what?

Well, that was the thing. She couldn't honestly think of any reason why a person would go into a dirty, dead-end crack between two buildings like that. Well, that wasn't entirely true. But she couldn't think of any reason that didn't involve things she'd never really associated with universities, like robbery, or murder, or …

She shook her head. Probably just being overly suspicious.

She sighed, and paced back and forth across the room a few more times, then, out of sheer boredom, turned back to the numbers on her chip.

They were arranged by value in credits, and by department, and she raised her eyebrows as she glanced through them.

Guess working at a university wasn't such a bad gig, if you got the right position.

At some point she wandered back over to the window, and glanced out at the narrow dead-end alley between the buildings. The frost had melted by this point, but—she was pretty sure she could see a dark shape, far back inside the entrance.

Wouldn't be able to see much from there, except … well, except this building. The records building, where she and Masha were working.

Again, the unease stirred in her stomach.

She shook her head and went back to alternating between pacing and flipping frantically through the pages of her com, trying to keep herself from going completely out of her mind.

She was not good at this. She was definitely not good at this, and she was grounded, and the more she thought about it, maybe being in university was basically the same thing as being in prison, and she needed to be in the air again, she needed it, and for a moment she thought she might actually go mad—

"Jez."

Masha's cold voice brought her back to the room, and she took a deep breath, forcing her hands to unclench.

She'd be fine. Hell, she'd survived weeks in prison. She could survive a couple days here. And anyways, the university was full of students, and if she knew anything about twenty-year-old kids, there's be plenty of places to buy sump. Maybe she could just go get smashed tonight, maybe that would help.

In fairness, it never actually had before. But there was always a first time.

Masha was, apparently, still talking.

"—go in there, I expect you to let me do the talking. Do you understand me, Jez?"

She scowled at Masha, and didn't deign to answer.

Damn everything to hell. Could you actually die from being stir-crazy?

If you could, she was definitely on her way out.

As they crossed the courtyard, she glanced over at the tiny, cramped alcove.

It was empty now.

She shook her head. Maybe she'd imagined it. Not like she hadn't been going half-crazy up there. Anyways, what had there been to look at in the records building? Just her and Masha, basically.

And then, finally, they were up the seven sets of stairs in the administration building, down a long corridor, and standing in front of a door covered with real wood paneling. Masha shot her one last glare, tapped firmly on the door, and then, without waiting for an answer, pulled it open and strode inside.

The room was huge, and almost empty. At one end of a long table sat a man, small and slightly built, but with a contained energy about him she hadn't expected in someone in a university job. Four other people who were probably board members sat on either side of him. All of them watched silently as Jez and Masha entered.

"Hello," said Masha, in her calm, pleasant voice. "I'm Masha, the government auditor, and this is junior auditor Jez. We're here to discuss our access to your internal records. I believe the university president spoke with you."

The man at the head of the table pushed back his chair and rose. He was smiling, but it wasn't a nice smile.

"Ah," he said, ignoring Masha and looking directly at Jez. "I had heard from the president of the university that you might be stopping by."

"Was it, perhaps, when you confirmed your appointment for this morning?" Masha's voice was still pleasant, but there was an edge to it.

The man ignored her again, and crossed around the table until he was standing only a metre or so in front of Jez. He had to look up to look her in the eye, but the expression on his face was one of such disdain that he might have been looking down from a damn captain's deck.

She grinned at him, showing all her teeth.

"So, Junior Auditor," he said, matching her smile, his eyes narrowed. "According to the president, you are the person I should be talking to. Since you seem to be the one with the most to say."

She probably shouldn't be grinning. But hell, she'd spent the whole damn morning trapped in a tiny room full of stuffy old information chips.

"Yep," she drawled, leaning against the table casually and ignoring Masha's furious gaze. Couldn't blame her for answering a question when the damn idiot had asked her specifically. "Guess she would say that. You should ask her next time about swamp rats."

The man was still smiling, but his eyes narrowed further. "I'm sure that the president would be happy to tell me all about her conversation with you, if I asked. But you see, I have very little interest in what you said to the president, or what you said to anyone else—I understand you say a lot of things to a lot of people. What I'd really like to know is, what exact protocol would you expect me to use to allow you access to our internal records? As I'm sure you're aware, I am unable to grant anyone access unless they are able to point me to the exact section under which they have authority. Because if I do otherwise, I could be on the line for losing my job."

Jez gave him a speculative look. That crap had probably been on the chip that Masha had given her to study, honestly. The one she hadn't got around to looking at yet.

From the corner of her eyes, she caught the expression on Masha's face. If the plaguer had a heat-gun, she'd probably have shot Jez already.

Jez turned back to the man, still grinning, and pulled up the holoscreen on her com.

"Well," she drawled, "I have no idea about sections and numbers and authorization and all that crap."

He gave a small smile of triumph and opened his mouth to reply, but she didn't give him time.

"Thing is, though," she said, pulling the holoscreen around between them, "guess while I was looking through your financial crap, I did notice something I found a little interesting. Thought maybe you'd like to explain it to me."

The man's smile didn't falter, but she could catch just a hint of uncertainty behind his eyes now.

She expanded the holoscreen, and drew a circle around a number at the top with the tip of one forefinger.

"Funny," she continued in a chatty voice. "Pretty sure this column is the total spending allocated to your department for salary and wages. And pretty sure this here—" she drew another circle, "is the wages you paid. Guess you thought people weren't going to look through it. Because unless you spent a few hundred thousand credits on getting the credits out to the people you pay, there's a pretty damn big gap in the information here." She slapped her palm over her com, and the holoscreen disappeared. She was still grinning.

He wasn't. In fact, he looked like he'd started to sweat slightly.

"Now, I'm not much of a numbers person," she said, hopping up to sit on the edge of the table. "But here's the thing. Masha here, she is a numbers person. And I'd be willing to bet that she could find some interesting patterns in there, if she were to take a look. Shame for that to go into the report she's sending back to the government, wouldn't it?"

"I—" he began, his expression growing increasingly desperate. From the corner of her eye, Jez noticed the other four board members shifting uncomfortably.

She shrugged. "No skin off my nose. I mean, I'm sure you have an explanation for it. Thing is, though, if we don't get access to your files, I guess we won't be able to put in any explanation when we write up our report, right Masha?"

Masha was looking at her speculatively now, one eyebrow raised. "No," she murmured. "I supposed we wouldn't, at that."

"So." Jez turned back to the man and slid off the table, landing with a thump on the hard floor. "Guess that's your final answer, then. Masha? No point in wasting our time with these idiots. Let's go talk to someone who might be a little more cooperative."

"Wait," said the man, holding up a hand. "I—I am sorry. I hadn't noticed the—discrepancy. I'm certain it's just an internal accounting error, hardly something that would be worth—"

Jez turned and stepped closer, so he was looking up and she was looking right down into his face. "Here's the thing, you dirty plaguer —if you don't want us to put that in our report—"

"As my colleague said," Masha broke in smoothly, "I'm certain you are correct as to the existence of an accounting error. However, it would be difficult for us to verify, without full and unfettered access to your internal records. If you can't grant us that, I certainly understand, but—" she shrugged delicately. "We will have to write something in our report."

The man glared at them, clearly torn. Finally, he sighed with bad grace. "I'm certain if we look, we will find some protocol under which you may get access to our internal records," he muttered, as if the words tasted bad in his mouth. "It may take several—"

"Well, Masha," said Jez, turning to her. "Guess at least we have something to put in that report we're sending in day after tomorrow."

"—hours," the man continued quickly, "but I'm certain I can grant you access by the end of the day."

Masha raised one eyebrow and studied him for a long moment. Jez grinned just a little wider.

Kind of nice, actually, seeing that icy stare turned on someone else for a change.

The man visibly shrank under Masha's gaze.

"Very well," said Masha. "I suppose that would be acceptable. I expect full access codes sent through to our coms prior to the end of the working day."

"Of course," the man muttered.

"And they'd better be the full access codes," said Jez, still grinning. "Because if not—"

"I fully understand the situation," said the man through his teeth.

"Just making sure," said Jez jauntily. "Hate for something to happen and you have no idea." She turned to the others at the table, gave them a cheerful grin, and sauntered out the door after Masha.

"Well," said Masha, when they were out in the hallway. She had a speculative look on her face. "That was—unexpected."

"What, that he gave us access?" asked Jez. "Figured he would eventually."

"No," murmured Masha. "That was not what I was referring to." She paused. "I—suppose I should say, today was not the utter disaster I expected it to be."

"You mean, I'm a damn genius?"

"For a junior auditor, I suppose," said Masha, with a slight smile. "I am curious to see what rumours are spreading about us by tonight."

11

Tae, day 6

"Tae!"

Tae glanced up from where he'd been bending over his narrow desk, and rubbed at the stiffness in his neck. He hadn't realized how long he'd been sitting here.

There was a tap on the door. "Tae? You in there?"

"Coming," he muttered, and stood, stretching. He hesitated for a moment, then shoved the tech he'd been working on under a pile of loose papers and pulled the door open a crack.

Dmitri stood there, with Vera and another boy he recognized— Leonid, maybe?

"Hey," he said stupidly, frowning at them.

"Hey yourself," said Dmitri. "We're going for dinner. You coming?"

"I—" he glanced helplessly back into the tiny room.

The truth was, he was exhausted, and he hadn't had a moment to even stop and think. He'd been in classes all day the whole week, and it wasn't until he'd gone to his first class that he'd realized that first, if he wanted any chance of blending in, at least with his professors, he'd have to figure out all the damn homework, and second, that he knew nothing about half the subjects Masha had enrolled him in. He'd barely slept the last two nights, and his eyes ached from reading.

"Come on, Tae," said Dmitri, lowering his voice persuasively. He glanced around the tiny room. "Are you trying to stunt your growth here? I haven't seen you outside in three days."

"I—there's a bunch of homework I have to—" Tae began helplessly.

The truth was—well, the truth was, he was sick of homework. He was sick of reading through information chips until his eyes were dragging closed, and then going through the hacked student records, and—and, well, if he was being honest with himself, there was something about Dmitri, his carefree, crooked smile, the way he walked, as if there was nothing in the world that bothered him, the easy way he made conversation.

"Well, it's your lucky day," said Dmitri, with that easy smile he had. "We're going to dinner, and then we're going to do a study group afterwards."

Tae stared dumbly. When he'd been on the streets, everything he'd taught himself he'd done in the dark, by the flickering light of his ancient com, after the other kids were sleeping and he was certain they were safe enough for the night. He'd never even imagined studying with other people.

"Come on," said Dmitri again, reaching out and taking him by the arm. "Don't make me drag you along. I will if I have to."

Tae was smiling despite himself, and Dmitri's smile broadened.

"There you go. I thought I'd seen you smile when you came with us last time, but I was starting to wonder if I'd imagined it."

"Alright. I'll come," said Tae. "Just let me grab my jacket."

When they reached the courtyard, five or six other students were waiting. They greeted Tae cheerfully, and he smiled back, in a dazed sort of way, even though he didn't remember half of their names. More students joined them as they walked, and by the time they reached the restaurant they'd been to a few days ago, their number had swelled to at least sixteen.

Tae found himself pulled off to one side by Vera, and she and a few of the other students somehow managed to pull a story out of him about a time he'd outwitted the police. They found it hilarious, and asked him to repeat it at least three times. Vera asked if he had a favourite subject, and when he said he wasn't too bad with tech, Leonid leaned closer. "Really? I've been fighting with my stupid tech homework for the last three days. You're coming to our study group, right?"

"I—" he glanced over at Dmitri, who was deep in conversation with another young man. "I suppose I—" he began.

"Excellent!" Leonid said, leaning over and patting his arm. "I'm counting on you." He paused. "I'm decent at gov studies, by the way. If you need a hand."

Tae tried not to let the dizzying wave of relief show on his face. "I —that's not my strong point."

"Good! Then we both win," said Leonid.

Vera leaned in as well. "That new chemistry professor!"

Every other conversation around the table ceased, and a sudden, haunted expression appeared on more than one face. Vera gave the table a meaningful look. "I swear, she's actually going to kill a student one of these days. That explosion last class? I thought we were all goners for sure."

Tae had to bite back a small smile. "I—don't think she'd actually kill anyone," he said. "At least, not on purpose."

Vera turned to stare at him. "Is that supposed to make me feel better?"

He gave a reluctant chuckle. "Sorry. I guess—I mean, I'm sure she's good at what she does. If she's not trying to kill you on purpose, she probably won't kill you on accident."

For a brief moment, he had the flash of a memory, Ysbel throwing an active ion bomb at him and telling him he had twenty seconds to disarm it before they all went up.

"I mean, unless you're not as good as she thinks you are," he amended. "But she seems like she's a pretty decent judge."

Vera was still shaking her head. "You say this like you aren't in mortal terror every time you walk into that room," she said.

Tae shrugged. "I grew up in a rough part of town, I guess," he said. "She's—not the worst I've seen."

Now they were all staring at him.

"Well," said Vera at last, "I propose a toast to Tae, the only student in this university who's not terrified by our new professor." She beckoned for the server, and everyone shouted their orders. "Yours is on me," Vera called over the din. Tae stared, still slightly bewildered, as a glass of sump was shoved in front of him.

"Not too much," Dmitri called over the friendly din. "I promised Tae we were studying afterwards. He'll never come with us again if I break my promise."

"One toast, then," Vera called back, rising and tapping her battered mug of sump with her spoon. "To Tae. May he never be blown up in his chemistry class."

"To Tae," the other students shouted, and then the conversation turned back to studies and gossip. Tae sipped his drink and sat back, watching the others. It felt strange, the easy camaraderie between the students, not having to be alert every single second, listening for a police drone. Or, in the last two months, a crime-lord weapons dealer's thugs, or prison guards, or prison gangsters, or a smuggler boss, or a core meltdown—the recollection of how long it had been since he had last relaxed crashed over him like a wave, and for a moment he had to blink against the encroaching exhaustion. He pushed his mug of sump away, feeling suddenly restless.

He'd been here long enough. He should really get back to his dorm room, get back to studying. They said they'd study together, but from the look of it, he'd get more done on his own.

When the others looked occupied, he pushed back his chair and stood, tapping his credit chip against the terminal for his bill. The others were talking so loudly they didn't notice, and he managed a slight smile as he watched them.

"Tae?"

He looked up, startled. Dmitri had stood and come over to him, and was watching him with a thoughtful look in his startlingly-green eyes. Tae looked away quickly and shook his head.

"Sorry. I just—I didn't know when I started how far behind I'd be, and I—" he trailed off. "Thanks for inviting me, but I should probably—"

"No, Tae, you shouldn't," said Dmitri, placing a hand firmly on his arm. "You look exhausted. You look like you haven't had a good meal since I saw you last. And you look like you're going to shrivel up and fade away without people around you. I've been around a lot of first-years, but you take the cake. I'm the one who showed you around, and I am going to feel personally responsible if you work yourself to death while the rest of us party, unheeding, below. Do you understand?"

Tae looked up, involuntarily, and found himself staring directly into Dmitri's eyes. For some reason he couldn't fathom, Dmitri's eyes seemed to catch his and hold them, and he couldn't pull his gaze away.

"I—" he began.

"You nothing," said Dmitri firmly. He turned to the boisterous group of students at the table and shouted, loudly enough to make himself heard, "Come on, we're studying tonight, if you didn't remember." He was smiling, and the easy smile carried through his voice.

No wonder all the other students liked him. It was something like what Masha did, but without any of Masha's cold calculation and dangerous intensity. Dmitri's smile was as open and friendly as Masha's was terrifying.

And as the others stood, with varying degrees of reluctance, finishing mugs of sump or one last bite of food, and trailed after Dmitri, Tae found himself coming along as well. Dmitri kept his hand casually on his arm, and strangely enough, Tae didn't feel the urge to shake him off, as he would have anyone else.

It was hard not to like Dmitri, to be honest.

They found an empty room in the student leisure complex, and spread out around the table, pulling out coms and holoscreens and eventually, lumping into groups. Tae found himself in a group with Vera and Leonid, and when he looked up a few minutes later, realized he was the centre of a growing group of awestruck students. He felt his face warming as he trailed off.

"Anyway," he muttered, "you can see if you wire it through that way, it's not actually a complicated problem."

Vera shook her head in astonishment. "You know," she said to no one in particular, "I've taken tech classes every term for the last two years, and I think I learned more about wiring a system in the last five minutes than I've learned from every single professor I had, combined."

He looked down. "I—I mean, it's just something I'm good at," he muttered. "Not a big deal."

"Well, I certainly think it's a big deal," said Leonid, leaning back and quirking an eyebrow. "Because if I'd failed this class, I think my parents would have pulled me. I'm aiming for a civil servant job, and you can't get one of those if you can't understand tech."

"No pilot jobs either, as far as I know," said Vera.

Tae smiled faintly. "I don't know. I know a pilot who isn't particularly good at tech. I think you just need to know enough to get by."

She raised her eyebrow at him. "You know a pilot? You think they'd come talk to us sometime? There's a bunch of us who want to be pilots, but I hear the exam is something else."

"I'm—pretty certain she didn't take the exam," Tae murmured.

Vera gave a slight chuckle. "For a first-year, you've got a pretty interesting background."

"I guess it's my turn, then," said Leonid, sitting up with mock reluctance. "Considering you saved me about seven hours of homework with that explanation. Here." He pulled up his holoscreen and pushed it around to the centre of the table. "Tell me what you're stuck on in gov studies."

By the time the group broke up, it was well past midnight. But somehow, he didn't feel nearly as exhausted as he knew he would have if he'd been hunched over his desk in his tiny room, trying and probably failing to figure out the facts he was supposed to know before he could even understand the homework.

"You're smart," said Leonid, grinning at him. "I've never seen someone pick that up so quickly. We study every couple nights. You want to come every time?"

"Um. I—I guess," said Tae. Vera grinned at him, and ran her hand down his arm.

"Any time you want to study, you can call me. Here, I'll send you my com number." She tapped her com to his. "Has anyone ever told you you're a genius?"

His face warmed again, and he looked down, feeling slightly awkward.

"Um. Thanks," he said. "I—guess I'll see you in class."

Her face took on that faint hint of terror again. "Damn. I wish you hadn't reminded me. I'm not sure I'll sleep tonight. I'm going to have nightmares about being blown into fragments in the middle of a chemistry lecture."

Tae smiled reluctantly, and she laughed.

"'Night, Tae."

"Good night." He raised a hand to the others, and there was a chorus of "good night"s and "see you in class". And then he turned to leave, feeling a warmth in his chest and lightness that he hadn't felt in—well, he couldn't really remember how long.

"Tae, wait," came a familiar voice as he was half-way across the darkened courtyard. He slowed, and Dmitri came up beside him. "What, you trying to run away?" the taller boy asked teasingly. "We live all of ten doors away from each other."

Tae smiled despite himself, and glanced over at Dmitri. He was watching Tae, and there was a soft friendliness to his face that Tae could never quite look at without feeling somehow that the world was a safer place than he'd grown up believing it was.

"Sorry," he said. "I just thought you'd be the last one to leave. You're quite the popular student."

Dmitri laughed, a low, soft laugh that made Tae, for no reason he could fathom, feel suddenly warmer than he had a moment before.

"You're one to talk. Vera couldn't take her eyes off you the whole night." He paused a moment. "You know," he said delicately, "if you wanted, I'm sure she'd be happy to spend some time with you. I think she likes you."

Tae felt his face heating again. "Oh. Um. I'm—I mean, she's very —I mean, but girls—I—I don't—"

Dmitri laughed again, that soft laugh, and again Tae felt that strange warmth in his stomach. "Ah. I have to admit, I was hoping you'd say that."

And he walked forward briskly, leaving Tae to puzzle over his words.

When they reached their floor, Dmitri paused in front of his door. For the first time since Tae had met him, he looked ever-so-slightly uncomfortable.

"Um, Tae," he said, looking away quickly, "I—I'll walk you home. I think I ended up with one of your com chips anyways, and I—I mean, I had a quick question about tech. If you have a minute. I know you're probably tired."

"That's fine," said Tae quickly. "I'm not actually that tired." He was exhausted, but for some reason, the thought of Dmitri walking him home was strangely appealing.

They walked down the hallway to Tae's room, and Tae unlocked the door.

For a moment, in the warm comfort of the evening, he almost missed it. Then he stiffened, shoving Dmitri behind him and grabbing for the modded heat-pistol he'd stashed in his pocket.

"What—" Dmitri began, but Tae gestured him to silence. Dmitri notice the pistol in Tae's hand, and his eyes widened.

Tae swore under his breath.

So much for making friends.

Still, better this than Dmitri being killed in his damn college dorm.

There was the faintest sound from behind the door, and he tensed, pushing Dmitri further back. Then the door swung open, and a tall figure grabbed his gun arm, shoving it up as he pulled the trigger. The blast sizzled through the air, leaving a dark burn mark across the pre-fab ceiling, and Tae was already dropping his weight against his attacker's hand, and with his other arm grabbing for their wrist— and then she laughed, and he recognized the voice, and his legs went weak with relief.

"Dammit, Jez," he said through his teeth, "what the actual hell are you doing here? I could have shot you!"

"Nah," she said, and even in the darkness he could see her grin. "I'm way faster than you."

He shook his head in exasperation. "That doesn't answer my question," he hissed. "What the hell—"

She glanced over his shoulder at the dumbstruck Dmitri.

"Hate to hurry things along, tech-head, but you and your boyfriend probably should get in here before—"

There was a sound from the hallway, and Jez somehow grabbed his jacket and Dmitri's at the same time, hauled them into the room with her, and slammed the door behind them.

"Lock it," she snapped, and he didn't bother to ask questions. He hit the lock, and heard it click shut, and then there was the heavy sound of something slamming into the door.

"Jez," he said through his teeth. "What the hell—"

"Sorry," she said, glancing around quickly. "Someone was trying to kill me. I tried to kill them back, but I think there were more than one of them."

"*Was* trying to kill you?" asked Tae, still through his teeth. "It looks to me like they still are. Who are they, and why are they after you?"

She shrugged, still grinning. "Pick a reason. I think I made a few people mad here at the university. And escaping Lena. And on the jailbreak. And on the heist, and when I escaped from prison the first time. And before I got thrown in prison. And—"

"OK! Fine. I get it. You're being chased by a bunch of people you don't know, and you decided to hide in my apartment."

She shrugged. "You weren't here. I didn't think you'd care."

"Well, I'm here now! So what are we going to do about it?"

Someone slammed into the door again, and it rattled on its hinges. Jez shut off the automatic light and glanced quickly out the narrow window. She made to swing herself up on the sill. He sighed in exasperation and grabbed her by the arm, and she turned, glaring at him.

"Don't you dare," he said. "You're not going out there to get killed, OK?"

"Come on, tech-head, this is me we're talking about. You honestly think they'd be able to—"

"Yes, as a matter of fact, I do! Now shut up and let me think."

Another hit on the door. It creaked alarmingly.

He caught a glimpse, over his shoulder, of Dmitri's stunned face.

Damn it to hell. Damn Jez and her damn problems to hell, he'd been actually having a nice evening, for once in his life.

He pulled up his com and did a quick scan.

Two—no, three—no four attackers, from the heat signatures. One outside the door in the landing, one farther down the hall, one guarding the door out, and one—

"Down," he hissed, grabbing Dmitri and shoving him to the floor as he and Jez dropped. The dirty glass in the window shattered, and something small and cylindrical and glinting menacingly landed with a clatter in one corner.

Damn, damn, damn.

He rolled and grabbed for it. His fingers recognized it before his brain did.

"Light," he said over his shoulder, and someone's com light flashed on.

He swore.

He had maybe five seconds. Not even time to throw the damn thing back out the window, and even if he did, who knew who it'd kill when it went off?

His fingers were already running over the sphere gently, exploring the delicate cracks where somehow it came apart … there. He twisted, and it popped open, and he grabbed one of the wires and yanked it free just as the timer on the display screen flashed "00:01." It flickered and died, and he sagged with relief.

"What was that?" asked Jez, with an obscenely cheerful curiosity.

"It was a damn ion bomb, you idiot," he growled at her. He glanced one more time at Dmitri, who—well, to his surprise, was the one holding the light for him. His face was grim and pale, but there was a determined set to his jaw.

"Not bad, tech-head," said Jez, raising an eyebrow appreciatively. "You'd think eventually people would get tired of trying to blow me up with ion bombs, really."

"No, Jez, I don't think they would, because right about now I'd like to blow you up with an ion bomb."

She turned to look at him. Her face had its usual reckless grin, but there was something serious in her eyes. "Listen, Tae. I'm going back out. Figure if I'm fast enough I'll get to the skybikes, and they won't be able to catch me on one of those. Don't plan on letting you get blown up for me. Stupid idea coming here anyways. Sorry." She turned and shot a quick grin in Dmitri's direction. "Nice to meet you. You picked good with Tae here. Bet he's a great kisser."

"Jez—" he groaned.

She was already half-way up to the window.

He shook his head and grabbed her arm again. "Listen, you idiot. You're not going out there. And yes, you should have come here, that's the whole damn point of having friends and I don't know when you're finally going to get that."

"If they were willing to put an ion bomb into a student dorm to get me—" she began, her voice more grave than usual.

"I know. We have to get you out of here, and we have to do it without them knowing." He was running his fingers over the ion bomb absently as he thought.

"I don't know about keeping them from knowing," said Dmitri, "but I think I know how to get her out of here."

Tae turned, surprised. "How?" he asked at last.

Dmitri pointed to the ceiling. "Ceiling panels. They're loose, and you can crawl through the vents. They're about a thousand years old, so there's plenty of room and loose screws. I could get us into my room from here, I'm pretty sure."

Tae stared at him for a moment, then nodded. "OK. OK, that's good, I just need to find a way—"

"You know," said Jez lazily. "Bet there's plenty of electronics on that ion bomb."

Whoever was on the outside must have decided the bomb wasn't going to go off after all, because they hit the door with a shuddering crash, and then, a moment later, there was the unmistakable hiss and sputter of a heat gun blast.

"Are these doors fireproof?" Tae asked sharply.

Dmitri shrugged. "I've never actually experimented with that." He looked slightly shell-shocked.

Tae turned back to Jez. "I'm not throwing a bomb out—"

"Not the bomb, tech-head. Just the inside."

He sighed and glanced back at the deadly device in his hand.

It was a terrible idea, but then again, when you were working with Jez, you tended to have to make do with terrible ideas.

"Fine," he said. The door hissed as another heat-blast hit it. "I'll hack your com signature into the mechanics. You take the rest of the bomb *don't even think about it Jez I know exactly what you're thinking* in pieces, and get rid of it in a safe place. Do you understand?"

"Got it, cap'n," she said with a mock salute.

"Alright. Just try to keep them from breaking down the door. I need about three minutes."

"On it," she said. She pulled a heat-pistol from her boot and sauntered over to the door. "Might want to stand back, lover-boy," she said over her shoulder to Dmitri, and Tae gritted his teeth.

He was actually going to kill her one of these days.

She hit the lock, paused a moment, then, as whoever it was behind the door hit the door again, she jerked it open. A muscular woman staggered into the room, off-balance, and Jez hit her in the nose. Blood sprayed across the room, and Jez grabbed her by one arm, lifted her up, and planted a fist directly under her sternum. The woman sagged, choking and gasping. Jez kicked her legs out from under her and, as she fell, dropped a knee into her stomach. The woman gagged, and Jez lifted her by one arm and one leg and half-swung, half-dragged her back through the open door, slamming it behind her. She hit the lock again, and grinned.

"Figure that should give you three minutes."

Tae was barely paying attention. He had his holoscreen up, and was typing frantically. Grabbing Jez's com signal was more complicated than it looked, mostly because of all the damn mods he'd put on it himself. He gritted his teeth.

In the corner of his mind, he heard a soft sound at the window. He looked up for long enough to grab Dmitri by the sleeve of his jacket and jerk him around behind him.

"Don't move," he said through his teeth, going back to his typing.

Jez was already at the window, taking careful aim. A heat-blast sizzled through the air, and there was a scream of agony from somewhere below them.

"Might want to hurry," said Jez over her shoulder. "Unless you want to be dealing with another ion bomb."

He hit the last few key-strokes, and blew out a breath of relief. "Got it." He glanced behind him. "Dmitri?"

Dmitri, eyes still wide, nodded, and stood carefully. He climbed onto Tae's cot and began feeling the ceiling panels gingerly.

"Hey lover-boy, bet I can help with that," said Jez. "Stand back."

To his credit, Dmitri stepped back smartly. Jez drew her pistol, aimed, and fired.

The ceiling panel melted.

She grinned. "There you go. Make your life a bit easier."

"Jez," Tae muttered, "you have never in the entire time I've known you made anyone's life easier."

"Maybe," she said, standing back and beckoning Dmitri ahead gallantly. "But I do make it a hell of a lot more interesting." She swung in after Dmitri.

"'Interesting' is not the word I'd use," gritted Tae. He shoved the pieces of the disarmed bomb into his jacket pocket that didn't hold the heat gun, grabbed the programmed piece of tech he'd salvaged from it, and flung it out the window. It flew in a long, glittering arc and fell to the ground somewhere on the other side of the commons. "Let's go," he said, hoisting himself up into the ceiling after them. "It won't take them long to figure out that's not you, and we have to be into Dmitri's apartment and you have to be out his window before they do."

Dmitri had been right—the ventilation ducts in the ceiling were easily big enough to crawl through. Dmitri led the way, pausing occasionally to get his bearings, and finally stopped beside a vent.

"Just a sec," he said. "Let me—"

"I could shoot it," Jez volunteered.

"Um. I appreciate the offer. But I'd rather not explain that to anyone," said Dmitri carefully.

A few moments later, he was pulling the vent aside, and the three of them jumped down. Jez dusted herself off, grinned at them, and unlatched the window. She glanced appraisingly out, shrugged, and pulled herself onto the sill, balancing there for a moment.

"Are—you just going to jump?" asked Dmitri, still sounding stunned. Jez grinned at him.

"Nope. Going to climb down." She looked out again, considering. "Or fall. Depending how good I am." She turned back to Tae. "That hack you did—are they going to be able to track my com?"

He rolled his eyes at her. "No, they won't be able to track you. I scrambled the signal from your com. But you'd better get down before they get visuals."

"Yep." She paused, and sobered for a moment. "Thanks, tech-head. I owe you one. I—didn't mean to bust up your evening."

He sighed and shook his head. "Jez. I'm not going to leave you to get killed by assassins, OK? Even if it busts up my evening. We're friends, remember? We've talked about this?"

"Yeah." She paused. "Um. Thank you." She turned back to

Dmitri. "He's a good kid, and he's my friend, so don't you dare break his heart or I'll come back and break both your legs and give you a scar that you'll carry around for the rest of your damn life. Got it?"

Dmitri nodded, in the stunned fashion of someone meeting Jez for the first time.

She grinned. "Good. See you around, tech-head."

She swung out the window, and was gone.

Tae stared after her for a few moments, mostly because he didn't want to look at Dmitri, which he knew was going to be the other option. Finally, though, when Jez was clearly long gone and he couldn't think of an excuse to put it off any longer, he turned slowly.

Dmitri was still staring at him like he'd grown a set of horns.

"Um," Tae began helplessly. "I. Um. You didn't have to—I'm. Sorry. I didn't mean—" He shook his head, something sick tightening in his throat. "Look, I'll go now. Thanks for the help."

"No," said Dmitri, seeming to finally shake out of his reverie. "You can't go back there. When they find out you tricked them, that's going to be the first place they look. Besides, what with the bomb and the fight and the heat-gun blasts—it might need a bit of cleaning up. Sleep here. You can have my bed, I'll sleep on the couch. We can—we can talk about this in the morning."

For the first time, Tae looked around the tiny apartment. It was identical to his in size, but Dmitri had clearly made it his own. In place of the large desk, there was a battered couch, and a shelf had been nailed into the wall above it that held ration packs and a few bottles of cheap sump. The dresser had been decorated with plastered-on slogans, and had careless phrases that Tae instantly recognized as chemistry formulas, tech symbols, math equations, and various other things a college student might need to memorize, scrawled across it in heavy black pen.

"I'm sorry about the mess," said Dmitri, half-apologetically. "I wasn't expecting company."

"Yeah. I—don't think either of us were expecting that. No one in their right mind expects Jez."

Dmitri stared at him for a moment, then broke into a soft chuckle. "I see your point," he said. He paused a moment. "She said something about skybikes. That's not the pilot you were telling Vera about, was it?"

Tae nodded ruefully, and this time Dmitri broke into a genuine laugh. "I imagine she didn't pass the exams," he said, when he'd finally recovered himself.

"She's a good pilot, though," Tae said, chuckling ruefully.

"I'll bet she is," said Dmitri, still smiling. "Alright, I know you're tired. Go on. I sleep on the couch half the time anyways. Seriously. I'm getting the better part of this bargain. At least the couch is soft. You've slept on the cots here."

And even though Tae knew he was lying, and even though he was pretty sure he'd messed up whatever chance at friendship or—well, or anything else—he'd had, he allowed Dmitri to half-bully him into the cot and took the blankets shoved at him, and was asleep almost before he had time to close his eyes.

He woke to dingy rays of late-morning sun falling across his face, and sat up in a panic.

Where—

The events of the previous evening filtered reluctantly back into his brain, and he dropped back onto the cot in abject despair.

Damn it.

Damn it to hell.

He half-contemplated burying his face in the pillow and just never getting up again, but that wouldn't be a great way to repay Dmitri, who'd let him sleep on his own damn cot while he took the couch.

Tae groaned, and sat up.

Dmitri was sitting on the couch, his holoscreen pulled up in front of him, but he looked up at the sound. Tae waited for the fear or the accusation or the disappointment in Dmitri's eyes, but instead Dmitri gave him the same friendly, crooked grin as always.

"You're up. I was hoping you hadn't just died of exhaustion."

"Sorry," Tae muttered, dropping his eyes. Somehow he couldn't bear to look into those green eyes, because somehow he knew that would make not seeing this person again much harder than it should be.

"You OK?" Dmitri sounded concerned.

"Yeah. I'm—I'm fine. I was just tired." He stood, still not meeting Dmitri's eyes. "Um. Thank you. For the bed. And—everything."

"Not a problem." He still sounded concerned. "Hey. You're not going to forget to eat breakfast, are you? Here."

Tae looked up in time to catch the rations packet that Dmitri tossed at him, and despite himself, Dmitri's eyes caught his.

He didn't look angry. He looked—worried, perhaps. Concerned.

Tae took a deep breath, and tried to smile. "I guess I was more tired than I thought. What time is it?"

Dmitri glanced at his watch. "1100 standard."

Tae groaned and cursed. "I missed all my morning classes."

Dmitri gave him that easy smile again. "Welcome to being a university student. Until you've slept in and missed a whole day of classes, you're still part of the uninitiated."

Tae smiled reluctantly, despite himself.

"Come on," said Dmitri teasingly, "don't worry so much. It's not the end of the world. I'll bet I know someone in your classes, and we can get you notes."

"Yeah," said Tae, still smiling, and then he remembered himself and dropped his eyes again, turning away. "Um. I guess I'd better head back, then. I—thank you. And—I'm sorry. About last night."

"Um. Speaking of last night. What—"

Tae sighed, glaring down at the carpet. "I—look, I told you a grew up on the rough end of town, OK? My friends are—they—get into trouble. A lot."

"And you—"

"I help them out. When I can. I honestly have no idea who was after Jez, but—" he shrugged helplessly. "She's kind of the sort of person who tends to have people trying to kill her."

He could feel Dmitri's eyes on him.

"Ah. I … see." He paused. "She's not—a criminal, is she?" He paused again, and shook his head. "You know what, don't even answer that question. Are you a criminal?"

"I—Look, I—grew up rough, OK? And my friends aren't always —but, I mean, I can't just—they—if they're in trouble, and I can help—" He glanced up without really meaning to.

Dmitri was still watching him, a strange expression on his face, and something in Tae's chest hurt, just a little.

He'd actually liked Dmitri. He'd actually, just maybe, started to hope that—

He shook his head at himself. He should have known better.

"I'm—I really am sorry," he mumbled. "I know you didn't sign up for anything crazy like this, and—well, I mean, you're—"

Dmitri stepped forward and grabbed his arm, turning Tae to face him. Reluctantly, Tae looked up and met his eyes.

For some reason his heart was beating strangely, and he was very aware of the pressure of Dmitri's hand on his arm.

For what seemed like a very long time, neither of them spoke. Then at last Dmitri shook his head in frustration.

"Tae," he said, "You know what? I grew up with both parents working in government, the boringest damn life you can imagine. And I meet you six days ago at the campus gates, and I've been trying to flirt with you since then. And I kept trying to ask you out, and you were so earnest and serious, and I couldn't decide if you were playing hard to get, or you were just that cute and innocent and oblivious, and I was trying to figure out what else I could do to make you see I was interested, I mean, I basically invited myself back to your room last night—and then I find out you're a person who carries a modded heat pistol in his jacket pocket and knows how to use it, and who pushes his friends behind him when there's danger, and who can disarm an ion bomb and hack like nothing I've ever seen before, and steps in to help his friends even if it means he might actually be blown up by an assassin—" he sighed, still shaking his head. "And I'm finally realizing I never even stood a chance." He let his hand drop. "I bet you have twenty guys falling over themselves for you."

Tae stared at Dmitri, dumbfounded and completely speechless. Finally he gave a short, incredulous laugh. "Dmitri. I … whatever it is you think about me, you're wrong. I don't know what I am, but I'm not that. I—I mean, I do what has to be done, that's all, and the rest of it … I've—I've never even kissed anyone, for the Lady's sake. I've been too busy my whole damn life trying to keep people I care about from being killed. Not like I didn't want to. Not like I didn't ever want to have a boyfriend, like a normal person, but I—" he gestured helplessly. "That, last night? That's basically my life. And you know what? Any time I meet someone I'd actually like to kiss, I immediately put their damn life in danger, OK? So I'm sorry. About last night. I'm sorry I'm not who you thought I was, I'm sorry I almost got you killed. I'm sorry about everything." He turned away quickly, biting down hard on the inside of his cheek to keep back the pathetic tears that were trying to fill his eyes.

It was a stupid thing to feel sorry for himself over, after everything he'd dealt with.

"Tac."

There was a tone in Dmitri's voice that made Tae turn back, despite himself.

"Tae." Dmitri's green eyes bored into him, and he couldn't seem to look away. Dmitri reached out a hand and, after a moment's hesitation, took Tae's arm, his hand sliding down to Tae's wrist. "Don't be sorry. Listen, Tae, I grew up in the middle of Prasvishoni. I never in my life had to worry about whether my friends would be killed. I honestly don't know what I would have done. But that—what you did last night, that was the most incredible thing I've ever seen. You, Tae, are the most incredible person I've ever seen." He paused, and Tae swallowed hard. He still couldn't look away. Dmitri's mouth turned up, just a little, in that crooked smile that made Tae's heart skip a beat. "And. Um. Tae. I've … I mean, I've always wanted to be someone's first kiss."

There was something in his expression, something vulnerable and hesitant. Tae took a deep breath, even though something seemed to be squeezing his chest. And then he reached out and slid his hand tentatively behind Dmitri's neck. The heel of his hand brushed Dmitri's jaw, and his skin was warm under Tae's hand, and Tae's heart pounded dizzyingly. He sucked in a short breath and pulled Dmitri's head down, quickly, before he could lose his nerve. And he had a flash of panic, as he leaned in, because he'd never actually kissed anyone before, and he wasn't actually certain exactly how—

and then his lips touched Dmitri's, and he realized kissing was something he must have known how to do all along.

And from the way Dmitri kissed him back—well, it was something Dmitri was pretty good at too.

When he finally pulled back, it took him a moment to remember where he was and what he was doing. He blinked, and shook his head slightly. He was smiling, and he wasn't sure he could stop even if he tried. Dmitri was looking at him, and there was a smile on his face as well, and a soft look in his eyes.

Dmitri blinked, seeming to come out of a daze. His smile grew wider and slightly teasing. "Your friend was right. You are a good kisser."

Tae could feel his face heating, but he was still smiling. He wasn't sure he'd ever stop smiling, ever again.

"Well. You're not too bad yourself," he said. He could still feel the warmth of Dmitri's lips on his. That was another thing he wasn't sure would ever go away, and he sort of hoped it wouldn't.

Dmitri leaned in and kissed him again, a short, familiar kiss that somehow felt almost as good as their first kiss because of the casual certainty of it, and took Tae's hand in his. "Well," he said, "I guess I should have thought of this in the first place. Who knew getting almost blown up by people chasing your crazy friend was all it would take to make you notice me?"

Tae's face heated more. "I—noticed you," he said softly. "From the first time I saw you I noticed you. I just—I mean, I figured you were probably—I mean, everyone seems to like you, so—"

"So you just ignored the fact I was practically throwing myself at you?" said Dmitri. There was that small dimple in his left cheek, and Tae was pretty sure that he could watch that smile forever without getting tired of it.

He shook his head and laughed ruefully. "I'm sorry. I guess I was a little dense."

Dmitri was still looking at him with that soft look in his eyes. "Not dense. Perfect. Besides, it was worth the wait. And the near-death experience." He paused, and looked Tae up and down. "And also, I don't think you can go out in that shirt. There's blood all over it."

Tac looked down. Sure enough, there was a fine mist of dried blood across his chest.

He sighed and shook his head. "She'd better buy me another one," he muttered, but he couldn't feel properly annoyed, because he was still smiling.

"Here. You can borrow one of mine until you get home. Unless you feel like walking through the dorm half-naked." Dmitri handed Tae a shirt, and, with the hint of a grin, turned his back as Tae changed.

"See?" Dmitri said over his shoulder. "I can be a gentleman when I want to be."

The shirt was much too big, but it was soft and comfortable, and Tae wasn't entirely certain he'd give it back.

"There. You look good even in my clothes," said Dmitri, examining him. "Alright. You should get back and get changed, if you want to get to your afternoon classes. And, um, dinner? Tonight? I have study group after, but I can cancel—"

Tae shook his head. "No, don't cancel. I need to study anyways, I'll come with you."

Dmitri gave him a fond smile. "Of course you'd say that. Save your friend's life, but don't get behind on your homework. I've never met anyone quite like you, Tae."

Tae was still smiling to himself as he closed Dmitri's door behind him. It wasn't until it had clicked shut that he looked up and realized at least half a dozen student, gathered in the common area, were all staring at him.

He glanced down, and realized suddenly how this must look—him staggering out of Dmitri's room, late in the morning, noticeably tousled and wearing Dmitri's shirt.

The other students were still staring.

He let out a long breath, set his jaw grimly, and turned down the hall, trying to ignore the whispers behind him, but he caught, "—half the school wants to be in Dmitri's pants, and it took him one week—" and "—only thing I don't envy is the hangover—"

He reached his door, and sighed. The outside of it was half-melted from heat blasts, and he knew very well that the inside would be covered in broken glass.

He'd have to figure out a way to explain this, somehow.

If he made it to his afternoon classes at all it would be a miracle, and he'd probably never live down the rumours.

One of these days, he was actually going to kill Jez.

But—

He touched his lips.

Somehow, even with all that, he was still smiling.

12

Lev, day 6, night

Lev jerked his head up to a sound at the window.

It was late. In fact—he glanced at his com.

Later than he'd realized.

But he still hadn't found any hint of whatever Klava had mentioned about Evka.

The noise came again, and he frowned. It sounded like a soft tapping, but his apartment was four floors up.

Cautiously, he stood and moved around the side of the room, keeping to the walls. He'd positioned the desk in his study so as to be all but unavailable from the window. He'd figured having a solid bookshelf between himself and any potential assassins would be helpful, at the rate at which he was currently making enemies.

The tap came again, and then a muffled whisper. "Hey! Genius! I know you're in there."

He froze, then stepped quickly over to the window, swinging it open. Jez pulled herself through.

He stared at her for a moment.

She was filthy, clothing torn, hair disheveled. Then he noticed the blood spattered across her shirt, and his heart stuttered.

"Jez," he said, pulling her the rest of the way through. "Are you alright? What happened? What are you doing"

She gave him a tired grin. "I'm fine, genius." She put her hand out and grabbed the wall to steady herself, and he swore, heart pounding.

"Tell me the truth, Jez," he said through his teeth. "What happened?"

"Relax. I'm fine." She took a deep breath. "Just been running hard, is all."

"And why, Jez," he said, enunciating each word, "were you running hard? And why is there blood on your damn shirt?"

She glanced down, seeming to notice it for the first time, and her grin widened. "Not mine. And because I figured running hard was better than getting killed. But—" she shrugged. "Don't worry. Tae said he scrambled my com signal, so they won't have tracked me here. Figured I'd better not go back home, though, since I was pretty sure they'd be waiting for me." She paused a moment, and dropped her eyes. "And anyways, I—well, guess I missed you."

"Jez! Who was trying to kill you? What—"

She shrugged. "I don't know. But they were willing to throw an ion bomb into Tae's apartment to do it, so I figure whoever it was was pretty serious."

He grabbed her by the shoulders and held her at arms length, looking her over for injuries. His heart was racing, like it did every time Jez was in danger, and the problem with that was that she seemed to be constantly in danger.

He didn't see any obvious wounds, and other than the circles under her eyes she didn't look like she was about to pass out or anything. He took a deep breath, going suddenly weak with relief.

"Jez," he said, dropping back into his chair. "Are you sure you're alright?"

She was giving him an odd look, as if she couldn't understand why he was reacting this way.

He shook his head in exasperation. "I worry about you, OK? It's not that strange."

She was still studying him. "Speaking of worrying about people, genius, how long has it been since you slept?"

He frowned, and rubbed a hand over his eyes.

Now that she mentioned it—he wasn't actually entirely certain.

"I—"

"You eaten anything today?"

He frowned again. He was pretty sure he had. Probably. Although in all honesty, he'd been fairly caught up with his research.

She rolled her eyes at him. "See? If one of us should be worried, it's not you."

"I'm not the one who was almost blown up by an ion bomb!" he snapped. He shook his head and turned away for a moment, because the panic that had flooded through him when he saw her reach out to lean against the wall was still jittering through his veins, and the exhaustion from however long it had been since he'd last slept wasn't helping.

This was ridiculous. Jez was a grown woman, and she could take care of herself, and she didn't need—

"Hey. Genius." Her voice was slightly more gentle. "It's fine. I'm OK. Really. I just—I just stopped by because I needed a place to stay until morning, OK?"

He sighed and reached out, catching her hand, and rubbed his thumb gently across the backs of her fingers. "I'm sorry, Jez. I just— I worry about you, OK? I—I care about you, and I worry about you, and—"

"Hey. Lev." She tightened her hand around his and yanked him to his feet, and there was a look in her eyes that made his throat go suddenly dry. She smiled slightly and grabbed his collar in both her hands. His stomach tightened, not unpleasantly, as she pushed him backwards, step by step, until his back was against the wall. She shoved him up against it, her body so close he could feel her warmth, and leaned in until her face was only a breath away from his. She paused there, her smile slightly predatory.

He could hardly breathe.

"If you're worried, you could always kiss me better," she whispered, almost into his lips.

His heart was skipping strangely, and her lips were so close to his he could almost taste her, and his brain seemed to have completely shut down. But then, he actually didn't need to think about what he was going to do next. He slid one hand around the small of her back and the other up into her hair, and then he pulled her against him hard and kissed her like she was water and he'd spent the last week in a desert. And she pushed him against the wall and kissed him back until he wasn't sure that his legs would hold him up.

He wasn't entirely sure how they'd moved from the wall to the large easy chair in the corner, only that it had been a thoroughly enjoyable experience and he'd do it again if offered the chance. But however long later this was, they were tangled together in the chair, and the buttons of his shirt were undone, and he was kissing his unhurried way from the corner of her jaw down to the hollow of her throat. Her head was tipped back against the chair, eyes closed, one arm flung out, and she was making small, pleasurable sounds that indicated she was enjoying this as much as he was.

And then an alarm beeped on her com, and she jerked up,

cursing. He pulled back far enough to allow her to see her wrist, and she narrowed her eyes and swore again, shakily.

"Is—" He cleared his throat and tried again. "Is everything alright?"

She gave a long, shaky sigh. "Yeah, but it won't be if I don't hurry up. I'm supposed to meet Masha in ten minutes in the records building."

"The—can't you just tell her you were almost murdered?"

She gave him a weary look. "You think she'd take that as an excuse? Guess you haven't worked with the bastard long enough."

Somehow, with clear reluctance, she managed to untangle herself from him, and she stood. Her clothing was disheveled, her hair mussed, and her eyes the sort of bright of someone who'd spent the last few hours making out with reckless abandon.

He didn't think she'd ever looked more attractive.

Honestly, all he wanted to do was pull her back down onto the chair and continue where they'd left off, and perhaps move locations again down the hall to his bedroom—

She was clearly having similar thoughts.

At last, though, she sighed, muttered something uncomplimentary about Masha, and turned back to the window. She paused a moment, and turned back.

"Hey genius. Catch," she said, and tossed something at him. He grabbed it instinctively, and she swung herself out onto the ledge, and was gone.

He sat staring after her bemusedly for a few minutes. At some point, he assumed, his higher brain function would return, but he wasn't sure when, and he wasn't sure he actually cared. Not as long as he could still feel her body against his and taste her on his lips.

He glanced down at his hand.

She'd thrown him a rations pack.

He smiled to himself and leaned back in the chair and closed his eyes for a moment, replaying every moment of the evening.

When he opened his eyes again, it was well into the middle of the day.

He yawned, stretched, and sat up, rubbing his eyes. Jez's scent, the faint smell of ship's grease and burnt ozone and ship interior, still clung to his clothing. He smiled to himself as he re-buttoned his shirt and pulled open the rations pack she'd thrown him.

Just as well, really. He'd come at the information better with a clear mind.

Although, to be honest, he wasn't sure his mind would be clear about anything but how Jez's body had felt, tangled up with his, and how very, very much he wished he was still kissing her.

He shook his head at himself, ruefully.

Not like they were trying to save the whole damn system or anything here.

He sighed and pulled open his holoscreen, bringing it around in front of him. He chewed on the rations square absently as he scanned through the information, although thoughts of Jez kept intruding on his mind.

The look in her eyes before he'd kissed her, teasing and dangerous. The feel of her, the angles and lines of her body, the hard, wiry muscles under her skin, the way she melted against him when he kissed her in exactly the right way …

He rubbed his eyes and peered down at the screen again.

This was not helping.

The jaunty way she walked, that smirk she had that irritated the hell out of him and somehow drove him completely crazy at the same time.

He'd been scrolling down on the holoscreen without actually reading any of the words for some time. He sighed, and scrolled back up.

It had taken him enough politicking to get this damn information. The least he could do was pay attention to it.

The way the taste of her lingered on his lips like salt, how—

He stopped abruptly.

There. That name. His eye had caught on it as he scanned half-heartedly through.

Evka.

He frowned and expanded the screen, making the paragraph larger.

He was almost certain the name should have been erased. Because after Evka had disappeared from the university, he'd never heard her mentioned again. And it wasn't for lack of searching. It was like she'd never existed. No faculty record, all the research under her name gone, her nameplate and her office changed over to a new professor like they'd been empty that whole time.

And now, here, deep down in the records of the Academic Standards department—her name.

He rubbed the bridge of his nose, peering closer. His breath was coming more quickly now, and he tried to force himself to be calm.

Evka.

How many years had it been since he'd heard that name? And how many years had he been looking for it?

It was thrown into the middle of a paragraph, something completely irrelevant. The history of the university, he was pretty sure, some curriculum from years back, and she was listed as one of the developers. But if she was here, there was just a chance …

He scrolled back up.

What he'd been looking at last night, before he'd been—distracted …

For a moment, his mind went back to the easy chair, the comfortable tangle of Jez's limbs with his, her strong hands pulling his face to hers—he shook his head, and peered back at the screen.

There. He'd been looking for the splice in the information, where whoever it was who was in charge of this department had hidden everything he didn't want the new upstart to see.

And he'd been very, very close to being able to pry that splice open.

He frowned in concentration. Really, Tae would have been better at this than he was. But he'd read up on all the specs on the university systems, from the moment he'd suspected they'd be coming back, because it was inevitable that someone would try to hide something from them, and it was imperative that they not be able to.

He bit his lip and typed in a few lines of code.

Tae would be able to do this by instinct, he was pretty sure. It wasn't just knowledge, it was a sort of intuition, and Lev didn't have it. But he did have access to a lot of information, and he did have a photographic memory, which meant …

Yes.

A whole new column of information scrolled out onto his screen, and he smiled to himself.

And there, half-way down the page.

Evka.

He scrolled down and began rapidly scanning the pages.

Her name was on this curriculum. That, in and of itself, wasn't surprising. He was certain she'd created at least half a dozen curricula in the short time he'd been at the school, studying under her.

But …

But this particular program. It was curriculum he'd never heard of, and he was certain he'd at one point memorized all the classes and subjects the university had ever offered.

They'd never offered this class.

Something cold crawled up his spine as he read.

No wonder they'd never used this. What they were teaching—and the way it was being taught—

He shivered slightly. He'd co-taught with her enough, and this was nothing like her classes. It was almost like something you'd teach to prisoners.

No, not prisoners. Something other than that. To someone who would obey every word you said. Either because they had no choice, or—

He sucked in a sharp breath as he caught another word at the bottom.

"Program," it said, and the word was capitalized, even in the middle of a sentence. "This teaching method should be usable when the Program is operational."

He glanced back up at the subject matter. The method had been so unnerving he'd hardly paid attention to what was being taught.

Government practical theory.

He sat back in his chair, and stared sightlessly at the ceiling for a moment.

He'd always assumed that Evka had been an unwitting participant in something. She'd been the one to champion his acceptance into the program, his mentor, the woman he trusted more than he'd ever trusted anyone besides his own family.

She'd practically been his family.

But this—this didn't look like the work of someone who'd been unwilling, or unwitting. Every sentence bore that thoughtful, inquisitive tone that had always marked her writing.

There was a sick feeling in his stomach.

He took a deep breath, and found he was clenching his fist hard around something, and when he looked down, he saw it was the empty packaging from the rations pack Jez had thrown to him.

For just one irrational moment, he needed Jez, he needed to be clutching her hand, and knowing that somehow she'd drag him out of this quicksand he seemed to have stumbled into. That she'd be there, and that he could close down his holoscreen and she could kiss him until everything was alright again.

He took a deep breath and opened his eyes.

No.

This was something he was going to have to deal with on his own.

He pulled the holoscreen back in front of his face, and tried to ignore the sickness in his stomach, the aching, desperate need for someone to hold onto as the words on the screen slowly, inexorably, turned his world upside down.

Jez, day 7

By the time Jez arrived at the records building, Masha was already waiting for her. Her arms were crossed, and there was a forbidding look on her face.

"Jez," she said, her voice icily pleasant. "I'm glad you decided to show up."

Jez managed a grin, somehow, despite everything that had happened over the course of the last twelve hours.

"I knocked on your door this morning," Masha continued. "As you did not answer, I assumed that you had come here early. It appears I was mistaken."

Jez drew in a long, shaky breath. She wasn't entirely certain whether the shakiness had come from almost being blown up, or from kissing Lev, or from the fact she hadn't slept in the last twenty-four hours, but she was feeling shaky, and cold, and one hundred percent not capable of dealing with Masha's crap.

"Guess you were," she said, sounding as unapologetic as possible.

"May I ask what you were doing?"

Damn nosey bastard.

"Well," she drawled, "guess you could. I might even tell you." She paused until she saw the small tightening around Masha's eyes that was the only outward sign of how much she wanted to actually shoot Jez, then she leaned back against the wall and let her grin widen. "I was busy. Kissing Lev."

"I see," said Masha, ice cracking off her voice. "And may I ask why you decided that kissing Lev was a good use of your time and the effort that the five of us have gone to for the past week and a half in order to get you into this university, rather than do what you are here for, which is trying to possibly figure out why the government wants to kill us?"

Jez smirked. "Guess you've never kissed Lev."

For a moment, she enjoyed the sight of Masha trying very hard to keep herself from actually exploding.

"Anyways," she added after a moment, "Figured it would be better than getting blown up with an ion bomb, which was probably my best option if I went back to my apartment. Seeing that someone broke in last night and tried to damn well kill me."

Masha stared at her for a moment. "Jez," she said at last. "So, what you are actually trying to tell me right now is that someone tried to kill you last night. And you didn't think to mention it?"

"Just bloody mentioned it," said Jez. "Anyways, basically everyone except you knew about it already. Seeing as Tae threw them off my track, and I hid out in Lev's apartment until morning."

"Kissing him," put in Masha.

Jez shrugged. "I was there, and he was there—"

Masha shook her head, her lips tight. "Jez. I need to know. What happened?"

For a moment Jez had to put out a hand and catch herself against the wall, a wave of dizziness washing over her.

It had been a long damn night, and she was exhausted, and all she really wanted to do was go back to her cot and curl up and, for some strange reason, cry. And instead she was here, facing an entire damn day of going through damn financial statements, and being interrogated by plaguing Masha. She gritted her teeth and scowled.

"Jez. Sit down," said Masha coldly.

"I don't need to plaguing sit down! I'm not plaguing hurt."

"Jez. Please."

She looked up angrily, and was slightly shocked to see what looked like actual concern in Masha's face.

"I'm fine," she muttered.

"At the very least, you had a long night." Masha unlocked the door into the archives and pushed it open. "Go on. Sit."

Jez gave her one last scowl, but pushed past her and sank down into one of the hard-backed chairs, suddenly unsure that her legs would continue to hold her up.

Masha closed the door carefully and stood, watching her. "What happened?" she asked again, finally.

Jez scowled. "Someone was waiting for me at my damn apartment with a heat gun. Thought I saw someone watching us the last couple days, and I guess I was right. I got out before they killed me, but there were a few of them, and—" she trailed off for a moment.

Now that she thought about it, she had almost been killed. More than once.

She gave a slight shiver. "Anyways, I needed a place to hide, so I ducked into Tae's apartment, because I thought he was out. But he came back, and they chucked an ion bomb through the window, then—"

"They threw an ion bomb? Through the window of a student dorm?" Masha's lips were pinched even tighter than they had been.

Jez shrugged again. "Tae disarmed it. Anyways, Tae scrambled the signal from my com, and then I figured I probably shouldn't go back to my room. So—"

"So instead you spent the rest of the evening with Lev," said Masha. Jez raised an eyebrow and grinned suggestively. Masha sighed, and Jez closed her eyes and leaned against the hard back of the chair, tipping her head back against the wall.

"Jez," said Masha finally, "are you certain you're unhurt?"

Jez grinned again, still somewhat shakily. "Yeah. I'm fine."

Masha pursed her lips. "It must have been the government," she said at last. "If it was someone from the university, disabling the tracking on your com wouldn't have thrown them for long. Either way, you can't go back to your apartment again."

Jez grinned again. "Guess Lev and I could probably—"

"No. I'd prefer Lev to be able to focus on something other than his planned leisure activities every evening," said Masha sharply. Jez smirked. Masha sighed.

"I'll look into getting you into a different apartment. I should be able to manage it, I think. In the meantime, I suggest we get to work. Apparently the university president has decided that you are, contrary to appearances, a genius who's acting stupid but is in fact playing some game of four-dimensional chess with the administration. We may as well take advantage of our newfound status."

Jez leaned back in her chair again, and closed her eyes, just for a moment.

There was a strange tightness in her stomach, and she couldn't decide if it was happiness or stark terror.

She should be worried about the attempted assassination, probably.

But—Lev.

She hadn't exactly planned on kissing him last night until neither of them could see straight. But he'd looked so worried, his dark hair tousled, his clothes disheveled, and he'd been holding her hand and looking at her with that concerned look in his eyes, and kissing him had suddenly seemed like a very good idea. And—well, she had to admit, the memory of it still sent electric prickles up her spine and made her whole body tingle.

But there had been something in his face when he'd seen her, a sort of relief. Like he'd known she'd come, eventually, and he'd needed her to.

And—what if she hadn't come? Because to be honest, she might not have. If she hadn't been running for her life from some lunatic ion-bomb-throwing assassin, she might have gone this whole time without even thinking of it. It wasn't like she never thought about him. She thought about him plenty, and especially she thought about kissing him, and how his hands felt on her body, but—well, she'd seen how Tae's lover-boy watched him, how Ysbel watched Tanya.

Neither of them would just not think to stop by to talk to whoever it was they were off their heads over, whenever they got busy or something happened.

And—that look in Lev's eyes, the certainty that she'd be there—

If she was being honest, that had been more unsettling than the assassination attempt. Because it wasn't like this was the first time someone had tried to kill her. Pretty regular occurrence, really. But someone who loved her? Who was certain about her, who knew, without even wondering, that he could depend on her, not to save his damn life, or whatever the crap else she might actually be able to do, but just to—be there?

That had never happened before, and even the thought of it made panic rise in her throat until she was sure she'd choke.

Reluctantly, she opened her eyes and pushed herself upright. Probably should go help Masha, after all that.

Anyways, maybe she'd get lucky, and the assassin, whoever it was, would get her before she had to deal with figuring out the mess that was her and Lev.

13

Ysbel, day 10

"Professor."

Ysbel looked up from her desk, into the face of the girl who'd helped Tae the first day.

She gave the girl a flat stare.

She still wasn't certain how Masha had talked her into teaching these children. And she was continually shocked by how utterly ignorant they were. None of them would have lasted one day on the *Ungovernable*.

"What is it?" she asked.

"Um. I." The girl looked frankly terrified. "Only. Our study group was looking at the problem you gave us, and I don't understand—" she pulled up the holoscreen on her com and expanded it to a page of hand-scrawled notes. Ysbel sighed and glanced through them, frowning to herself.

She was—mildly impressed, actually. She hadn't thought any of these students were bright enough to figure out the problem she'd set them, even though it was one of the most basic formulas you'd use for an explosive. But the girl hadn't been that far off, honestly.

"Here," Ysbel said, tapping a spot on the holoscreen. "That's your problem. You have the numbers switched."

The girl frowned at the screen for a moment, then her face cleared in relief. "Oh. I see that. Thank you." She looked up quickly, as if suddenly remembering who she was talking to. "I mean. Um. I'm sorry for bothering you."

Ysbel studied her for a moment in faint amusement. "I'm not actually planning on murdering you, you know," she said at last.

The girl stared at her, then shook her head and muttered something in a disbelieving voice.

"What was that?" asked Ysbel.

The girl froze, and Ysbel was suddenly certain she hadn't meant to say whatever she'd said out loud.

"I—" She swallowed hard.

"Yes?" said Ysbel.

"I—I said—" she swallowed again. "I said, you—you could have fooled me." She had a look on her face of someone about to go to the firing squad. Ysbel stared at her for a moment, trying to keep a blank face. And then she cracked, and snorted with laughter.

The girl was still watching her, terror and confusion mingling on her face, and then she seemed to realize what had happened, and her body sagged in relief, and Ysbel had to look away, wiping tears of laughter from her eyes as she chuckled.

"I'm sorry," she said, once she had regained her composure. "It was just very funny. The look on your face."

The girl was still staring at her. "You—" she began uncertainly. "You—this whole time, you thought this was funny?"

Ysbel shrugged. "Well, you have to admit. It was kind of funny."

"You had every single one of us convinced that you'd actually kill us if we got an answer wrong, and you thought it was funny?" The girl's voice was now shaded with incredulity.

"I told you at the beginning of class," said Ysbel patiently. "I never had any intention of killing any of you. I did warn you that if you got a problem wrong and mixed the wrong compound, the explosion might kill you. But I was very clear that I had no intention of killing you myself."

The girl was still looking at her, her face registering the kind of shock of someone who had, against all odds, survived something that should have killed her.

Then her shoulders began to shake gently, and for an alarming moment Ysbel thought that perhaps she was crying, and she honestly had no idea what to do with a student who was crying—and then she realized the girl was laughing, helplessly.

She grinned. "What is your name, girl?" she asked after a moment.

"Vera," said the girl, when she'd finally recovered herself. "I'm Vera."

"Well. I am happy to meet you, Vera. I hope you manage not to blow yourself up before the class is over."

"As do I," said Vera, her face mostly straight. "Um. Thank you, professor."

"It is not a problem," she said, with a slight smile.

Once Vera was gone, Ysbel finished scooping the rest of her materials into her padded bag, latched it closed, then followed Vera out the door.

As she stepped out of the classroom, she heard faint voices from around the corner. She frowned and paused.

"—if you'd like to pass your classes this semester, that is."

It was a male voice, and she was fairly certain she recognized it as one of the other professors she'd met in one of the staff meetings.

If she recalled, it was not a professor with whom she'd been impressed.

"I—I can't—" there was a momentary pause.

This voice she did recognize. Vera.

She sounded afraid.

"Professor Ivanov. I need this grade. I can't be sent home, and my family can't afford to send me if I don't get my scholarship for next term. I'll work as hard as I need to, but I can't—they're my friends. I can't give you information on my friends."

She sounded on the verge of tears.

Ysbel raised an eyebrow. She walked quietly down the hallway towards the sound of the voices.

"Well, Vera." The professor's voice was smug and self-satisfied. "I guess you'll have to make a choice, won't you? Because I promise you that your grades in my class will be enough to stop you completely from any sort of—"

Ysbel stepped around the corner and cleared her throat.

Vera and the professor looked up at the same time.

Ysbel let every trace of emotion drop from her face.

"Professor," she said, in her flattest voice. "I am very sorry to interrupt. But, I believe I heard you talking to one of my students."

"Ah." The professor looked, suddenly, very nervous. "I—she and I were—discussing her grades. I assume you know the reason. And I don't know what you heard, but—"

Ysbel fixed him with a stare, and his voice faltered.

"Listen to me, professor," she said, enunciating each of her words carefully. "I am very protective of my students. And if I hear, even one time, you threatening one of them, ever again, I will make it so your family, or whoever it is stupid enough to want to bury you, will have to scrape bits of you off the ceiling. Do I make myself perfectly clear?"

He was staring at her as if he'd been completely paralyzed, only the muscles in his jaw working. At last he seemed to remember how to swallow, and he swallowed hard.

"I—are you threatening me?" To his credit, there was still some bluster in his voice. "You're new here, professor. You don't know what can happen to professors here who get into things they don't understand."

"Thank you for informing me. But no, I am not threatening you," said Ysbel. "I'm giving you options. I thought you might like to know the consequences of whatever choice you made." She paused. "And believe me. Blowing you into vapour is something that I could do without even thinking about it. If I thought about it, I could come up with something that would probably be just as permanent, but much more painful. Now. Do I make myself clear this time?"

He nodded, his adam's apple bobbing alarmingly.

"Good," she said. "Now. I suggest you find somewhere else to be."

He nodded again.

Vera was staring at her with a kind of awe.

She gave the girl a slight smile, and to her surprise, Vera paused, waiting for her. With a shrug, she walked up to the girl, and once she'd reached her, Vera turned and gave her a small smile, and fell into step beside her.

"Thank you," said Vera, after a few moments. "I assume you wouldn't have actually murdered him either?"

Ysbel raised an eyebrow. "What makes you think that?"

Vera studied her, as if unsure whether or not to laugh.

They walked in silence for a few more moments. Finally, Ysbel said, "Why was he asking you to tell him about your friends?"

Vera frowned. "I don't know. It's not just him, though. There are a few professors asking. If anyone has ever said anything … seditious. About the university, about the government. Read any restricted books. Things like that."

Ysbel frowned. "Do they ask this often?"

Vera shook her head. There was concern clear in her voice. "I don't know. But—" she paused, and lowered her voice. "But apparently people have disappeared from campus. They disappear, and then no one ever talks about them again. You never hear their names again. It's like they never existed."

Ysbel's heart was beating faster. "And does this happen often?"

Vera shrugged. "I don't know," she said softly. "But the professors have been asking about students more often than they ever have before."

"When did this start?"

"The professors asking? I don't know, maybe … a month ago? Month and a half?"

A cold chill ran down Ysbel's back.

Right around the time that someone put that tag on Jez's file, in prison.

Right around the time Lena started after them, sent by the government.

"And the disappearances?"

Vera glanced around quickly. They were outside the building now, and still a ways away from the nearest clump of students. The girl lowered her voice further. "I don't know. But—well, apparently there was one eight or nine years ago. I don't know if it was a student or a professor. No one knows who it was. But lately there have been rumours."

Eight or nine years.

Right around the time that Lev's old professor had been

kidnapped.

"And the rumours are that whoever it was made the wrong person angry?" asked Ysbel. Vera shook her head.

"No," she said in a low voice. "The rumours are, she's the reason other people disappeared. She was behind it, somehow."

Ysbel stared at her. "She somehow started this, and then disappeared?"

Vera shrugged. "That's all I know. But—" she shivered. "I'm not planning on telling any professors about what my friends talk about over dinner."

"Good," said Ysbel. "If any of them ask you, I am happy to blow them up for you. It would not even be a problem."

Again Vera shot her that look, as if she wasn't certain whether or not Ysbel was serious. Then she smiled, a wide, friendly smile.

"You know, professor," she said, as she turned off towards the maths building. "Tae was right. You're actually not that bad." She paused. "I—might come ask for help again after next class. If you don't mind."

Ysbel smiled to herself as the tall girl strode away down the walkway.

Perhaps these students of hers weren't so terrible after all.

Then she sobered.

The other professors knew something, at least some of them did. There was a reason they were asking about the students, whatever it was. And she'd studied the syllabus chip from Professor Gurin, and she was almost certain what he'd had the students researching had to do with Jez's strange metal. Was he trying to learn something from them? Or did he want them to know enough to understand the consequences, when—well, when whatever it was that was coming finally came?

On top of all that, there was something here, something about Lev's old professor. Who perhaps had not been as innocent as Lev had assumed.

The thought sent a small shiver down her back.

14

Jez, day 12

Jez's com buzzed loudly, jolting her out of a sound sleep.

Damn that Masha. Jez slapped her com, mumbled some profanity through a yawn, and said, "What do you want, you plaguer? You had me reading through your number crap all day. Can't I even get a decent night's sleep?"

"Which 'plaguer' are you referring to, Jez?" Ysbel sounded slightly amused. "You're on the general line."

Jez squeezed her eyes shut in a vain attempt to push the fog from her head. "Well, guess there are a few of you to choose from, then."

"What is it?" Tanya came on next, her voice crisp and businesslike, and promising dire things to whoever or whatever was trying to make trouble.

"Lev found something." It was Masha's voice. "Is everyone on?"

"Tech-head?" asked Jez. "Haven't heard from you yet."

There was no answer.

She frowned. Usually Tae was the first to answer.

"Has anyone seen Tae today?" Lev asked, worry clear in his voice.

There was a long pause, and Jez pushed herself into a sitting position, rubbing hard at her eyes.

"I can't get him on the private line either," said Lev finally.

Jez stifled a groan and rolled out of her cot.

This wasn't like tech-head, and suddenly she felt just as worried as Lev sounded. "I'll go over and—"

"Hello?"

It was Tae.

She rolled her eyes and dropped back onto her cot

"Tae?" Lev sounded relieved. "Are you alright? What—"

"Um. Yeah. I'm fine." Tae sounded—happy. Almost dreamy.

Jez snickered. "Hey tech-head. Tell your lover-boy hi for me."

Tae sighed. "Jez—"

"We all know he's there, Tae. Shall we take you off the call so you can get back to whatever you were doing?"

"We were studying." Tae sounded annoyed.

"'Course you were." Jez grinned broadly. "Bet I can guess what you were studying, though."

"We were studying chemistry," he said, exasperation clear in his tone.

Jez snorted with laughter.

"I mean, for class!"

She laughed louder.

"Jez," Masha broke in coldly. "When you're quite finished—"

"Hey, no judgement here. His lover-boy's cute. If I was Tae, I'd be studying chemistry too."

"Jez—" Tae's voice was strangled.

"Alright, that's enough, you two," grunted Ysbel, amusement clear in her voice. "I don't think Masha called us so that we could talk about Tae's boyfriend."

"All I'm saying is, I haven't seen someone so off their heads over someone for a long time. That kid definitely has a thing for our tech-head. In fact—"

"Jez." Ysbel's voice was flat.

Jez smirked.

"Alright. Lev, tell us what you found," said Masha, in a tone of strained patience.

Lev's voice was steady, but Jez could hear the hollowness behind it.

"I think I know where the records are," he said. "But it's going to be hard to get to, and once I'm there, I doubt I'll be able to bring whatever I find back out. I think our best bet will be going in together."

There was a moment's pause. At last Masha said, "I agree with you. When were you thinking of doing this?"

"Tonight," he said in a flat voice. "Whatever this is, it's dangerous. We need to figure out what's happening, and we need to do it quickly. We don't have time to wait."

"I agree," said Ysbel. "I've been hearing things from my students. Whatever it is that's coming—I don't think it's far off."

"Very well," said Masha. "It's 0200 standard right now. I doubt we'll find a time that's less busy."

"Tae was pretty busy," Jez chimed in.

"Jez, next time I'm just going to let you get blown up by the ion bomb," said Tae through gritted teeth.

"As I was saying," said Masha, "this is probably the ideal time. We'll meet behind the records building in twenty standard minutes."

Jez fidgeted restlessly with the cuff of her jacket. She and Masha were concealed in the shadows under the back entrance to the records building, and she was pressed uncomfortably close to the woman. She could smell the worn fabric of Masha's jacket, the same old-leather smell she'd grown used to over the past couple months. It still made her stiffen reflexively, but—well, somehow, working together with this woman, day in and day out—it hadn't made them friends. She wasn't sure she'd ever be actual friends with Masha. But it had somehow made them feel a little less like enemies.

"Masha?"

She glanced up. Ysbel appeared in the entrance, silhouetted against the guttering artificial lamps that were supposed to illuminate the campus, but generally seemed to only make things darker. A second later, Tanya slipped in behind her.

Jez grinned, despite the worry sitting heavy in her gut. She'd never seen someone move quite so quietly as Tanya did, and who could so clearly kill every last one of them without breaking a sweat. It was actually very hot.

"Who are we still waiting for?" asked Ysbel.

"You two are the first," said Masha tersely. Ysbel nodded. She turned to Jez after a moment.

"Does Tae really have a boyfriend?"

Jez grinned. "If he doesn't, it's not because the other kid wasn't trying."

Ysbel gave a soft chuckle. "I was wondering who it was that kept dropping him off to class. He looks nice."

Jez shrugged. "He managed to survive having an ion bomb chucked at him. Figure he can't be all bad."

Ysbel chuckled again. "Well. I will see what I can do. It would be good for that boy to have friends his own age. Who aren't trying to kill anyone."

Tae arrived a few moments later. He slipped into the entrance, and even in the darkness she could see his glare.

"Hey lover-boy," she whispered.

"Jez," he said through his teeth. "Are you the one who started the rumours about me?"

"What rumours?" she asked, still grinning.

"The ones where I'm actually a former youth model-citizen and have a boyfriend on every planet in the system."

Ysbel made a noise that sounded like she was trying very hard to choke back a laugh. Jez shrugged.

"Just trying to do you a favour. Figure it's not going to hurt your social standing."

He let out a long, exasperated breath. "Jez. I think I can handle my own social standing. Not to mention that after your damn exploits a week ago, now everyone in the whole damn school thinks I'm sleeping with Dmitri—"

"Aren't you?" she asked, grinning. "Might want to get a move-on, tech-head."

"We just barely—I—Jez, you need to learn how to mind your own damn business!"

"Hey, you do me a favour, I do you one. I thought that's what friends did." She was still grinning.

Actually, it felt good to see him like this, flustered and dreamy and actually happy.

He was still sputtering when another figure appeared in the entrance way.

"Lev?" asked Masha. He nodded wearily and stepped inside.

Jez frowned. In the darkness, she couldn't see the look on his face, but there was something in his posture, something weary and hopeless.

"We should go," he said quietly, and pulled up the holoscreen on his com. "There's a vault under the records building. I believe they'll be somewhere in here." He expanded the screen and touched a small grey section. "I have the specs on the security. Tae, I've sent them through to your com."

Tae pulled up his holoscreen, frowning in concentration. "I've written a hack for external and internal security systems. Their security in this place is—not very good. But I don't know if I can override the blast doors. I used Masha's key to create a lock-pick, but that's the best I can do."

"As long as it gets us inside, Tae, that's all we need," said Masha briskly. She glanced around at the others. "Let's go."

They filed after her through the back entrance, through the dark hallways of the deserted building, and to the locked door in the back. Jez bit her lip, and glanced at Lev as they walked.

He looked stunned, like someone in shock.

Whatever it was he'd found in those records, it wasn't good. And somehow, the sight of him like this made her heart hurt, just a little.

She fell in beside him. "Hey. Genius. You OK?"

He turned, and tried to smile at her, but even in the darkness she could tell his heart wasn't in it.

"I'm fine. Just—a little more than what I was expecting."

She grinned. "What, you were expecting not to almost be killed at a damn university?"

"No," he said quietly. "I was fully expecting to be almost killed. I told you, I grew up here." He paused a moment. "I suppose I wasn't expecting to realize how bad things were, and how much I didn't notice."

She bumped him with her shoulder. "Cheer up, genius. At least you didn't spend your teenage years running jobs for a smuggler boss."

This time he did manage a slight smile, but it didn't reach his eyes. "No, I suppose you're right. I'm beginning to wonder, though, if what I did was actually any better."

They'd reached the stairwell. The stairs going up were clear, but there was a locked door blocking their descent. Tae stepped forward and clipped his lock scrambler onto the door. It whirred for a few moments, then clicked. Masha reached out gently and pulled the door open, and they stepped down into the darkness.

Tanya led the way. The dim light on her com illuminated a few steps in front of them, and threw dark shadows off the narrow walls. The air smelled of mildew and damp, and had the stale flavour of a place where people didn't often come. Jez walked as quietly as she could, placing each foot down softly on the bare, crumbling pre-fab blocks of the stairs, but their footsteps still managed to seem abnormally loud in the stillness.

"What are we looking for down here?" asked Ysbel in a soft voice.

"I'm—not completely certain," Lev whispered back, his voice echoing off the walls. "But there's something down here that my old professor was working on, before she disappeared. Whatever it is, I think it will give us some idea of what the government was using her research for."

Jez's heart was pounding, and she bit down hard on the inside of her cheek.

Usually, she'd be happy to be actually doing something. But there was something about this silent, claustrophobic darkness that made something cold and unpleasant crawl up her spine, and a sick knot from in the pit of her stomach.

Something about this was wrong. Cold, and emotionless, and wrong.

They must have gone at least six floors down when Lev held up his hand to stop them. He stepped around Tanya and led them out of the stairwell and into a long, narrow corridor. It was dimly lit with blue emergency lighting, and the walls on either side were bare prefab. Lev hesitated a moment, glancing around, then walked quickly over to one of the doors set back into the corridor walls.

"Tae. It's this one."

Tae nodded and came up beside him. The blue light made his face look gaunt, accentuating the hollows under his eyes and cheekbones as he bent over the lock. He scanned his com quickly over it, pulled up his holoscreen, and frowned at it for a few moments. Then he typed something in quickly, held it to the connector end on his lock scrambler, and clipped the scrambler to the door.

Again, the soft whirring and the click.

Lev reached out and pushed. The door swung open, and they stepped inside.

Masha was the last one in, and closed the door behind her, and Lev reached over and flicked on the light. Jez blinked against the sudden brightness, swearing under her breath as her eyes adjusted.

And then she looked around the room.

It wasn't a large space—maybe the size of her apartment with all the walls removed. There were industrial-style shelves against the walls on both sides, and in the back there was a desk with a large piece of tech on it that she didn't recognize, and beside it, several large compartments, rectangular and emptied, like boxes stood on their sides. Each had a transparent covering, secured with a lock, and each was empty. And beside those—she cocked her head. Beside those, there were an assortment of mechanical parts, none of them completely familiar, but all of them—well, all of them things she'd probably seen before, working on ships' components.

She glanced quickly at Tae and saw the same confusion on his face.

She shook her head uneasily.

So maybe she wasn't a tech person.

Still—still, the sense of unease she'd been feeling was stronger here. It was silly, really. Not like a piece of stupid tech could be evil.

But something about the whole setup of this room felt off, somehow.

Lev walked forward, frowning. His movements were slow, like someone sleepwalking, but the expression on his face was one of sharp intensity. He reached out a hand to the piece of tech, then glanced at Tae.

"Are you certain the security is off?"

"I hacked in and over-rode the systems," said Tae, and the concern in his voice mirrored the strange unease crawling through Jez's stomach. "Let me do a quick scan to make sure."

For a few moments no one moved. Then Tae nodded, still frowning. "Security is off. You should be fine to touch anything. But be careful."

Lev nodded, and, after a moment, ran a hand softly over the piece of tech. He slid his hand down the side, as if it was something he was long familiar with, and a moment later there was a faint whir. Jez tensed, but then she noticed it was the machine itself blinking to life, a light glowing in one corner. A moment later, a holoscreen flickered to life above it.

Across it, a long line of numbers and letters and symbols stretched out in a complicated pattern. Lev, still moving like someone in a trance, reached out his hand to the screen and ran a finger along one of the lines of text.

"Lev?" asked Masha softly. "Can you read that?"

"I wrote it," he said quietly, not looking away from the screen. "At least, I helped write it."

Ysbel had stepped forward as well, and she was frowning at the screen.

"Down there. At the bottom." She turned to Tanya. "That's—"

"That's the composition of Jez's stolen cargo," said Tanya, her own voice quiet. "What is that?"

"Tell me, Ysbel," said Masha quietly, her voice sharp. "What did you find when you tested that material?"

Ysbel shook her head. She was still staring at the screen as well, as if there was something about it that once you understood it, it had the power to hold your gaze and not let it go.

Jez shivered again. Suddenly, she wanted nothing more than to get the hell out of this tiny, cramped underground room.

But—the others were here, and she'd be damned if she was going to leave them to face whatever the hell this was alone.

"It was a strange composition, but nothing I believed was dangerous," said Ysbel slowly. "A metal alloy, but something that could be dissolved easily in water. It was slightly magnetic, and would hold a charge easily and for a long time. But I don't know what it would be useful for. Certainly I don't know why someone would be willing to try to kill Jez over it, and blow up any place that might still have a trace of it left."

Jez reached into her pocket slowly and ran her fingers over the small, round ball, heavier than it looked, in the pocket of her jacket.

Someone had been willing to kill her over this. Willing to kill her, and however many hundreds of people who'd had the bad luck to be living in the same apartment complex she was three years ago. She could still see the flash of a sight, as she was running for her life, of her neighbour, the old woman lying on the floor, a pool of red spreading out around her throat.

And whatever it was, whoever it was, it had something to do with this tiny room, the strange piece of tech, the lines of text scrolled down the holoscreen.

Lev turned abruptly, as if broken out of his reverie. "Wait. Ysbel. You said it would make a compound that was water soluble?"

"Yes. And highly chargeable."

Tae frowned. "Anything that highly chargeable would be something you could use to program," he said slowly. "Hypothetically, if you had an alloy like that, you could use it in all sorts of tech, because if it holds a charge, it will hold information. But—"

Lev grabbed for the table, his movement so sudden that Jez jumped. His face had gone bloodless, his expression slack with horror. He looked like he might fall over.

"Lev?" she said, taking a step towards him. "You OK?"

He didn't seem to hear her.

"I know what this is," he said quietly. He took a deep breath and straightened. "I believe I know what this is."

"What?" Masha's voice was sharp.

"Jez? Do you still have that material?" he asked. She nodded and took a few steps closer to him, even though for some reason whatever it was set up at the end of the room was almost physically repellant to her. She drew it out of her pocket and held it out, and he took it, rubbing his fingers gently over the material.

"I don't know how I didn't see it," he said quietly. "When I was here. In university. I don't know how I didn't realize."

"What is it, for heaven's sake?" asked Ysbel, her accent thicker than usual.

Lev looked up, as if he'd just realized the rest of them were there. His face was haunted, but he managed a small smile. "This equation. It's the one I was working on with Evka, while I was in graduate school here." He paused. "Ysbel," he said at last. "You said this is water soluble, and highly chargeable, correct?"

Ysbel nodded.

"I assume, if this were to build up in sufficient quantities in a substrate, because of the nature of it, it could re-form, more or less, correct? As in, you would be able to find a way to attract all the bits of the alloy back to one part of the substrate, although it would have been dissolved and distributed throughout before, correct?"

Again, Ysbel nodded.

"And Tae said it could be programmed. Which makes sense." Lev paused again, and for just a moment Jez wondered if he was going to fall over. But he didn't, just stood there watching them absently.

"You could take this," he said, still running his fingers over the material. "You could take this, and you could program something into it. You'd need—how much of it would you need, Tae, to get a basic program?"

Tae was watching Lev, his face creased in concern. "I'm—not completely sure," he said at last. "I'd have to work with it. But I suspect not much. A few micrograms would probably be sufficient."

Lev nodded, and turned back to Ysbel. "So. You take this material. You dissolve it into a gas. Or, you dissolve it into water, or you dissolve it into the components of a rations manufacturing plant, put it in the spray you use on plants. It really doesn't matter. Gas is probably the most efficient, because you can control the dosage better."

"Dosage?" Ysbel was still frowning, but Jez could see the look on her face, the look of someone realizing something she desperately does not want to realize.

"You spray the gas into the air. People breath it in, it goes into their bloodstream. It's programmed, of course, charged to respond to certain electric signals."

"It would congregate in the brain stem, yes?" said Tanya softly. "To charge it to respond to those electric signals—that would be simple."

Lev nodded. "Yes. And when there's enough of it, enough to be able to run whatever programming it's been encoded with—it's connected to the main system." He patted the piece of tech beside him absently. "Not this. They'll have a bigger system somewhere. It would be a massive database, and the capacitors would have to be huge."

Jez glanced around again, feeling unaccountably close to panic. There was the realization in Tae's eyes now as well, the lines around Masha's eyes that told, as clear as words, how horrified she was.

And, if Jez was being honest with herself, she knew too, she just didn't want to think it, because if she thought it, maybe it would be true, and she didn't want it to be true.

"And then—well. Why would you have any need for prisons then, or police, or anything else?" continued Ysbel softly.

"Wherever you are in the system, they'd be able to find you," said Tae. "You couldn't hide. Whoever controls that database controls the life of every person in the system. And if you do something wrong —" He glanced at Lev.

"What could you program into something like that?" asked Lev distantly.

Tae shrugged helplessly. "You could cause headaches. You could put through an electric charge that would short out the target's higher brain functions, turn them into a vegetable." He glanced at Tanya. "That chip in your head, Tanya. The one we shorted out when we escaped prison. It would do that, but it would be a million times more sophisticated than that. And with something like this material? Once enough of it had built up in people's brain stems, there would be nothing that could get rid of it."

Lev nodded. "Control the database, control the system. And no one, ever, could escape."

For a moment, Jez couldn't breathe.

Someone always able to find her, no matter where she went or what she did.

She'd never be free. Never again in her life, and nor would anyone else, and no matter how fast the *Ungovernable* could fly, no matter how far into deep space she went, they'd be there, in her head. She felt dizzy, suddenly unsure of how exactly she was staying on her feet. She was pretty sure the others were talking, but she couldn't hear them through the panic. And then someone caught her by the arm, and a low voice whispered, "Jez. Are you alright?" and she took a deep breath, and then another, and somehow the hand on her arm anchored her back to reality.

Lev.

She glanced over into his concerned face, still drawn and haunted, the hollows under his cheeks that seemed to have grown much sharper over the last few days—was he eating anything at all? She wasn't certain he was.

And here he was, comforting her.

Like she was the one that needed to be comforted.

She took a deep breath and managed a grin, shaking off his hand. "I'm good, genius. I'm fine."

He nodded, still watching her, and a slight nausea rose in her stomach.

She should have been the one comforting him, probably. If this had been Dmitri, or whoever it was Tae was soft over, Tae would have been the one doing the comforting, she was certain of it.

But this was her, and she didn't do relationships, and she didn't know how to do relationships, and there was something in Lev's eyes when he looked at her, that calm assurance, and she suddenly wanted to turn around and run as fast and as far as she could. Because the thing was, he deserved someone who'd know what to do right now, who'd have gone over to his apartment and held him while he fell apart, and who could be patient and steady and actually be there, the way he believed she would.

She was breathing too quickly again, which wasn't helping how dizzy she already felt, and damn it to hell, he was still watching her —

She reached out and caught herself against the wall and closed her eyes for a moment. There was a pause, then she felt his hand on her arm. The pressure and the weight of it steadied her, and when she opened her eyes again, she'd somehow managed to shove down her panic, at least enough that she could look Lev in the face.

"I'm good," she said jauntily. "I'm fine. You should probably worry about yourself, genius."

He watched her for a moment, then managed a small smile before reluctantly releasing his grip on her arm and turning back to the others.

Now that she was actually paying attention, Masha was talking.

"—any idea of the timetable on this?" she asked, in her brisk voice.

Lev glanced at the equation and shook his head. "There's nothing here that tells me that. But—" he scrolled down, glancing through the long lines of the equation. "But it's complete. It wasn't when I left. It is now. They could put this into play at any time."

"I've been hearing rumours," said Ysbel slowly. "My students. They're saying that something big is supposed to happen in the next couple weeks."

"Tae?" asked Masha. Tae nodded.

"I've been hearing the same thing. No one knows what it is. It's just campus gossip, really. But they say there's some big event happening in a couple weeks, that the university is keeping quiet."

"And they've told the security guards that we're going to be needed soon," put in Tanya.

"Did they give you a date?" asked Masha.

"No. But I have been talking to the other guards, the ones who have been here for a long time. They are guessing whatever it is will happen within two weeks."

"That would fit in with what I've been hearing," said Ysbel. "Tae?"

Tae nodded.

For a moment, there was silence. Then, finally, Ysbel said, "So. What do we do? I suppose we can't just blow this room up and be done with it?"

Lev shook his head. "No." His voice was distant. "They'll have all the information stored away in servers somewhere, and probably multiple back-up copies. We can't get rid of it by blowing up anything that's in this room." He touched the piece of tech again, lightly, as if trying to reassure himself that it was real, or that he was.

They were quiet again. Finally, Masha said, "Well, we'll have to think of something. Because I'm not sure about the rest of you, but I'd prefer the government not be able to find and kill me whenever it believes I pose an inconvenience." She turned to Ysbel. "Is there anything you know of that could change the way this alloy reacts?"

Ysbel frowned slightly. "I don't know. But it's possible."

"I can help you," said Tanya. "If I know you, my heart, you already have plenty of chemical components you've stockpiled. Am I correct?"

Ysbel turned and gave her a smile that was so full of tenderness that again, Jez's stomach twisted.

"We can't destroy the information," said Lev slowly. "At least, I don't currently know a way to do that. But it's just possible we could corrupt it."

"How?" asked Masha.

"I could re-write the equation, just enough to make it useless, and find the specs to how they're going to distribute the gas, and where and when. And then, if Tae can hack into their system and create a virus, we may be able to overwrite the equation that they have with the false one I write. And if Ysbel is able to find a chemical formula, we can spoof the chemical composition as well. It's just possible we could do it."

Ysbel was nodding. "I think I could do that. Here, I have access to all sorts of materials and testing equipment. I believe between Tanya and I, we could do this."

"I—I should be able to write a virus," said Tae slowly. The old, familiar look of strain and worry was back on his face. "It will be complicated, but I think I could do it." He paused. "We'd need to come back here. I'd need physical access to the network in order to plant the virus, and I doubt I'll be able to get that off a com."

Lev seemed to have regained control of himself. "That should work, then," he said, his voice its usual calm. "I'll re-write the equation, Ysbel will work on the formula, and Tae will create the virus. And in the meantime, Masha, I'll need you and Jez to find me everything you can dig up on this program. Tae will need specs, and I doubt they'll be anywhere I can access them."

"Can't you just overwrite the equation with a bunch of crap numbers?" asked Jez, swallowing hard.

Lev shook his head. "No. That would temporarily shut it down. But they'd re-write it, and it would be back online far too soon. We need something that will make them think this doesn't work. It will have to be very close to the original, and I need to know who worked on the original if I'm planning to fool them."

"I believe that's something we can do," said Masha quietly. She glanced at Jez, and Jez nodded. She looked quickly around at the six of them, illuminated by the harsh artificial light, and had to bite down another wave of panic.

It would damn well have to be something they could do. Because if it wasn't—well, if it wasn't, there wasn't a chance they'd survive whatever the hell was coming next.

15

Lev, day 14

"Lev."

He glanced up from his holoscreen at the voice in his earpiece, and tapped his com. "Yes?"

"The board is meeting today at 1500 standard. As you are the newest member of our board, we would like a report on what you've found in your, ah, review."

Maxim's voice had a grim tone to it. Lev smiled to himself.

"Of course. I'll be happy to attend, and I'll be certain to bring a report on what I've found."

"Thank you."

The com line shut off abruptly, and Lev sighed and leaned back in his seat. He pressed the heels of his hands into his eyes for a moment, then shook his head, stood, and stretched.

It was—what time was it? He glanced down at his com again. 1100 standard.

He hadn't even noticed the light creeping through the grungy curtains in the study.

Even when he was looking around the room, the lines of the

equation danced in front of his eyes.

He'd been right. It was the exact equation he'd been working on with Evka when he'd last studied here, but finished. They'd worked on it for eight months together, and had been no more than half-way done. Well—they'd been no more than half-way done before Evka had disappeared, and he'd erased the entire thing and replaced it with something that looked legitimate, but was nothing but gibberish.

And somehow someone had re-created it, and he wasn't certain how, and the more he thought about it, the more he was certain that he really didn't want to know.

At any rate, the important thing was, he needed to memorize the entire thing and understand it inside-out so he could figure out what parts he could tweak to make it still work, but not do what it was intended to do.

And somehow, in the next four hours, he had to also put together a report on what he'd found on the university system in his curricular review.

He took a step, then grabbed onto the table to steady himself. He managed a wry smile.

He was getting as bad as Tae. He couldn't actually remember how long it had been since he'd slept, but then, he'd been so engrossed in what he was working on that he wasn't sure he'd have noticed anyways. He blinked hard.

At this point, a nap might be his best option if he was planning on being prepared.

As he stumbled into his bedroom, he noticed something on the window sill. He frowned and opened the window cautiously, then he smiled slightly to himself.

It was a bundle of ration packs, tied together with ship's twine, with a note shoved into the bundle. The messy scrawl was unmistakable.

"Hey. Genius. Eat something."

He shook his head and stood staring out the window for a moment, a faint smile on his face.

He could still, if he closed his eyes, feel her body pressed up against him, her hands on his back, her lips on his.

He wasn't entirely sure what it was about her. It wasn't like he hadn't been attracted to people before Jez. There had been women in university, and then when he was working in the government, and it had always been a mutually-enjoyable experience.

Well, most of the time. Unless they were trying to murder him, which had happened.

But it had never been more than a pleasant distraction, something he could wake up and shake off and put aside until a convenient time.

And then there was Jez. Jez, with her cocky grin and her swagger and that way she had of getting under your skin until you couldn't decide whether you wanted to kill her, or couldn't live without her. But whatever she was, it wasn't something you could ignore. She was the most alive person he'd ever met. Maybe that was it. You couldn't be around Jez and not feel completely alive. You couldn't be around Jez and want to be cautious, or careful, or prudent, or analytical, because she was an entire force of nature all on her own. She was messy, and loud, and ridiculous, and completely unapologetic, and until he'd met her he'd had no idea that in the entire system, she was exactly what he wanted. What he needed. What he could no longer imagine his life without, because without her, everything else suddenly became colourless and tasteless.

It was ridiculous. If he was being honest, it was terrifying. Because he'd gotten by his entire life without needing anyone. He was smart, and he was very, very capable of getting by on his own, and he had always managed until now. And then Jez had exploded into his life like one of Ysbel's bombs, and from the moment he'd first seen her in Masha's tiny office, with one black eye and a bruise across her cheekbone and that snarky grin, he'd realized, without even knowing he'd realized it, that something had irreversibly changed.

He sighed and glanced down at the ration packs, and gave a small smile.

She was right, though.

He pulled one open, shoved it quickly into his mouth, and set an alarm on his com.

1500 hours. He'd have to be there, and he'd have to be very, very prepared. Because he was almost certain that whatever it was they were planning, it wasn't because they liked him.

He arrived outside the boardroom at 1450 and tapped lightly on the door. There was no answer, so he pushed it open gently. Chairs were set around the long table, but the room was completely empty.

He frowned to himself.

He'd read up everything he had on Maxim's file, before he came here. Apparently, the man was always ten minutes early to every meeting.

He settled himself in one of the hard-backed wooden chairs, glancing around the room. It was old-fashioned, with actual wood trim, and for some reason the sight of it reminded him of the *Ungovernable*, and the thought of the *Ungovernable*, of course, reminded him of Jez.

He sighed and closed his eyes for a moment, trying to re-focus his brain on the statistics he'd brought, rather than the way she tasted on his lips.

He almost didn't catch the faint click of the door locking. He jerked upright, jumped to his feet, and strode over quickly, trying the handle.

No luck.

He glanced quickly around the room. No other exits. The room was windowless, and the only door was the one he'd entered through.

He bit down hard on his teeth and swore softly.

This certainly wasn't the first time someone had tried to ambush him. What were they planning?

There was a soft hissing, and he glanced up again to see faint steam hissing from the ventilation pipes.

He gave a small, grim smile.

So. That was how they'd decided to kill him.

He rummaged quickly in the pocket of his jacket and pulled out the mask he'd placed there before he came, securing it over his face.

At least he knew it wasn't whatever the hell they were developing in the basement—it wasn't ready to be run yet. So this would be just regular poisonous gas, presumably.

He scanned the air quickly with his com, shook it, and glanced at the readout.

It would kill him if he breathed it, but it shouldn't harm his eyes or burn his skin at this concentration. Although he'd definitely want to take a shower after this.

He shook his head.

He was almost disappointed. Either they still had a very low opinion of him, or they had no imagination to speak of. He sighed, sat back in his chair, and pulled up his holoscreen, brushing away the clouds of gas when they obscured his view of the screen.

No point in wasting time, with the amount of work he still had to get through.

When the alarm in the hallway finally began to clang, he glanced up from his holoscreen. Five minutes. Plenty long enough to kill him, and then make it look like it had been an accident.

They were treating him like they thought he'd never set foot in a university before this.

There was a loud pounding at the door, and for a moment he contemplated ducking behind a chair. Still—they weren't likely to come in with heat guns, considering the composition of the gas, unless they had almost as much disregard for their own lives as they did for his.

He turned back to his holoscreen.

The door broke open a moment later, and two masked security guards stumbled inside. They glanced around the floor, clearly looking for a body, and it wasn't until he cleared his throat that they noticed him.

They both stared.

"Do you need something?" he asked politely.

They were still staring.

"If you don't—" he said, glancing pointedly at the holoscreen in front of him. Finally, one of them seemed to find her voice.

"I'm—I apologize. We were told that there may have been someone in the room when the security system locked it down. We were told to come retrieve a body.

"Well, I'm sorry to waste your time," he said pleasantly. "However, as you can see, there's no body available for retrieval, and I am, in fact, waiting for a meeting which was supposed to have begun—" he glanced down at his com, "five minutes ago."

"Uh." The woman glanced around helplessly. "I—can let them know you're waiting."

"If you would," he said, with a polite smile they probably couldn't see through the mask.

The ventilation fans kicked in a moment later, and by the time a pale-faced President Maxim entered the room, it was entirely clear. Lev looked up, removed his mask, and smiled in a perfunctory way.

"Ah. There you are. I was under the impression that the meeting was at 1500 hours."

The president was staring at him, but, he noticed, Klava was watching him shrewdly.

He wasn't entirely sure which one of them was behind this.

And he wasn't entirely sure that, in the grand scheme of things, it really mattered.

"I—we were on our way to the meeting, and we were told that there had been a malfunction in the building ventilation system, and gas had vented into the room. We were told the doors had locked automatically as part of the emergency system."

"I'm glad to see you alive, Lev," said Klava dryly. "I was afraid you might have been affected."

Lev met her gaze, his expression bland enough that Masha would have been proud. "I'm fortunate to have had a mask on me when the venting began."

She gave him a slight raise of her eyebrows, an acknowledgement between combatants.

"Well," she said, walking to the table and taking her seat. "I suppose, since we're all here and since you risked death to bring us your conclusions—the very least we can do is listen to your report."

He nodded, and waited for the others to take their seats.

They did, in a sort of stunned silence, and he smiled internally. They were likely unaccustomed to getting reports from people they'd attempted to murder minutes earlier. Then again, they probably should have reviewed his resume a little more closely.

Klava, at least, had done her research. There was a faintly-impressed look in her eye, but certainly no surprise.

When they were seated, he stood and pulled up his holoscreen.

The report he'd prepared was bland, and peppered though with platitudes, and as dry as he could possibly make it.

But then, that wasn't the real reason they'd asked him here. Besides trying to murder him, of course.

When he'd finished, he shut down his holoscreen and pulled back his chair, but the president held up a hand.

"A moment, Lev," he said. He seemed to have regained his equilibrium, and his voice was cold. "Before you sit down, I wonder if you might explain this." He pulled up the holoscreen on his own com, and flipped to a screen full of dense text.

Lev glanced over it quickly. His heart was beating slightly faster now.

This was the part that was always going to be the most delicate.

"It appears, Lev, that since you arrived at the university, and since you were granted access to the files, that someone has been searching through records that are clearly marked as highly classified. As you are, I am certain, aware, the classified designation was not given by the university, but by the government itself." He leaned forward slightly on the table. "Which would make access of those records not only academic misconduct, but a crime."

Lev managed to keep his expression neutral, but his palms were sweating slightly.

He'd been careful. He'd been very, very careful. But somehow, standing here facing these people, seated around a table in a room that was likely much too grand for what their budget would afford—this reminded him all too clearly of the moment when he'd been arrested for, ironically, the exact same crime.

Ten months in prison, most of it in solitary.

At the time he'd managed it. At the time, he'd been able to focus on recalling and reading all the documents he'd memorized, parsing through them for information on the problem he'd been working on when he'd been arrested. But now? After meeting Jez, after spending months in deep space, after experiencing a sort of flight and a sort of freedom he'd never dreamed of before—he was no longer sure he could bear it with equanimity.

"That is a truly unfortunate coincidence," he said at last. "However, I'm not certain what explanation you expect me to give."

Maxim leaned farther forward, narrowing his eyes. "I expect you to tell me the truth, Lev. Why were you accessing these records?"

Lev raised an eyebrow at him. "President. As I'm very certain you are aware, you gave me all the access codes I have. Unless you mean to suggest that you mistakenly provided me with codes to access illegal data, I'm not certain how you expect me to explain this."

Klava was still watching him, head on one side. She seemed slightly amused. Finally, she spoke.

"I believe we could solve this problem without much argument," she said. "Lev." She gave him what was likely meant to be an apologetic smile, but he could see the note of challenge in it, and the enjoyment. "As I'm certain you are as innocent as you proclaim yourself to be, you will have no objection, I'm sure, to allowing me to inspect your com." The emphasis she put on the word 'innocent' was the tiniest of barbs, but it didn't really matter.

He smiled tightly. "I was under the impression that my employment here would not require me to give up my personal privacy. A personal com search is rather a drastic measure, don't you think?"

Klava shrugged. "Perhaps. But then, a crime against the government is rather a drastic accusation. I would hate to make it against someone who was innocent."

The threat was hardly veiled. Apparently, whatever pressure the government was putting on the university was enough to make them willing to bend all sorts of social norms. In addition to attempting murder.

Although, in fairness, if his recollections of university life were accurate, not attempting murder was hardly a social norm here.

"Come now, Lev, surely you'd have no objection to me taking a look."

And there was nothing he could do about it.

Slowly, he removed his com. Klava didn't take her eyes off his face the whole time, and he made a conscious effort not to allow any of his emotions to show.

Just over a year ago, he'd done the same thing, removed his com and handed it to a line of auditors almost as grim-faced as this woman.

He dropped it to the table with a 'click' that was clearly audible in the now-silent room. The other board members were leaning slightly forward, straining to see what would happen next.

Klava picked the com up, flipped it open, and pulled up the holoscreen.

The room was deadly silent.

She flipped through the files on the screen, until she came to a small file, hidden in one corner.

He forced his hands to be still, despite his racing pulse, forced the bland, polite smile to remain on his face.

She pulled it open.

Across the screen, pages and pages of government reports. She was scanning through them quickly, and maybe, just maybe—

She paused, and, a moment later, tapped on one thick file.

It opened.

Behind it, a folder.

He closed his eyes for a moment, and opened them in time to see her watching him.

With the slightest hint of triumph to her expression, she tapped the folder.

It opened.

A file, and on it—

He almost snorted with a mix of laughter and giddy relief.

Klava's face turned suddenly cold with anger, and around the table, someone coughed in a failed attempt to disguise a laugh.

The folder was full of large, full-colour pictures of barely-clothed people lounging in what appeared to be tiger-skin unders.

Klava slapped her hand down on the com, and the holoscreen disappeared. "I would like to know, Lev, if you believe it is appropriate to look at underclothing models during time when you are being paid by the university."

"I do apologize," he said, keeping his head down to avoid bursting into a fit of completely uncontrollable laughter. "However, I have been very careful to only look at underclothing models when I was no longer on the university's time." He was almost shaky with relief.

Tae was a damn genius. He'd told Lev he'd put in a spoof, but Lev hadn't had any idea of the details.

"Well, I'm not sure how I managed to pull it up, then, while looking through your files—"

"If you recall," he said in a mild voice, raising his head, "that is my private com you are looking through. I'm fairly certain there is no university policy dealing with what I can look at on my private com, as long as it is not illegal. Now, if I may?" He held out his hand.

She narrowed her eyes and watched him for a long moment. At last, grudgingly, she dropped the com into his outstretched palm.

He looked around at the board members, still transfixed in their seats.

"Now," he said, and this time he let ice creep through the bland politeness of his voice. "You asked for a meeting with me, and you asked me to present a report. I did exactly as I was asked to do. You, however, wittingly or unwittingly, put me in what was certainly a life-threatening situation. If you knew of it far enough in advance not to come into the room, there was no reason why it should have taken the security guards five minutes to arrive and break down the door, and no reason that no one should have tried to warn me. And then you insinuated that I had been accessing classified documents, a crime that would send me to prison, and you took my private com and searched through it in an open meeting.

"I believe," he turned to the president now, and his voice softened with the threat, "that there are university protocols against that behaviour. I believe that constitutes much, much more than academic misconduct. I believe that any one of these things taken separately could comprise a report to the government board of education." He paused a moment to let his words sink in. Then looked directly at Klava, and smiled. "I expect this will be the last time something like this happens while I am on campus," he said softly, his voice almost friendly. "If it is not, then the report I have prepared will go straight back to the government headquarters. And if you were paying attention while you were reading my report— which I doubt you were—you would have seen it there. Everything I've found on each one of you, all there, in standard government cypher."

He strapped his com onto his wrist in the silence. "I expect you to leave me alone," he said, once he'd finished. "I expect full cooperation from here on out. And if I do not get it, then you can expect that there will be consequences."

He turned and walked out of the room, leaving a dead silence in his wake.

When he reached his apartment, he carefully closed and locked the door, then quickly scanned the room for bugs.

They were there, of course, but only the ones he'd already blocked with Tae's hack.

He sighed, and sat back in his chair, pulling the blinds closed to shut out the dim afternoon light. Then he pulled up the screen on his com again.

He flipped through to the file Klava had pulled up, and then, carefully, maneuvered to the file hidden behind it, pulled it open, swiped past Tae's spoof, then scrolled down to where he had left off, where a new sheaf of documents began.

He frowned as he scanned through the text.

The program he and Evka had been working on had been going on for much longer than he'd supposed. Twenty years, at least.

And even after glancing at the first few paragraphs, he realized that reading the history behind it was going to make him sick.

16

Tae, day 15

"Tae? Tae, you in there?"

Tae blinked, and looked up. "What is it?" he mumbled.

"Tae. It's me. Open the door."

Tae sighed, and pushed himself to his feet. He wasn't certain what time it was, and he didn't have the energy to try to find out. Instead, he stumbled to the door and pulled it open.

Dmitri stood in the doorway, a worried look on his face, a bag of something in his hand. The smell wafting from it made Tae suddenly realize how long it had been since he'd last eaten.

"Tae." Dmitri reached past him and flicked the room light on, and Tae blinked against the sudden glare. "Can I come in?"

Tae nodded, wordlessly, and Dmitri stepped through the door, pausing to drop the bag on the desk, which was cluttered with bits of tech and chips and notes Tae had scrawled when he was trying to keep track of what he'd been doing.

Dmitri's glance took in the room, then moved to Tae, and Tae could feel his face warming.

"Dmitri. I—I'm sorry. I've been—Look, I'm really sorry."

Dmitri shook his head and took a step closer, putting a hand on Tae's arm. His face was—not accusing. Concerned.

He tipped Tae's chin up with his other hand, and looked him over critically. "Tae. Tell me the truth. When's the last time you slept?"

"I—" he frowned. To be honest, he didn't actually remember. Dmitri shook his head, his lips tightening.

"I've hardly seen you in three days. Listen to me, Tae. This isn't how things work around here."

Tae dropped his eyes. "Dmitri, I'm sorry. I—"

"No." Dmitri's voice was firm. "I thought we'd agreed. We're boyfriends, right?"

"I—" He felt the familiar sick knot of guilt in his stomach. Because of course this would happen. Of course he'd finally start seeing the kindest, most attractive boy he'd ever met, and then he'd have to drop everything, and hurt Dmitri, or else let his friends die. And he couldn't let his friends die.

"Do you know what that means?"

Reluctantly, Tae met his eye.

He was—smiling?

"It means that if you have a problem, it's my problem too, OK? It means we take care of each other. It's not that complicated. I've seen you. You take care of everyone. You take care of that crazy pilot friend of yours, you take care of every student in our study group— and now I'm here to tell you that it's your turn to be taken care of."

Tae stared at him, not quite certain he'd heard right. Dmitri gave a small, amused smile.

"Honestly, Tae, it's not that strange of a concept. Now, sit down."

Tae did, too bewildered to protest.

"I brought you dinner. So what we're going to do is, you're going to eat. You're going to eat all of it, because I doubt you've had anything other than ration packs since you disappeared three days ago. And once you're done eating, you're going to go to bed, and you're damn well going to sleep through all your morning classes until you don't have any more circles under your eyes, and if I have to stand here the whole night and watch you to make sure you do, so help me, I will."

Tae was still blinking up at Dmitri, too surprised to respond.

Dmitri chuckled softly. He leaned in and gave Tae a quick kiss. "Do you know you're absolutely adorable when you're surprised? Now, eat. And while you're eating, tell me what's gone wrong."

Finally, Tae's brain managed to compute what Dmitri had said. "I —but—" he started. Dmitri laughed and turned his chair to face the desk, then opened the bag, pulled out the carton of food, and opened it.

"I'll hand-feed you if I have to," he said, his voice joking, but with a tone in it that made Tae believe him.

Still slightly in shock, he glanced down at the food—something crisp-fried and breaded and smelling delicious—and picked a long stalk up and put it in his mouth. Dmitri watched him with raised eyebrows until he'd chewed and swallowed and picked up a second piece.

Tae's brain finally caught up with his body, and his stomach was loudly informing him of how hungry he was, and for a few minutes he ate without talking. Dmitri lay back on the cot, and every so often Tae glanced over at him. Dmitri had his hands behind his head and was watching Tae with a soft look on his face, and for some reason the sight of Dmitri laying on his cot made his heart beat slightly faster.

He sighed and shook his head, pushing the empty carton away. "Dmitri. I—I'm sorry I've been so busy the last few days. I didn't mean to—"

Dmitri pushed himself up on his elbows, flashing Tae a crooked smile. "Tae. Stop apologizing. I know you well enough to know that whatever it is, you're worried sick over it." He sat up and leaned forward, resting his elbows on his knees, and his voice softened. "What happened?"

Tae looked at him for a long time.

This was stupid. It was ridiculous. He was in this university as a plant, and he was only going to stay long enough to plant a vicious virus into one of the university's top-secret research projects, and if anyone had any idea what he was doing right now he'd be thrown in jail so fast he wouldn't have time to catch his breath, and his friends were a group of crazy ex-convicts who basically couldn't wake up in the morning and go for breakfast without breaking seventeen different laws, and every person even slightly associated with him was in very plausible danger of being violently killed.

And still, somehow, he wanted to open his mouth and tell Dmitri every damn thing, something about the soft look in his eyes and his crooked smile and that damn dimple—

"Hey, Tae," said Dmitri softly. "It's OK." And he realized there were tears of exhaustion forming in his eyes, and he brushed them away quickly.

But—he had to tell him something, so he sighed and tried to smile. "It's nothing. I—got some news. Friends of mine. They were —they were looking into something dangerous, and the government got wind of it, and they asked me to help them get out of trouble." He shrugged helplessly. "And I'm behind in all my classes, and I just —I'm sorry. I just haven't had time to breathe."

Dmitri had cocked his head to one side, and was looking at him in concern. "You have more friends who are in danger? Tae, I know nothing you do should surprise me anymore, but—what's going on?"

"I—" he shook his head, and decided to stick as close to a true story as he could. "I have street-kid friends. The government has been cracking down on them lately, and they've been—disappearing. The police come after them, and they take them away, and we don't hear from them ever again."

Dmitri was still staring at him, and there was a slightly horrified expression on his face. "I—didn't know. I—I'm so sorry. Is everything alright?"

Tae shook his head tightly. "I don't know. I'm doing my best. I think—I think something might be happening soon. Something dangerous. Like—like you all have been talking about. And I'm afraid it might—they might—" he broke off.

It wasn't a lie. The thought of that gas, permeating Masha's abandoned hangar bay, had kept him awake staring at the ceiling long past when he'd wanted to be asleep. Once the street-kids were infected, cleansing the city of them would be a matter of typing in one simple command, and then sending a group in to pick up the bodies. And he wasn't nearly naive enough to believe that anyone in the government would hesitate one second to do just that.

The thought was enough to make him regret the food he'd just eaten.

"Anyways," he said, gesturing helplessly at the pile of tech on his desk, "I—I haven't had much time, is all. I'm sorry."

Dmitri tightened his lips in a gesture of frustration, shaking his head. He stood abruptly. "Tae. No. I'm sorry I didn't know. I should have come up here the first night you didn't come to dinner with us." He sighed. "Right now, Tae, you're going to bed, but we are going to talk about this in the morning."

"I—"

Dmitri reached down and offered his hand, and at last Tae took it, pulling himself to his feet.

"Tae, listen to me," said Dmitri. "I can't do what you can do. But I can at least make sure you can do what you can do, and if that means I bring you food and sit here until you fall asleep, I'll do it. OK?"

Tae blinked up at him for a minute. There was something strange in his chest, fear and worry and guilt and something else he didn't recognize.

And then he caught the tiny hint of a dimple in the corner of Dmitri's mouth, the concern in his eyes, and he finally realized what it was.

Happiness.

He leaned forward slightly, and kissed Dmitri, and Dmitri wrapped his arms protectively around Tae's back, and for the first time in a very, very long time, the heavy brick of worry that had been sitting hard and unyielding on his chest, seemed to lift, ever so slightly.

When he woke the next morning, he blinked and peered around, disoriented. Light was filtering in through the window, and when he glanced at his com, he swore and sat up quickly.

1200 hours. He'd slept a full eleven hours, and he'd missed classes, and—

Something on his desk caught his eye, a scrawled note. He stood and picked it up.

"Tae," it read. "You've just woken up and are panicking because you slept too long and missed your classes. Honestly, I don't know how to explain to you how normal it is to sleep through your classes. But if you weren't like that, then you wouldn't be you, and I've discovered I adore you. So, I will just say, please stop panicking. Vera is taking notes for you in chemistry, and Leonid is taking notes in gov theory, and you already know more than the tech teacher, so you don't have to worry about your tech class. I'll leave breakfast outside your door. Call me when you're up."

Tae frowned and rubbed the sleep from his eyes, then pulled open the door. True to Dmitri's word, there was a plate of sweet mashed tubers, now cold, sitting there.

He smiled slightly, and picked it up. Under it was another note.

"I'm serious, Tae. Call me. Don't make me come hover outside your door for the whole day trying to figure out if you're awake."

He closed the door with his elbow and hit his com, smiling despite himself.

"Tae?" Dmitri answered instantly.

"Um. Thank you. For last night. And for breakfast. I—"

"Tae, seriously. Don't mention it. I thought I explained this to you last night. That's kind of part of being boyfriends, OK? You up?"

Tae sat down at his desk and leaned back, the muscles in his shoulders relaxing slightly. "Yeah. I'm up. But I need to—"

"No. Before you do anything, hold on a minute. I'm coming up right now."

Tae waited, bemused, until there was a tap on his door. "You decent?" came Dmitri's voice.

Tae opened the door.

"You're dressed. Good." Dmitri grabbed him by the hand. "We're going down to the study room."

"What?" Tae frowned in confusion.

Dmitri smiled teasingly. "Tae, you're an actual genius, I've seen you work. I'm not sure why you're having so much trouble understanding what I'm saying to you. Come on!" He pulled Tae out into the hallway, and finally, Tae followed.

When they reached the study room, Dmitri paused for a moment, smiled broadly, then pushed the door open. Tae looked inside, and felt his mouth drop.

Vera, Leonid, and all the others were there, but they didn't have their usual study materials open on their holoscreens. Instead, there was one holoscreen, expanded to fill half the table, and on it was a long list, starting with, 'Food? Place to sleep?' and ending with 'Overthrow the government?'

Tae stared at it, then at the students, then at Dmitri.

Dmitri grinned. "I hope you don't mind. I told the rest of them what was happening to your friends, and we've been brainstorming ideas."

"Overthrow the government?" Tae said blankly.

Dmitri chuckled. "Alright, one or two of us might have gotten a little carried away."

Tae shook his head wordlessly. Of course he, personally, had only a few weeks before agreed to help Masha actually overthrow the government, but it sure as hell wasn't the first thing he would have listed if he was making a list of how to help street kids being harassed by police.

"Come on in, Tae," said Vera, her smile as wide as Dmitri's. "We've been waiting for you."

He entered, still dumbstruck, and when Dmitri pulled out a chair for him he almost fell into it.

"Here's the thing," said Vera, turning the holoscreen to face him. "We always sit around and talk about the government, and how much we hate it, and how corrupt it is, and how we'd never do what our parents do, just going along with it to stay safe. We've talked about that over our sump for years. And then here you come, and you don't even have to talk about it. You just—" she gestured with her free hand. "You just go in and damn well start taking it apart! So here's the thing. We're brainstorming what we can do, and we're still working on it. But none of us can hack like you can. So we figured, while we're working on coming up with a plan, the very least we can do is make sure you're not worried about your homework. So." She swiped across the screen, pulling up a new list. "We've set up a new schedule. We're rotating taking classes for you—here's the notes rotation, we'll send them to your com as soon as class is done. If you don't have time to do the homework, here's the list of who'll do yours as well as theirs. We're going to mix it up so you don't have the same answers as the same person more than once in a row, but I'm making sure no one in the rotation gets below ninety percent average, because we don't want to bring your grades down too much. And here," she flipped the screen again, "I made a list of everyone who was going to bring you food, but Dmitri nixed the whole thing, because he said that was his job, thank you very much, since he happens to be your boyfriend."

Dmitri slipped an arm around Tae's waist possessively, and shot him a quick grin.

Tae just stared. At last he turned to Dmitri.

"Did you—did you know they were—"

Dmitri shook his head firmly. "Listen, Tae. You told us you'd grown up in the rough part of town, and we all just treated it like it wasn't a big deal. And none of us bothered to even consider what that might mean for you. I can't believe you've been dealing with this all on your own, but that stops right now."

Tae shook his own head stubbornly. "No. Dmitri, listen. I almost got you—I mean, I got you in enough trouble the other day. You don't cross the government without risking some very serious consequences, and I can't put you or anyone else in the kind of danger again."

He wasn't certain if Dmitri had mentioned the incident with the ion bomb to anyone else, and he sure as hell didn't want to bring it up if he hadn't. There were enough damn rumours flying around campus about him, what with Jez's interference.

"Tae. Listen to me." Dmitri caught his gaze. "Like I told you. We're your friends. I'm your boyfriend, for the Lady's sake. I remember during that—incident you're talking about, you said something. You said something about friends not doing that to each other. We're not going to let you kill yourself with worry and lack of sleep, OK? I'm not going to let you. So you might as well get used to it."

Tae stared at Dmitri, then around at the others.

"Come on," said Vera, grinning and swiping the screen back to the list that included, 'overthrow the government.' "You'll know better than any of the rest of us what we can do to help."

"We are going to help you, Tae, whether you like it or not," said Dmitri. "So. Do you want to help us figure out what to do? Or would you rather Vera try to overthrow the government?"

Tae looked around again, helplessly. At last he sighed and shook his head, but he couldn't seem to stop the smile that was spreading across his face.

"Alright," he said, leaning forward. "Alright, show me what you have."

17

Ysbel, day 17

Ysbel watched the students file out of class.

In the weeks since she'd been here, she was actually starting to get to know their names.

Vera gave her a quick smile as she stood. Ysbel smiled back reluctantly. Then, sighing to herself, she cleared her throat.

The students stopped as if they'd been frozen.

Apparently, she was still somewhat intimidating.

"I am going to be in my office at 1500 hours if you need to ask me questions about the homework," she said, her voice loud enough to carry over the sound of shuffling papers. "I would prefer you asking me questions to you getting blown up, which is probably what will happen if you try to do the homework without asking me questions. You can go now."

The students stood frozen for a moment longer, staring at her with expressions that said they weren't sure whether or not she was joking and they were too terrified to take a chance. Then, one by one, they resumed their slow shuffle towards the exit.

Ysbel sighed again, and looked after them with a sort of fondness.

She'd probably actually regret if one of them blew themselves up at this point.

She'd be spending the rest of the day working on a chemical formula that would do what Lev wanted it to do. She'd spent every spare moment of the last three days working on it, and she still had plenty of work ahead of her. Not that she couldn't do it. She was quite certain that she could—she'd solved much more difficult problems in the past, although admittedly those had been creating weapons, not sabotaging them. The question was only, could she do it in time.

She sighed.

And—well, the problem was, she'd somehow also become invested in making sure her idiot students didn't get themselves blown up, injured, or blackmailed by the other professors.

She walked quickly down the hallway to her office, and smiled when she opened the door and saw Tanya perched on her desk, eye protection on, carefully measuring granules into a test tube. She looked up as Ysbel walked in, and smiled back.

"Ysi." She slid off the desk, carefully replaced the excess granules into the beaker on the table, and leaned in for a kiss. Ysbel kissed her back, then held her off at arms length, looking at her.

"You're different, Tanya," she said at last, with a small smile. "I think this is the first time I've seen you not looking worried."

Tanya gave her a quizzical look, then a small, wry smile. "Well, my heart, it is a little difficult not to be worried all the time when you're raising children in a prison." She paused. "I believe this time here, in the university, is the first time I've been away from the children in five and a half years."

Ysbel sobered. "I'm sorry, my love. I didn't—"

Tanya shook her head and pressed a finger to Ysbel's lips. "That was not your fault. When we were together, we raised the children together. And when we were apart—" her words faltered for a moment, and Ysbel could sense the pain behind them, and it echoed the pain that clutched at her own chest whenever she stopped for a moment to remember.

"When we were apart, I did the best I could. And I love those children, but—it's not easy. You get used to it, but it's not easy."

Ysbel nodded again and pulled Tanya close, and Tanya relaxed into her.

"I feel like this is the first time I've been able to be a person, not just a mother," she whispered into Ysbel's shoulder. "The first time in a very long time."

Ysbel held her for a while, feeling their hearts beating in tandem.

So much she'd never know. So much about this woman who she'd loved for as long as she could remember that she'd never know, and so much she'd carried that Ysbel couldn't take from her.

But—well, but now she had the rest of her life to try, and that was enough.

Most of the time, that was enough.

She sighed and loosened her grip on her wife. Although, if they didn't come up with the chemistry equation quickly enough, the rest of her life might not be all that long.

"I suppose we'd better get back to work," she said reluctantly, and Tanya sighed and nodded, a faint smile in the corner of her mouth.

"I'm not on duty for another four hours. I'll stay and help. If you want me to, that is." She shot Ysbel a teasing glance, and Ysbel grinned back wickedly.

"Well, my love, four hours is a long time. I'm happy to have you stay, but I will tell you, I'm not completely sure we'll be working the entire time."

Tanya laughed, shaking her head in mock despair, and Ysbel watched her, and for a moment she could hardly breathe, thinking of how lucky she was, how unbelievably lucky she'd been to find Tanya, and then, after that horrible day five years ago, find her again.

She didn't realize how long they'd been working until the first timid tap on her door. She frowned, glancing at her com.

1500 hours. Of course. She'd promised the students, and those of them who were brave enough or desperate enough to show up probably deserved the help.

"I'm sorry, my love," she whispered to Tanya. "It's my students."

Tanya looked at her with the hint of a teasing smile, but she just nodded. "Alright Ysi." She glanced around. "I'll go into the back room and keep working while you talk to them."

Ysbel kissed her quickly, and Tanya grabbed the test tube and the materials they'd been working with and slipped soundlessly into the back as Ysbel opened the office door.

Vera stood there, with three or four other students. They all looked faintly terrified, although Vera looked slightly less terrified than the others.

"Come in," said Ysbel in a flat voice, and, with nervous glances at each other, the students stepped into the office, huddled together as if they were worried they'd be attacked the moment they stepped through the door.

Ysbel walked back around the desk, pulled her chair up, and sat down.

The students stood in their tight cluster, eyes wide with a sort of abject terror and the look of someone regretting all the life choices that had brought them to this point flashing across their faces.

"Well?" she asked, somewhat impatiently.

There was a collective swallow. Then Vera stepped forward.

"Professor. We've been working on this one problem, and we're having some trouble."

"Alright, show it to me, then." She looked at them for a moment, and sighed. "If I'd wanted to kill you, I would have done it already. Since you are still alive, I clearly do not want to kill you. So sit down."

"Um. Professor." Vera had a look of slight amusement gleaming through the fear on her face. "I think we're all just hoping you won't change your mind."

Ysbel scowled at them. "If you don't sit down and tell me what you need, I might."

They jumped for chairs like something had bitten them, and Ysbel sat back and watched them with faint satisfaction. When they were all seated, Vera pulled up a holoscreen on her com and brought it forward.

"Here, professor. We couldn't figure out this part of the formula."

She frowned as she looked at it. There was something familiar about the scrawled writing on one of the problems.

"You study with Tae?" she asked at last. "I haven't seen him in class lately."

The students glanced at each other quickly. Finally Vera said, very obviously trying to keep her tone light, "I'm not sure what you're talking about. He was sitting just behind me today. I can't remember, he might have had to slip out early."

"Is he skipping class and you're helping him with his homework?"

There was another long, fraught silence.

"Um," said Vera at last, with a sort of forced, reckless brightness to her tone, "I don't know why you'd think that. I'm certain he's been there for every class."

"His handwriting keeps changing every time he turns in his

homework, for the last two or three days."

"I—think he's been a bit stressed lately."

She stared at the students.

They stared back at her.

They were clearly terrified, and clearly none of them was going to rat Tae out anyways, even though they all clearly were under the impression it might cost them their actual lives.

She felt her mouth turning up into a smile, despite herself. "Well," she said at last. "I am glad Tae has managed to be at all his classes. And I'm glad he's managed to finish all his homework, despite the fact that he is clearly very stressed." She paused a moment. "And," she added, more softly, "I'm very, very glad he's found friends like you. Not everyone is so lucky."

There was a sort of communal release of breath from the other students, and she smiled to herself and leaned forward to study the holoscreen.

She might have missed the sound, if she hadn't been listening for it with half an ear. She shoved her chair back, jerked the heavy desk around so it stood between the students and the door, and shoved it over, test-tubes exploding in shimmering fragments of glass as they hit the floor. The door slammed open, and three masked figures burst inside, heat-guns drawn.

"Down," Ysbel hissed at the students. She reached into the pouch she carried around her neck, pulled out a soft pocket of explosive gel, and turned.

"Shoot me, and this whole building goes up," she said softly, into the sudden silence. "You have no idea how many explosives I'm carrying on me. And believe me, one drop of this lands on you and I promise, there will be no time for you to find out."

The masked figures froze.

To one side of her, she caught, out of the corner of her eye, a slender, shadowy figure slip from behind the back office door. She smiled to herself.

Good. She would actually prefer not to have to leave a crater the size of Masha's hangar bay in the university grounds.

"Now," she said, in a friendly fashion. "I suggest you drop your heat guns and walk out of that door right now."

They were still staring at her. One of them made to lift their gun, the slightest fraction of movement in the muscles of their arm. And then they dropped bonelessly to the ground. Before the other two had time to turn, Tanya dropped them as well, and then straightened, smiling that faint, wistful smile.

Lady and Consort, she loved that woman.

"Well," said Ysbel, stepping over to the bodies and nudging one with her foot. "I could drip some of this onto them and we could take them somewhere private before I hit the control and set off the explosive."

Tanya smiled at her fondly. "Ysi. There's nowhere private like that in the university. You know that. I'll take care of them. I may not even have to kill them."

"You say that like it's a good thing," Ysbel muttered, and Tanya laughed and kissed her.

The students were still cowering behind the overturned desk.

"Do you need help?" Ysbel asked her wife briskly. Tanya shook her head.

"No, my heart. I have an antigrav, and I am perfectly capable." She smiled one last time, pulled the antigrav out of her pocket, and draped the three bodies onto it.

"But, I could borrow your jacket, if you don't mind."

Ysbel smiled, pulled the spare explosive components she generally kept in her pockets out, then handed it to Tanya. Tanya tossed her jacket and Ysbel's over the bodies, gave Ysbel one last smile, and left, pushing the masked figures ahead of her with one leg.

The door closed behind her, and there was a long, long moment of silence. At last, slowly, the students rose from behind the desk, their faces slack with a mixture of terror and shock. Ysbel shook her head, leaned over, and with an effort, righted the table. She dragged it back to where it had been, picked up her chair from where it had fallen, and resumed her seat.

The students were still staring at her, unmoving.

She sighed. "Listen. I am a very busy woman. I am more than happy to help you with your homework, but I can't make my office hours any longer than they already are. So. If you would like me to look at your question, kindly pull up your holoscreen and show me again where you got stuck."

"I—you—" began one of the students. "The security guard—"

"Yes. We are very lucky she was here."

"You carry explosives. In a bag. Around your neck," said Vera, in a faint voice.

"Yes, well it's a padded bag," said Ysbel, with faint irritation. "Believe me, I've seen enough people get blown to fragments that I am very careful."

Vera nodded, in a stunned sort of way.

"People with heat-guns—they just—they—"

Ysbel gave a long sigh. "Yes. People with heat guns tried to kill me. I am very aware of that. As I said, I have no interest in me being killed or in you being killed, so I stopped them, and the security guard dealt with the problem. And now," she glanced at her com, "we have exactly twenty standard minutes of office hours left, and then I need to get back to my work."

One of the students pulled up the com again and tapped, in a dazed fashion, at the point in the equation where they'd gotten stuck. Ysbel leaned forward again.

"Ah," she said. "I think I see your problem."

When the students filed out of the office, twenty minutes later, she noticed, behind their terror, a sort of awed respect. And for some reason, she couldn't help but smile.

Once they'd gone, she tapped her com. "Tanya?" she asked.

"Ysi."

"What did you find out?"

"They're all still alive. I took them to Masha, and she questioned them. I don't think they knew who you were, they were only following the government tracking signals. We can't let them go, because now they will have narrowed down who they were tracking to you, me, and those students." She paused. "Masha gave them something to put them in a coma for a few days, and I dropped them at the hospital."

"Well, my love," said Ysbel quietly, looking over the chemical components she'd re-spread across her desk. "If we don't figure this out in the next three or four days, I have a feeling it won't really matter."

18

Jez, day 17

Jez glanced over at Masha in the darkness.

Masha was looking straight ahead, and didn't meet her gaze. Which was just fine by Jez.

The thing was, when Masha had told her what they needed to do that night, what probably should have happened was, Masha should have told her to stay home, and Jez should have told Masha to shut up, she'd do it herself because she was a hell of a lot better than Masha at that sort of thing, and besides, she wasn't a damn cautious bastard like Masha was.

But instead, Masha had asked, quietly, if Jez would mind coming along, and Jez had been so shocked that she'd just nodded and hadn't said anything about how she'd rather work alone.

They were hidden in the dark shadows of a narrow entry way, just outside the math theory building. Outside where Lev's old professor had once had her laboratory.

A laboratory that, apparently, was still in use.

If there were records on the program, they were likely not stored there. But it was possible it would hold a clue as to where they were stored.

The night air was cold on Jez's skin, even through the jacket and the scarf she'd pulled over her head.

"How much longer?" she whispered.

"I don't know." Masha's voice was resigned. "But about ninety seconds less than the last time you asked me."

Jez sighed heavily. "I told you I was crap at waiting."

"Well, I'm afraid you're going to have to learn," Masha snapped.

Jez rolled her eyes and bumped her heel against the wall.

She was definitely not ever going to be good at this.

Plaguing Masha didn't even look cold.

"You grow up in this dump of a city?" Jez whispered, when she couldn't stand the silence any longer.

Masha turned, studying her. "Yes," she said at last, and Jez raised an eyebrow. She hadn't actually expected a response.

"Family still live here, then?"

"No," said Masha shortly, in a tone that did not invite questions. Jez frowned.

She hadn't actually pictured Masha as having a family. But she must have, somewhere.

Anyway, she knew what it was like not to want to talk about your family.

She glanced sideways at Masha again. The woman was staring straight ahead, her face fixed, and Jez felt a sudden, unexpected jolt of sympathy.

"Hey," she said at last. "Don't know if it makes you feel any better, but my damn family kicked me out on my fourteenth birthday."

Even as the words left her mouth, she could feel her shoulders tensing.

Stupid damn thing to say. Now Masha was going to say something like, "I don't blame them," and honestly, she'd gotten over it a long time ago, at least she told herself she had, but the words would still cut at something inside her like knives.

But Masha didn't say anything.

Jez's muscles were still tense, and she tried to relax them. Maybe the plaguer was waiting for a better time, when Jez wasn't ready for it and it would hurt more.

It had to have been at least a couple hours by now. She glanced down at her com.

Three minutes.

She leaned back against the wall, closing her eyes, and forced herself to breathe deeply.

"I'm—sorry. That was wrong of them."

Jez jerked her head up. Masha was watching her, and she still couldn't make out her expression.

Was she joking, maybe? Or had she actually just—

"I—lost my parents," said Masha at last. "When I was young. I know it's not the same, but—I'm sorry."

Jez stared at her, speechless. Finally, she shook her head. "I—I'm sorry too. I mean, that your parents died."

Masha gave a small, humourless smile. "Not died, actually. Murdered. By the government, and the mafia."

Jez was silent, and so was Masha.

Finally, Jez glanced sideways at her.

Who was this woman? She was pretty damn sure that if someone had murdered someone she cared about, she wouldn't have gone to work for them.

And Masha had, for years.

"Alright," said Masha quietly, at long last. "If Tae's scanner is to be trusted, I think that's the last of them out of the building. Let's go."

Jez nodded, grinning as her muscles tightened with a familiar excitement, and started after Masha.

When they reached the door Masha typed in a code. There was a soft click, then the door swung gently open.

Silently, they stepped inside and started up the dark corridors. Jez had glanced through the map Lev had sent them, and she was pretty sure she could figure out how to get where they'd need to be.

Eventually.

She slipped the heat pistol from her boot and held it lightly in her hand, the weight of it comforting against her palm.

And then they were in front of a door, and her heart was pounding so fast she could hardly stand it. Masha stepped past her and typed something into the pad.

"What are you doing?"

Jez spun, blinking against the sudden, bright artificial light.

Damn.

She sprinted the three steps forward to where the corridor turned and grabbing for where a hand must be holding the light. Her hands closed around an arm and she jerked it up at the same time as she brought her elbow around hard at temple-height, and the body attached to the arm collapsed. She yanked the light free and turned it on it's former owner—a security guard, apparently, who now lay groaning softly on the floor—then put a foot hard on his wrist, where he was trying, weakly, to bring his com up.

In the background, she heard Masha muttering into her own com. The man's eyes fluttered open, and she pointed the light directly into his face. He squeezed his eyes shut again against the brightness, and she grinned. If the damn plaguer was going to blind her, she figured he deserved at least the same treatment.

"Wouldn't move, if I were you," she drawled quietly, but her heart was pounding. If the plaguer'd gotten a call out, things were about to get a hell of a lot more interesting—

And then a figure materialized silently out of the darkness in front of her, and she jerked her heat-pistol up with her free hand—

"Shh."

It took her half a second to recognized Tanya's voice. She lowered the heat-pistol, still grinning, and Tanya put a finger to her lips. She reached into her security-guard jacket and pulled out a bottle of something, then stooped and held it to the weakly-struggling guard's nose. He went limp, and she straightened.

"I will take care of this from here. It looks like one of my fellow guards was drinking on duty. Good thing I found him." She paused. "Did he see you?"

"Not clearly, certainly. Jez acted admirably quickly," came Masha's calm voice from behind her. Jez frowned in surprise at the words, but even in the darkness, she could see Tanya's faint smile.

"I would have expected nothing less from our pilot." Tanya bent, lifting the man to his feet with his arm around her neck. He was significantly larger than Tanya, and she staggered slightly under the weight, but got her feet under her. "Don't worry, I won't let him hear the end of this. Drinking on the job, running into the corner of the wall and knocking himself out—" she turned her faint smile on them again, then made her careful way down the corridor, supporting her unconscious companion.

Jez turned slowly back to the door. Masha was watching her appraisingly.

"Thank you, Jez," she said at last. "That was well done."

Jez stared, but Masha had already turned back to the locked door.

It swung open, and Masha stepped inside, hitting the light on her com. Jez, still slightly stunned, followed, looking around her quickly as she did.

It took a moment for her mind to compute what her eyes were seeing. And then it did, and she felt suddenly sick.

The room was filled with those same boxes she'd seen downstairs, only now, for the first time, she realized what the hell they were. Because some of them were the right size for an adult, and some of them were child-sized, and they all had a space where a tube could be hooked in, and gas vented into the chambers.

And they looked like damn coffins.

"They—" she started, her voice slightly unsteady. "There were kids—"

Masha nodded grimly.

Jez's breath was coming quickly, too quickly. She clenched her fists, trying to steady her breathing and hold back the nausea.

She really, really didn't want to think about who or what might have been in those boxes, and why.

One glance at Masha, though, and she knew Masha had thought about it. Masha, at some time in her long, long, uneventful career in government, had thought about how the government she worked for ran its programs, how it tested them, who was and wasn't expendable. And she'd known the answer, and it had sickened her.

Just like the thought of what they'd done to her parents must have sickened her.

And she'd kept right on doing what she was doing, day in and day out, not showing even one sign of how sick it made her, until she'd managed to find exactly who she wanted on her team, and get a government-approved mission to break them out of prison, and then —and then she was going to use them to take down the whole damn thing.

She'd never actually thought about Masha like that before. She'd thought about her as an irritation, as someone trying to force Jez to be something that she wasn't, as the mastermind behind half of the plans they pulled off, the force against which Jez pushed herself off—but not like this. Not as a person, who was just as horrified at all this as she was, but who had somehow managed to work through it until exactly the perfect time.

The woman was already going through the room with a businesslike air, and, swallowing back her horror, Jez joined her.

And then, finally, Masha said, "I think I found something."

Jez looked up. Masha was standing over what looked like a small information-retention box. She tapped it, and a holoscreen appeared, glowing in front of them.

Over the screen scrolled a long list of numbers and letters. Masha scanned it quickly, then gave that grim smile. "I know where they keep the information storage chips," she said brusquely. "I think we've done what we need to."

Jez nodded. But as they made their silent way out of the building, she couldn't help casting another glance at Masha, this woman who, she realized, she didn't actually know at all.

19

Lev, day 18

It was well past dark.

Lev wasn't actually certain how long he'd been sitting in the darkness, staring at the string of letters and figures on his com. It might have been minutes, or hours, or years.

He thought he might throw up, and there was a sick shakiness that had spread through his whole body.

Evka.

His mentor.

His friend.

But he couldn't un-see the words glowing on his holoscreen. Even if he closed his eyes, they were carved across the back of his eyelids.

"Suggest conscripted street children used for first-cohort tests. If successful, and if mortality rate within acceptable limits, suggest scale up to student body. Students without parental or other influence first choice. Will create list of acceptable subjects."

If mortality rate within acceptable limits.

It was Evka's spare, concise phrasing, not a single extraneous word. He would have recognized the sentence structure even if he had no idea what he was reading.

How many deaths was "acceptable limits?" He closed his eyes for a moment.

"Suggest conscripted street children used for first-cohort tests." The words burned behind his eyelids, searing into his brain even with his eyes closed.

"Evka," he whispered. "What were you doing?"

He opened his eyes again, and read through the words in the memo one more time, even though he'd memorized them by now. The date was a few months before Evka had disappeared.

Street children. Conscripted street children. He'd known Tae long enough to have a fairly good guess what that meant. But here? In his own university, the place he'd grown up in since he was a child—the first place in his life that he'd ever actually felt like he fit in, like he belonged. He'd grown up here, cheerful and unawares, devouring knowledge like he'd been starving, eating and sleeping and dreaming his studies and blissfuly, gloriously, desperately happy to be here.

And Evka, who had taken him under her wing. Who had forced the university to accept him, when he graduated from his undergrad at sixteen, who had brought him along with her, co-taught classes with him, patiently explained concepts he didn't understand, championed his acceptance as a professor. More than that. Had brought him dinners, sometimes, when he had no credits left on his meagre stipend and he was almost dizzy with hunger. Had bought him a new jacket, the first time in his life he'd ever worn something new.

She'd been like a second mother to him, and, if he was being honest, he'd probably thought of her more than he'd thought of his own mother.

And the whole time, the university had been experimenting on street kids.

The whole time, Evka had been experimenting on street kids.

She'd mentored him, stood up for him to the university administrators, made sure he was cared for and safe, and then she'd gone back to her research, on human beings.

He thought for a moment he might throw up.

He'd been feeling like he might throw up since he first started reading this file.

But—well, he had to finish this equation. And to finish the equation, he had to understand what Evka had been doing, so that he could understand how she'd written it.

And so, finally, with an effort that was almost physically painful, he turned back to the holoscreen.

He read with a strange feeling of detachment. He could almost believe, as he scanned farther and farther down, that he was watching someone else reading, watching someone else's entire life being shredded, word by word. Watching someone else half-curling into his seat at the physical pain the words cut into him.

It hadn't just been street kids. It had been, certainly, and he somehow managed to not think too hard, not see through that spare, familiar prose the terrified children, dragged into a laboratory. It had been students like him, as well, students with no family or no influence, students who didn't have parents to complain, or whose parents didn't have the money to cause problems.

And as he read, even though he was searching for it, he couldn't find one shred of remorse. He couldn't find one hint that what she was doing struck her as wrong, as sick and awful and physically repellant.

And he was searching.

Because, if this was true, she'd not only mentored him. She'd saved him. She'd kept him from suffering the same fate. She'd never told him, never mentioned it to him. They'd worked together as colleagues. As friends.

And all the time—

Finally, he sat back in his chair and gently tapped his com, shutting off the holoscreen.

The words, though, kept scrolling relentlessly through his brain.

It hadn't just been her. It hadn't begun and ended with Evka. For a program of this size—half the university administration would have had to have known. And would have had to have said nothing, as terrified, ragged children were brought in, under the cover of darkness or some other guise. And the professors as well—the scope of this research, they must have at least known of it. Or even if not, they must have heard rumours.

And done nothing.

Or maybe they'd been as blind as he had, as a young student. As blind, or as willfully stupid.

And he had been on the verge of joining them.

He'd mourned that dream for almost seven years. He'd still, secretly, mourned it, even though he'd told Jez he was over it and it was fine. And she knew it as well as he did.

And now—to come back and to realize what he'd dreamed of his whole life was something that would have made him a monster. A willing monster. That's what they taught here—logic divorced from morality or compassion, because morality and compassion didn't serve the government's purpose, or the university's, for that matter. They wanted people who could think, yes, but not people who gave a damn what they were thinking about, or what the end purpose of their work was. And he'd been the perfect student. He'd done exactly what they'd wanted him to do. He'd been a perfect student, then he'd moved seamlessly on to being a perfect government employee, as perfect students were meant to do, and he'd almost killed Ysbel's family and sent her wife and children to grow up on a prison planet, and it hadn't mattered to him because nothing mattered to him, because that was the whole damn purpose of this place.

He closed his eyes and clenched his fists against the sick panic that was knotted in his stomach.

He'd lived here for how long? And he hadn't noticed the rot. Somehow, for as smart as he'd always thought himself, he'd been blind to the rot, growing right under his feet.

But now he could see it, and he couldn't imagine how he could have missed it before.

Maybe he just hadn't wanted to. Maybe he'd been just as wilfully blind as the rest of them.

For a long, long time he sat there, fighting the panic and the nausea, and thinking that maybe this time he would actually go mad and there was nothing he could do about it.

He took a long breath, then another, then another.

No. He wouldn't fall apart. Because he couldn't fall apart, because everyone else was depending on him not falling apart, Tae, and Masha, and Ysbel, and Jez—

And for a moment the thought of her seemed to cut every tendon in his body, and he needed her. He needed Jez, and he needed her here, and he needed to feel her, and he couldn't survive one more second with the words from the holoscreen haunting in front of his eyes without hearing her voice.

He tapped his com.

It was too late, and she was probably already asleep, and for a moment he hesitated. But when he closed his eyes, even for a second, Evka's words glowed behind his eyelids.

"Jez?" he said finally into the com. He noticed, absently, that his voice was shaking.

"Lev?" She sounded half asleep, and he cursed quietly.

"Sorry. I—didn't mean to wake you."

"What's wrong?" Her voice was groggy, and worried. He managed a small smile, and took a long breath, trying to calm his heartbeat.

"Nothing, Jez. I'm sorry for waking you up. I'll talk to you in the morning."

There was a long pause. Finally she said, sounding slightly more awake, "You're a crap liar, genius. What happened?"

"I—" He closed his eyes for half a second. "I need you, Jez," he said at last, quietly. "Please. I—I just need you here."

"Be there in a jiff," she said, her jaunty tone doing nothing to hide the worry in her voice.

He squeezed his eyes shut, cursing under his breath.

He hadn't meant to ask her. He'd meant to tell her to go back to sleep, heavens knew they all needed their sleep these days. He dropped his head in his hands and tried to breathe, tried to think of nothing for a few moments.

There was no reason to ask her to come running over to his apartment the moment he found something disturbing. It was stupid, and selfish, and—

There was a soft knock at his door, and he jerked his head up.

"Hey. Genius. Let me in." Her voice was a loud whisper.

He stood slowly, feeling like his legs were too heavy to lift, and somehow made his way to the door. When he opened it, she slipped inside and shut it behind her. Then she turned to him, and the sharp concern in her face took him aback.

Had he really sounded that awful?

"Lev. What's wrong?"

He sighed, and tried to smile. "I'm sorry, Jez. I—it's not really anything, I just—"

She was looking at him appraisingly. Finally she shook her head, shoved him down onto the couch, and sat crosslegged, facing him. She put her elbows on her knees and her chin in her hands and raised an eyebrow.

"Look, genius. You called me up at 0300 Standard, and you sounded like someone had arrested your grandmother, and I ran all the way over here even though, by the way, I was having a very good dream, and you are damn well going to tell me what's wrong."

He stared at her for a moment, and then, despite himself, he began to chuckle, softly at first, and then the chuckle turned into a laugh, and he was laughing silently, with tears streaming down his cheeks, and even though he knew it was probably some sort of hysteria, he couldn't help himself. And Jez reached out, gently, and touched his arm, and he grabbed her hand like it was a lifeline and somehow he managed to get himself under control.

"Lev," she said quietly, but there was steel under her voice. "I need to know. What's wrong? Because I'm about to damn well take this university apart with my bare damn hands."

He shook his head, that strange, shaky lightheadedness still thrumming through him.

"No, Jez. It's fine. I just—" He paused, and reluctantly he caught her eyes. "Jez," he said quietly, his voice choking. "Jez, I—they were —experimenting. On street kids. On students, and I was here, and I was working for them, and I had no idea."

Her eyes widened for a moment with the same horror he'd felt. Then, with an effort, she gave him a small smile, the expression cut with sympathy. "Hey, genius. That's rough. I'm sorry."

He managed a haunted smile in return. She watched him for a moment, then reached into her jacket pocket and pulled out a flask.

"You sounded pretty bad on the com. So I brought some sump. In case you wanted to get drunk or something."

He managed a smile that was a little more genuine. "I—appreciate the sentiment. However, I'm not certain that getting drunk will help this particular problem."

She shrugged. "Worth a try." She paused. "Or," she added, "we could both get drunk and then have sex. That might help."

She stopped talking abruptly. There was a moment of fraught silence as they stared at each other, and there was a sudden panic behind Jez's eyes. And he wondered, somewhere in the back of his brain, when joking about sex with Jez had become something incredibly awkward, and not a joke at all.

At last he managed a weak chuckle, and her shoulders dropped with the released tension. She shook her head, leaned in, and gave him a soft, lingering kiss. Then she tucked her knees under her, scooted closer, and curled up next to him, trying, unsuccessfully, to stifle a yawn.

"Well," she said, "if you don't want to get drunk and have sex, I suppose we could do this."

He put his arm around her, and she snuggled into him, and some piece of him that had been cut out finally settled back into place, and for the first time in a long, long time, the tight muscles in his neck and back begin to relax. He took a long, deep breath, trying to stop the shaky feeling in his muscles. She looked up at him, blinking sleepily, and he leaned down and kissed her, and she kissed him back, and if before he'd been drifting in deep space, he felt like someone had finally thrown him an anchor-line. And then she nestled her head into his shoulder, and he put his arms around her and just held her as her breathing slowed and her heartbeat evened out. And even when he knew she was asleep, he still held her, because somehow the feel of her wiry body in his arms made the glowing words from the holoscreen just a little more manageable, the sickness in the pit of his stomach a little more bearable.

And somehow, he found his own head nodding slightly, his own eyes drifting shut and opening again with more and more reluctance, and somewhere in his sleepy brain he realized that falling asleep next to Jez was maybe the only thing in the world that he wanted to do right now.

And then he didn't remember anything after that, except that even in his dreams he knew he didn't want to let go of her, maybe ever.

When he woke with a start a few hours later, he had no idea what time it was, or what had woken him. Somehow during the intervening time Jez had ended up curled up with her back against his chest and her head pressed into his shoulder, and he had sprawled out against the arm of the couch, still holding her. She was asleep, one arm flung out over the edge of the couch, her black hair sticking out in all directions, her face peaceful in a way it never was unless she was asleep or at the controls of the *Ungovernable*, and for a moment he was almost weak with the thought of her here, next to him, and he had to close his eyes for a moment, because this was ridiculous, and he needed to get a hold of himself.

And then he realized what had woken him.

There was a knife, sticking into the cushions of the couch. It was only a hair's breadth from Jez's throat, and it was pinning a folded piece of paper to the couch cushion.

He went suddenly very, very cold. Carefully, he wrapped his hand in the sleeve of his shirt and pulled the knife free.

Inside the folded paper was a com chip. He studied it for a moment, then maneuvered himself upright without waking Jez and slipped the chip into his com with hands that shook slightly.

The holoscreen pulled up, and when he saw the face there, everything else became suddenly unreal.

It was Evka. Older, certainly, the lines on her face deeper than they had been when he'd worked with her, and she'd mentored him. But unmistakably her.

The woman he'd spent the last nine years mourning. He'd been investigating her death, or trying to, when he'd come across the information chips which had eventually landed him and his entire family in jail.

And here, somehow, a recording of her. Alive.

His breath caught in his chest. He recognized the scene behind her as she spoke, quietly, into the recording.

When she'd recorded this, she'd been here. Metres away from him.

"Hello Lev," she said, and the familiar way she said his name made his heart pound harder than ever. "It's been—quite some time. I admit, I was very surprised when you turned up here. I heard that you had been thrown in jail, and I was very sorry for it. And when I heard about your death—believe me, Lev, that I was heartbroken. And now—" she shook her head. "Here you are. I haven't told my department yet, although I'm certain they'd be very interested to hear it. And," the holoscreen version of Evka glanced down, to where, he assumed, she would have seen Jez, and a slight smile appeared on her face. "Not your usual type, if I remember correctly. But very sweet, nonetheless."

He almost choked at that.

Jez was many, many things, but this was the first and probably the last time he'd ever heard her described as 'sweet.'

Evka looked back up at the screen, and her face went grave. "Lev. During the time we worked together, I did everything in my power to protect you. I liked you, and I admired you, and you were—are—intelligent beyond any student I'd ever worked with. You could have done great things. I imagine you still can. And so, because I cared for you and still care for you, I will warn you   leave this alone. Leave it. You have no idea what you're getting yourself into." She paused, and gave him that faint, fond smile he remembered so well. "Of course, if you're anything at all like the sixteen-year-old student I mentored, you heard those words and heard a challenge. But listen to me, Lev. This is not a game. This is not an intellectual puzzle. This is something that has been in the works for years, and no matter how much I care for you personally, if you try to get in the way of it, you will be destroyed. And, as I say that, I realize that you'll hear a challenge there as well. So listen." She paused. "This girl, who's curled up next to you on the couch. As you're listening to this, there's a timer counting down on an explosive. It's planted subcutaneously into the skin of her neck—a tiny bit of wipe-on freezing, and she didn't feel a thing. I had originally thought to use it on you, but this seemed more appropriate. It will go off in—" she paused. "Three minutes and twenty-eight seconds from now. You can try to remove it, or you can try to disarm it." She gave him that fond smile again. "Lev, I hope this proves I'm not joking. Leave thi—"

He didn't wait for her to finish, just slapped his hand down on the com, shutting off the recording. Frantically, trying not to wake Jez, he parted the mussed hair at the base of her neck.

He could see it, the almost-imperceptible needle prick.

He swore under his breath, suddenly lightheaded with panic.

How many minutes left? How many seconds?

He had to think. There had to be an answer. He knew Evka, she wouldn't have set him a puzzle with no answer.

Cut it out, or disarm it. But he'd need a razor blade to cut it out, even if he figured what she'd used and knew what he was looking for and managed not to set it off as he removed it, and the knife she'd left wasn't sharp enough for that kind of surgery.

That left disarming it. But how the hell was he supposed to disarm something when he had no idea what it was or how it worked?

He closed his eyes for a moment, forcing himself to take a deep breath.

She'd injected it into the skin in the back of Jez's neck, that's what she said. And she'd said it was an explosive.

Alright, that was a start. Some explosive device small enough to be injected in with a needle.

And she'd said three minutes and twenty-eight seconds from a certain time on the chip. Which meant she had an exact countdown from when he played the chip. So something about putting the chip into the com—no not that, he could have put the chip into the com, and there could have been several seconds between when he did that and when he started listening to the message. It was something about starting the chip playing.

He gritted his teeth and closed his eyes, trying to remember every detail of the video. What she'd said, what she'd done. Had there been anything in the bottom of the screen?

He replayed it in his mind.

Yes. That moment when she looked down to one side, when he'd assumed she was looking at Jez. There, in the corner, where her eyes had been focused, there had been a small line of numbers.

A formula.

He squeezed his eyes shut harder, trying to visualize every one of the numbers.

What was she trying to tell him? What—

"Lev?" Jez's voice was sleepy, and it jerked him out of his reverie. He opened his eyes. She was looking up at him, and there was a sleepy smile on her face, and at any other time at all that smile would have turned his insides to mush and he wouldn't have been able to help himself kissing her until they were both flat on the couch again, but right now it only shot the panic in his brain that much higher.

"Don't move, Jez," he snapped. "Just—don't talk, don't move."

She frowned at him in slight confusion, but shockingly, did as he asked.

He gritted his teeth. Maybe thirty seconds left, this couldn't be the last time he looked at Jez, this couldn't be the last time he saw her—

No. He had it. He knew what Evka had been telling him.

He grabbed for the com, slapped it on, and pulled up the video, scrolling frantically through the still-shots until he got to the one he was looking for. Just the smallest glitch, like the recording com had flickered for a moment, but he was certain that if he—Yes! There. He pulled up, from the memory on the com, a long line of numbers. Frantically, he scrolled through them.

Ten seconds.

Where was it, where was it—

Eight seconds. The weight of Jez's head on his leg was too heavy and far too light all at the same time.

There. There it was. Now to disrupt it, he'd have to—

Five seconds.

He touched the screen, and, almost not daring to breathe, typed in a one-word command.

The screen flickered, and flashed green, and Evka's face appeared again.

"Well done, Lev," she said quietly. "It appears you haven't lost your touch." Her face sobered. "But I promise you, next time it will not be something you can win. So I say again, and I hope this time you will take me seriously—leave this, Lev."

The screen flickered and died, and for a moment he felt weak with relief, every muscle in his body gone completely limp, and he collapsed against the back of the couch.

"Lev?"

Jez still hadn't moved from where she was lying, and for a moment the panic almost choked him again. He grabbed her, pulling her into an embrace so tight that finally she shoved him back.

"Hey. Genius. I still need to breathe, remember? Can I sit up now?"

"You can sit up now, Jez. I'm—sorry."

She sat up at that, rubbing the back of her neck absently. She glanced around his apartment, then up at him. "You OK?" she asked softly. "You didn't sound too good last night." She frowned. "You don't look too good right now, either. Something happen?"

His heart was still pounding strangely. "Jez," he said quietly. "I— someone almost killed you. While we were sleeping."

She stared at him, still rubbing the back of her neck. "What? Who?"

"My old professor," he said, and even as he said them, the words sounded unreal. "She's still alive. And—I think she's behind all of this."

20

Tae, day 19

Tae glanced up at the noise from outside. Then he stood up so fast he knocked his chair over, and crossed quickly to the narrow dorm window.

Below him, a full-fledged protest was going on, students carrying signs and shouting.

His stomach tightened.

He recognized some of them. Especially the ones leading the protests, and starting the call-and-response.

"You take them," Vera shouted, her husky voice carrying over the crowd, "You take us!" the students called back enthusiastically.

"You fight them," she shouted, "You fight us!" the students chanted back.

Tae stared. Then he slapped his com. "Dmitri!"

"Tae?" Dmitri's voice was slightly smug.

"Dmitri! What are they doing? This is a terrible idea! I've got to get down there, talk to Vera. She's—"

"Tae! Relax. Sit tight, I'll be right over." He paused a moment, the grin still in his voice. "I didn't go to the protest myself, because I thought you might need some emotional support."

"Dmitri—"

The com shut off, and Tae was left staring in blank panic at the window.

Dmitri knocked at the door a moment later. When Tae let him him, he laughed softly.

"Tae. You look like you've seen one of the seventeen demons."

"I—they don't know what they're doing. They have no idea what the government is capable of. I've got to stop them. We're got to stop them, I have no idea how many of them are already in the database —"

"Tae. Shhh." Dmitri took him by the shoulder and turned him around. He studied Tae for a moment, then leaned in and kissed him gently. "It's alright."

"It's not alright! It's—"

"Tae! Listen to me." Dmitri was still smiling, but his green eyes were serious. "You have friends who are being kidnapped by the police. You grew up somewhere where you watched your friends being taken, and you couldn't do anything about it. But now you're here. We're here. We're not going to let it happen anymore." He shook his head. "The government isn't going to be able to take us the way they took your street-kid friends, OK? We have families, some of our families are in government. They can't just disappear us. We're the best people in the system to be able to do this."

"Dmitri, listen." Tae was breathing too quickly now, his heart pounding. For a moment, he saw Ivan's face, from prison, friendly and tired and concerned. "I know people who've been thrown in prison for protesting. They were taken to a prison planet and locked up for years, for doing this exact thing. You can't—"

Dmitri shook his head. "Tae. You need to understand this. This is exactly the kind of thing we've been wanting to do for years. Ever since we came here as innocent little first-years, with grand ideas in our heads. Vera isn't going to stop, and neither is Leonid, and neither am I. We started this because of what you said, but Vera's been looking into it more, and I have too, and there's something bad going on. There's something the government's doing with street kids that it doesn't want us to know, and we fully intend to stop it, alright? I can't go around knowing these kinds of things happened to anyone, let alone my boyfriend, and I didn't even try to stop it."

Tae glanced from Dmitri to the window and back. Dmitri's expression was stubborn, his handsome face set, but there was something in his eyes, something kind and ever so slightly worried, as if he didn't care what the government thought, but he cared, very much, what Tae thought. And despite himself, Tae felt his heart rate slow, and his mouth twitch up into a small smile. Dmitri gave a relieved smile in return.

"I was worried you'd be angry or something," he said, pulling Tae in for a hug. "I—we wanted to do something. Vera's been spreading the word to all the students she knows, and I've been as well, and everyone we've talked to is angry." He paused. "Did you know that there was a time they used to bring street kids here, to the university, and use them as test subjects? Not recently, of course, fifty or sixty years ago, but still—" He broke off, shaking his head. "I can't believe I've studied here for almost three years now, and I had no idea. Anyways, everyone was angry, and they needed to let off steam, and Vera thought a protest would be better than putting pre-fab bricks through the windows of every building on campus, which is what some of the students wanted to do." He paused, a little shamefacedly. "She may have also had to talk me out of that idea."

Tae's smile widened, despite himself, and Dmitri chuckled.

"Sorry, Tae."

"For what?" Tae asked, shaking his head.

Maybe Dmitri was right. Maybe the students here were protected enough that they could shout and blow off steam without getting arrested and disappeared.

Dmitri had told him, his first day here, how when the police were called on drunken university students, at worst, they'd throw them in a cell to sleep it off and release them in the morning, and more likely, they'd simply open the dorm lock for them and tell them to go to bed.

He sighed shakily, and Dmitri smiled at him, the dimple appearing in his cheek. "Alright, you," he said. "Sit down, and I'll show you your homework. No, wait. I'm going to get you dinner first, because it's 1900 hours, and I'm certain you haven't eaten yet."

"I—I have some rations packs," Tae began lamely, but Dmitri waved his protests away.

"No. You are going to eat an actual meal, because believe it or not, I'd prefer to cuddle with someone who wasn't wasting away from eating nothing but ration packs. I know you're busy, so sit down and work while I bring it back, if you have to. But I'll expect at least one very decent kiss for my efforts, so book that into your schedule."

Tae smiled again, and it was strange how the expression felt so familiar on his face these days.

Dmitri studied him critically. "I think we've been doing a good job, Vera and I. I can't even see the circles under your eyes anymore, and I think you've slept through almost as many classes as I had at this point in my first term." He gave Tae a grin, turned, and headed out the door.

"Take my credit chip," Tae called after him.

Dmitri turned in the hallway and winked at him. "Tonight's on me. You can pay tomorrow if you want."

Tae shook his head, watching Dmitri go. He was still smiling softly to himself, because he couldn't seem to help it when he was around Dmitri.

He sighed, picked up his chair, and turned back to his work. He was almost done with the virus, and he'd almost finished hacking through into the system, and both things only needed a little more of his time. But he found that instead of focusing on the virus, like he had planned, there was a corner of his mind that was focusing on the kiss Dmitri had promised when he returned.

He frowned, and shook his head.

Lev had called on the general line that morning, sounding more shaken than Tae had ever heard him. He'd explained, in a voice that was clearly supposed to be calm, what had happened, and Tae had heard the helpless panic under it, and for a moment, picturing Jez dead on Lev's couch, he'd felt an echoing panic. And Lev had told them they needed to get finished, now, because his old professor knew he was there. He was going to do everything in his power to convince her he'd given up, but he didn't think it would fool her for long. So their timeline had changed from days to hours, and Tae still wasn't quite finished.

He didn't look up at the sound from the corner, a few moments later, just smiled to himself. "Dmitri?" he said.

"How did you know I was here?"

Tae froze.

Dmitri's voice had come from the hallway.

The sound, whatever it was, had come from across the room, by the window.

Carefully, casually, he stood, tapping off his com. He picked up the scattered chips that held the projects he'd been working on, and pocketed them, then he walked, still casually, towards the door.

He was certain the noise of his heart beating would give him away, and every step, he was certain he'd feel something sharp between his ribs, or a heat-gun blast in the small of his back. But somehow he reached the door, stepped through it, and pulled it shut tightly behind him. Then he sagged against it.

"Tae?" said Dmitri, coming up to him. Tae straightened and shook his head quickly, holding a finger to his lips. He jerked his head down the hallway.

Dmitri, to his credit, didn't ask questions, just led the way to his own room, let them both in, and shut the door. Then he turned to Tae, a worried look in his eyes.

"What happened?"

"There was—there was someone in my room," said Tae in a low voice. "I don't know who, and I don't know what they wanted."

"Probably nothing good," said Dmitri grimly. He paced up and down the narrow walk-way between his bed and the couch for a moment, then turned back to Tae. "You're sleeping here tonight, and probably for the foreseeable future."

Tae frowned. "I—"

Dmitri grinned slightly. "Don't worry, Tae. I'm not propositioning you. Although," he added, "I wouldn't have any objection to propositioning you. But I'll sleep on the couch, and you can take the cot, like last time. You can't go back to your room, anyways."

"I can't stay here, either! If they found me there, they'll find me here, and I don't care what you say, I won't put your life in danger again if I can help it."

Dmitri shook his head stubbornly. "Fine. We'll find another solution for tomorrow night. But they haven't found you here yet, whoever they are, so you're as safe here as you'd be anywhere else.

I'll stay up if that would make you feel more comfortable, and keep a lookout. But you need a place to sleep, and I know you need to finish whatever it is you're working on. Alright?"

Tae looked around helplessly. But Dmitri was right. There was nowhere that would be safe, and there was no way he was going to talk Dmitri into agreeing that he should sleep rough until this blew over.

Until they finished what they were here to do, and he left.

The thought hit him, suddenly, and took his breath away.

Until he left. Until he left here, and he never saw Dmitri again, those green eyes, that dimple, the friendly, easy smile.

He closed his eyes for a moment and breathed deeply.

Until he left, and finally, for the first time since they'd met, Dmitri was safe.

Even that thought didn't quell the sickness crawling in his stomach.

21

Jez, day 19

"Alright, Jez," said Masha. "Once I'm inside, you'll have about fifteen minutes to get in, get the information chips, and get out."

There was a strange, concerned tone in her voice, like there had been ever since Jez had apparently almost died because of Lev's creepy old professor or whatever and Ysbel had to cut the damn explosive out of the back of Jez's neck, and Jez wasn't entirely certain how she felt about it. But—well, somehow, since that night they'd broken into that old lab, she'd found she looked at Masha a little differently too.

"Got it," said Jez, forcing a grin.

"I hope I don't have to remind you what happens if this goes wrong."

"Nope," said Jez cheerily. "You'll die, I'll die, everyone else in the crew will die, and then the government will put some sort of crap into everyone's food and water and probably kill all of them too."

"Yes, Jez," said Masha, with what could only be described as a sour note in her voice. "I'm happy to hear you have so much equanimity about the prospect."

"Don't sound happy."

Masha sighed heavily. Jez was still grinning, but she could feel the nervous energy running through her fingers like electricity.

Because they had to make this work. Because Ysbel, and Tanya, and the kids, Tae, with his hair constantly falling in his face and his scowl and his new boyfriend, and Lev—She closed her eyes for a moment.

Lev.

The thought of him flooded her with the same nervous energy as the thought of what she was about to do just now.

Everything about him was—well, perfect, but also perfectly wrong. And she could hardly sleep at night, thinking about kissing him, and about what it would be like waking up in his bed, and every time she looked into his eyes it was like he was the only thing in the entire system, and then every time she looked away, and realized what she'd just been thinking, she was so cold with terror that she almost started shaking.

And damn it, she didn't have time to deal with that crap right now.

She took a long, deep breath, and tried to steady her hands. Masha looked at her curiously.

"Are you alright, Jez?"

"Fine," she said, pasting her jaunty grin back onto her face.

Come to think of it, breaking into the top secret files in the damn university records department would be a hell of a lot less terrifying than trying to figure out how she was supposed to handle whatever was happening between her and Lev.

Masha cast her one last appraising glance, then straightened her jacket, walked smartly to the door of the records building, and stepped inside.

She'd left her com on, so Jez would hear where she was. Jez tapped her heel restlessly against the corner of the building until she heard the smooth voice of the record board president saying, "Of course, Masha. We're happy to show you—"

She grinned to herself, pulled the mask down over her face, and started for the back of the building.

The tall evergreen, which she'd noticed the first day they'd arrived, stood much closer to the building than was probably safe. Still—she wasn't about to complain.

Once she was in the shadow of it's massive trunk, she glanced up appraisingly.

Nearest limbs to the ground were a good five metres up. Still, that only made things more interesting. She rubbed her hands on the seat of her pants, rolled her shoulders, and shimmied up the thick trunk like she was going up the slide-pole in a raid on a cargo ship. She caught the first branch easily, and pulled herself up.

Through her earpiece, she could still hear the dull murmur of Masha's conversation with the president.

"—and as you know, it is our mandate to examine the records of every department, as we are trying to ascertain—"

She rolled her eyes as she climbed. Leave it to Masha to actually pay attention to crap like what their mandate was.

Although, it was probably a good thing that she did, because Jez sure as hell had no intention of doing it.

She glanced down through the branches as she pulled herself up. She had to be a good three stories off the ground now. The branches were getting thinner, the tree trunk itself growing narrower.

She'd figured, looking up at it, that it wouldn't quite reach. But, better than trying to scale the damn building herself.

She kept climbing.

She was getting closer now—when she glanced across to the building, she was almost eye-level with the fourth floor windows. One more story up.

The branches she was holding onto now, though, bent precariously at her weight, and a sudden gust of wind sent the tree swaying alarmingly. She closed her eyes at the motion, smiling despite herself. It was actually a bit ridiculous to think that this was the closest she'd been to flying in—well, in weeks.

She sucked in a quick breath, fighting back the sudden, irrational panic at the thought.

It would be fine. Get this done, get out, and then she'd be back in the sky and everything would be alright.

Right now she had to focus on the job at hand.

Cautiously, she pulled herself up a few more branches. She was getting near the top of the tree, and she was still not quite high enough to get into the window she was looking for. Granted, she could just try for a window on the fourth floor, but according to what Masha had said, fourth floor was offices, and there would be a good chance she'd burst in on some university bureaucrat.

She sighed, and pulled herself a little higher.

The trunk now was slender, barely thicker than her arm, and every movement made it sway crazily, but … there.

High enough.

She glanced over at the window.

OK, she was high enough, but she was a good four metres from the side of the building.

She grinned, the familiar rush of adrenalin almost as good as a drug.

Hell. This was the kind of thing she lived for.

Cautiously, she leaned out, away from the building.

The tree swayed with her weight, tipping her outwards, and for one heart-stopping moment her foot slipped on the branch she was standing on. Then she caught her balance and, holding her breath, leaned back towards the building.

This was the test. Because if she was out too far, the tree wouldn't swing back, and then—

But it did, slowly at first, then, as gravity caught at it, faster.

This was going to work.

She pushed the tree back and forth a couple times, like a kid pushing a swing, and with each sway, it brought her closer to the building.

Not close enough, of course. She'd still have to jump. But then again, this was kind of her specialty.

Unlike looking through pages and pages of damn financial documents.

She swung the tree away from the building again, and then leaned back hard, pushing it back towards the building.

Probably the best chance she was going to get.

She crouched, and at the tip of the tree's sway, shoved herself away from the tree with both feet, aiming for the window sill. The tree sprang upright behind her, one of the branches catching at her boots, and she swore, knocked momentarily off-balance, and then she slammed into the side of the building, too far to the right, and she was falling—She grabbed for the sill, and caught it with one hand, and for a moment was dangling helplessly against the side of the building. The rough cement of the window sill cut into her hands, and the muscles in her shoulder screamed at the strain.

"—we are, of course, highly interested in the amount of funding that is distributed to the cafeteria systems. I'm curious if you believe that the subsidies for services there are an effective use—" Masha's voice droned on through her earpiece.

She swung her body experimentally. Her hand on the windowsill slipped slightly at the movement, and she froze.

She glanced down.

On the bright side, from this height she probably wouldn't have to worry too much about breaking anything—if she hit the long stretch of cement beneath her, she'd be dead long before she had to worry about another six damn weeks of healing another broken arm.

Still, when push came to shove, she wasn't entirely certain that was all that good of a consolation.

She tried again to swing her body, and again her hand slipped, just a fraction of a centimetre.

Again, she froze.

Well, nothing for it. Not like hanging here from one hand was a sustainable long-term option. She took a deep breath, pulled her legs up carefully against the wall, then kicked herself up and sideways as hard as she could. As her grasping fingers slipped off the edge of the sill, she managed to catch it with her other hand, and pull herself part-way up onto her elbows. She rested there for a moment, panting, the skin on her arms torn from the rough cement, then she pulled herself up a little higher, until the sharp edge of the sill was cutting into her belly and she could afford to pull one of her hands free. She rummaged in her pockets and pulled out Tae's lock-scrambler, and barely caught herself again as she started to slip. She took a long breath, balanced herself once more, and tapped the lock-scrambler against the window latch.

Then she swore, loudly.

The damn thing wasn't locked. It had been sealed shut.

She narrowed her eyes, looked at the lock-scrambler calculatingly, braced herself, then, with a sharp jerk of her hand, hit the solid glass pane.

The rebound almost knocked her off her precarious perch, and she had to grab for the sill with both hands to keep from falling four stories to the cement courtyard below.

She took a deep breath, rearranged the lock scrambler so the sharpest edge was pointing out, and tried again.

Again, she had to grab with both hands to keep herself from falling to her death, but this time a tiny impact-crack appeared where the lock-scrambler hit.

On her third try, the impact-crack was replaced with a spiderweb of hair-thin cracks, and on her fourth try, the glass shattered.

She grinned, pulled herself all the way up onto the sill, now that the window pane wasn't blocking her way, and stepped carefully over the knife-sharp edges of glass and into the room.

Tae had been right. Lock scramblers were pretty handy devices after all.

"—had been worried that they'd have an upward impact," Masha was saying. Jez was pretty certain she'd said the same phrase at least twice before, which was odd, because—

Damn.

She'd been trying to warn Jez that they were on their way up.

Jez glanced at her com. She was supposed to have at least five more standard minutes, damn it to hell. And—she looked quickly around the room, the shattered window, the glass sprayed across the floor, the trail of evergreen needles, bark, and debris that she'd brought in with her.

Well, she was here now, may as well get the damn information chip.

She scanned the shelves quickly. Where had Masha said it was?

There. The box on the top shelf. She grabbed a chair, spun it around, and jumped up, snatching the box down. She tipped the chips out into her hand, shoved them into her jacket pocket, slammed the lid back on the box and shoved it back into place.

There was the click of the door lock releasing.

She jumped down off the chair, spun it back into its place, and leaned against it with a cocky grin as the door swung open, and a tall man with a white beard and greying hair stepped into the room, flanked by another man and a woman, and followed by Masha.

He made it three full steps into the room before he seemed to notice anything amiss. And then he stared, his shocked gaze taking in the full extent of the chaos that had overtaken the once-immaculate records room.

His eyes, at last, landed on Jez, and seemed to stick there.

She realized, belatedly, that a large twig was hanging from her hair and down the side of her face.

She grinned at him, even though he probably couldn't see it through the mask. "Hey. Nice to meet you."

He just stood there, staring.

The man behind him recovered himself first.

"What are you doing?" he asked, his voice a mix of shock and outraged disbelief.

Jez grinned easily. "Been a long day. Thought I'd take a break in here. I was planning on some peace and quiet, but looks like you plaguers can't stay out of a room long enough to give a person time to breathe."

His face went a sort of dark purple colour, and Jez grinned wider.

They'd probably all be killed as soon as he regained his equanimity, but in the mean time, this was actually pretty funny.

"I'm going to call security," said the bearded man, finally seeming to recover himself. "I will call security, and they'll arrest you and search you. And let me tell you, they will turn you over to the police in a heartbeat, and believe me, the police know exactly how to get you to tell the truth about what you're doing here."

Jez was still grinning like a lunatic, and her heart was racing and every muscle in her body was drenched in adrenalin.

Three dead administration bureaucrats probably wasn't the best solution, but then it would be a murder rather than a robbery, and hell, they might catch her but it should throw them off the scent of the others.

She was just tensing to grab for the heat pistol in her boot when Masha cleared her throat. It was a small, polite noise, but it somehow managed to be loud enough to make every person in the room turn to look at her.

"Excuse me," said Masha, her face that bland, competent pleasantness that was completely unreadable. "I'm sorry, but would someone please explain to me what exactly is going on here?"

The three administrators looked from her to Jez in something like blank astonishment.

"I don't mean to be rude," she continued, her voice sharpening slightly, "But as a government auditor, I must insist that you explain to me how it is that you have decided that leaving a broken window in the middle of a records department was a good use of resources."

Jez was staring at her too now.

For half a second, she caught Jez's eye. She flicked her eyes briefly towards the open door, and suddenly, Jez grinned.

Whatever you wanted to say about Masha, she had the most damn gall of anyone Jez had ever met.

"And furthermore," said Masha, warming to her subject, "I would like to know how you intend to replace information chips that have been exposed to the weather, as these ones no doubt have." She strode over and pulled the chair sharply out from under Jez's elbow, almost knocking Jez onto her butt, and swung it around briskly to where Jez had placed it moments before.

All three administrators were now staring at her as if at some new species of space-creature, who they weren't sure if it knew how to communicate, or was just making babbling sounds from it's own gaseous digestion process.

Jez slipped quietly behind them and towards the door. As she slipped out, she caught a glimpse of Masha pulling down the box that Jez had emptied with one hand, and with the other, surreptitiously replacing the information chips with a handful she'd grabbed from who knew where.

Jez grinned to herself, turned, and ran.

Getting out involved intimidating two administrators and breaking another window, but when she reached the courtyard where she and Masha had agreed to meet, yanked off the mask, and combed the majority of the evergreen needles and branches out of her hair, she only had to wait a couple of minutes before Masha arrived.

The woman looked as cool and competent as ever, but there was a slight glint of something in her eye that Jez recognized, with shock, as humour.

"Well, that was slightly more exciting than I had planned," she said at last. Jez grinned at her.

"That's what makes it fun," she said.

Masha looked at her for a moment, and then, to Jez's undying astonishment, she actually smiled.

"Well, Jez," she said at last, "you may be right, at that."

22

Lev, day 19

Carefully, Lev typed in the last few keystrokes, then sat back, breathing a long sigh of relief.

He was done.

Because the thing that Evka hadn't anticipated, when she'd threatened him and tried to kill Jez, was that, in order to make the puzzle she'd set him breakable, she had to give him something she'd worked on. And when she showed him her most recent work, she'd shown him the key to her thinking. The key to what she'd done with the equation he'd worked with her on so many years ago, and he'd finally, finally see where he could break it in a place she'd never notice.

He smiled to himself grimly. He could still feel the ghost of the panic of earlier that morning, looking at Jez's sleepy smile and realizing it might be the last time he ever saw her alive, unless he broke Evka's code.

And he'd damn well broken it now.

His com buzzed, and he frowned, tapping it on.

"Lev." It was Masha, and she sounded grim.

His heart seemed to stop for a moment.

"Is Jez alright?" he managed.

"Jez is fine. But listen. We got the chips, and looked through them. They've put the timeline forward. Far forward, I don't know how far. We need to get in there as soon as we can. Have you finished the equation?"

"I'm done," he said. He stood quickly and looked around. Nothing he needed to take, since everything he needed was on his com file and in his head. "What's the plan?"

"We go in now, tonight. I don't know if we have any other option, at this point."

"I'm on my way," he said shortly. "I'll meet you behind the records building."

He tapped off his com, grabbed his jacket, and glanced around one last time at the spare faculty apartment. Despite himself, he found a wry smile on his lips.

How many years had he dreamed about this? And now here he was, and he'd found the whole thing was such a mess of corruption that it made his government job look clean, and—well, and somehow he still felt a slight pang of nostalgia and regret for what might have been.

He shook his head, stepped out the door, and closed it firmly behind him for what was probably the last time.

By the time he arrived, the others had already gathered They were grim-faced and silent, their expressions telling him Masha had already explained to them what had happened. Tanya slipped in a moment after he did, and glanced around.

"Is this all of us?" she asked. Masha nodded.

"Is everyone finished their assignments?" Lev asked in a sharp whisper. Ysbel and Tae nodded.

"Alright. We'll go down there, and Tae will hook into the network. We'll feed Ysbel's formula into the virus first, and then my equation. Then Tae, you'll upload it into the system. With luck, it will overwrite everything before anyone notices, and as long as no one catches it during the actual overwrite process, it should be virtually undetectable. Is that correct, Tae?"

Tae nodded, without speaking.

"Masha, I assume the chips you and Jez stole have the program codes? You'll have to give them to Tae to input, otherwise it will be obvious someone from outside accessed the system."

"I have them with me," said Masha, in that calm voice. She glanced around. "Is that everything?"

He nodded.

"Very well," she said. "We don't have time to waste."

They made their way down the silent corridors to the narrow stairwell, and again Tae's lock-scramble whirred and clicked. The dark staircase was as eerily silent as it had been last time, but the still, stale flavour of the air tasted different somehow.

He pushed back the unease crowding the back of his mind.

They'd been down here only a few days ago. That was likely the only reason for the difference. Almost certainly the only reason.

Tanya stepped in front of the group when they reached the bottom of the stairs. She and Jez exchanged glances, and Jez drew her heat pistol and fell to the back.

Neither he nor Ysbel protested. Because, in all honesty, if there was someone either ahead of them or following them, he was pretty certain that Tanya or Jez could take care of them in a spectacularly competent fashion.

The door to the room was exactly as it had been the last time they'd been down here, but as Tae stepped forward to the door, Lev couldn't stop the spike of anxiety.

There was something different here. Something had changed, and he wasn't sure how he knew, but he did.

Something was wrong.

For a moment, he caught Ysbel's gaze.

If it was booby trapped, if it was an explosive, she'd be the one who'd know it.

"Scan the door first, Tae," said Masha quietly. Tae pulled out his com and scanned the door quickly, then the surrounding door frame and the room beyond. He shook his wrist, checked the screen, then glanced up at them, shaking his head.

"If they did something here, it wasn't with any tech my scanner will pick up," he whispered.

"Go ahead then," said Masha. Tae set the lock-pick, and when it finished whirring and the door clicked, he put a hand on the handle.

"Let me," said Tanya, stepping in in front of him. He hesitated a moment, then stepped back, letting her push the door open.

And it wasn't until the door swung open that the parts of the puzzle fell into place. And when Tanya gave a small gasp, he knew, without having to look, what she'd seen.

But he looked anyways, the heavy dread in his stomach hardening into despair.

The room, small and cramped and bare, was exactly how he remembered it last time. Exactly the same, except—

"It's gone," said Tae at last, into the silence.

Lev didn't say anything, just stepped past Tae and Tanya into the room.

He knew Evka. If he hadn't fooled her into thinking he'd given up, she'd know he was planning on taking this out. And she'd know better than to wager against him.

But he needed something, anything, to confirm what he'd already guessed.

He scanned the room, distantly.

And there, under the desk where the machine had been hooked up. The power module.

"Tae," he said. "Can you come over here, please?"

Tae came, his face a sort of sickly grey in the blue of the overhead lights. Lev gestured at the power module.

"Do you think you can pull up the activity on that over the past twenty-four hours?"

Tae nodded again, and knelt, tapping the connector on his com to the bare metal port on the module.

The room was silent as he worked. Lev didn't bother looking over his shoulder at the others. They'd have realized the same thing he had.

Tae pulled up the holoscreen on his com, and Lev glanced dispassionately at the report that scrolled across it.

He didn't feel sick, yet, although he knew that would come, eventually. He felt nothing but that same, dispassionate despair.

So, Evka had won.

She'd always been smart. There had been a reason he'd liked her so much.

"What does it say, Lev?" asked Ysbel, her accent thick with worry.

"It says," he said distantly, "that they came in this morning and powered it up. It needs just over twelve hours of running time to go through the system checking for bugs, and to integrate the equation."

"And then?" asked Ysbel, but from the tone in her voice, he knew she already knew the answer.

"And then, they run it," he said quietly. "There's really no need to power it up otherwise."

He turned back to the others, finally, and noticed, again, dispassionately, the dawning looks of shock and horror on their faces. "My guess is that when they realized what we were after, they decided to adjust the schedule. They'll skip the test run, and simply distribute the gas through the city. And of course, they can't do that from inside the University of Prasvishoni, so they've taken it somewhere else."

"Can—can we—" Jez's voice was horrified, and slightly sick. He shook his head, and managed a faint smile.

"I don't know where they've taken it. We can find out, I'm sure, but that would take—hours, days, maybe. They're venting the gas tonight." He glanced back at Tae's holoscreen. "I'd guess in about thirty minutes. I'm sorry. I think we've lost."

23

Tae, day 19

Tae stared at Lev, trying, somehow, to make the words he was saying mean something different.

They'd lost. The government had taken the machine, and was going to flood the city with airborne particles that would congregate in the brain-stems of every person in Prasvishoni, and from the moment that happened, every movement any of them made would be scrolled across a screen somewhere, and the moment any person in this city of millions made a mis-step, punishing them would be as dispassionate and as easy as a keystroke on a holoscreen.

But that wouldn't be the first thing.

The first thing that would happen would be that every street kid in Prasvishoni would die.

He leaned against the table leg beside where he was crouched, feeling suddenly dizzy.

He'd failed them. All of them, for good this time. He'd been here, in university, laughing and studying and sleeping in and *dating*, for the Lady's sake, and he'd failed his friends, and they were all going to die. Every other time, every other failure, he'd been able to push the thought away, tell himself that one day he'd make it back to the city, and then he'd manage to make everything alright.

But not this time. In thirty minutes—well, probably closer to a few hours, by the time they breathed in the infected gas, by the time the tiny, airborne, water-soluble particles managed to dissolve into their bloodstreams and congregate in their brainstems in a high enough concentration to be able to send a shock that would kill them, instead of just stun or damage or disable them—he wouldn't be able to fix things for them, ever again.

Slowly, he stood up. One glance at Ysbel and Tanya's faces told him they'd realized the same thing he had.

"Do you think Caz and Peti could get them out of the city?" he asked softly.

Tanya, her face very pale, shook her head. "No. I'm certain they will have closed down the gates. I trained as an agent for the Internal Security Committee, remember? I know how they work. If anyone tries to get out now, they'll be shot down."

Masha nodded. "I'm sorry, but Tanya's right."

He closed his eyes for a moment and leaned up against the table.

He was going to die too, of course, but that hardly seemed important.

"Tae?" He jumped at the voice in his earpiece, and hit his com.

"Dmitri?"

"Tae, where are you? I didn't hear you go out. Is anything wrong?"

For a moment, he was tempted not to tell him. How do you tell the first boy you've ever kissed that you're going to die in a few hours, and the street kids he'd been protesting for just hours earlier were also going to die, and probably everyone who attended the protests were going to die, and that unless he changed everything about himself so that he would be a perfect government employee, he was going to die as well?

But then again, how did he not tell him?

"Tae?"

"I'm—listen, Dmitri. It's—not good. Something happened."

There was a pause on the other end of the line. "Does this have to do with your pilot friend? Or your street kid friends?"

"Both," he said, after a moment. He shook his head recklessly. Honestly, it hardly mattered now if Dmitri knew. "Listen, Dmitri. I'm—not what you thought I was. I'm not really a student. One of my friends forged my documents. I'm a street kid, and an ex-convict. And that pilot, and my other friends you haven't met, they're all ex-convicts too. We're all wanted by the government, and if they knew who we were and where we were, none of us would last five minutes. We came here because there's a program the government is keeping very, very secret, and we assumed that whatever it was was going to be bad, and we had to stop it. And, well, we were right. It was bad. But we're too late. We can't stop it, because they've taken the machine they're going to use for it, and we don't know where it's gone, and in about thirty minutes it won't matter anymore." He stopped for a moment, unable to continue.

He could picture the confusion in Dmitri's eyes, the hurt. The look of disbelief and betrayal. And despite everything, despite the fact that his whole world had crumbled, the picture still had the power to cut him.

"I'm sorry, Dmitri," he said, finally, into the quiet on the line. "I— I'm sorry. I wish I hadn't had to lie. But I promise, I—what I felt about—about you. That was—that was never a lie. That—"

He broke off, biting down hard on his molars.

"Tae?" said Dmitri at last. His voice was cautious. "You there?"

"Yes," said Tae shortly.

"Tae." Dmitri took a long breath. "If it was anyone other than you who told me that, I'd assume they were lying to me. No, I'd be certain they were lying to me, because that's the most fantastical story I've heard in a very long time, and I had to study Orlovski for my literature class, so that's saying quite a bit." He paused a moment. "But Tae. I know you. And if there's anyone in the world who would forge documents and sneak into a university as a student, and in the process, by the way, make me go completely off my head for them, so that they would be able to shut down a clandestine government program before it could kill them or their friends—well, quite frankly, that person would be you."

He gave a soft, slightly incredulous chuckle. "Please, tell me you're telling the truth, and you didn't just make me confess that I secretly had fantasies of you being some covert undercover anti-government justice fighter."

Tae stared at his com for a moment. "I—No. No—I—no, that was the truth."

"Good." Dmitri sounded faintly relieved. "I feel slightly less awkward now." There was a moment's pause. "So. Tell me, what do you need me to do?"

Tae frowned. "I told you. There's nothing we can do, because we don't know where they took the machine."

"I think," said Dmitri, a slight note of smugness creeping into his voice, "that you've underestimated our mutual friend. I'm calling Vera, and we'll meet you. Where are you?"

"In—in the records building. In the basement."

"Of course you are," said Dmitri, and Tae could hear his grin. "Do you know that Vera and Leonid and I spent our entire first year trying to figure out how to break in and see what was down there?"

He paused a moment. "We'll meet you outside, on the west entrance. Five minutes."

Tae nodded, in a stunned fashion.

Everyone in the room was staring at him.

"Tae," said Masha cautiously. "What exactly was that about?"

"I—I'm not completely sure," said Tae carefully. "I think one of my friends might have seen where they took the machine."

Again, they all stared.

"Where?" Lev snapped, finally seeming to realize what he'd said. "Do you know?"

Tae shook his head. "I—no. They were going to meet us by the west entrance in five minutes."

Lev looked around quickly, the vacant despair of earlier completely gone from his movements. "Let's go, then."

"Yep," said Jez, a wide grin stretching across her face. "Guess all that studying chemistry paid off after all, tech-head."

And he was so dizzy with a sudden, disorienting hope that he didn't even bother to scowl at her.

Dmitri was quicker than his word—by the time the six of them got to the west entrance, Dmitri, Vera, Leonid, and three or four other students were already there, shivering in the cool of the night air. Dmitri smiled when he saw Tae, and even with everything that had just happened—was still happening—something about that smile made his muscles relax, and an answering smile spread across his own face.

"Tae!" Dmitri stepped forward and pulled him in for a quick, tender kiss. "We're here, and I was right. Vera has some information."

Vera was staring at the six of them. "Professor?" she said at last, in a dumbfounded voice.

"Yes," said Ysbel, with faint satisfaction in her tone.

"Dmitri said—he said all of you were ex-convicts?"

"Well, yes, that is true," said Ysbel.

"I—" she was still staring at Ysbel. Finally, though, she shook her head. "Alright Tae, here's the thing. The fact that I know that Professor is with you makes me much more comfortable telling you this. Although Dmitri just informed me that he'd personally watched you disarm an ion bomb, so I would probably have told you anyways."

She paused a moment, gathering her thoughts. "So, when we were protesting today, I caught sight of an unmarked government transport. We thought, what better way to get our message across than to get in their way, so a few of us ran over to it. The pilot hit the engine and flew low, and knocked a few of the students over, and I was really angry. So I ran out after it, for as long as I could. It wasn't flying fast, and I don't think the pilot noticed me. But anyways, the reason they were flying so low was that they pulled into a building just a couple of blocks that way." She pointed.

Lev was watching her, his head tilted slightly, as if trying to absorb every piece of information. He looked in the direction she pointed, frowning slightly. "A tall building?" he asked at last. "Rectangular, with a parking area on the roof?"

Vera nodded.

Lev turned to the others, his voice sharp and businesslike. "I know where they've taken it. Masha, the Upravleniya building. It was converted from a manufacturing plant fifty years ago."

Masha nodded slowly. "Assuming the venting system was still intact, that would make perfect sense."

"Alright," said Lev. "Let's go."

"Tae," said Dmitri softly, taking his arm. "Are you going to be alright?"

Tae tried to smile. "I—hope so."

Dmitri studied him for a long moment, and there was worry and pain behind his expression. Finally he touched Tae's cheek, gently, and leaned in for a soft, lingering kiss.

"Tae," said Tanya softly from behind him, and he nodded, unable to speak.

"You have to go," said Dmitri, still looking at him with that mix of tenderness and love and pain and worry. "Go on. Save everyone, that's what you do."

Tae managed a weak smile. Then he turned to Tanya's tug on his sleeve, and set out at a sprint after the others.

24

Jez, day 19

Jez grinned as they sprinted down the narrow university walkways, out the entrance, and into the street.

This, here, this was the kind of thing she liked. Screw all that crap about finding information and re-writing a bunch of stupid equations and figuring out some dumb chemistry crap. Although, honestly, that part probably wasn't that bad, considering that it was Ysbel in charge of that, and she probably made some damn good explosives out of it.

Either way, she was basically crap at all that. Comforting Lev when he was so stressed out that she could see his hands shaking, navigating this new and rather uncertain relationship with Masha, figuring out what of all the hundreds of hidden threats stalking them was important and which was not—she was crap at all of it. But this, right here—this, she was good at.

She slapped her com as she ran. "Hey tech-head, stop kissing your boyfriend and get a move-on."

"Jez—" Tae's voice was choked, but still managed to hold his customary trace of annoyance.

She glanced over her shoulder.

He was on his way, running after the rest of them, with Tanya beside him.

And suddenly, inexplicably, through the adrenalin pounding in her brain and jittering through her body, the lunatic grin on her face that she couldn't help and wouldn't even if she could, something warm and happy flooded through her chest.

Because no matter what Lena had said, no matter what she'd thought when she first came here—they were a crew. They took care of each other. They looked after each other, and protected each other, and she'd damn well punch anyone in the damn face if they thought for one second they'd hurt one of her crew.

Who'd have guessed, two months ago, that she'd not only be part of a crew—she'd actually enjoy it?

Not her, that was for sure.

They rounded the corner to the university entrance and pounded out into the streets, and then Ysbel, who was in the lead, pulled up sharply. Jez almost collided with her before she saw what Ysbel had seen. Masha, too, came to a panting halt next to them, looked out over the streets, and, to Jez's actual shock, swore.

The streets, which should have been deserted this time of night, were lit with flashing lights, and crowded with police officers.

"Your old professor, Lev, seems the type not to take chances," said Masha, through pinched lips.

"That, or someone thought that an unknown gas filtering through everyone's windows during the night might cause a mass panic," said Lev grimly.

Ysbel reached down and pulled out a couple modded snub-nose pistols from her jacket pocket. "Well," she said, "I suppose we shoot our way through."

"No time," snapped Lev. "According to my calculations, we have about twenty minutes left. I know a way the police shouldn't know about. Follow me."

Jez raised an eyebrow as he glanced around, then stepped quickly forward into a small narrow alley.

She caught him up as he jogged down the darkened streets, ducking through alleys and clambering over rotten piles of garbage.

"How'd you know about this place, genius?" she asked.

"I am wondering the same thing myself," said Ysbel from behind them. "For some reason, I don't see this as the ideal study area."

"I—" Lev sounded almost embarrassed. "I—there were times, while I was in university, that I found it—prudent to be able to get around without interference from the authorities."

Jez stared at him for a moment in unadulterated delight as they ran. "Wait. So when you were in university, you were one of the troublemakers? And you needed to be able to get through the streets without the police finding you?"

"I was a lot younger at the time, if you recall," he said breathlessly, his words clipped with faint annoyance.

Ysbel chuckled. "Well, Lev. It appears you have some stories to tell us when we're back in the *Ungovernable*," she said.

"I told you—" he said, in faint exasperation.

Jez caught up to him and elbowed him, hard enough that he staggered slightly sideways. "Hey genius, that's actually kind of hot. Did you ever get shot at?"

He glanced at her with clear annoyance on his face. "No, Jez," he said patiently, "I didn't get shot at. As I'm certain I have mentioned before, I hate being shot at, and I avoid it whenever I can."

"Until you met me," she said, still grinning.

"Yes. Well, I still avoid it as much as I can, within the rather limited parameters within which I now work," he said through his teeth.

"Nah, you're not fooling anyone," she drawled. "You wouldn't know what to do with yourself if people weren't shooting at you on a regular basis."

"Well, I'm beginning to think I'm never going to get the chance to find out," he muttered, breathing hard. He stopped abruptly, and peered down a dirty alley off the narrow street they were running down. The others came to a stop behind him, and he swore softly through his teeth. Jez followed his gaze.

"This is as close as I can take us," he said softly.

On the other side of the alley, the street was so full of police officers Jez wasn't entirely certain they'd be able to thread themselves through even if they didn't all happen to be very wanted criminals.

"Listen," said Tae, coming up beside them. He was still breathing heavily, but he seemed, at least, to have regained his composure. "I have a lot of practice getting by police. We just have to get half a block down, correct?"

"That's right," said Masha. "We'll want to get in the back entrance to the building, so we'll have to get through to the alley behind it."

"Aright," said Tae, frowning. He watched the street outside for a moment, biting his lip. "OK. I assume they'll be waiting for anyone who looks like they don't belong. Normally we might be able to blend in, but I don't see anyone here who's not an officer. So our best bet is to wait until there's some diversion, and then step out—"

"A diversion like this?" asked Ysbel. She reached into her shirt and pulled something out of the padded bag she wore around her neck. She balanced it in her hand for a moment, twisted it, then stepped quickly down to the alley entrance, leaned out carefully, and threw it down the street.

For a moment, there was silence. Then a loud *boom* reverberated through the streets. The officers in the street in front of them shouted and pointed, and for a moment there was utter chaos.

"I—yes. That would work," said Tae, in a slightly dazed voice. Then he shook his head, straightened, and stepped forward into the roiling street.

Somehow, he was right—despite the fact that she actually bumped into two officers, and was roundly cursed by the second, no one challenged them, probably on the basis that no one would be walking through the square right now if they weren't either supposed to be there, or completely stark mad.

Which, on reflection, wasn't completely wrong, so she'd give them that.

They followed Masha into the narrow alley, then down around to the back of the building. Where the front of the building was well-lit, the back was lit only with a flickering artificial lamp, the bulb buzzing and sputtering weakly.

"I don't have a code," said Masha shortly. "Tae, how long will it take you—"

"I don't believe we need one," said Tanya. She gave them a small smile, which broadened slightly when she turned to Ysbel. Then she looked up at the side of the building, braced herself, and with almost unnatural agility, started up the side, her fingers finding purchase in the cracks between the pre-fab bricks that Jez wasn't entirely certain even she could have managed. Jez stared at her, then over at Ysbel, and Ysbel shot her a smug sort of grin.

Yep, so Tanya was also very hot.

Above them, Tanya had reached a second-story window. She reached up and hit the glass with a quick, sharp motion, and Jez heard the tinkle of shattering glass. Tanya pulled herself up over the ledge, paused on it for a moment, looking back at them, then disappeared inside.

There was a shriek, abruptly stifled, and then nothing.

They stared at each other for a few moments, only Ysbel managing to look completely calm and completely confident. And then the door beside them rattled and swung open, and Tanya, looking as unruffled as ever, stood in the doorway.

She wasn't even breathing heavily.

Jez closed her eyes in a sort of blissful delight.

Yes, if you had to be on a damn crew, well, this was a pretty good choice.

"Come on," said Tanya. "You'd better get in here. But it's not going to be easy—I think every person who's ever worked here, and more besides, are all here right now. They've even brought the Minister of Labour along for the spectacle."

Lev gave a brief, distracted nod. "He's a high party official. There's no way they're going to let this go through without someone high up watching it. But we can't take any chances. The moment they know someone's interfered, it will be only a matter of time before they find the bug and reverse it."

"Do we know where we're going?" asked Ysbel. Lev pulled up the holoscreen on his com, the faint green glow of it illuminating the dim lighting of the narrow back entrance way. He pulled up a diagram. "Here's the specs. The logical place to put the machine is —" he expanded the diagram with two fingers. "Right here."

Ysbel swore. "Perfect. So we have to get through the exact centre of this building, right through the main entrance. And we have to do it with no one noticing."

Jez glanced at her com.

They were down to about ten minutes.

Then she grinned. "Hey genius. You remember way back when we were pulling that job on Vitali?"

"That was two months ago. Yes, I do."

"OK, well remember when we went in to the pleasure planet to kidnap that idiot weapons dealer? And there were those ships, and you were worried because they'd see us going in?"

He stared at her, realization slowly dawning on his face. "That's— actually not a bad idea."

She smirked. "Don't act so shocked, genius."

"What isn't a bad idea?" said Ysbel impatiently. "If you remember, we are on a time limit here, and as much as I love playing guessing games—"

"Well, see, Ysbel," Jez drawled. "Figure they're not going to be all that worried about people sabotaging the gas machine if they're also worried about someone trying to assassinate the damn minister."

For a moment, Ysbel stared at her as well. Then, slowly, a smile spread across her face.

"You know, you idiot, for a complete lunatic, you come up with some good ideas sometimes."

"Jez and I will take this," said Masha brusquely. "If you get into the room before we get back, I believe the rest of you will be needed to take down the program."

Ysbel pulled two snub-nose pistols from her jacket and held them out. "These should convince people that you're serious." She pulled a gas-bomb out of the pouch around her neck and held it out as well.

"How many of those do you keep in there, anyways, Ysbel?" asked Jez.

Ysbel gave her a flat look. "More than enough, pilot-girl. Now, get out of here."

Jez gave her a mock salute, then turned to Masha.

"Shall we?" Masha murmured.

Jez grinned. "Figure maybe we shall, you bastard."

Masha gave her a long-suffering look, then turned down the corridor. "Very well. Follow me. I believe I have an idea of where they'll have taken the minister."

Lev grabbed Jez's hand as she turned away. She looked at him, shocked, and he pulled her in for a quick kiss.

"Don't—don't die, OK?" he whispered, and let go of her.

For a moment she stood there, blinking. Then she swallowed hard, turned, and headed after Masha.

The nice thing about striding down a corridor with a snub-nose modded heat pistol in one hand and a gas bomb in the other was that you didn't actually need to worry about being inconspicuous. And the thing was, Jez had never actually been all that good at being inconspicuous.

But making a hell of a lot of noise? That, she was very good at.

Masha, to Jez's everlasting astonishment, was actually pretty damn good at it too. Even Jez might not have wanted to cross the grim, wild-eyed woman striding down the hallway beside her.

"You know, Masha, you look almost as crazy right now as I always figured you were," she murmured out of the corner of the mouth. Masha shot her a brief, amused glance.

The first group of people they came across, what looked like a group of damn office drones, took one look at them, screamed, and ran for their lives, muttering desperately into their coms as they fled.

Jez drew a deep, satisfied breath. "Shooting's going to start pretty quick here," she murmured.

"I am aware of that, Jez," said Masha in a prim voice.

From around a corner, a laser blast cut the air in front of them, burning a thin line across the wall to their left. Jez shoved Masha down as another laser blast fizzed through the air, followed by the staticky buzz of a heat pistol blast. Jez rolled, yanked out her own pistol, and fired in the direction the attack had come from.

The back-blow from the blast shoved her back with a white-hot wall of heat, and, as she lay stunned, blinking in shock, she could hear the faint, tinkling sound of overheated pre-fab crumbling as it cooled.

Masha grabbed her by the arm and jerked her to her feet. "I suspect that Ysbel is correct," she muttered as they ran, ducking low, towards the stairwell, "If that didn't convince them that we're serious, I'm not certain what would."

They sprinted up the stairwell, but before they'd even gotten to the top, boots pounded down from overhead.

"Stand back," said Masha, in that calm voice. She reached into her boot and pulled out another pistol, this one a narrow-bore that Jez had never seen before. She took careful aim and fired.

A laser blast whispered out, so bright it left jags of lightning across Jez's eyeballs, and an entire section of the staircase simply disappeared.

She stared.

Masha gave her a bland smile and holstered the gun. "I asked Ysbel to make me something like this," she said. "I thought it might come in handy."

And suddenly Jez was left to grapple with a world wherein Masha —cautious, scheming, over-controlling Masha—had decided that a gun that could vaporize a staircase was a very specific weapon that she would likely have use for in the near future.

She shook her head, grinning suddenly.

Honestly, though, that was a world she could get used to.

When they reached the vaporized section of stairs, Jez retreated two stairs down, bounced on her toes, then ran up and leapt, legs pumping, and managed to grab hold of the edge of the landing above. She swung her body up, glanced around, then yanked off her jacket and dropped to her belly.

"Grab on, you bastard," she called, and Masha glanced calculatingly at the jacket, took a couple of steps back herself, and then jumped. She caught the jacket, and Jez hauled her up. The moment her head appeared over the edge of the landing, she let go with one hand and grabbed for a pistol.

"Stay down, please, Jez," she said. Jez flattened herself to the cement, and scorching by-blow heat singed the hairs on the back of her neck.

"You can get up now," said Masha. Jez pulled back up onto her elbows, yanked Masha the rest of the way onto the platform, and turned.

Behind the blackened doorway, she could hear breathless cursing.

"They were trying to get behind you while you were distracted," said Masha pleasantly. She glanced at her com. "We're fairly close. I think perhaps you should go first, as you seem to have a knack for—making an entrance."

Jez grinned and picked up her pistol.

In this case, 'making an entrance' consisted mostly of her striding into the room, firing a blast into the air that probably melted all the heating vents, and shouting, "alright you damn plaguers, we're planning to kill the minister, mostly because he's a damn bastard. So unless you want to be melted into actual damn floor grease, I suggest you stand the hell back."

It was surprisingly efficient, if the object was to cause mass panic.

It was also really funny.

"I think that may have done the trick," murmured Masha quietly. She aimed and fired her 'very specific' weapon at one of the support beams. What remained of the beam tottered alarmingly, and there was more screaming.

Jez looked around appraisingly and shot one more heat blast into the roof for good measure. Then she turned and pushed after Masha through the corridors, which were now very full of people running in every imaginable direction, screaming loudly, and with absolutely no attention to spare for two ragged university auditors. Besides, Masha had already holstered her heat-pistol, and something about the businesslike length of her stride, and the sharp, distracted politeness of her, "Pardon me, please let us through," made people part for them like water parting for grease.

Jez shoved her own pistol away and matched Masha's stride. "You know," she whispered, "whatever it is that you do there? That's actually pretty damn useful."

Masha turned slightly and gave her a considering look. Finally, she actually smiled. "Yes, Jez. I have always found it to be. But—" she shrugged slightly. "Your—rather unconventional skills are, as you so aptly put it, pretty damn useful as well."

"What, you mean threatening to blow the hell out of the Labour Minister?"

"Precisely," said Masha, turning to face forward again. "Please, pardon us. We need to get through rather urgently."

Jez grinned to herself as she followed.

25

Tae was just straightening from where he leaned, panting, against the wall in front of the door when Jez and Masha arrived, also breathing heavily.

Whatever the two women had done, it had been effective. The hallways and even the massive main entrance had been completely empty as he and the others sprinted through them.

"Hey slowpokes," said Jez, grinning. There were dark smudges on her face, and the hair on the back of her neck looked like it had been singed half-off. "Thought we were in a hurry here."

Despite the fact that he felt like he hadn't caught his breath at all in the last twenty-some-odd minutes, Tae scowled at her on instinct.

"I suppose, Tanya, you can't get us through this door?" asked Lev, also breathless. Tanya shook her head.

She didn't look breathless at all. In fact, she looked as refreshed as if she'd just woken up after a good night's sleep, and for one brief second he felt that renewed terror he felt every damn time that he remembered that in addition to being Ysbel's wife, and a kind, but stern mother to Olya and Misko, she also happened to have trained as an Internal Security Committee agent and could kill any one of them without breaking a sweat. But her expression now was grave.

"I'm sorry. I looked at that diagram Lev sent, and there's no windows."

Lev nodded. His face was tense as he glanced at his com. Tae sucked in a last long breath, then straightened and leaned forward, peering at the lock.

Not something he could do with a basic lock-scrambler, but—well, if there was anything to say for the last two damn months he'd been with this crazy crew, it had given him plenty of practice hacking locks on a time-limit.

He touched his connector to the lock, and pulled up the holoscreen. "Specs," he snapped. Lev had already pulled up his own screen, and by the time Tae had hooked into the lock, had sent them over.

Tae squinted at the specs, typing carefully. There was security here, an overlay, but that shouldn't be too hard to get through, and then the lock.

He gritted his teeth, feeling the tension ache through the back of his skull. Just once, it would be nice to actually have time to hack through one of these properly, instead of getting through on swearing, desperate prayers, and sheer luck.

He muttered a prayer to the Lady as he hit the final key. It blinked, blinked again and—he let out his breath. They were through. He closed his eyes in relief as the lock clicked.

"Let me go first," said Tanya quietly. "We don't know what's inside, but I'm certain it will include plenty of people who want to kill us."

Tae stood to one side as Tanya opened the door and slipped past him inside.

"No one is shooting right now, anyways," she whispered back over her shoulder.

Tae took a deep breath and followed her through the door, the others close behind.

It took him a moment to get his bearings.

They were about three stories up, on a metal frame walkway over a large, open room. In the top and the bottom were large ventilation pipes, and huge, ancient industrial-style fans to push the air through. Far down below, he could just make out a table, with what looked like the machine on it, hooked into a large tank. But … He frowned, a sudden unease gripping his chest.

Where was everyone? There should have been scientists and government officials crowded around the machine. The room should have been so packed there'd hardly be space to get through them.

But it was completely empty.

Had they guessed wrong, and it wasn't scheduled for tonight after all?

And then he realized, and as he turned, he saw that Lev had realized the same thing, saw his eyes widen. Tae was already moving, grabbing Tanya by the arm as if he could somehow shove her out of the way of the danger, even though he knew, already, even as he did it, that he was too late—And then there was a hissing rush, and a massive plume of gas hissed up from the machine, and down from the pipes and tubes in the ceiling, and he was completely enveloped in it. He choked and coughed and then, because he didn't have any choice, he sucked in a long breath.

The gas filled his lungs, colourless, tasteless except for a faint, metallic tang that he could smell and taste in the back of his throat, and he tried to choke it back up, wave it away. But it was too late. Even as he tried, he knew it was too late.

He blinked hard, rubbing his eyes against the smoke. And then, consciously, he relaxed, drawing in full breaths.

Their was no point in fighting it, really, not anymore.

The fans had creaked and groaned to life, and were already blowing the gas out through the vents, spreading it throughout the thick city air. Even if someone somehow managed to avoid breathing it in, even if they could somehow secure their doors and windows so tightly, find a mask that would keep the tiny gas particles out of their lungs, it was too late. It would drip in through the pores in their skin, infiltrate the water they drank and the food they ate. The students, the street kids—everyone. No one inside Prasvishoni was safe. Not ever again.

He looked around him, with a faint smile of despair on his face.

And his crewmates. All of them.

How many hours did they have? Three? Four? How long before they gas they'd been choking on congealed in their blood, congregated in their brain stem?

It didn't really matter. Every one of them was a corpse walking.

The people in the building, the people that Jez and Masha had distracted, would be here eventually, would find them. But really, whether they died now or died in four hours' time, it was no longer a matter of if.

It was only a matter of when, and how.

26

Lev could taste the slight tang of metal in the back of his mouth, the metal that would kill them all as surely as poison.

It was a strange feeling, the sensation of your lungs pulling in something deadly, and knowing it, but not being able to help it. They could have done—something, maybe, before. Not now. They were all infected, and there was nothing that he or Ysbel or Masha or any of them had found that could reverse that.

He found his mind was strangely clear, even after everything.

He glanced over at Tae, and he saw the same weary, resigned smile on Tae's face that he felt on his own.

"Well, Masha," Lev said at last. "I suppose it's been a good run. Honestly, I wouldn't have believed we could do what we did, if you'd told me this two months ago."

He didn't look at Jez. He couldn't bring himself to look at Jez, somehow.

Tae tapped his com. He was speaking in a low voice, but besides the soft *hiss* of the gas the room was silent, so his words were clearly audible.

"Dmitri," he said quietly. "I—just wanted to let you know. We've —I failed. We didn't get to it in time." He paused a moment, swallowing hard. "I—guess I just wanted to say I'm sorry. Don't bother protesting anymore, please. Because they'll find you now. There's no way to stay safe, except not to attract attention."

Tae must have hit the general button on his com, because the response came, not through his earpiece, but through his com.

"Tae!" It was the voice of the young man who'd kissed Tae as they'd left. "Tae, listen. We're out here right now. Look, I don't know what happened, but whatever happened, you need to get out. We're trying to make a distraction for you, but—I don't know how long this will last. The police are holding back for the moment, but I think they're losing patience." Behind his words, Lev could hear shouts, screams, the sound of voices amplified and muffled through police coms.

Tae stared down at his com, his face going bloodless.

"No," he managed at last, "Dmitri, you have to get out of there. Get back to the university."

"Little late for that." Dmitri's voice was trying to be cheerful, but Lev could hear the fear behind it.

Tae reached out one hand and grabbed a railing, as if to keep himself from falling over, his knuckles strained around the metal bar. He looked like he might pass out.

Lev glanced quickly around. Ysbel and Tanya were standing close, Ysbel's arm on Tanya's, as if their touch was the only thing keeping them upright. He'd never seen Ysbel so pale in his life, and Tanya's face was twisted in a sort of agony he could only imagine.

Of course. Their children, back at the hangar bay, who would die without even their parents there to comfort them. Die with Tae's street kid friends, alone and terrified.

Masha—there was a blank despair to her face he'd never seen there before, a slight twist to her lips, as if the metal that would kill her left a strange, unpleasant taste in her mouth. She was watching Tae as well, and then, for some reason, she glanced over at Jez, and despite himself, Lev followed her gaze.

Jez was still looking around frantically, the expression on her face almost a match for Tae's. In her eyes he could see that helpless, hopeless horror of being trapped, of never getting free.

It wasn't death that terrified her, he knew her well enough to know that. It was this kind of death, the kind that you could never get away from, that no matter how far you went or how fast you flew, you could never escape. A prison you carried with you, wherever you went, however hard you tried.

She turned and caught him watching her, and somehow she managed to twist her face into the approximation of a grin.

"Hey genius, guess that's what we get for being late," she said. But there was a stark fear behind her eyes that she couldn't hide, and the sight of it made him suddenly, violently sick.

No. No, this wasn't happening, because he'd be damned before he let Evka hurt Jez.

He'd be damned, and he'd damn this whole system with him.

"Tae," he said slowly. "Tae, hit your com. I need to talk to Dmitri."

Tae glanced up from his com. There were tears glistening on his cheeks, and he wiped them away hurriedly. "What?" he asked dumbly.

"Please."

Tae looked at him a moment, then hit his com. "Dmitri? My friend wants to—"

"Dmitri," said Lev, taking a step closer. "Can you hold the police's attention for a few minutes?"

"I think so." Dmitri's voice was grim.

Tae was gaping at him. He turned frantically back to his com. "No, Dmitri. You need to get out of there, now!"

"Sorry, Tae. I don't think we can anymore. But we can probably hold their attention for long enough for you to get out."

"No! Dmitri—"

The com cut out. Tae stared at it, then at Lev, and there was a sort of horrified betrayal on his face. Lev stepped across the narrow walkway and took Tae by the shoulder. The younger boy looked at him, eyes swollen from tears, dark hair sticking to the tear streaks down his face.

"Tae," he said curtly. "Dmitri was right. It was too late for them the moment they stepped into the street. Any police officer with a recording com will be able to pinpoint every last one of those students. Unless we do something, four hours from now they'll be as dead as we are."

There was something ice-cold inside of Lev, but right now he hardly cared.

"So—"

"So we go in, right now. We take that damn machine apart, and we hack Ysbel's and my formulas into it. They'll know we've done it. We can't turn back the clock. But your virus will overwrite everything in the system. They'll have to go through and pick my modifications to the equation out number by number. It won't stop this. But it will give us time, and right now, that's the best we have."

"Lev. I'm certain you've already considered this, but however busy Tae's friends are keeping the police outside, it's not going to be long before someone comes back in here to check on things."

"And that, Masha," said Lev, turning to her with a faint, distant smile on his face, "is exactly why you and Jez and Tanya will be running interference. As much damn interference as you can manage."

Jez's expression was slowly changing from one of terrified desperation to one of shock, then to one of absolute delight.

"That, genius-boy, is probably the best idea you've had yet. Right, you damn bastard?" She turned and grinned at Masha, and despite himself, Lev raised an eyebrow.

Well.

He was capable of imagining a lot of things, but he'd certainly never imagined this.

"Ysi, my heart?" said Tanya, with a faint smile of her own. "Would you please give me some of your explosives?"

Ysbel smiled fondly at her wife. "I would give you anything you asked for, you know that." She pulled the padded bag from around her neck and handed it to her wife. "I suppose I don't have to tell you to be careful?"

In response, Tanya leaned in and kissed her.

Lev found he was smiling slightly, despite himself.

"Hey. Genius."

He turned. Jez was beside him, and she grabbed his face in both her hands and kissed him, a long, slow, sensuous kiss that set his head spinning and his pulse racing and a jolt of visceral disappointment when at last her lips left his.

"Can't let them have all the fun," she whispered.

Tae, beside him, was looking fixedly in the opposite direction. "Lev," he said through his teeth, "I don't mean to interrupt anything, but we have maybe five minutes before someone is trying to break down the door here."

"Yeah," muttered Lev. He was, for a moment, not completely

certain his voice still worked, and damn it to hell, the last thing in the world he needed to be thinking about right now was how Jez's body had felt, tangled with his on the easy chair—

Jez winked at him as she turned away, and for a moment his entire brain melted down.

He squeezed his eyes shut, sucked in a quick breath, shook his head, and started after Tae, who was already making his way at a half-run down the maze of walkways and steep metal stairs towards the ground floor.

Evka had tried to kill Jez.

Evka was still damn well trying to kill Jez, and he'd be damned before he'd let that happen.

The certainty sat in his veins like ice.

When Lev reached the ground, Ysbel at his heels, Tae was already at the machine.

"Lev, come on," he snapped. And of course, Tae hadn't been kissing anyone on the walkway because the boy he would have been kissing was outside, probably being beaten by the police, if nothing worse was already happening.

The thought was enough to sober Lev. He shook his head to clear it, and sprinted over to the machine.

He glanced around quickly, pulled up one of the uncomfortable metal chairs, and took a seat in front of the machine. Tae pulled up a chair beside him, and Ysbel stood behind them.

"Alright, Tae," Lev murmured. "Get me into the system. I think I'm going to enjoy what I'm going to do next."

The moment Tae had hacked him in, Lev pulled up his holoscreen. He was smiling to himself.

"Alright, Evka," he said quietly. "Round two."

He pulled up the pages of the equation on the holoscreen,

scanning through quickly.

Change one number here. Another here. Switch the equivalent.

He probably shouldn't be enjoying this quite so much, but there was a cold, hard anger inside him, like there'd been when he'd seen Jez beaten half to death by the guard on the prison planet.

Someone would suffer for this, and he felt very, very good about that.

Someone was hammering on the door behind him, then Jez's cheerful voice. "Hey you plaguer, we're busy right now. Besides, not sure I'd let anyone as ugly as you in here even if we weren't."

The unmistakable hiss of heat-blasts.

He was a third of the way through the equation.

Tae, beside him, had already hacked Ysbel into the system, and, under her direction, was re-writing the chemical formula. Too late to save anyone in Prasvishoni, but it would stop them gassing anywhere else until they pinpointed the error.

"Stand back." It was Tanya's voice, clipped and matter-of-fact, then the slam of a door and a muffled explosion.

"Jez. They're coming through—" Masha's voice, tight with worry.

"Not any more they aren't," in Jez's drawl. Another exchange of heat-blasts.

From the corner of his eye, he saw Masha stumble back from the door, heard Jez curse.

He was three quarters of the way through.

"Hurry it up, genius." Jez's voice was tense. "They're bringing backup. And Masha's hurt."

But he didn't have time to focus on that, because he had to finish this equation, because that was the only way any of them or their friends got out of this alive.

Anther muffled explosion, and more swearing from Jez.

"Lev?" asked Tae, beside him.

"Just give me one minute—" he murmured.

Another explosion.

"I'm finished. I'm going to help them," said Ysbel in a matter-of-fact tone. She shoved back her chair and sprinted towards where her wife was struggling with a figure in police gear.

"Done," Lev said, hitting the final key. Tae pulled the holoscreen over and typed in a quick command, and the screen went suddenly blank. For a moment, he and Lev stared at each other.

"Did it work?" asked Lev.

"It damn well better have," muttered Tae. He glanced around quickly.

Lev tapped his com. "Jez. What's happening?"

Her voice was unusually grim. "Masha's down. She's alive, but she's lost a lot of blood. I'm holding them off at this door, but it's not going to last for long."

"Tae," said Lev. "Can you override the locks?"

"I—suppose," said Tae. "But that's not going to work. They'll just take down the doors."

"Not if we do it first." He hit his com again. "Ysbel?"

"What do you need?" Her voice was strained, and when he glanced up, he saw why. She was in the process of throwing an unconscious figure back through the open doorway, and into an oncoming rush of other police-garbed figures.

"I assume you can set an explosive that can take this place down?"

Ysbel snorted through the com. "Lev. I could have set an explosive to take this place down by the time I was four years old. However, we all happen to be inside this place at the moment."

"I know. And Tae's going to make it look like we stay here."

Ysbel slammed the door, then turned to look at him as someone on the other side of the door slammed something large and heavy into it. There was an appraising look on her face. "I believe I see what you want to do," she said.

"Tae?" asked Lev quietly. Tae nodded.

"I think I can. It will take me a minute or two."

"Set something to go off in five minutes' time, then, Ysbel," said Lev into the com. "We're going to take this building down."

She looked at him one last time, said something in a low voice to Tanya, then stepped away from the door. Tanya stood back as the door burst open, then stepped forward smartly and did something with her hands that he couldn't see. The first figure dropped to the ground, and three more tripped over the body, and before they could get up, she'd dropped them as well, then shoved the whole pile back through the door, slamming it shut behind them.

Ysbel stood in the centre of the room for a moment, looking up at the support beams. Then she smiled grimly and set to work, tucking explosives carefully into the corners between the beams and the floor.

Tae looked up, his face drawn. "Doors are sealed. Lev, I'm going to hack into the alarm, get the building evacuated."

Lev shook his head. He could still feel that slight smile on his face. "No, Tae. Don't bother."

Tae frowned. "Lev. If I don't set the alarm—"

"They'll all die?" Lev shrugged slightly. "They're monsters, and to be honest, Tae, I'd be very happy to see that happen."

Tae was still staring at him. At last he shook his head. "Lev. I'm not going to let you—"

Lev stood, and closed his eyes for just a moment.

His whole damn life had been a lie, a lie made by people like the people outside here right now, made to take people like him, like

Tae's boyfriend, and turn them into complacent, amoral drones, who didn't question and did exactly what they were told. And, if he was being brutally honest—maybe they'd succeeded with him.

But then, maybe they'd succeeded too well.

"You're not turning on the alarm, Tae," he said quietly, putting his hand over Tae's. "I'm not going to let you."

Tae stared into his eyes, his expression a mixture of shock and horror, and probably one day Lev would feel guilty about that, but right now he felt absolutely nothing.

And then the alarm went off, the jangling and clanging resounding through the massive room and bouncing off the walls and sounding through the entire building.

He turned.

Ysbel stood behind him, the end of the alarm-pull in her hand.

She let it go, not taking her eyes off his.

"Lev," she said quietly. "I'm a murderer. I killed thirty-five people once, in cold blood. But you're not."

"Ysbel—"

She shook her head. "You're not what they tried to turn you into. Remember that." She glanced over at Jez, crouched beside Masha, face drawn with worry. "Besides, she deserves better than that. You deserve better than that."

She turned, and walked off towards Tanya.

Lev watched her go. Finally, he turned back to Tae.

There was no condemnation in Tae's eyes, just a sort of weary sympathy. He gave Lev a small smile. "I have all our com signals hooked into the machine. Once we get out, they'll read that we were here the whole time." He paused, and reached out, putting a hand on Lev's arm. "Come on. Let's go."

Lev took a long breath. Then, at last, he nodded, and they turned and sprinted up the stairs towards where the others were gathered.

292

27

Ysbel, day 19

Ysbel glanced over at Lev in the darkness, as the six of them ran in a half-crouch down the inside of the huge ventilation pipes. Well, the five of them, since she was currently carrying a half-conscious Masha on her back.

She'd never seen him like this before. She'd come close, once, when they were in jail and Jez had been almost killed, but this was something different. This wasn't just anger. This was a sort of cold hopelessness.

She didn't blame him. He'd always missed what he'd left behind here. And then to find out the whole thing was a lie, a facade covering fetid rot—it would be enough to shake anyone.

He didn't meet her eye, or anyone else's, and she shook her head.

Now wasn't the time to worry about that, honestly.

"Here," said Tanya, coming abruptly to a halt. "Out." Ysbel stepped around her and glanced down.

They were two stories up, and the ground below was solid concrete.

She shook her head, and lowered Masha gently to the ground.

"I'm going to jump," she said grimly. "Lower Masha, and I'll catch her."

Tanya nodded, and Ysbel braced herself and leapt out, tucking her shoulder. She hit the concrete hard and let her momentum carry her into a roll, and when she got to her feet, she was almost certain that she hadn't broken anything important. Jez came next, and popped up with more ease than Ysbel had. Then again, she was several years younger, and likely had more experience than any of the rest of them in leaping off of high places while people were trying to kill her. Lev landed hard, and Tae managed a roll as well, and then Ysbel caught the half-conscious Masha as Tanya lowered her on a makeshift cord sling. And then the building lit up, as if in slow motion, prefab bricks shattering and spraying into the air, fire jetting up from the centre of the building, and at the same time Tanya leapt.

For a moment she hung suspended against the sky, the explosion lighting the night behind her, and Ysbel's breath caught in her throat, because she couldn't lose Tanya again, and if she lost Tanya again she'd lose herself because she knew that she couldn't possibly live one more day without this graceful, beautiful, perfect woman.

And then Tanya landed in an effortless roll, and Ysbel breathed again. She hoisted Masha on her back and they ran, ducking their heads as the flaming prefab bricks fell around them.

When they turned the corner of the building, a scene of total chaos met their eyes. Flares burned overhead, lighting what could only be described as a brawl—university students struggling with police, the police with their shock-sticks and gas, the students with whatever came to hand, throwing bits of prefab bricks and concrete, grabbing the officer's shock sticks, using their protest signs as weapons. Vera had climbed onto the entrance arch of one of the nearby buildings and was shouting directions to the students below. Tae slowed involuntarily, and she didn't have to look at him to know the expression on his face.

Then, through the crowd, a tall figure with sandy hair turned towards them. He saw Tae, and his haggard face broke into a smile of relief. He mouthed "Go! Quickly!"

Tae started towards him, almost involuntarily, but Jez grabbed his arm. "Not right now, tech-head," she said, steering him down the street. "We'll come back for them."

Tae was resisting her, pushing back, trying to get to the riot.

"Tae," said Ysbel, and he turned to her, his eyes wide and panicked. She waited until he caught her gaze. "Tae. Those are my students. We won't leave them like this, I promise."

He glanced between her and Jez, and then, finally, he nodded, the movement a quick jerk, and stopped trying to fight.

"Back to my office," Ysbel panted. They turned into the university entrance and ran down the almost-deserted walkways. Apparently the entire population of the university had either locked themselves into their dorms, or were on the streets. Here and there a student ran down the walkways, carrying a placard or shouting, but there was no one around when they reached the science building.

Once inside the office, Ysbel laid Masha gently down on the floor. The woman was breathing, but unconscious. Jez had tied a rough, makeshift bandage around her chest, and blood was still seeping through it, but she looked stable, at least. And there wasn't time to check farther, because her students were outside right at this moment, getting beaten by police with shock-sticks.

Tanya glanced at Ysbel's face. "I'll take care of her," she said, kneeling beside the fallen woman.

"I'll get the sky-bikes then," said Jez, grinning. "Come on, tech-head." She grabbed Tae's arm, and they raced from the building.

Ysbel opened her case and tucked some additional gas bombs into the pouch around her neck, and shoved a couple stun-pistols into her jacket.

"Ysbel. I'll come with you, help Tae get everyone in," Lev said. His voice was still that emotionless calm of earlier, and she assumed it would be until they were finally out of danger.

Jez and Tae were already waiting outside. Tae scooted back, and Ysbel swung up in front of him as Lev slid on behind Jez.

"Let's go," said Jez, grinning at them. Then she leaned forwards and shot off.

When they reached the street outside the flaming building, the riots were still going full-bore. They dropped Tae and Lev on the periphery, then Jez winked at her, and they shot forward into the centre of the action.

Three police bikes pulled in behind them, but Jez darted between them, somehow knocking two of the officers off their bikes. The third swerved wildly to avoid her, and had to pull up to keep from running into a building.

Ysbel glanced around. They were still packed too tightly for gas bombs.

"Jez. Get over here," she called on the com, pulling a stun-gun out of her jacket. As Jez swerved close, she tossed the lunatic pilot the weapon.

"It won't kill them, but they'll have a headache in the morning," she called after her. Jez gave her a mock salute, and even in the crazy light of exploding flairs Ysbel could see the gleeful grin on her face. She shook her head.

That girl had far too much fun knocking people out.

"Tell your friends to fall back as soon as they can," Ysbel muttered over Tae's line. She pulled out her own stun-gun and took careful aim. A police officer who had been standing over a student, shock-stick raised, collapsed. The student glanced up and saw her, and Ysbel gave him a small smile. He stared, then smiled back in a disbelieving and slightly terrified way.

"Go on!" Ysbel called to him. "Get out of here. Tae will get you back."

And then the officers turned their heat guns on her, and she dove back in, grim-faced and smiling.

Perhaps that idiot pilot wasn't so wrong after all.

By the time she and Jez had taken out half a dozen police officers, the officers seemed to realize that, as between the unarmed students and the two maniacs on skybikes, the skybikes were the bigger concern. As they turned to face the new threat, Dmitri and Vera herded the students down the street away from them. Ysbel slapped her com to Jez's line.

"It's about to get hard to breathe in a minute here."

Jez gave her a jaunty nod. It was clear she was thoroughly enjoying herself.

Ysbel armed a gas bomb with a quick twist, and tossed it into the heaviest mass of police officers. It exploded in a thick cloud of smoke, and the officers fell back, coughing and waving their hands in front of their faces, before one by one, they collapsed.

When they reached the gates of the university, Tae and Lev were standing off to one side as the students streamed through. Dmitri and Vera stood with them. They were breathless, and they looked somewhat the worse for wear from their encounter with police, Vera leaning heavily against the archway, her left leg bent gingerly as if she couldn't bear weight on it, and Dmitri with a shallow cut over one eye, blood dripping down the side of his face. But they both had elated smiles on their faces.

"Hey tech-head!" Jez called as they landed beside them. "Kiss him, already!"

"Jez—" Tae turned to her in complete exasperation. Dmitri grinned at Jez, turned Tae's face back towards him, and pulled him into a kiss, and Tae seemed to suddenly and completely forget about his objections.

When Dmitri finally pulled back, he studied Tae with a look that was so tender, and mixed with so much wistfulness, that Ysbel almost had to look away. Then Dmitri gave a small, wry smile.

"I got blood all over you," he said, with a laugh that sounded like he was choking back tears. Tae smiled back at him, and Ysbel could see the tears glistening in his eyes as well.

"I—it's fine."

"I'm going to miss you, Tae," Dmitri said, quietly.

Tae reached out, almost in a daze, and brushed the blood from Dmitri's face. "I'm—sorry. That I have to leave."

Dmitri shook his head. "Don't be. I think I knew it from the moment I first saw you. Certainly since I watched you disarm an ion bomb in your student dorm. You're like—you're like a meteor. You're too brilliant and burning and—and beautiful for just an ordinary person like me to expect to hold on to." He smiled slightly, through his tears. "I just—I'm glad I got to have you, for a little. I'm glad I was your first kiss. I'm glad I got to wake up to see you sleeping in my bed."

"Tae!" exclaimed Jez delightedly.

Tae turned away from Dmitri for a moment and glared at her, tears still glistening on his cheeks. "Jez. Shut up. He was sleeping on the couch."

Ysbel smiled despite herself.

Jez was still grinning in absolute delight. "Not sure if anyone ever told you this, Tae, but that's not how sex works. Guess you and I should have a little talk one of these days."

"Jez—" his voice was strangled, but he closed his eyes for a moment and brushed the tears from his cheeks, and Ysbel glanced surreptitiously at Jez.

Maybe that idiot was more perceptive than she'd given her credit for.

Tae, at least, seemed somewhat more composed when he turned back to Dmitri.

"I'll—I'll never forget you," he said, in a voice that was almost a whisper. "And—well, tell the others thank you for me. I'll hack into the police cameras before we go, erase the footage. The government shouldn't be able to track who was out there tonight. At least—" he paused, the typical worry shadowing his face again. "At least, not for now," he finished finally. "And we'll keep trying to figure something out so we can fix this for good."

Dmitri reached out one last time, cupping Tae's cheek tenderly. "I know you will, Tae. I know." He dropped his hand finally, and reached up to wipe away his own tears. "Alright, go on, you hero. Go save the entire Svodrani system."

Tae nodded, but for a few moments neither of them moved. Then, at last, Tae turned away, wiping futility at his eyes.

"Come on, let's go," he said, his voice half-choked, and Jez gestured him onto the back of her bike with a jerk of her head. Lev climbed on behind Ysbel, and they shot through the gate and back towards the science building. But Ysbel could see Dmitri looking after them until they turned a corner and were out of sight.

When they arrived back in Ysbel's office, Masha was propped against a wall. Her face was grey with pain, but she managed a pleasant smile as they entered.

"How is she?" Ysbel asked bluntly. Tanya raised an eyebrow.

"She'll need to be seen to when we get back to the ship, but she hasn't lost enough blood to kill her yet." She paused. "Ysi, I've packed up all your materials. Is there anything else you need?"

Ysbel glanced around quickly. "I don't think so. I'm not entirely sure what our next move is."

"I also went through the school chemical supplies in the back room and took everything I thought you might use."

Ysbel smiled at her gently. "You know, Tanya, I adore you."

Tanya gave her that wistful smile, cut with a hint of mischief. "Considering we are married and have two children, I am glad to hear it."

Masha pushed herself upright with an effort. "Ysbel. Our plan has not changed. The speed at which we have to carry it out might have." She hunched forward abruptly, face twisting in pain, and Jez dropped down beside her, swearing under her breath.

"Damn idiot," she muttered, and Ysbel gave a slight smile.

Who would have thought?

Masha recovered herself, and managed to straighten once more. "At any rate, I believe there's nothing else we can do here. I suggest we remove to the hangar. Between the information I have and the information I'm certain Lev possesses, we'll make a decision on our next move."

Ysbel glanced over at Lev. He still had that distant, slightly lost look on his face, and something inside her twisted, just a little, to see him like that. Jez seemed to see it too, because when she stood, she slipped her hand into his. He grasped it, knuckles white.

"Well," said Tanya, glancing around. "We should leave, before we get anyone else into trouble."

Ysbel glanced over at Tae, who was typing furiously into his holoscreen, scowling in concentration. Once again, she felt an odd warmth in her chest to know that her students were being taken care of by someone so thoroughly competent to take care of them.

"Tae? Are you ready?" she asked.

"One second." There was a pause, then he looked up, a grim smile on his tear-streaked face. "There. I took down the entire damn police surveillance system, and shredded it. They won't be getting that video feed."

She raised one eyebrow.

Every so often, she was reminded of how bad of an idea it would be to cross any one of the members of their little crew.

She smiled, and slipped her arm around Tanya. "Alright. Let's go home."

As their bikes approached the hangar bay, Ysbel closed her eyes for a moment, letting the night wind blow across her face.

It still held that faint metallic taste that lodged in the back of your throat.

Jez slowed abruptly. Ysbel slowed as well, frowning.

And then something hard and cold squeezed her chest.

There was someone standing outside the entrance to the hangar bay, someone she didn't recognize. He was medium height, but with the kind of lean muscle that showed that he could hurt someone if he wanted to, and the look on his face of someone who had wanted to often, and had.

"Hey, you bastard," said Jez, her voice tight. "What the hell you think you're doing here?"

He gave her a long, calculating stare. "You Jez Solokov?"

"Not sure it's your business, you dirty plaguer."

He nodded, as if she'd confirmed a suspicion. "These others then. They must be," he glanced down at his com. "Masha, Lev, Tae, Ysbel, Tanya."

"I said—" Jez's heat pistol was already in her hand, her posture tense, and Ysbel yanked a pack of explosive gel out of the pocket of her jacket. Her heart was pounding so hard she was almost dizzy. Tanya's arms had tightened around her, but now they loosened, as if she was getting ready to jump from the bike.

"No need for that," said the man with a faint, ugly grin. "I'm not going to stop you going in."

Ysbel took a quick, steadying breath. "If I find out that you've hurt any one of the people inside that hangar—" she began, her voice flat and emotionless. The man glanced at her, and she felt a grim satisfaction at the quick flash of fear in his eyes. He spread his hands quickly. "Everyone inside is safe. I swear it. I'm here to protect them, that's all. Go in, you can see for yourselves."

Ysbel slid off the bike and stalked over to him, a modded snub-nose pistol in her hand. He froze, but didn't try to run. Which was probably a good thing for him, because considering the mods she'd done on this particular pistol, he would have been lucky to have left a stain on the concrete.

"You go in first," she said. "Drop your weapon and put your hands on your head."

He complied, and she shoved him ahead of her into the hangar.

Inside, the children were huddled on the floor, and her eyes scanned frantically for Olya and Misko. She felt almost guilty at the sick relief that flooded through her when she saw them, safe and unharmed, in the centre of the huddle. They broke free when they saw her and Tanya, and ran to them. She scooped up Olya, who was white-faced and trembling, and Tanya grabbed Misko, who clung to her neck like he'd never let go.

And it wasn't until she was clutching Olya to her, and she was able to breathe again, that she saw Tae's face, and she realized that the street kids weren't all there, after all.

One was missing.

The girl, the younger of the two siblings who'd been taking care of the other children. Of her children.

"Tae," said the older boy, Caz, getting slowly to his feet. His voice was unsteady, thick with a sort of sick despair. "It's alright. Everyone's safe, for now."

"Where's Peti?" Tae whispered.

The man standing in front of Ysbel turned cautiously to face them. "The girl's fine. My boss found these kids just before a group of police officers did. Promised to protect them, and we did. Bit of luck, us finding them, because the thing is, we were looking for you. So we were happy to help. But my boss, he didn't want to lose you, so he asked for a volunteer to come with him."

Lev slid off his bike and crossed to the man in two quick strides, the same cold, emotionless look on his face as when he'd been about to bring a building down on hundreds of people, and Ysbel had stopped him.

"Tell me," he said in that passionless voice, "where you took her. And tell me that she's alright. Because if your boss hurt one of Tae's friends, I promise you, wherever he is and whoever he is, I will find him, and he will die for it."

The man looked suddenly very, very uneasy. "I—he didn't hurt her, I swear it. She's been treated like a guest. We don't want her, don't have any use for her at all except to make sure that whoever the boss wanted comes along. Just wants to talk, that's all. He'd have no reason to hurt her."

Lev studied him for a long moment. "I hope," he said pleasantly, "that that is true."

"It's true," said Caz, almost in a whisper, and the anguish and the guilt in his voice made Ysbel's stomach twist. "All of it's true. The police were on their way, we could hear them coming, and we were trying to get everyone out, and then these people showed up. And —" He swallowed hard, letting his gaze drop. "And one of us needed to stay with the other kids, keep them safe, and Peti said—she said I was the oldest, I needed to stay with them, so she'd go. And—" he paused a moment, and then finally, defiantly, looked up, meeting Tae's eyes. "And I let her," he said at last, quietly.

Tae nodded, looking shell-shocked.

"Who is your boss?" asked Lev at last. "And who was he looking for."

"I think," said Masha's faint voice behind them, "I know the answer to both those questions."

28

Masha, day 19

Masha's head was spinning, slightly, and for a moment she swayed on her feet. Then someone grabbed her elbow to steady her, and Jez's voice whispered, "Easy there, you bastard."

Masha looked over at her fondly.

Of all the strange things to have happened …

She turned back to the cold, furious Lev, the stricken Tae, the grim Ysbel. And the man, standing in front of them.

So. They'd finally found her.

"Grigory Korzhakov," she said, her voice as calm and as pleasant as she'd trained it to be, no matter what the circumstances. She ignored the quick intake of breath from Lev, the hiss of air through teeth from Ysbel.

Even if you weren't familiar with the mafia, you'd recognize Grigory Korzhakov's name.

"Masha Volkova," said the man. He wasn't familiar himself, but she recognized the edge of the tattoo that just showed over his shirt above his collarbone. "Or should I call you Mari?"

"Masha," she said, despite the cold that settled into her chest.

"I'm afraid I don't know you, but I know Grigory. You say he's given his word not to harm Peti?"

The man nodded. "All he wants is your word you'll come. And he didn't want you to wait too long, seeing as you're such a busy woman, so he thought he'd borrow the girl. But she'll be treated as a guest, probably better than what she has here." He gestured around the grease-stained floor of the deserted hangar bay. "And certainly better than what she'd have gotten if the police had gotten a hold of her. Nothing bad will happen to her at all, as long as he has your word you'll come."

Masha nodded, although the movement made the room sway. "As you can see," she gestured in a self-deprecating way at the blood soaking through her shirt and staining her pilot's jacket, "I am not entirely disposed at the moment. But I give him my word I'll come, the moment I'm able to."

The man studied her appraisingly. "Shall we say … two weeks?"

"I am afraid I don't heal quite as quickly as all that. Three."

The man considered, then nodded. "Very good. Three weeks. We'll be expecting you, and the girl will be waiting. Nothing at all to harm her, for three weeks."

The threat in his words was clumsy, but clearly apparent.

Masha closed her eyes for a moment and leaned against Jez, steadying herself. When she was able to open her eyes without the room spinning around her, she looked over to Ysbel.

"You may let him go," she said. "I believe he's telling the truth."

Slowly, reluctantly, Ysbel lowered her weapon, and Lev stepped aside. The man reached into his pocket, and froze when heat-pistols appeared in the hands of all five of the crew members as if by magic. He raised his hands.

"Just getting out a chip with directions," he said, in a slow, careful voice.

"Figure I can do that just as well as you can, you scum-sucker," said Jez. Carefully, she let go of Masha's elbow, and Masha steadied herself inconspicuously against the skybike. Jez sauntered over, pistol still drawn, and shoved her hand into his jacket pocket, emerging a moment later with a chip.

"This it, you bastard?"

He nodded, and Jez handed it to Masha, without taking her eyes off the man.

"Now," said Ysbel, in a soft voice that managed to hold an amount of menace that probably shouldn't have been possible, "I suggest you get out of here before I do something that you will regret. Because I promise you, I will not regret it at all."

The man opened his mouth to protest, caught sight of Ysbel's face, and closed it again quickly. He started towards the door, then turned and caught Masha's eye.

"Three weeks," he said. Then he disappeared out the door.

Jez caught Masha's elbow as she swayed.

"Thank you, Jez," she said quietly. "Could you help me sit, please?"

Everyone in the room was watching her, but she wasn't entirely certain how much longer she could remain on her feet without passing out, so she figured that this was the better part of valour.

Once she was sitting, her back pressed against the concrete wall of the hangar, she tipped her head back for just a moment, letting the world steady around her.

Grigory Korzhakov.

She should probably feel some emotion. But at the moment, all she could feel was a vague relief that she was sitting, and she no longer had to focus on staying on her feet.

But then again, perhaps that was an emotion in and of itself.

"Masha?" asked Lev at last, in that same distant, pleasant voice.

She opened her eyes and smiled slightly at them, despite the sickness coating her stomach and the inside of her throat. "Yes, Lev?"

"Were you planning on telling us what the hell is going on?"

She took a deep breath.

They were her crew. That had become indisputable, no matter what she would have originally preferred.

And she wasn't certain how much she could tell them.

"It's the mafia, as you will have surmised," she said at last. "However, I have full confidence that Peti will be fine. I know Grigory—know of him, at the very least—and she will be treated with every respect."

"For three weeks," said Lev softly.

Masha nodded.

Caz still looked haunted. Tanya and Ysbel were holding Misko and Olya, and Tae was sitting with one arm around the youngest street-kid girl and the other around her teenage brother, his face hollow.

"Tae," she said, in as brisk a voice as she could manage. "I'll get her back for you. I promise. Grigory has asked to meet with me, and I have no objection to doing so." Somehow the words came out without a tremble. And she waited for Jez to contradict her, to tell the others what she knew about Masha's past.

But she didn't. She caught Masha's gaze and quirked an eyebrow, and didn't speak.

Tae turned his face to her, and what she saw there almost did make her sick.

A sort of weary trust.

"I believe you," he said quietly. He turned to Caz, reached out and put a hand on his arm. "If Masha says Peti's fine, you can trust her."

And when she glanced around at the others, she saw variations on the same expression on each of their faces.

So it hadn't been just her who'd changed.

How had this happened? And when had it become something that disturbed her, instead of something she could take in her calm stride? Because that had been the point all along, hadn't it, get them to trust her?

Somehow, she still managed to smile.

"So. It appears, then, that our next step has been planned for us. If Jez doesn't mind playing transport pilot, I will go meet with Grigory and find out what he wants." She paused, and glanced around once more, taking one last steadying breath. "I—believe the easiest thing at this point, and certainly the most efficient, is for Jez to drop me off in exchange for Peti. That way you can take her back here, and I will stay to find out what exactly Grigory would like to discuss."

And there it was—their way out.

She'd offered. All they had to do was accept.

"No," said Jez flatly. "Look, you bastard, you want me to just drop you off on your own in the middle of the damn mafia? Not sure who you think you're talking to, but it's not happening. If you go in, you'll damn well need someone along with." She paused a moment, and grinned. "Anyways, thought we'd figured out that I'm the smart one here."

Masha gave a small, wry smile despite herself.

"I agree," said Ysbel. "I wouldn't let any of these other idiots go into something like that on their own. I won't let you either. So, you may as well forget that idea."

Tanya looked up and met Ysbel's eyes with a slight smile. "As I have said before, I am not leaving my wife, ever again."

"I'm with Jez and Ysbel," said Lev.

Tae looked over at Caz for a moment, then turned back to Masha. "I'm coming too. I told you. I trust you that they'll keep Peti safe, as long as you come when you said you would. But I don't know if they'll keep you safe, and I'm not willing to risk it." He gave her a small smile.

And for a moment, Masha was completely speechless.

She closed her eyes for a moment, and had to blink back a sudden stinging of tears.

"Well," she said finally, "if you're certain this is what you'd like to do, I suggest we—" she faltered for a moment, vision turning suddenly hazy.

"I suggest you damn well lie down, you plaguer," said Jez. "We know what we're doing. We can figure out details tomorrow."

"Perhaps you're right," murmured Masha.

They could pin down details tomorrow.

And then—well, and then she'd take her motley crew of geniuses and misfits directly into the lair of perhaps the most powerful and dangerous man in the system.

They'd all volunteered. She hadn't even had to ask.

The thought should probably have been gratifying, but she couldn't shake the sick feeling in the pit of her stomach.

29

"Ysi."

Ysbel looked up, blinking out of her reverie, and Tanya laughed softly, kissing her on the cheek. "Who are you worrying about?"

Ysbel smiled reluctantly, glancing around their small cabin on the *Ungovernable*. Caz and the others had opted to sleep outside in the hangar bay, but she found she'd missed this place.

"It's not like I don't have enough options," she said.

It was true. The list of people she had to worry about—that she cared enough for to worry about—seemed to have grown to a size that was becoming slightly unmanageable.

"How do you do it?" she asked, turning to her wife and brushing the hair back from her face. "You've always liked people. How do you worry about so many people at once?"

"You liked those students, didn't you," said Tanya. "I thought you might. You are not nearly as cranky as you like to pretend."

"I am much crankier than I like to pretend," Ysbel grumbled. She hesitated a moment. "But yes. I did like those students. And Tae's street-kids, I like them too."

Tanya kissed her on the forehead, then gave her a faint smile. "I'm going to go make sure Olya is sleeping and not keeping Misko up. I'll be back in a moment."

Ysbel nodded, and Tanya slipped through the door separating the two cabins.

Ysbel looked after her for a moment, shaking her head slightly.

She still wasn't entirely certain when Masha's crazy scheme to take down the government had become personal for her. But she no longer pictured an abstract revenge for something that had happened in the past. Now she pictured Vera, and Peti, and Tae's boyfriend Dmitri, the ragged street-kids huddled in the hangar bay.

She pictured Tae, as they ran past the protesting students, when she told him to go on, and promised him they'd come back. There had been that slight moment of hesitation in his face—and then he'd come. Because he believed her, because they were more than crewmates, they were friends.

It had been so long. Five and a half years of not feeling, not caring, blocking out everything except thoughts of revenge on the people who had killed her family. Cutting herself off from every other person, because the pain of it was too great. When she'd blown up the shuttle station, she hadn't felt even the faintest pang of regret for the thirty-five deaths.

But—perhaps now, she might.

She remembered, for a moment, Lev, the cold, distant look on his face back in the government building. She'd recognized that look— the look of someone whose life, or everything they thought was their life, had been stripped away.

But the difference was, of course, when she'd lost Tanya and Olya and Misko, she'd been alone.

And Lev—wasn't alone. He wouldn't be.

Tae would almost certainly stop by to check on him, sometime tonight. Jez would, too.

She gave a faint grin. Jez would possibly do more than check on him.

And she, Ysbel, would be there, when he thought he'd lost everything and had nothing left to lose, and she'd stop him, again, and again, and again, as many times as it took, until he realized everything he hadn't lost.

She smiled to herself, and stood. She slipped into the children's room and stood beside Tanya, looking down at their children.

Maybe that was the difference, in the end. Maybe that's what had finally changed. Lev wasn't alone. And—nor was she.

Nor were any of them.

She slipped her arm around Tanya's waist, and Tanya leaned against her shoulder, and Olya and Misko slept peacefully in the cots, and outside the street-kids slept on the pile of cot-pads and blankets, draped over each other instinctively, even though they no longer had to worry about keeping warm.

She was smiling, a peaceful smile she hadn't felt for a long while.

Tae sat with his back shoved up against the wall, his knees pulled up to his chest and his face shoved into his hands.

He wasn't certain why, after twenty damn years of never even having the time to cry, he couldn't seem to stop crying now.

It was stupid. Peti was going to be alright. He'd managed to talk to Caz, managed to convince him that what Masha said was true. The street kids—his kids, the ones he'd promised to protect—were safe, finally. Not forever, but for now, and with everything else that was going on, 'safe for now' was far better than anything he'd expected.

And his university friends were safe, and Dmitri—

He clenched his teeth hard against the tears, but he couldn't stop them.

Dmitri.

He'd never planned on meeting someone like him, on kissing him, on—well, on having someone care about him. Like he was something special, not just a street kid ex-convict who never seemed to get enough sleep and never seemed to be able to stop worrying about something or other. Dmitri had been—beautiful. And Tae had known, from that very first moment he saw him, that this would never actually work, that he'd have to leave, that the worlds they lived in were too different, but just for a few weeks it hadn't seemed to matter.

And now here he was, sitting in his cabin crying his damn eyes out.

There was a tap on the door, and he sat up quickly, scrubbing at his eyes in a futile attempt to disguise the fact he'd been crying. The door opened a crack, and Jez peeked in.

"Oh good, you're awake," she said, grinning. She came in without waiting for an invite, and dropped down on the cot beside him. He tried to look away in a half-hearted attempt to hide his tear-streaked cheeks and swollen eyes, but she put a hand on his shoulder and said, her voice a little more gentle, "Hey. Tech-head. It's OK. Nothing wrong with crying."

And for some reason he was crying again, and he dropped his face back into his hands.

Jez leaned back against the wall beside him and left her hand on his shoulder and just sat there for a while while he sobbed, and her presence was strangely comforting.

Finally, he raised his head slightly and took a long, shuddering breath. Jez shoved a tissue at him, and he wiped his eyes and blew his nose and scrubbed the salt from his cheeks with the sleeve of his jacket, and somehow that made him feel a little more human again.

"That lover-boy of yours?" Jez asked.

He nodded wordlessly.

"You know," she said thoughtfully, "I could kidnap him. I could go back there, have him here by tomorrow morning."

He turned quickly. "No! You can't—"

"Bet I could." She was grinning.

"No Jez! You can't kidnap him."

She raised an eyebrow. He sighed.

"Jez. I appreciate the thought. But I—would really rather you didn't do that."

She shrugged and settled back against the wall. "Well, if you don't want me to—"

She actually sounded disappointed.

He stared at her for a moment, then shook his head and broke into a half-hearted chuckle, and she grinned back at him.

They sat like that for a while. Finally, she said, "Tae?"

There was a strange note in her voice, and he looked up quickly. "Yes?"

She paused, fiddling with the edge of her jacket. "I—you and Dmitri. You—I mean, you were good for each other."

He managed a faint smile. "Yeah. I guess so."

"I mean—the way he treated you. The way you treated him. I—where did you learn to do that?"

Tae frowned, and shrugged. "It's not something you learn, Jez. It's just—it's how you treat people. If you care about them." He turned to look at her. She didn't meet his gaze, just stared down at her jacket like there was something vitally important hidden in the lining.

"Yeah."

They were silent again for a few minutes. Finally she looked up, her face serious. "You OK, tech-head? Really?"

He smiled again, a little more genuinely this time. "Yeah. I'm OK." He paused, and took a deep breath. "I—I mean, Dmitri was —he was—amazing. But—I mean, it couldn't be forever. Where we came from, what our lives were like—it was too different. But, I'm glad. That I got to know him. Even if it was only for a few weeks."

Jez nodded, tipping her head back against the wall and closing her eyes. "Guess it was probably easier now, anyways. Easier than if you'd waited longer before you had to leave, right?"

"I—suppose so," he said, looking at her curiously.

She nodded, then sat up suddenly, her usual crazy grin pasted back on her face. But there had been something in her expression, before she'd hidden it under a grin, something a little wistful and a little sad.

"I'm glad you're OK, tech-head," she said. "I—was worried about you. And don't worry, we'll get Peti back for you."

"I know," he said softly, with a small smile. "We all will."

"Yeah." After a moment she pushed herself to her feet, but turned back with her hand on the door handle. "You sure you don't want me to kidnap Dmitri? It'd be easy, I'd just—"

"I'm—very sure."

She shrugged. "To each their own, I guess." Then she slipped out, closing the door behind her.

He stared blankly at the closed door for a few minutes, but somehow he found there was a small, watery smile on his face.

It had been—different, at the university. For the first time in his life he'd had friends his own age, not just people to take care of. He'd gone out drinking and laughing and talking over dinner with them, had come home late and slept through his classes, slept as long as he needed to, every night, for weeks. He hadn't actually known how that would feel, before then. He'd had a boyfriend, and they'd kissed and held hands and sat side by side studying, Dmitri's arm tucked around him.

And it had been good. It had been better than he'd dreamed it could be. And he was going to miss it, and he wasn't entirely sure if it would ever stop hurting.

But—he glanced around at his tiny, familiar cabin.

Jez was probably back in the cockpit already, because she couldn't seem to help herself. Ysbel and Tanya were next door with the kids, and outside the ship, his kids—the kids he'd promised to take care of, who counted on him, who needed him—were sleeping somewhere warm and soft and actually safe.

He closed his eyes and pictured Dmitri again, his soft smile, that friendly, cheerful innocence.

Maybe in another life, that would have been all he needed.

But it wasn't his life. He knew too much, about how the world worked, about what was happening in it, about what needed to change and how he needed to change it, to ever be content in a place like the university. Even though he wanted to, even though he wished he could.

The universe was too wide, and he'd seen too much of it.

This, here, this was his life. He'd made his choice. And—well, even after everything, even after a whole damn evening of crying his eyes out—he'd probably make the same choice again.

Because this—in its own, strange, crazy, exhausting way—this life of his was good, too.

Jez slumped back in the pilot's seat, staring blankly out the cockpit window, fingers resting almost unconsciously on the controls. The *Ungovernable* wasn't running, but the familiar feel of the controls under her hands made everything feel like somehow it was going to be alright. That despite everything that had happened, and everything that was going to happen, there was something in her life that was perfect and right, something she could always depend on.

Something she wouldn't screw up, because she couldn't screw it up, because she was as much a part of it as it was of her.

Her mind was racing, and she couldn't seem to slow it down.

Lev.

Kissing him, holding him, falling asleep curled in his arms, waking with her head on his lap. The way his face had softened with a sort of desperate relief when he'd seen her that night he'd called on his com, and she'd thrown on her boots and jacket and sprinted halfway across campus to reach him, because she'd heard the pain in his voice and she couldn't bear that he hurt.

Even the thought of him made her faintly dizzy.

How had this happened? How had she let this happen?

And it wasn't just Lev, either. This whole damn crew. She'd realized it at some point during this whole thing. Maybe it was when she saw Masha go down, blood blossoming from her side, or maybe when she'd seen that stupid mafia thug at the door of the hangar bay and she'd realized she'd take the whole damn system apart to save Ysbel's kids, or Tae's friends.

She was part of this crew now. And she couldn't run away, because she'd tried that already and it hadn't worked, and it wouldn't even be so bad if she didn't care about them so damn much. She couldn't handle this, she couldn't handle being trapped, and being stuck, and maybe she was just going to go completely crazy, because she couldn't do this, she absolutely couldn't, and she couldn't leave either—

She splayed her hands on the controls, heart pounding, trying to slow her breathing. She took a long, deep breath, and then another, and then another.

Tae's exasperated scowl when she teased him about his boyfriend, Ysbel, shaking her head in a mix of amusement and affection, the strange, tentative thing that felt almost, a little bit, like friendship, that had begun to grow between her and Masha, of all people.

The thing was, no matter how terrifying it was … she loved these people. Desperately, helplessly, like she'd never let herself love anyone. She hadn't meant for it to happen, because she knew all about people, and she knew people were basically awful, and they didn't stick around when you needed them, and that if you let yourself care about them, they'd hurt you. She wasn't a damn idiot.

But the problem with this crew was, they didn't do what they were supposed to. They didn't get fed up with her and walk off, they didn't hate her, no matter how irritating she was, and they didn't leave when things started to go sideways. They just—stayed. They stayed, and helped her put things back together, no matter how many times she broke them. They'd put her ship back together, when she'd thought it would be impossible. They'd put her back together.

And—well, and the worst part of it was, as terrifying as the thought was, as much as being trapped sent something crawling under her skin and tightened off her breath—she didn't actually want to leave them.

So she'd make it work. Somehow.

Because she didn't know what else to do.

Her breathing had somehow steadied, her heart-rate evening out. She could feel the controls under her fingers again, soothing and comfortable.

Her ship.

Even if she was trapped, even if she didn't know how to handle any of this, even if maybe she might actually go crazy, she had her beautiful, perfect angel, and somehow it would be alright.

And then there was Lev.

She took a deep breath, and managed a small smile.

Lev.

She loved him.

That was the thing. She loved him, and she'd probably never stop loving him, no matter how much she tried.

And she couldn't do this. Not to him, not to her.

"It's not something you learn, Jez," Tae had said. "It's just—it's how you treat people. If you care about them."

And she didn't know how that worked. She didn't know what it felt like. She wasn't like Tae, someone steady and dependable who you could count on to be there today and tomorrow and the day after that. She didn't know how not to panic and run as soon as the person she'd been sleeping with started to actually care about her. She was crap at relationships, and if she tried, she'd screw it up, just like she had with every other relationship she'd had in her life, and she'd hurt Lev, and if there was one thing she'd learned over the past few weeks, it was that she couldn't bear to hurt Lev.

She closed her eyes again.

Before, maybe she would have ignored it, told herself it would all work out somehow, he was a grownup and he could take care of himself. Before she realized how much his pain hurt her. Before she realized that seeing him happy—seeing him alright—had become maybe the most important thing in the whole system to her.

Masha'd been willing to wait years, work for people she hated and never say a thing, even though it must have been killing her inside, because she knew what she wanted was worth whatever it would cost. That had never been something Jez was good at.

But maybe she was learning.

If she tried, she could still feel the ghost of his lips against hers, the pressure of his hands on her back, the warmth of his body pressed against her. And for half a moment, she was tempted to pretend that she didn't know how it would inevitably end.

But—the longer she didn't tell him, the more she'd hurt him when she finally did. Hurt herself, too, although at this point there wasn't an option that wouldn't hurt. And at the end of the day—well, maybe that was what love was. Caring about someone enough that you wanted them to be alright, even if it tore you to pieces.

Lev walked slowly into his familiar cabin on the *Ungovernable*. He pulled back his chair and sat carefully. There was something fragile and brittle inside his chest, and he was terrified of what would happen if it broke.

He placed his hands on the edges of the chair, and the cool wood against his hands reminded him that he was here on the *Ungovernable*, not drifting through space, untethered from every damn thing he'd ever known or wanted or believed.

Everything still felt distant, slightly unreal.

Evka. The university. The familiar, enjoyable politicking and backstabbing and contests of wits that had been the predictable undercurrent to his life. To the life he'd dreamed about, yearned for, that he'd always unconsciously turned back towards, no matter how far he'd been driven away from it. And the professor he'd spent nine years mourning, nine years searching for answers as to why she was kidnapped and presumably murdered.

But of course, she wasn't murdered. Instead, she was the murderer.

He tightened his hands on the edges of the chair, but it wasn't working as well as it had been at grounding him here, holding him from losing himself.

Then again, he wasn't entirely certain it mattered anymore.

There was a tap on the door. He blinked, glancing around, then called, in a voice that was somehow calm, "Come in."

Ysbel pushed open the door and entered, and he managed a pleasant smile.

"Hello Ysbel. What do you need?"

She walked over and dropped down on the edge of his cot, putting her elbows on her knees, and he watched her in polite, detached silence.

"Lev," she said after a moment. "Tanya is bringing Olya in to say goodnight. But I thought I'd come in first. How are you doing?"

"I'm fine, thank you, Ysbel." It was a ridiculous statement, but he said it with a straight face, and he had to fight the urge to break into hysterical laughter.

Ysbel shook her head. "I've told you this already, but you are terrible at lying."

He smiled again, politely. "I suppose that means I need more practice."

"No, you idiot. It means you need to stop it, because there's no point." She paused. "I'm not going to leave until you tell me the truth, you know."

He held onto the pleasant smile for a moment longer, and then he couldn't anymore. He closed his eyes and dropped his head to his chest, and stayed there for a moment, as if perhaps if he didn't look up, he wouldn't have to face everything again. At last he took a deep breath and lifted his head. "You're right, Ysbel," he said in a low voice. "I'm not fine. I—honestly don't know if I will be."

She cocked her head to one side. "And why not?"

He gave a brief, incredulous laugh. "Ysbel. I'm the one who damn well sent your family to a prison planet for five years. Do you have to ask that? I am exactly what they made me. I wanted everything the university had to offer, and—" he spread his hands. "Everything I wanted, Ysbel. I finally got to see what that was."

She was silent for a moment, and for some reason, he couldn't look at her.

Because, of course, it was one thing to know who you were. And it was something else, something infinitely more painful, to look at a woman who had been your friend, and who you'd hurt beyond what should have been possible, and who had somehow forgiven you, and see confirmation of that in her eyes.

"Lev," she said finally, her voice deep and amused.

Despite himself, he glanced up in shock.

"For someone who is supposed to be a genius, I think you're missing something fairly obvious." She paused, raising an eyebrow. "You say your old professor was helping to create this program, yes?"

He nodded warily.

"And so presumably, when we were in that building, she was there somewhere, trying to make sure her project went off without a hitch. As was the minister, as were however many other people from your university."

He nodded again, the familiar sick feeling coating his stomach.

"And where were you?" she asked, quietly. "What were you doing?"

He stared at her for a moment, not entirely certain he'd understood her words.

"I thought you were supposed to be very smart. Think about it," she said, pushing herself to her feet. There was a faint, amused smile on her face.

She walked to the door, then paused a moment, turning back. "You know who you are, Lev. We all know who you are, because after the last few months we've spent, it's hard not to. And somehow, none of us have killed you yet."

From outside the door, he heard Tanya's voice.

"Lev? Are you in there? Olya woke up, and she won't go back to bed until she gets to say goodnight to you."

"I know he's in there," said Olya, slightly self-important. "Uncle Lev never leaves his desk light on unless he's in his room."

Lev shook his head fondly, stood, and crossed to the door, pulling it open. Tanya and Olya were waiting outside, and he knelt so he was at the eight-year-old's eye level. "Hello Olya. How are you?"

"I'm doing well, Uncle Lev," she said primly.

"Are you alright?" he asked softly. "When those people came, and Peti went with them—are you alright? Because it's alright to be afraid sometimes. Even when you're very brave you can be afraid sometimes."

She swallowed. "I was—a little afraid," she said in a small voice. He put a hand on her shoulder.

"I was a little afraid too," he said. She nodded, and for a moment neither of them spoke.

"But I'm not afraid anymore," she said.

He nodded. "I—might be," he said. "Just a little. But not as much as I was."

She raised her eyebrows at him. At last she nodded matter-of-factly. "That's good."

He smiled. "I think it is. Goodnight, Olya. I'm glad you came. I missed you."

"I missed you too, Uncle Lev," she said, and hugged him tightly around the neck.

"Alright, Olya, you said goodnight," said Tanya patiently. "Time for bed."

Reluctantly, Olya released her grasp. She gave Lev a long-suffering look, then allowed Tanya and Ysbel to shoo her down the corridor. Tanya shot an amused glance at Lev over her shoulder and mouthed 'thank you,' then herded Olya into the room and closed the door after them.

He smiled and closed his own door, then walked over to the cot and sat down, leaning back against the wall.

He wasn't sure how long he sat there after she'd left. But he was still sitting there when someone else tapped at the door.

"Lev?" Tae's voice had a familiar hint of concern.

"Yes?"

The door opened a crack, and Tae peered inside.

He'd clearly been crying, but he seemed to have regained his composure. "Lev. Just—wanted to check on you. You doing alright?"

Lev smiled slightly. "I—don't know. But I think I will be."

Tae nodded, an answering rueful smile on his face. "Yeah."

"You?" asked Lev after a moment. Really, Tae should be the one they were all worried about right now, not him, what with Peti gone. But he looked—different, somehow. Peaceful. Like despite everything, he was pretty sure things would turn out.

"Same as you, I think," said Tae. Lev smiled again.

"That boy was good for you, Tae."

"Yeah," said Tae, a soft smile on his face. "Yeah. I think he was." He sighed, and glanced around. "You look tired. You should probably get some sleep. You know Masha—as soon as she's not unconscious, we're not going to get two seconds of rest for probably the rest of our lives." He paused. "Anyways, I'm going to bed. Just wanted to—" He shrugged. "It was—a long day. For all of us."

"Thanks, Tae," said Lev softly, and Tae gave him a brief smile before he pulled the door shut.

The cold numbness inside him, that fragile, brittle thing inside his chest, had shrunk, somehow. Not gone, but—manageable.

He still felt lost, disconnected from everything he'd thought he was and knew. But—well, but now he felt like maybe there was a path back. Maybe he hadn't been lying to Tae. Maybe he would be alright, eventually.

A wave of exhaustion crashed over him, and he closed his eyes and for a moment wasn't sure if he'd open them again, maybe just fall into his bed and not move until his life made sense again.

And somehow, with that thought, came the memory of Jez curled up into his shoulder on the university couch, eyes drifting closed. And he realized, suddenly and desperately, that he needed her, he needed her so badly that it was almost a physical pain. He reached, almost instinctively, for his com, because even hearing her voice would be something, and he needed something, the need so strong he could taste it.

Then, slowly, he let his hand drop.

She'd be just as tired as he was. She was probably sleeping, and she needed her sleep, and even though his whole body ached with needing her, he was going to let her damn well sleep.

He tipped his head back against the wall and closed his eyes again, trying to think of something other than Jez, her body, her lips, her cocky grin and her loud laugh and the way her hair stuck up on one side when she'd just woken up, the soft look in her eyes sometimes when she looked at him, the sharp, intelligent aliveness of her.

There was a soft knock on his door, and then it swung open before he had time to respond.

"You still up, genius?" came Jez's quiet voice.

He sat up so quickly that he had to catch himself on the edge of the bed. "Jez?"

"Who'd you think it was?" She slipped inside, and the sight of her sent a rush of desperate relief through him that almost made him dizzy.

She came and sat next to him on the edge of the cot, close enough that their shoulders touched. She bumped him, hard, and he had to grab the side of the bed to keep himself from falling over. She snickered, and he smiled, reluctantly. Then she turned to him, her eyes serious.

"Lev?" she said quietly.

He closed his eyes and pulled her into his arms, and her body fit with his like it belonged there, like it always did. He kissed her, desperately, and the warmth of her and the shape of her was a lifeline that he was clinging to, and if he let go he'd never find his way back again.

Finally he pulled back and he looked at her tangled in his arms, the dreamy half-smile on her face that always lingered there for a moment after they'd kissed.

And he felt again that sharp spike of panic, of seeing her, sleepy-eyed and smiling, her head on his lap, and knowing that she was going to die in seconds if he didn't somehow figure out a solution, blood and shattered bone and her dark eyes glazing over and her wiry body going limp in his arms.

He let go of her abruptly, panic choking off his breath.

"Lev?" she said, confusion in her voice. "What's wrong?"

He swallowed hard, forcing himself to breathe in. "It's—nothing. Just—it's been a long day."

She studied him for a moment, appraisingly, then sat up and leaned against the wall beside him. "Yeah," she said at last. "Guess it has been."

They didn't talk for a while. She was fiddling with the cuff of her jacket, a strange, regretful look on her face.

"Lev?" she said finally. He turned to her.

"Yes?"

She looked up, and her face was weary. "Lev. I—need to talk to you. About something."

He closed his eyes again for a moment.

Jez, lying on his lap, blinking up at him with that sleepy smile, the panic jolting through him.

How the hell could he justify that?

He needed her. That wasn't the question. He needed her, and he wasn't sure he'd survive without her. But the point was, he didn't just need her.

He loved her.

And no matter how selfish and self-centred he was, he couldn't justify that. He couldn't handle that fear for this woman who, he realized with a sudden certainty, he loved more than he'd ever dreamed he could love anyone.

And the thought, even for one second, that she might get hurt precisely because he loved her—it made him sick.

He'd have to tell her. He'd have to somehow make her understand that no matter how badly he wanted her with him, he wanted her safe and alive even more than that, and the possibility that somehow, loving him might get her hurt, paralyzed him, choked him.

He opened his eyes. She was looking at him, weary and determined and a little sad, and he was so tired, and damn it to hell, he just wanted one night without having to think or explain or hurt. Just one night.

"Jez," he said, cupping her cheek with one hand and trying to smile. "I—I'm happy to talk to you, about anything you want to talk about. But—could we do it tomorrow? Right now I just—I—"

She nodded, her eyes never leaving his. Then she leaned in and kissed him, gently.

"Yeah," she whispered. "It can wait until tomorrow."

And he put his arms around her, and she nestled her head into his chest. And he held her as her breathing slowed and steadied, her wiry muscles relaxing against him, as his own eyes began to drift shut. As he slumped sideways, finally landing on his pillow, Jez still clutched in his arms, as she turned in her sleep and curled up against him, her head on his shoulder, her lanky body fitting perfectly into the hollow of his side.

And he held her as he drifted off to sleep, and she was an anchorline, and just for now, just for tonight, he wasn't lost anymore.

Masha turned restlessly on her cot. Tanya had bandaged her wound expertly, and despite the loss of blood, that wasn't what was keeping her awake.

This crew was hers now, heart and soul. What she'd been planning for since the beginning.

Grigory Korzhakov.

She'd been telling Tae the truth. She'd heard of him, in her years of working with the government, she'd worked across from him many times. Because the old saying, that the mafia was the biggest branch of the government, was much more true than the people who made the joke wanted to believe. It had all been the truth.

What she hadn't mentioned, of course, was the fact that she'd known him—or known of him—for much longer than that.

Since she was seven years old, crouching, wide-eyed and terrified, under a kitchen table with splintery wooden legs, the long table cloth almost, but not quite, hiding the gruesome scene taking place in front of her. He'd stood casually over the bodies of her parents, laughing with the woman beside him, and she'd heard the woman call him Grigory.

And she'd never forgotten that name.

He hadn't been the head of the mafia at the time, of course. That had come years later. But she'd watched him ever since that day. And when she'd had to work with him, in the government, she'd done it, somehow, without losing her calm demeanour and pleasant smile. Because she knew that, one day, she'd kill him. Or he'd kill her.

And now he'd come looking.

It was possible, of course, that he knew her because of her work in the government. Possible that he still had no idea who she was or where she'd come from. That's what her crew would think.

But it wasn't.

"Mari," the man had said.

She hadn't used that name since she was seven.

She lay back, staring sightlessly at the ceiling.

Whatever it was she'd put in motion with the job on Vitali, it had been like tipping a boulder off a cliff. And she'd done it intentionally, knowing exactly what she did. But it wasn't until now, watching it gathering speed, smashing everything in front of it in its wild, bouncing, careening course, that she truly realized what she'd known, intellectually, the whole time.

Whatever was coming next was raw destruction, a destruction that couldn't be tamed or controlled or steered. And it would crush everything in its path.

THE END

ENJOYED THE BOOK?

I HOPE YOU'VE ENJOYED Insider Threat, the fourth book in The Ungovernable series. Thank you for reading!

I have a small favour to ask you: Would you please leave a review on Amazon? It may seem like a silly thing, but reviews are very important to authors like me, as they help other people find my book, which in turn helps me to keep writing. Even a line or two would be unbelievably helpful.

The series continues with Firewall.

In the mean time, if you subscribe to my mailing list, I'd love to send you an exclusive short story prequel featuring Jez Solokov, *Devil's Odds.* I'll also let you know about future launch dates, giveaways, and pre-release specials. And I always love to hear from my readers, so feel free to drop me a note!

If you'd like claim your free short story and subscribe to my newsletter, head over to my website: www.rmolson.com

Also, feel free to connect with me on Facebook: https://www.facebook.com/rmolsonauthor

or Instagram: https://www.instagram.com/rolson_author/